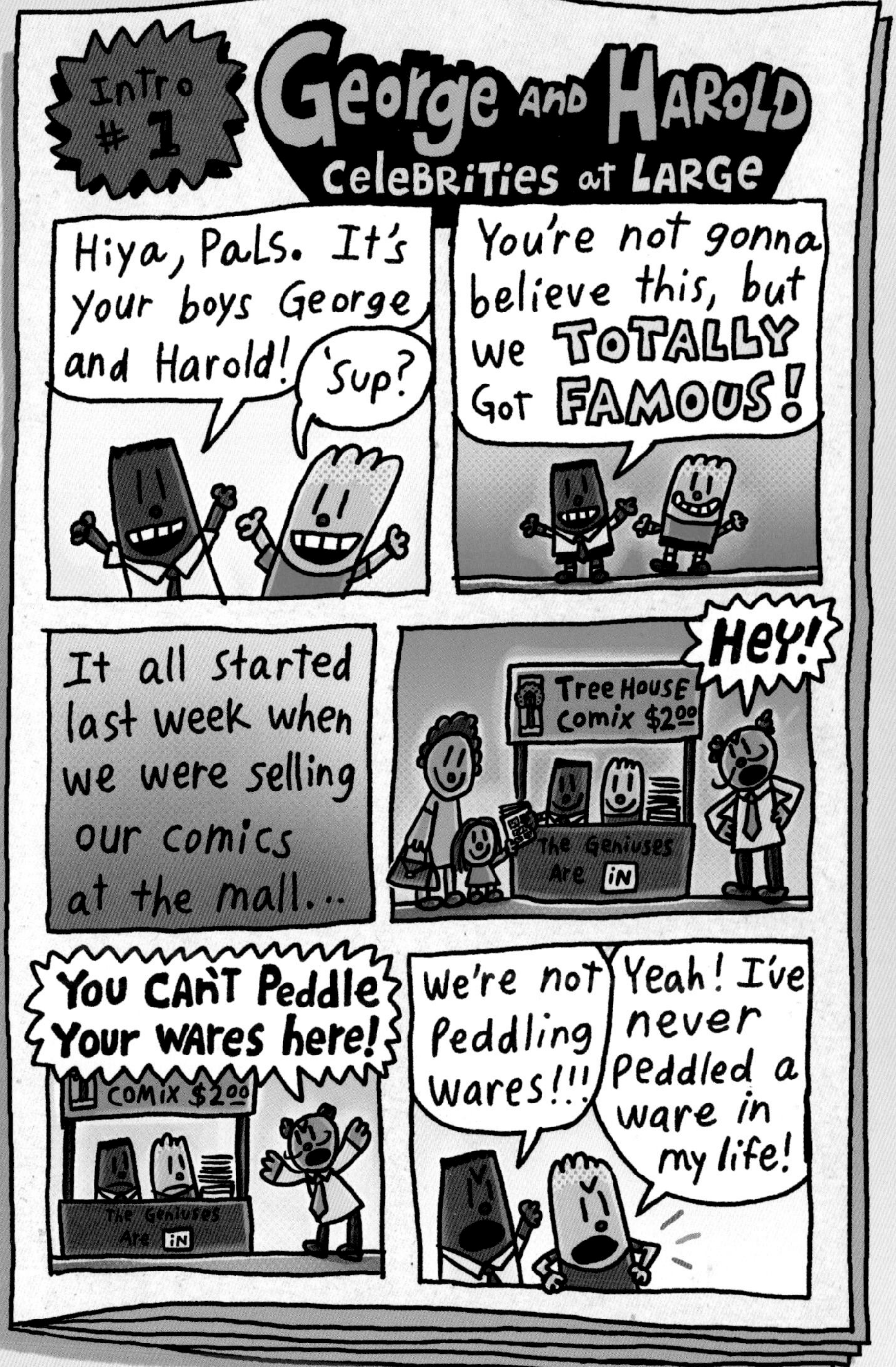
Intro #1
George and Harold
Celebrities at Large
Hiya, Pals. It's your boys George and Harold!
'Sup?
You're not gonna believe this, but we TOTALLY Got FAMOUS!
It all started last week when we were selling our comics at the mall...
Hey!
Tree House comix $2.00
The Geniuses Are iN
You CAN'T Peddle Your wares here!
COMix $2.00
The Geniuses Are iN
We're not Peddling wares!!!
Yeah! I've never Peddled a ware in my life!

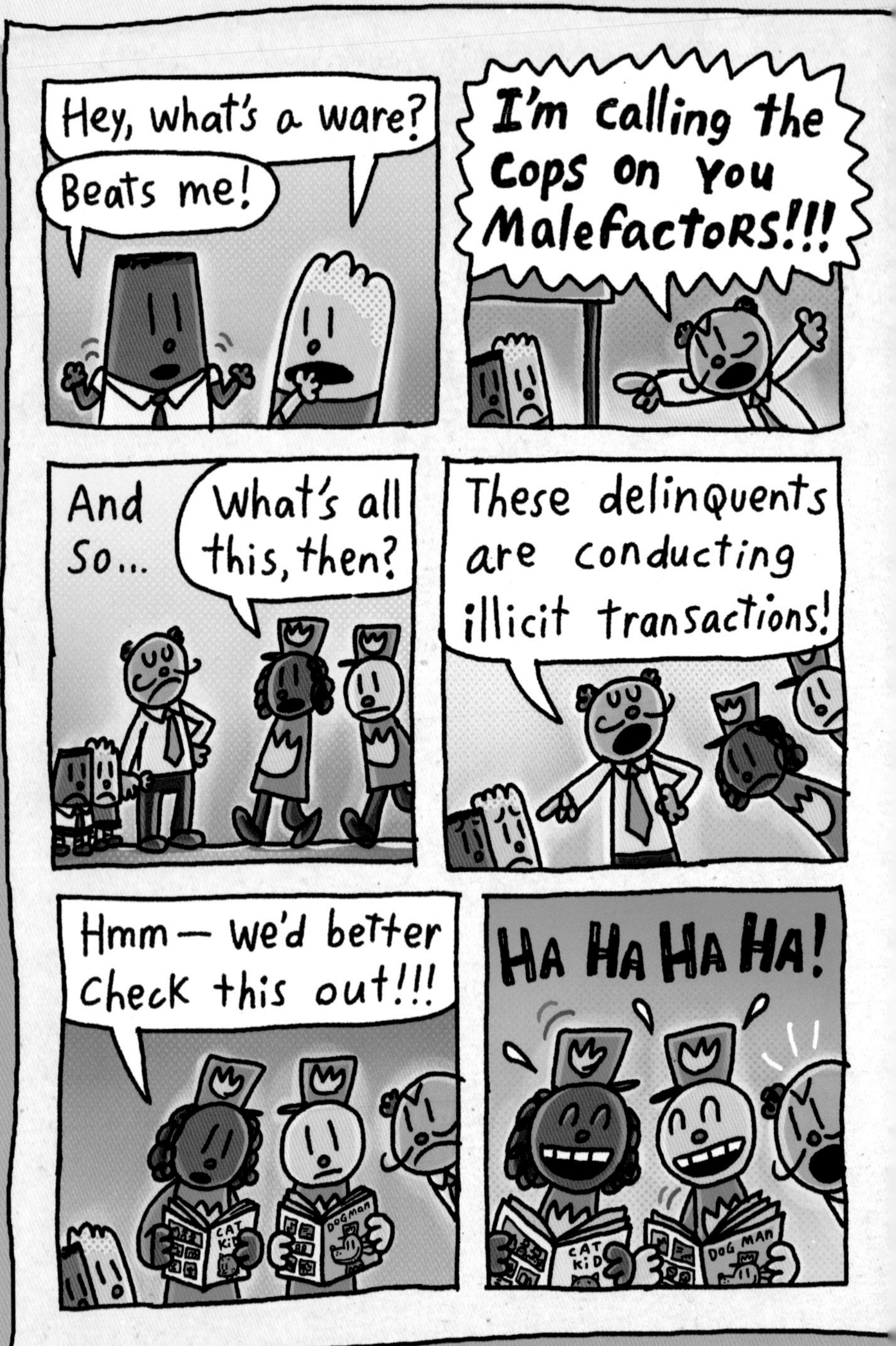
Hey, what's a ware?
Beats me!
I'm calling the cops on you Malefactors!!!
And so...
What's all this, then?
These delinquents are conducting illicit transactions!
Hmm— We'd better check this out!!!
HA HA HA HA!
CAT KID
DOG MAN
CAT KID
DOG MAN

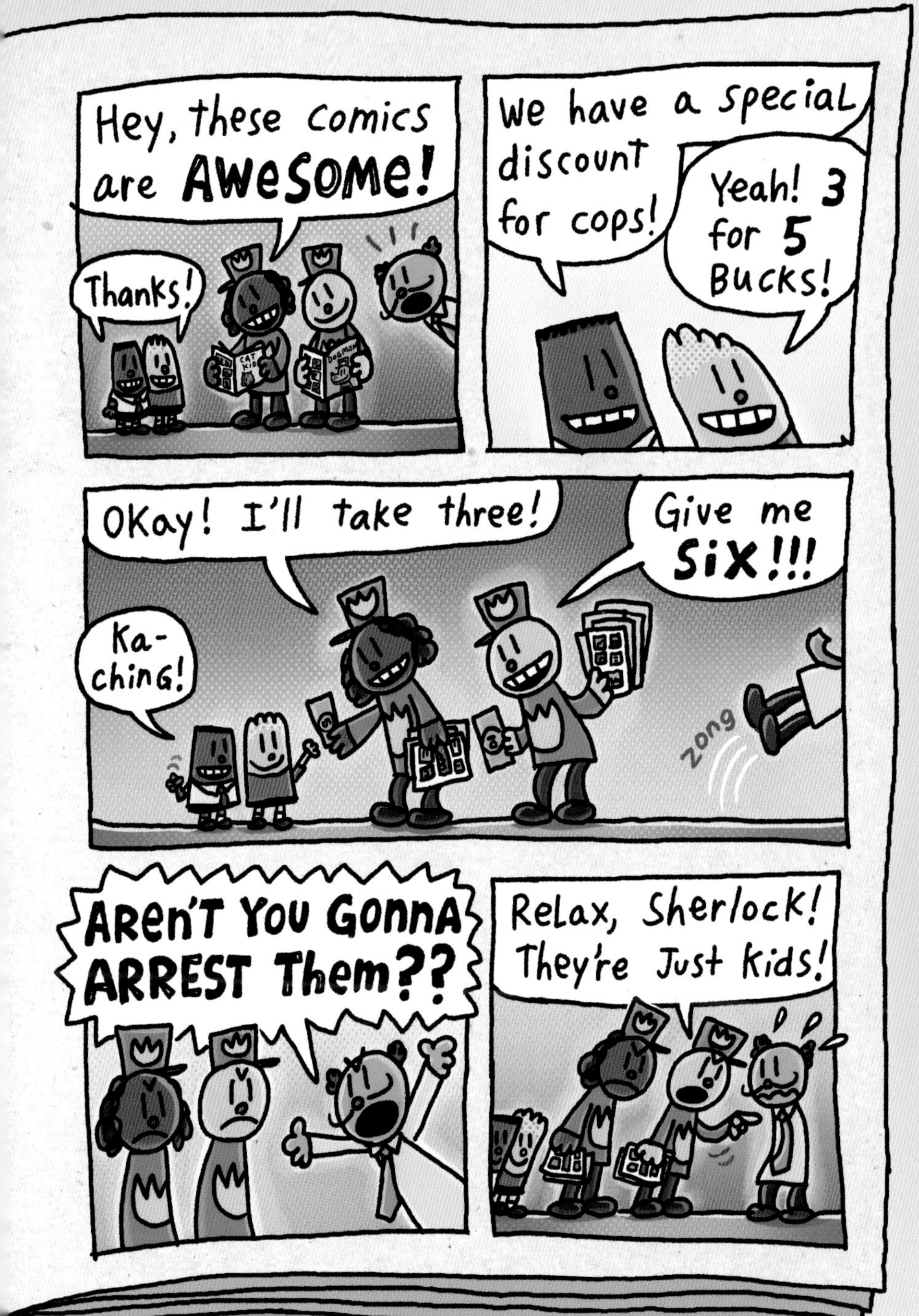

Hey, these comics are AWESOME!
Thanks!
CAT KID
DOGMAN
We have a special discount for cops!
Yeah! 3 for 5 Bucks!
OKay! I'll take three!
Give me SIX!!!
Ka-chinG!
ZONG
AREN'T YOU GONNA ARREST Them??
ReLax, Sherlock! They're Just Kids!

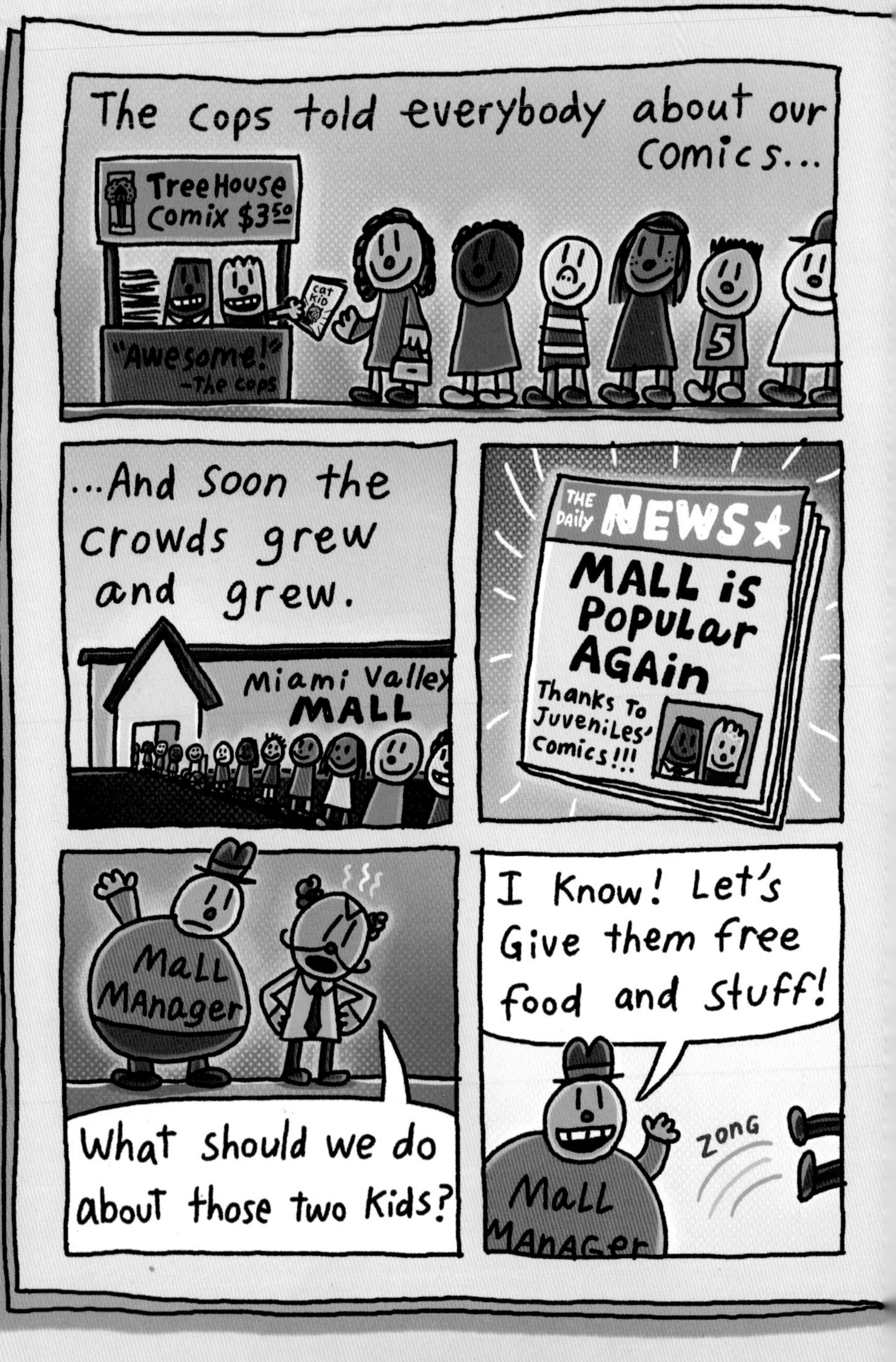
The cops told everybody about our comics...
TreeHouse Comix $3.50
Cat Kid
"Awesome!" -The cops
5
...And soon the crowds grew and grew.
Miami Valley MALL
THE Daily NEWS
MALL is Popular AGAin
Thanks To Juveniles' Comics!!!
Mall Manager
What should we do about those two Kids?
I Know! Let's Give them free food and stuff!
ZONG
Mall Manager

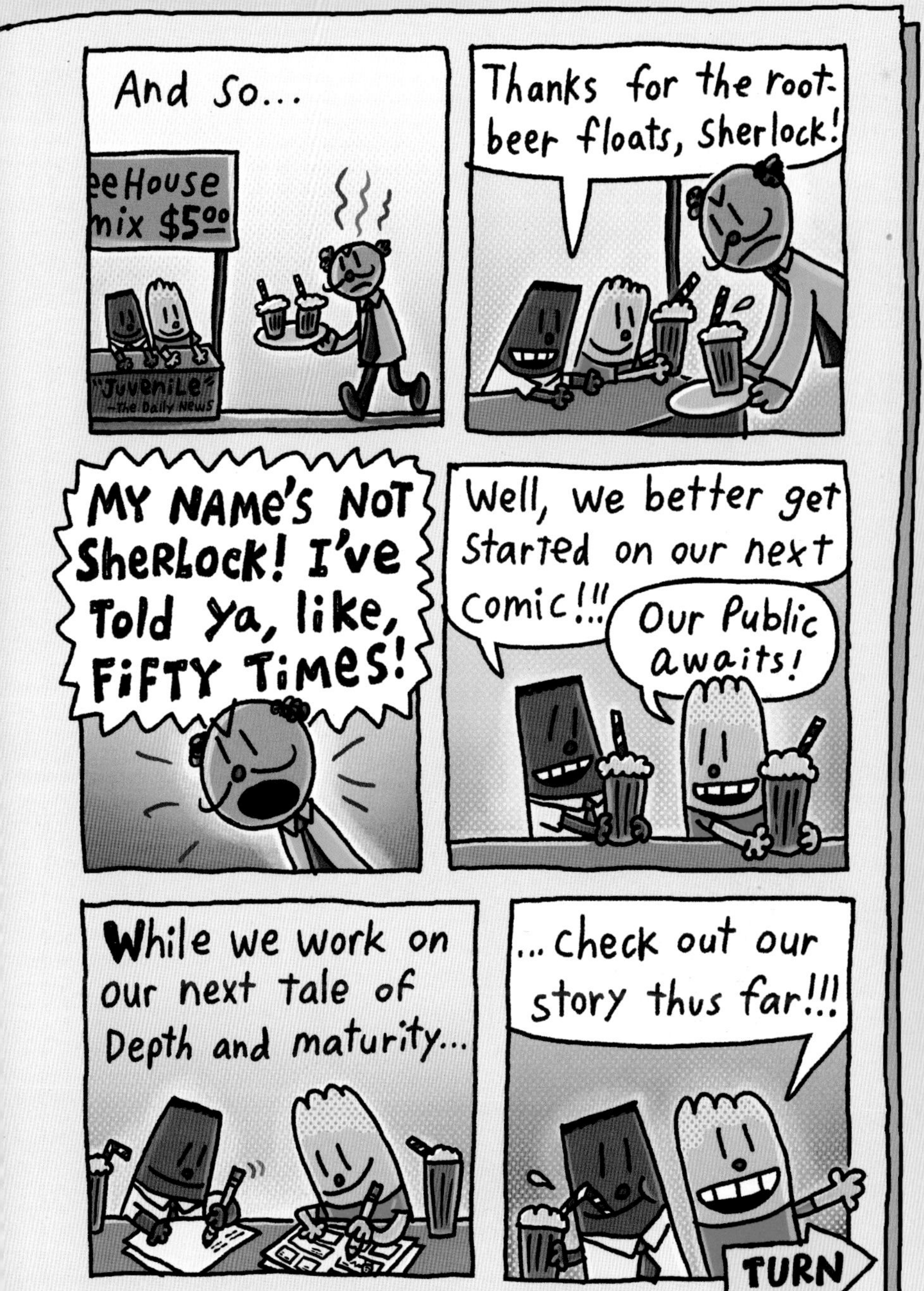
And so...
eeHouse
mix $5.00
"Juvenile"
—The Daily News
Thanks for the root-beer floats, Sherlock!
MY NAME'S NOT SHERLOCK! I'VE TOLD YA, LIKE, FIFTY TIMES!
Well, we better get started on our next comic!!!
Our public awaits!
While we work on our next tale of depth and maturity...
...check out our story thus far!!!
TURN

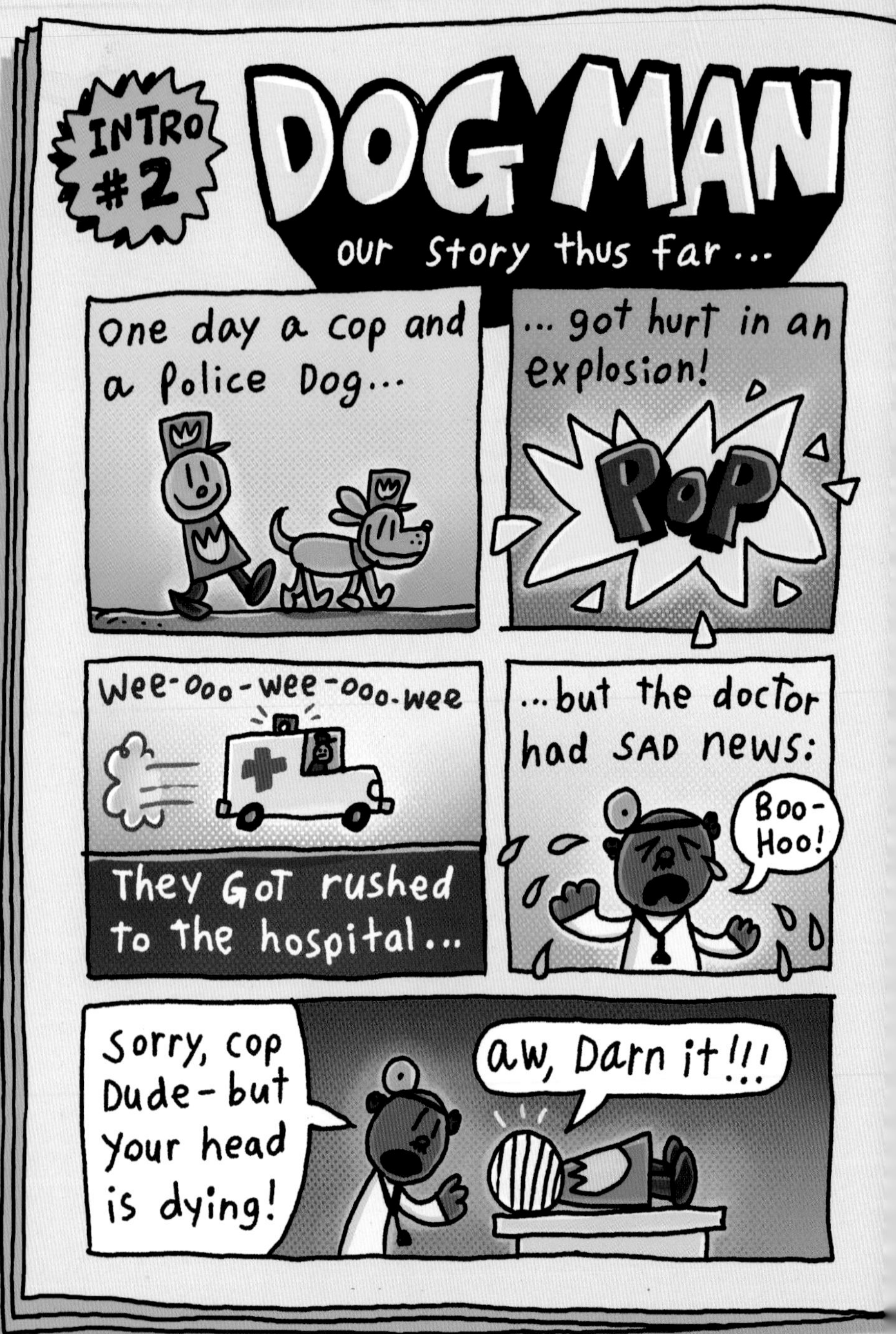
INTRO #2
DOG MAN
our Story thus far...
One day a cop and a Police Dog...
... got hurt in an explosion!
POP
Wee-ooo-wee-ooo-wee
They GoT rushed to the hospital...
...but the doctor had SAD news:
Boo-Hoo!
Sorry, cop Dude- but your head is dying!
aw, Darn it!!!

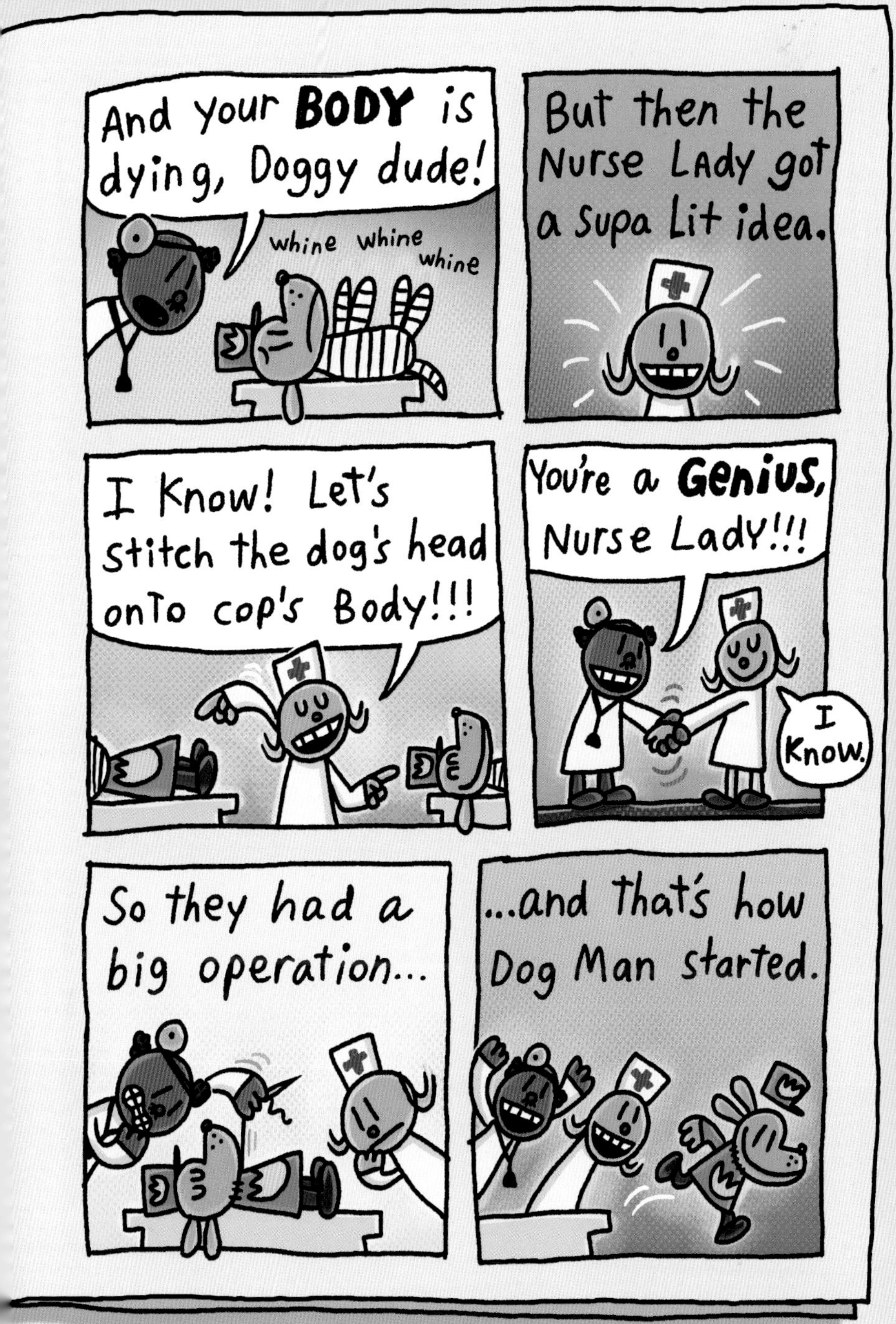

And your **BODY** is dying, Doggy dude!
whine whine whine
But then the Nurse Lady got a Supa Lit idea.
I Know! Let's stitch the dog's head onTo cop's Body!!!
You're a **Genius,** Nurse Lady!!!
I Know.
So they had a big operation...
...and that's how Dog Man started.

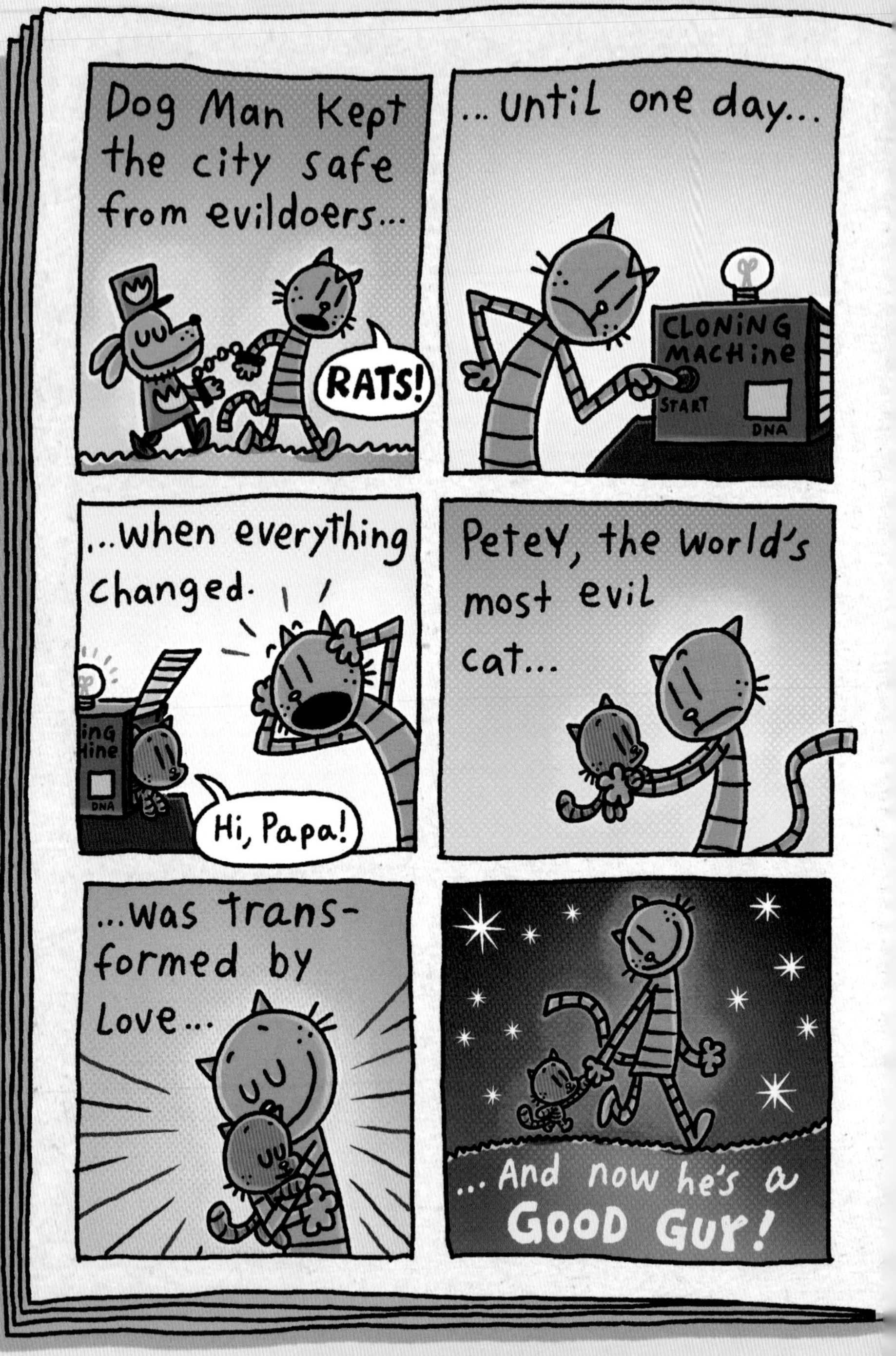

Dog Man Kept the city safe from evildoers...
RATS!
...Until one day...
CLONING MACHINE
START
DNA
...when everything changed.
Hi, Papa!
DNA
Petey, the world's most evil cat...
...was trans-formed by Love...
... And now he's a GOOD GUY!

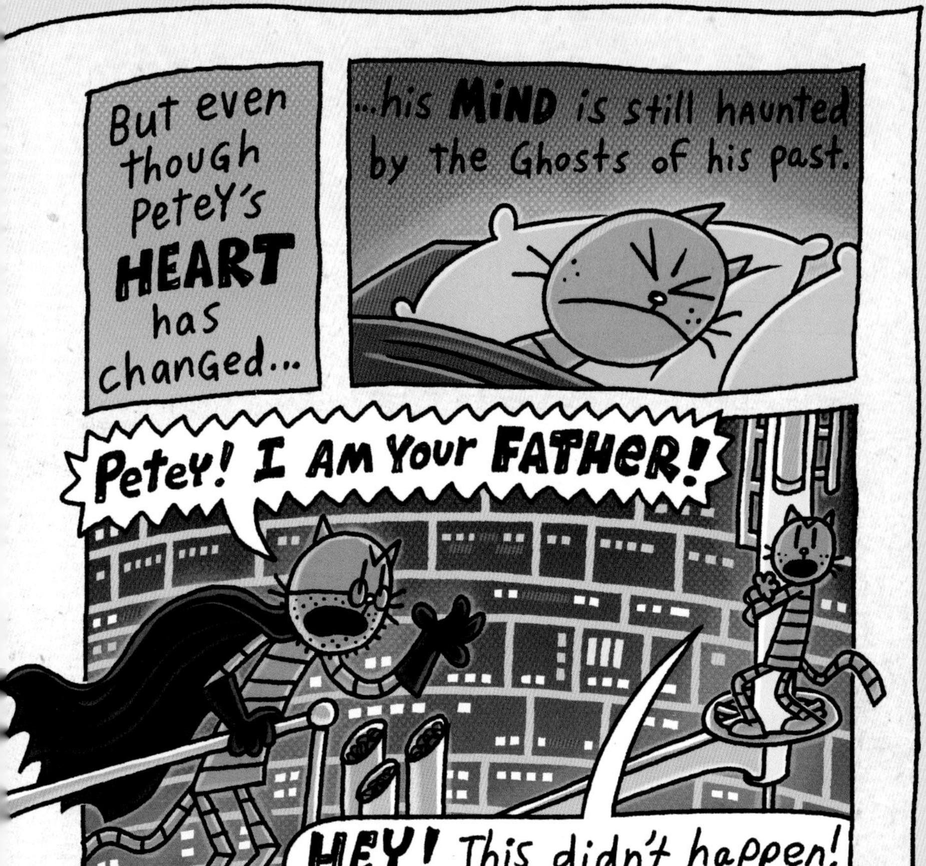
But even though Petey's HEART has changed...
...his MIND is still haunted by the Ghosts of his past.
Petey! I AM Your FATHER!
HEY! This didn't happen!
If Petey is gonna continue to DO GOOD...

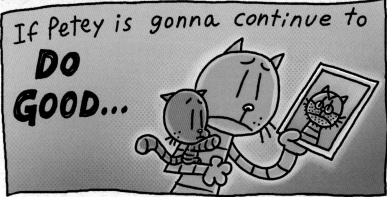

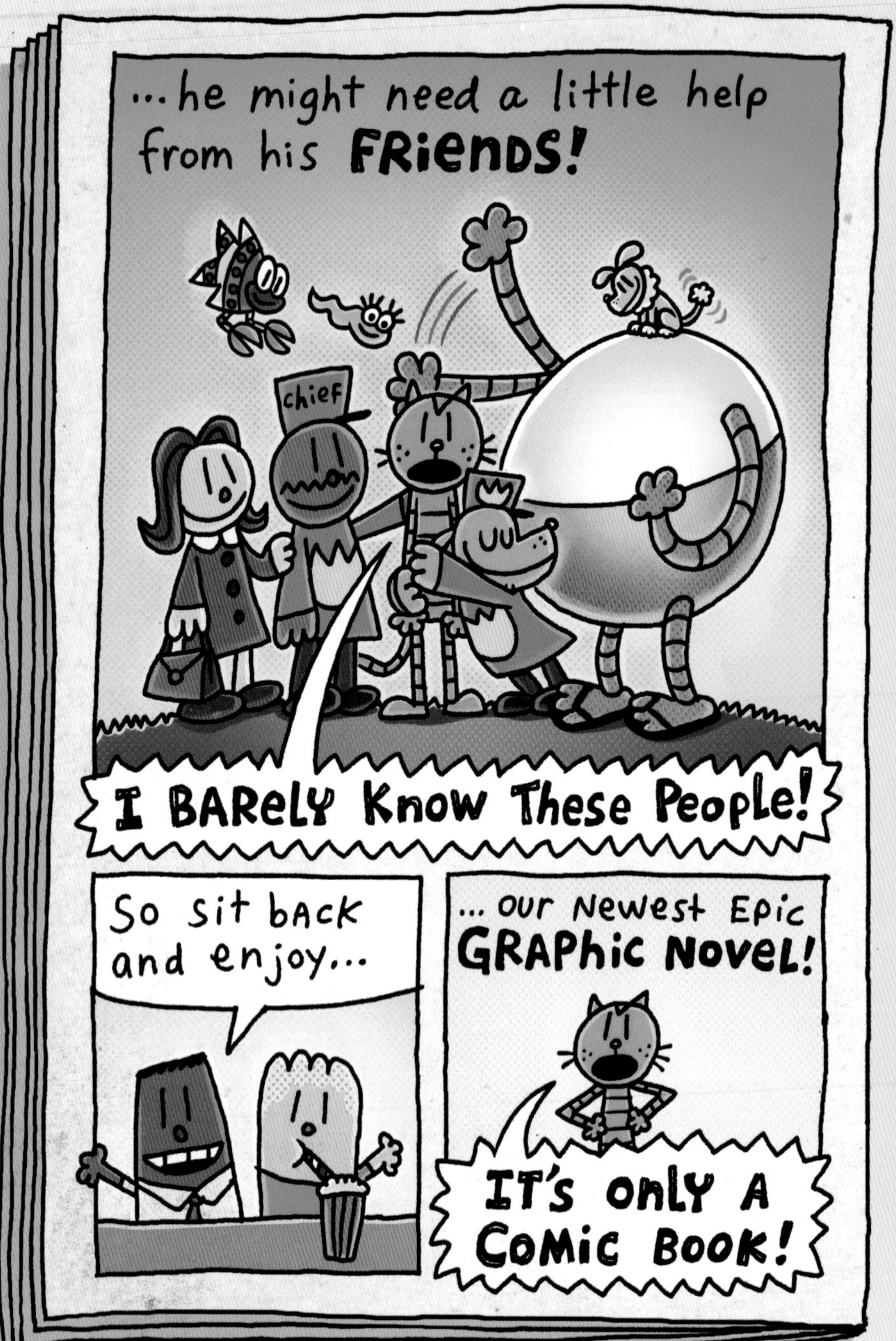
...he might need a little help from his FRIENDS!
chief
I BARELY Know These People!
So sit back and enjoy...
...our Newest Epic GRAPHIC NOVEL!
IT'S ONLY A COMIC BOOK!

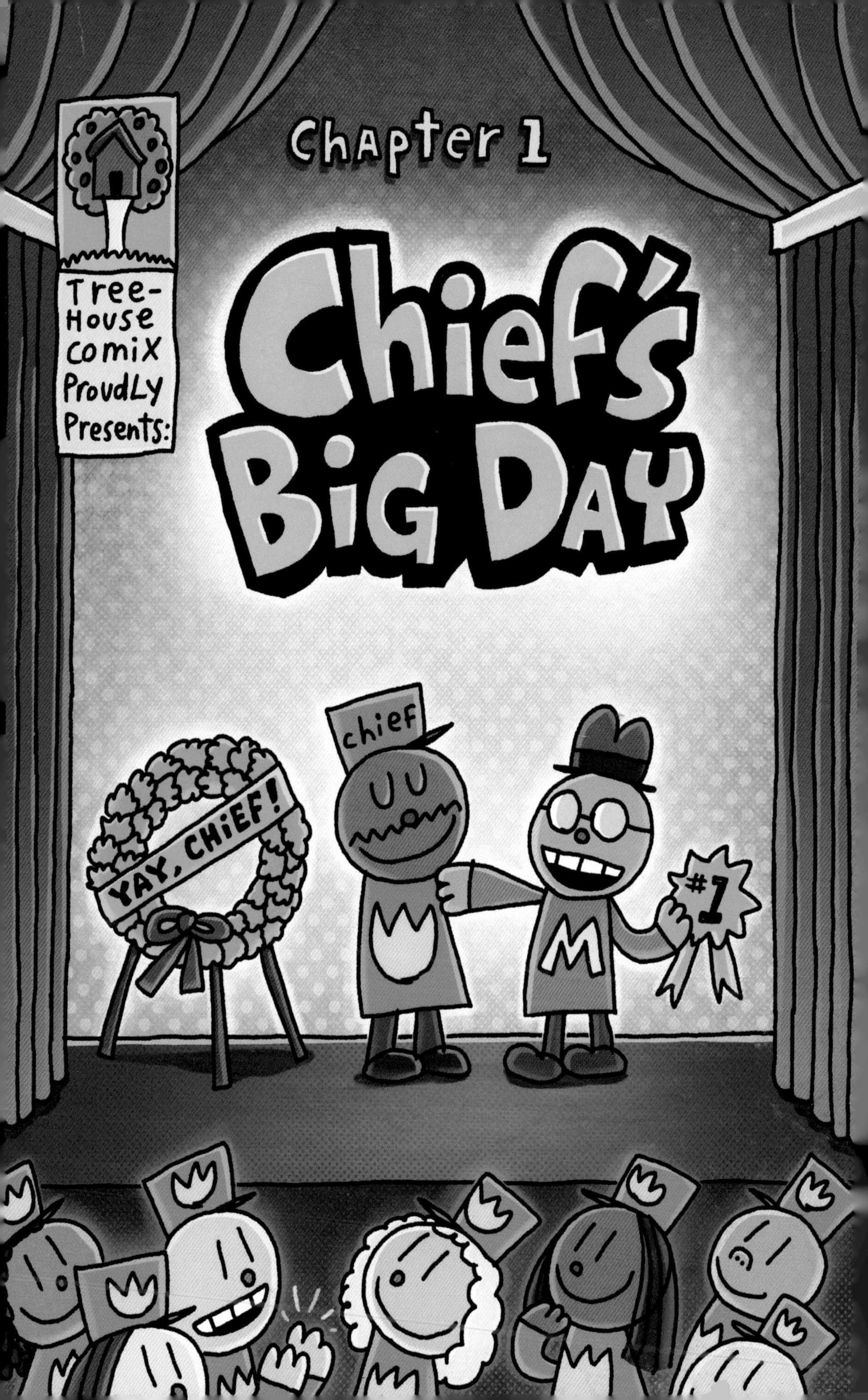
Tree-House comix Proudly Presents:
Chapter 1
Chief's Big Day
chief
YAY, CHIEF!
#1

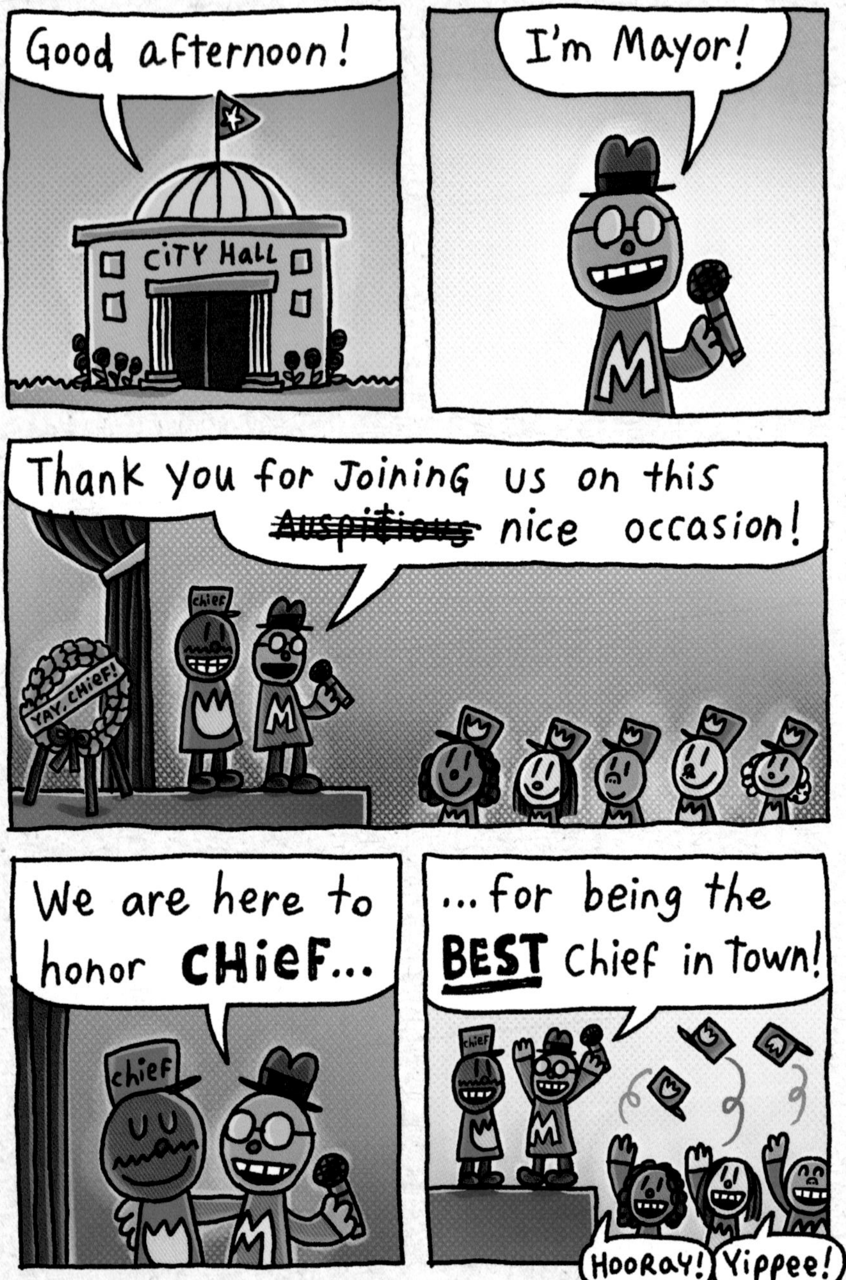
Good afternoon!
CITY HALL
I'm Mayor!
Thank you for Joining us on this ~~Auspitious~~ nice occasion!
chief
YAY, CHIEF!
We are here to honor **CHIEF...**
chief
...for being the **BEST** Chief in town!
chief
HOORAY!
Yippee!

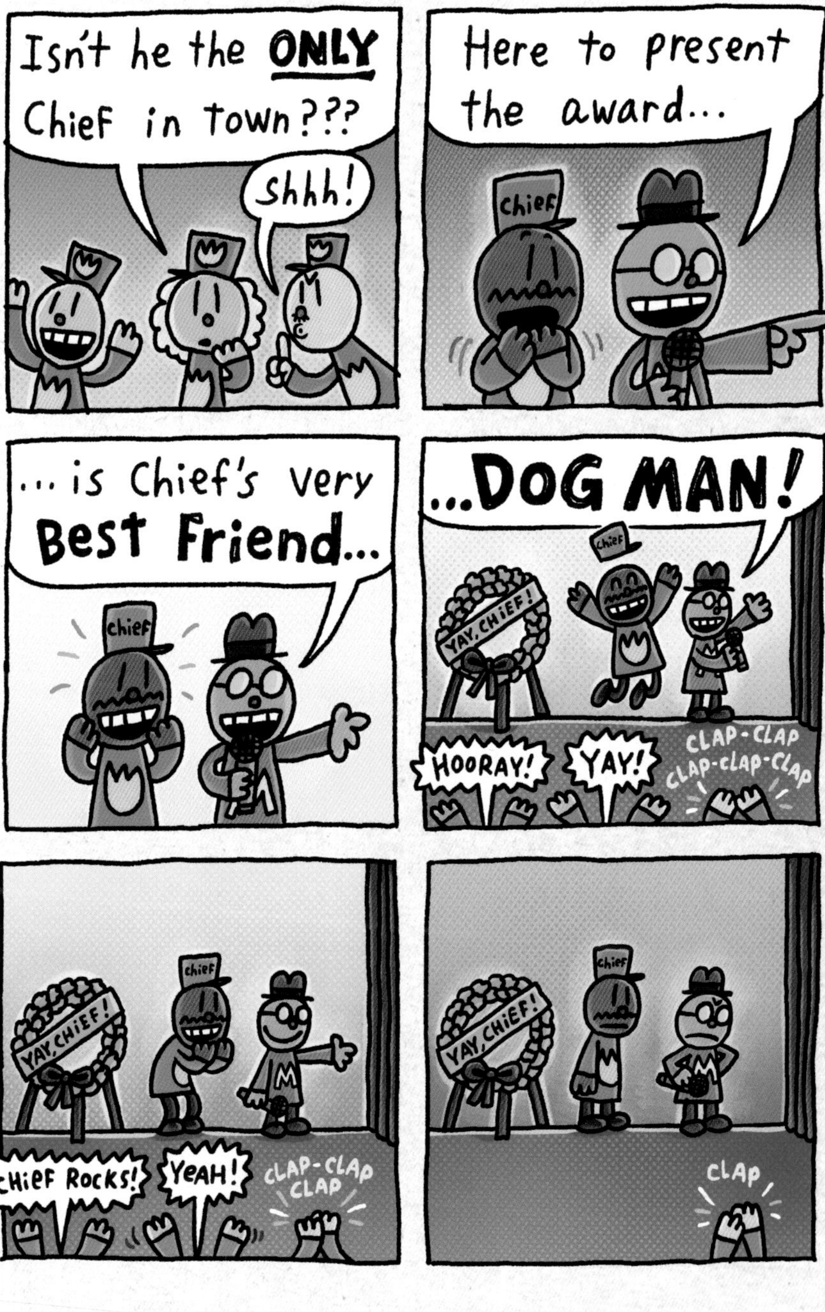
Isn't he the ONLY Chief in town???
Shhh!
Chief
Here to present the award...
... is Chief's very Best Friend...
Chief
...DOG MAN!
Chief
YAY, CHIEF!
HOORAY!
YAY!
CLAP-CLAP
CLAP-CLAP-CLAP
Chief
YAY, CHIEF!
CHIEF ROCKS!
YEAH!
CLAP-CLAP
CLAP
Chief
YAY, CHIEF!
CLAP

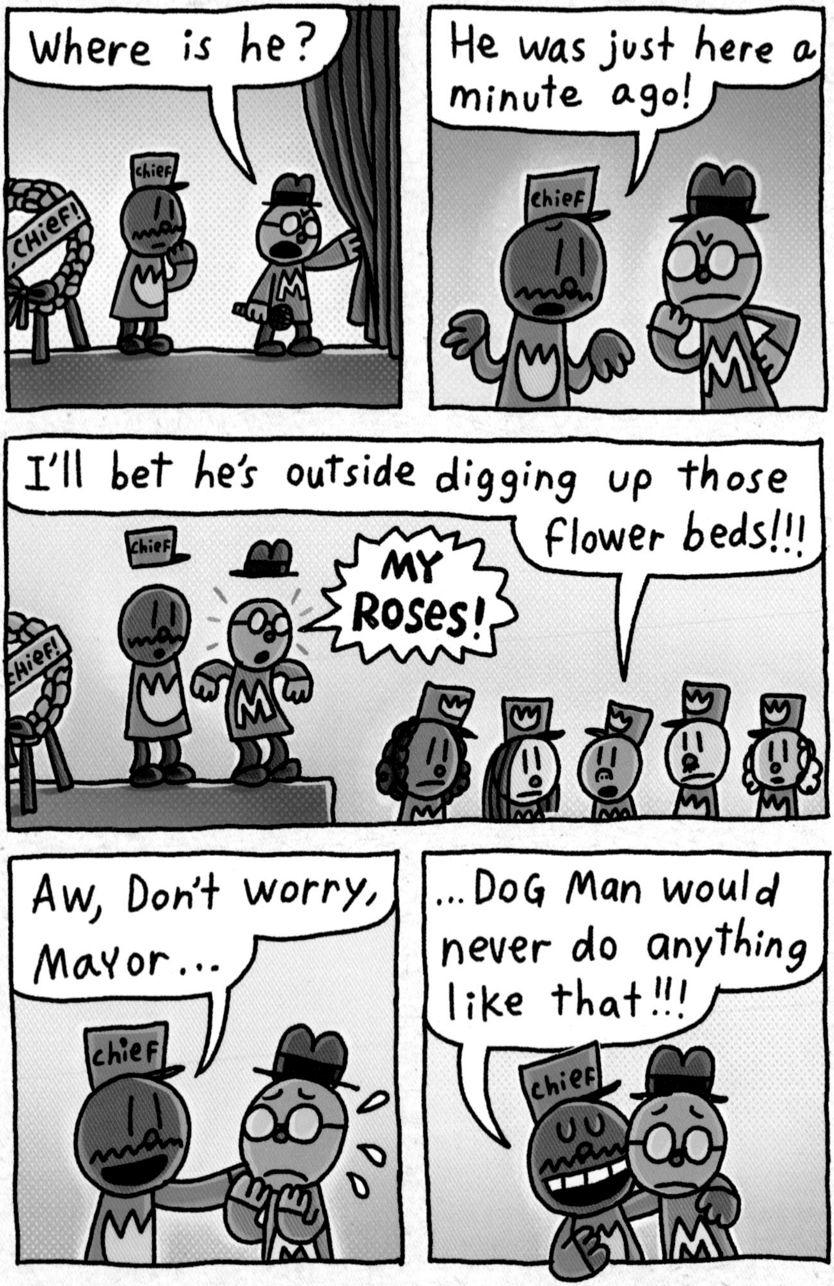
Where is he?
He was just here a minute ago!
I'll bet he's outside digging up those flower beds!!!
MY ROSES!
Aw, Don't worry, Mayor...
...DOG Man would never do anything like that!!!

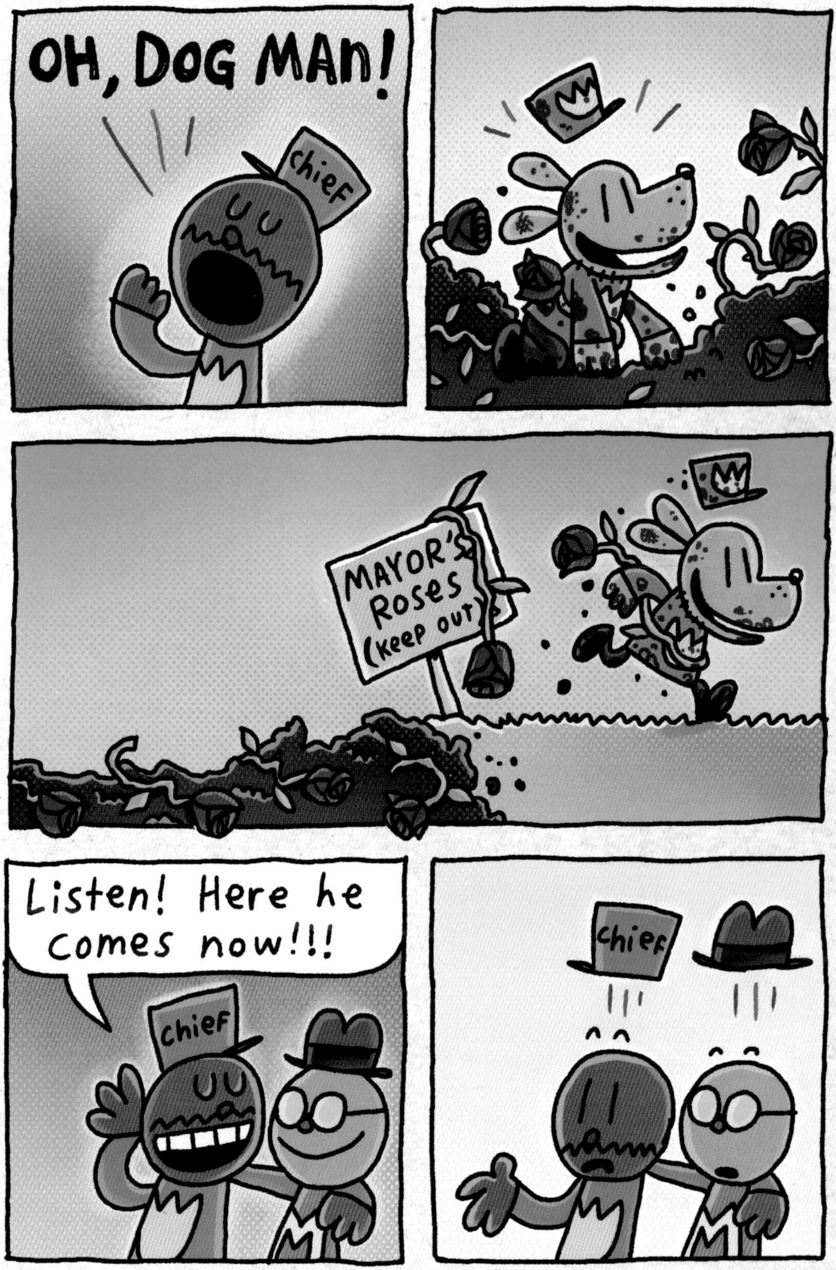
OH, DOG MAN!
chief
MAYOR'S Roses (keep out)
Listen! Here he comes now!!!
chief
chief

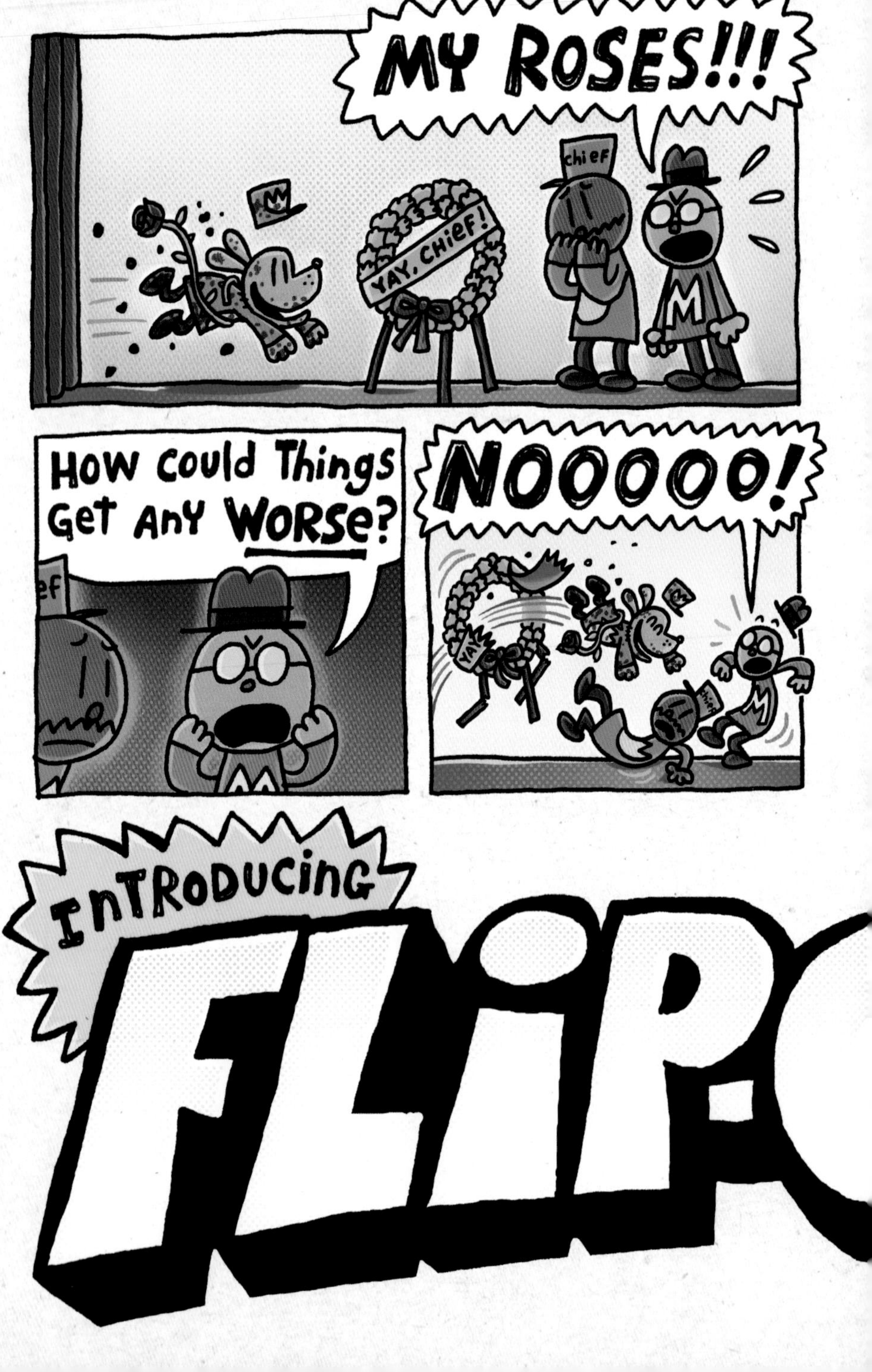
MY ROSES!!!
CHIEF
YAY, CHIEF!
M
How Could Things Get Any WORSE?
NOOOOO!
YAY
INTRODUCING
FLIP

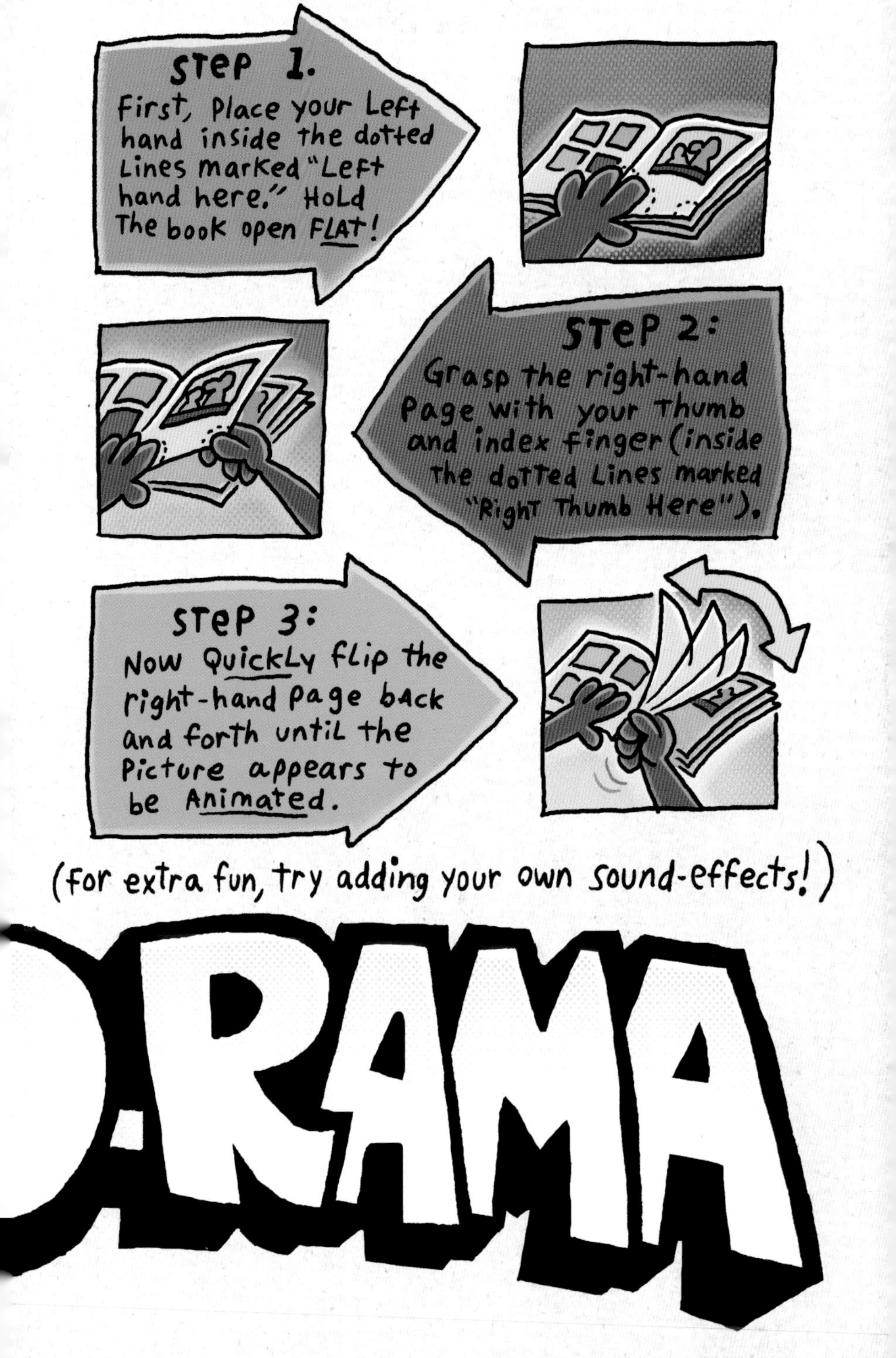
STEP 1.
First, Place your Left hand inside the dotted Lines marked "Left hand here." HoLd The book open FLAT!
STEP 2:
Grasp the right-hand Page with your Thumb and index finger (inside the dotted Lines marked "Right Thumb Here").
STEP 3:
Now QuickLy fLip the right-hand Page back and forth until the Picture appears to be Animated.
(For extra fun, try adding your own sound-effects!)
RAMA

ReMemBeR,

While you are flipping,
be sure you can see
the image on page **23**
AND the image on page **25**.

If you flip quickly,
the two pictures will
start to look like **ONE**
ANIMATeD cartoon.

Don't forget to
add your own
sound-effects!!!

Left
hand here.

Right
Thumb
here.

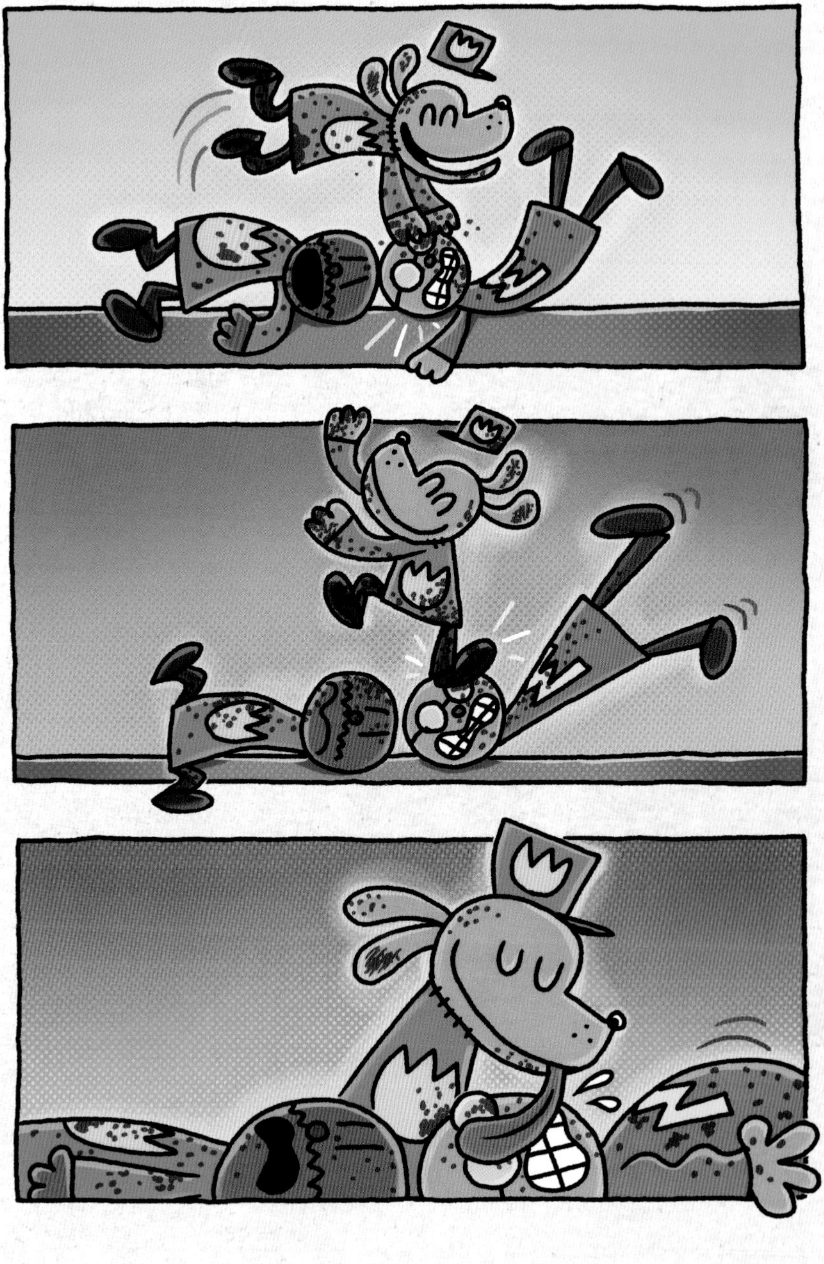

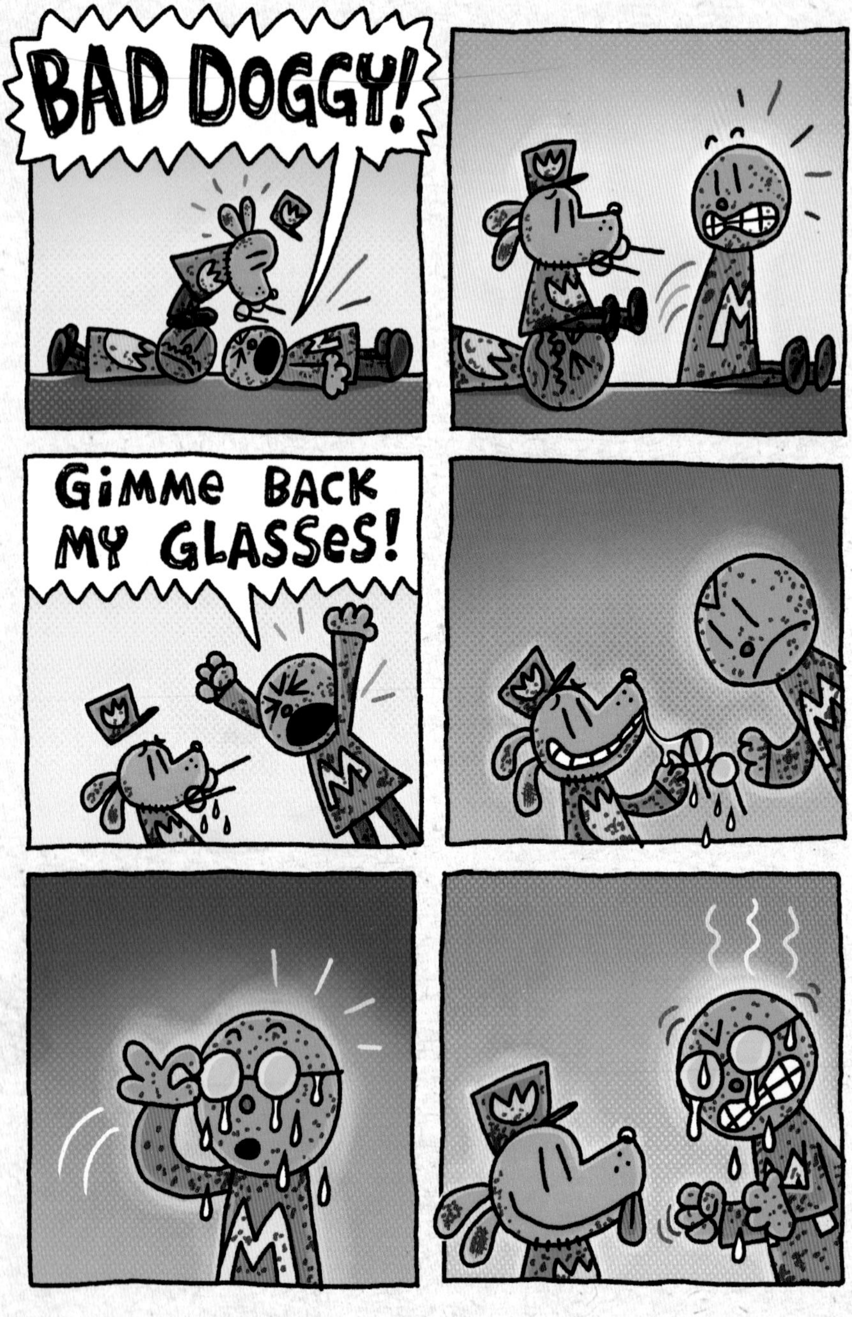
BAD DOGGY!
GiMME BACK MY GLASSeS!

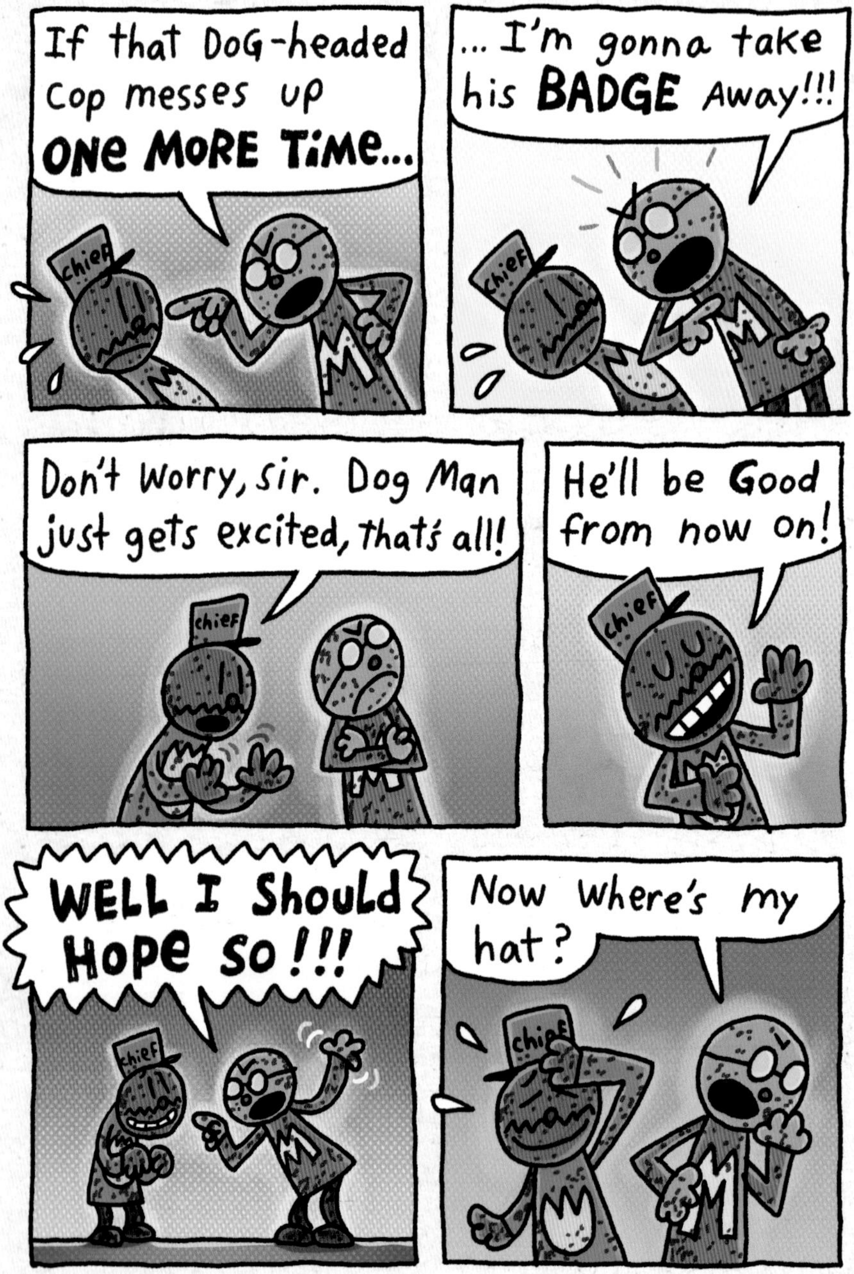
If that DOG-headed Cop messes up ONE MORE TIME...
... I'm gonna take his BADGE Away!!!
chief
Don't worry, sir. Dog Man just gets excited, that's all!
chief
He'll be Good from now on!
chief
WELL I Should HOPE SO!!!
chief
Now Where's my hat?
chief

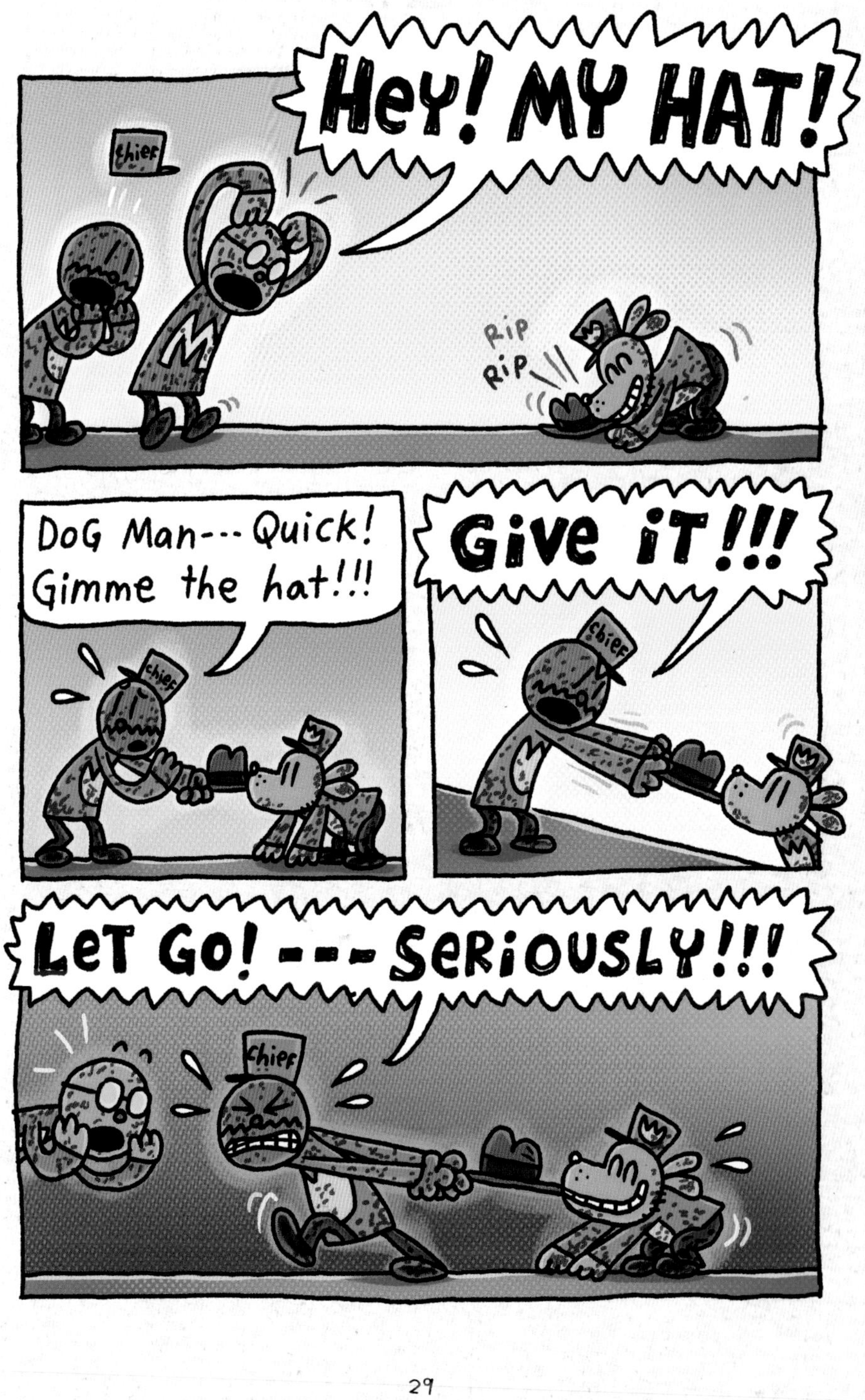
Hey! MY HAT!
chief
Rip
Rip
DoG Man---Quick! Gimme the hat!!!
chief
Give iT!!!
chief
LeT Go! --- SeRiOUSLY!!!
chief

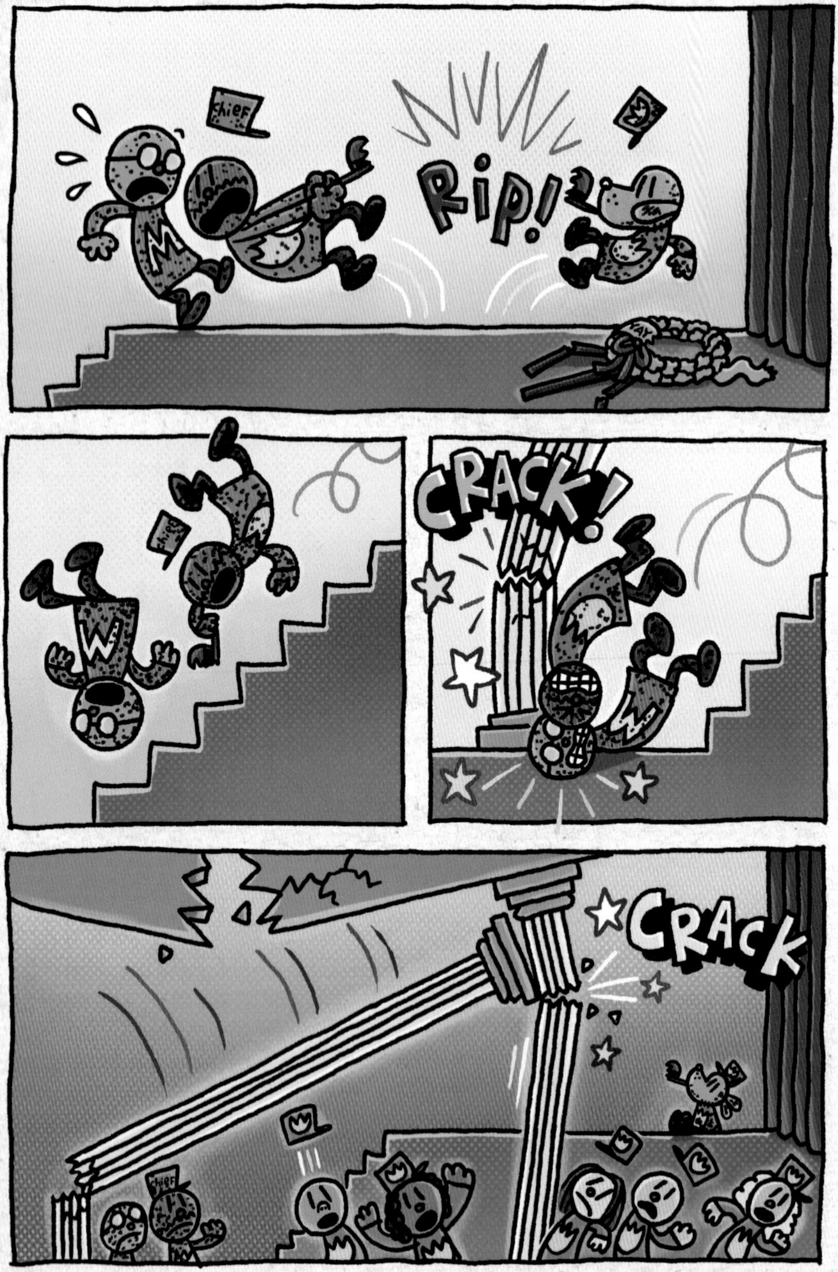

CHIEF
RIP!
CRACK!
CRACK

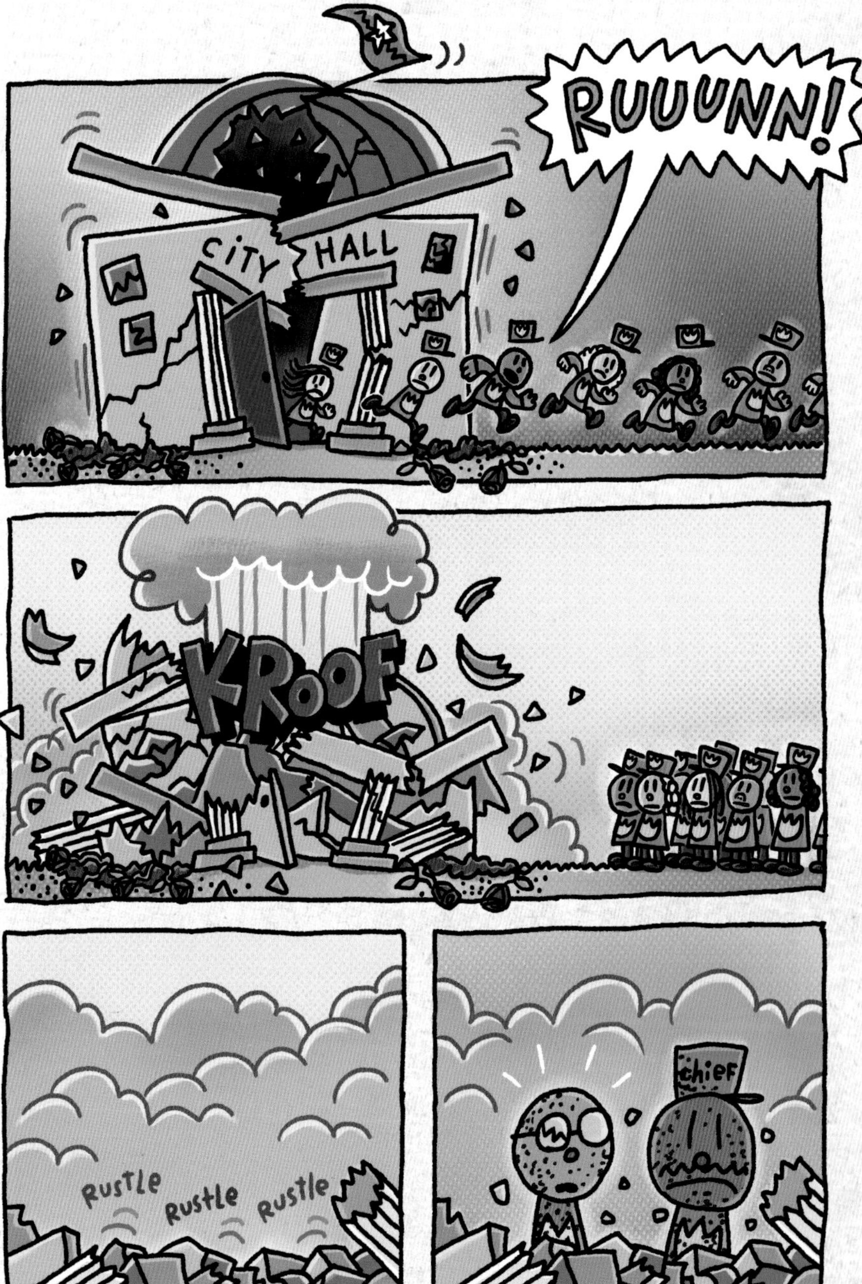
CITY HALL
RUUUNN!
KROOF
RUSTLE RUSTLE RUSTLE
CHIEF

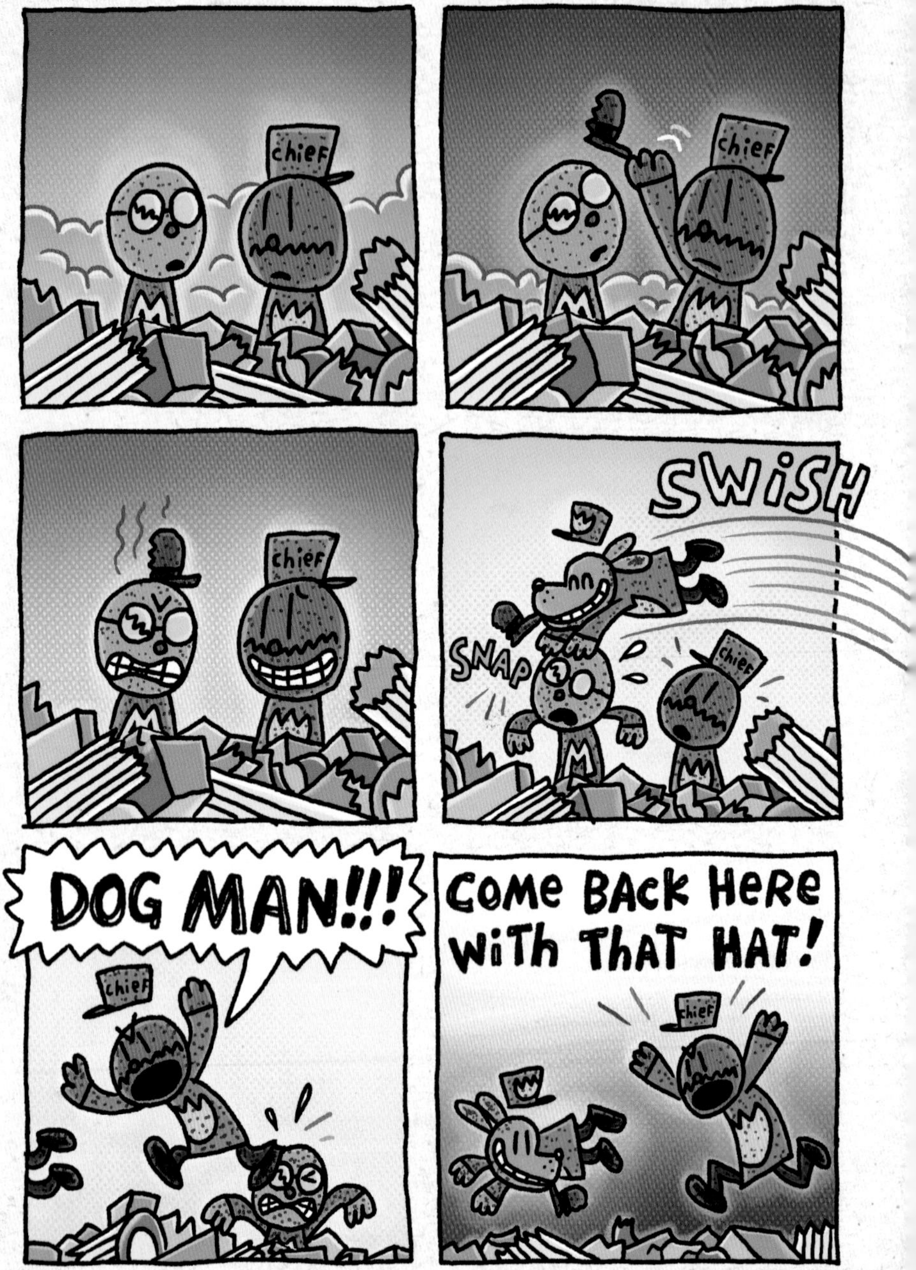
chief
chief
chief
SWISH
SNAP
chief
DOG MAN!!!
chief
Come Back Here With That HAT!
chief

CHAPTER 2

The Saddest CHAPTER Ever Written

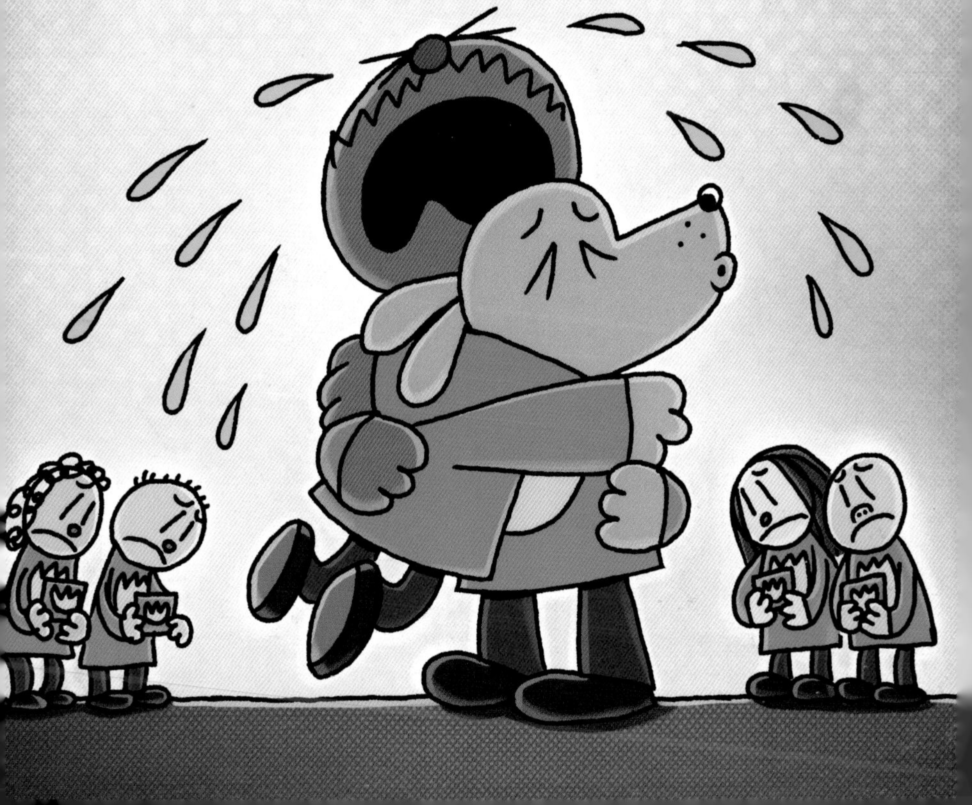

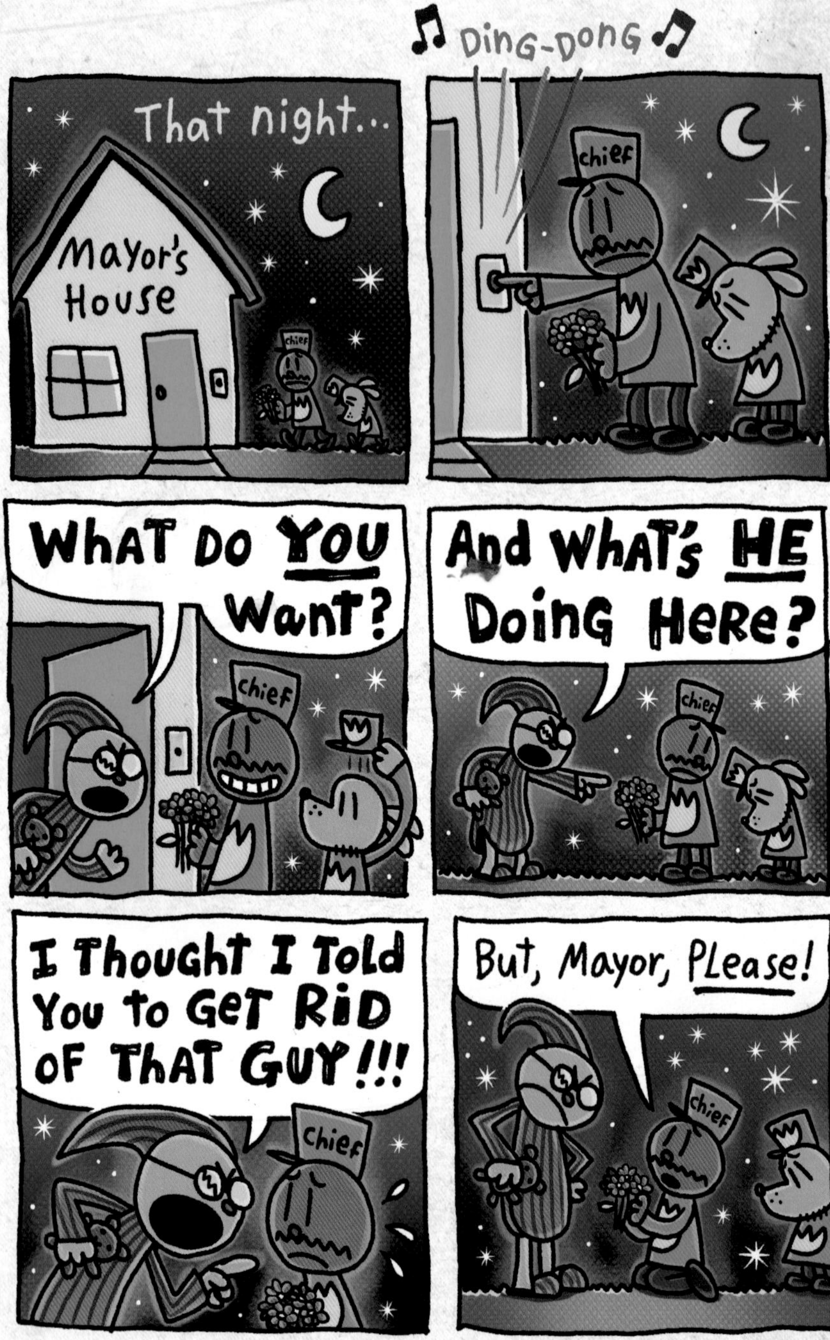
That night...
Mayor's House
chief
DING-DONG
chief
WHAT DO YOU Want?
chief
And WHAT'S HE Doing Here?
chief
I Thought I Told You to GET RID OF THAT GUY!!!
Chief
But, Mayor, PLease!
chief

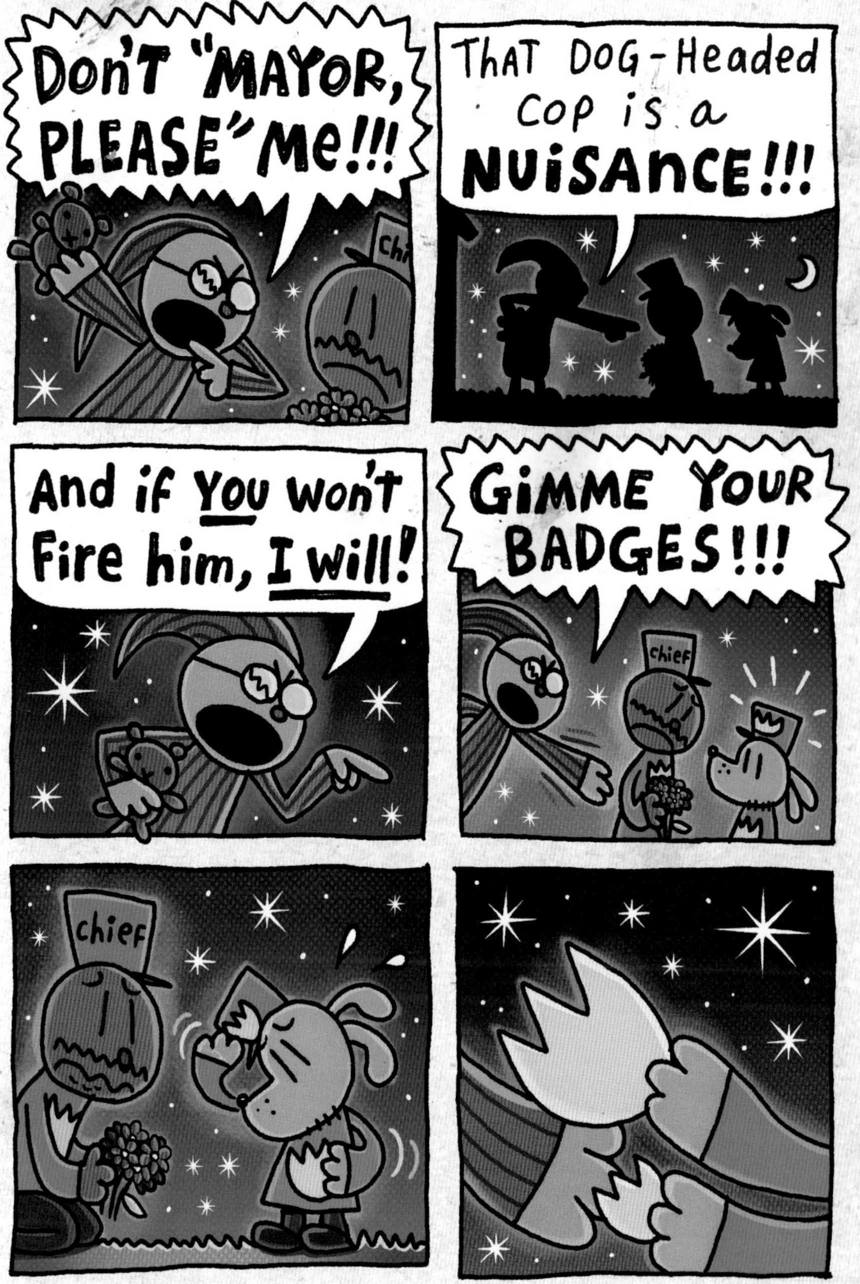
Don't "MAYOR, PLEASE" Me!!!
THAT DOG-Headed cop is a NUISANCE!!!
And if YOU won't Fire him, I will!
GIMME YOUR BADGES!!!
chief
chief

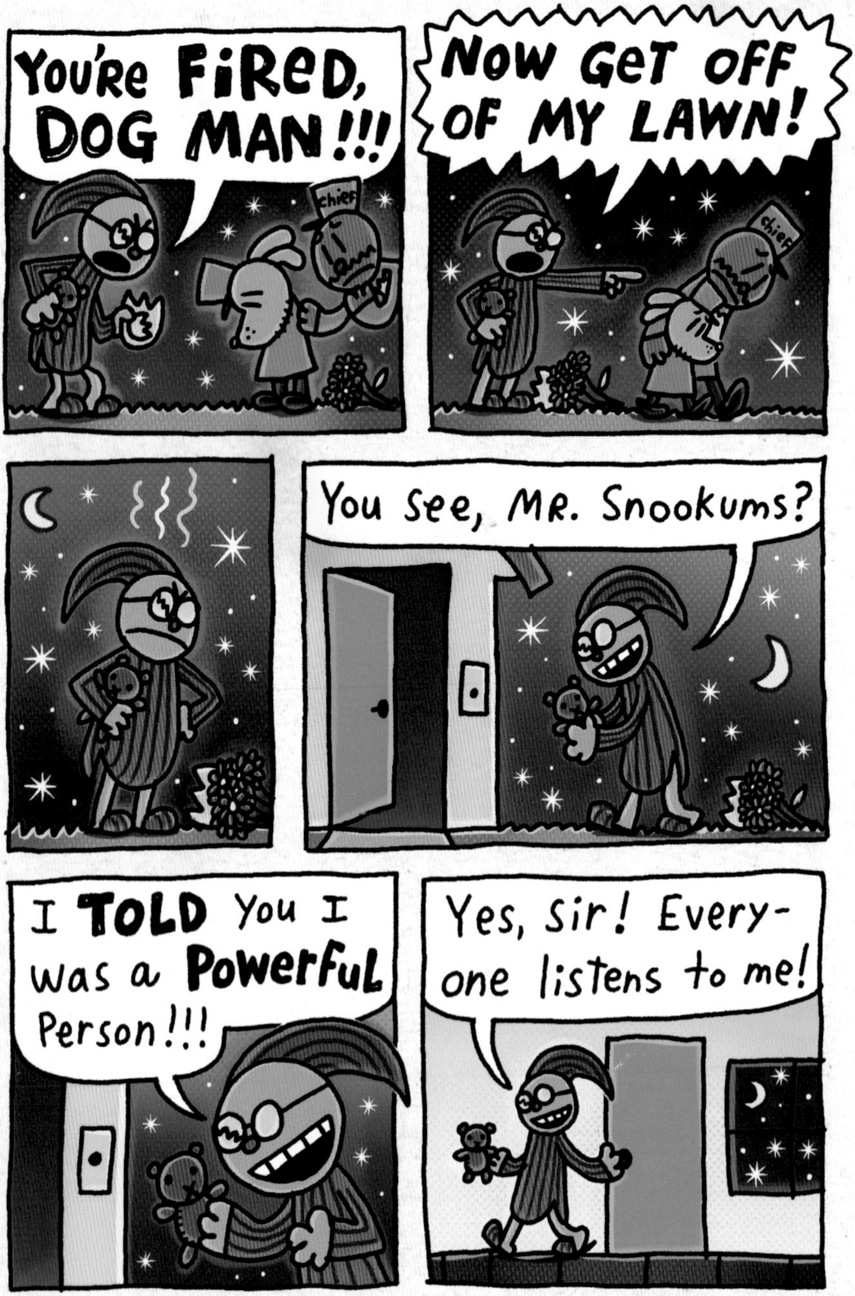
YOU'RE FIRED, DOG MAN!!!
chief
NOW GET OFF OF MY LAWN!
chief
You see, Mr. Snookums?
I TOLD You I was a Powerful Person!!!
Yes, Sir! Every-one listens to me!

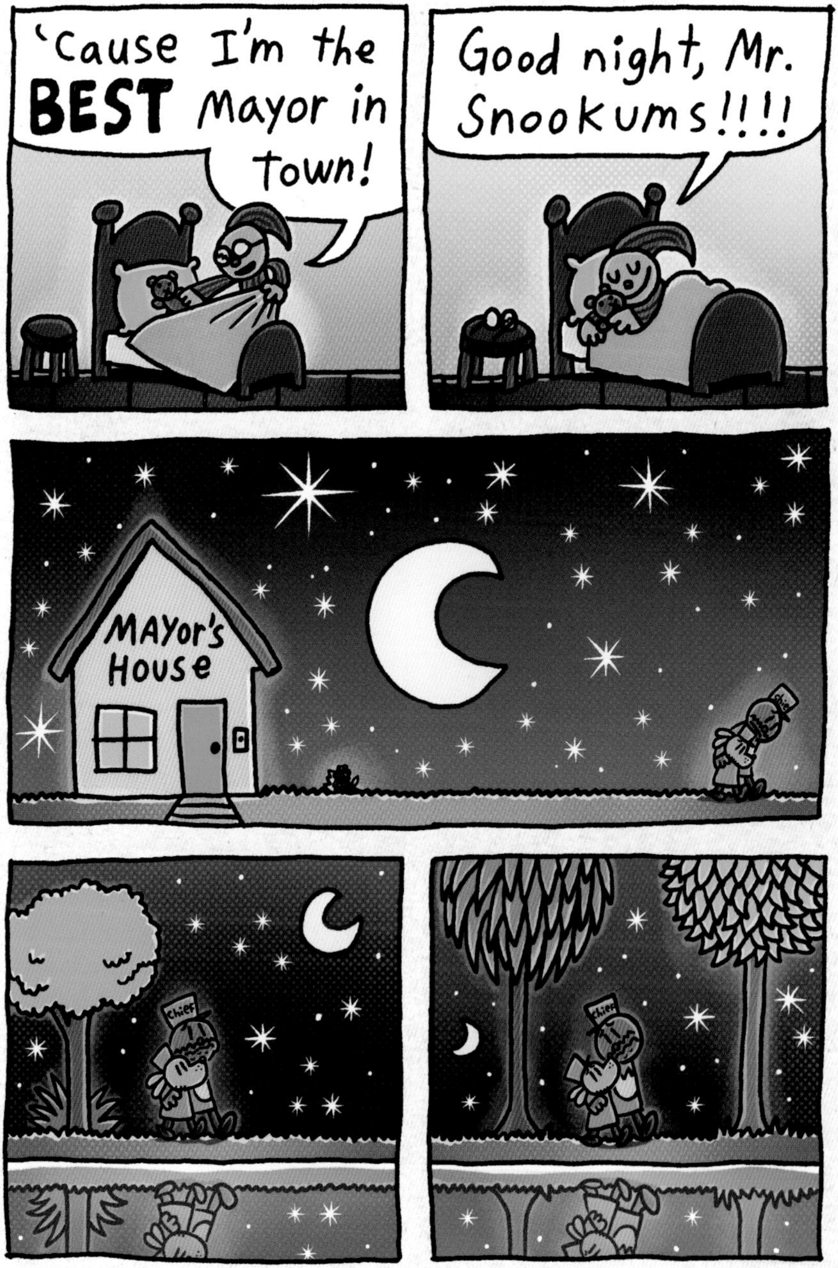
'Cause I'm the BEST Mayor in town!
Good night, Mr. Snookums!!!!
MAYOR'S HOUSE
CHIEF
CHIEF
CHIEF

38

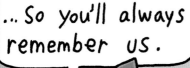

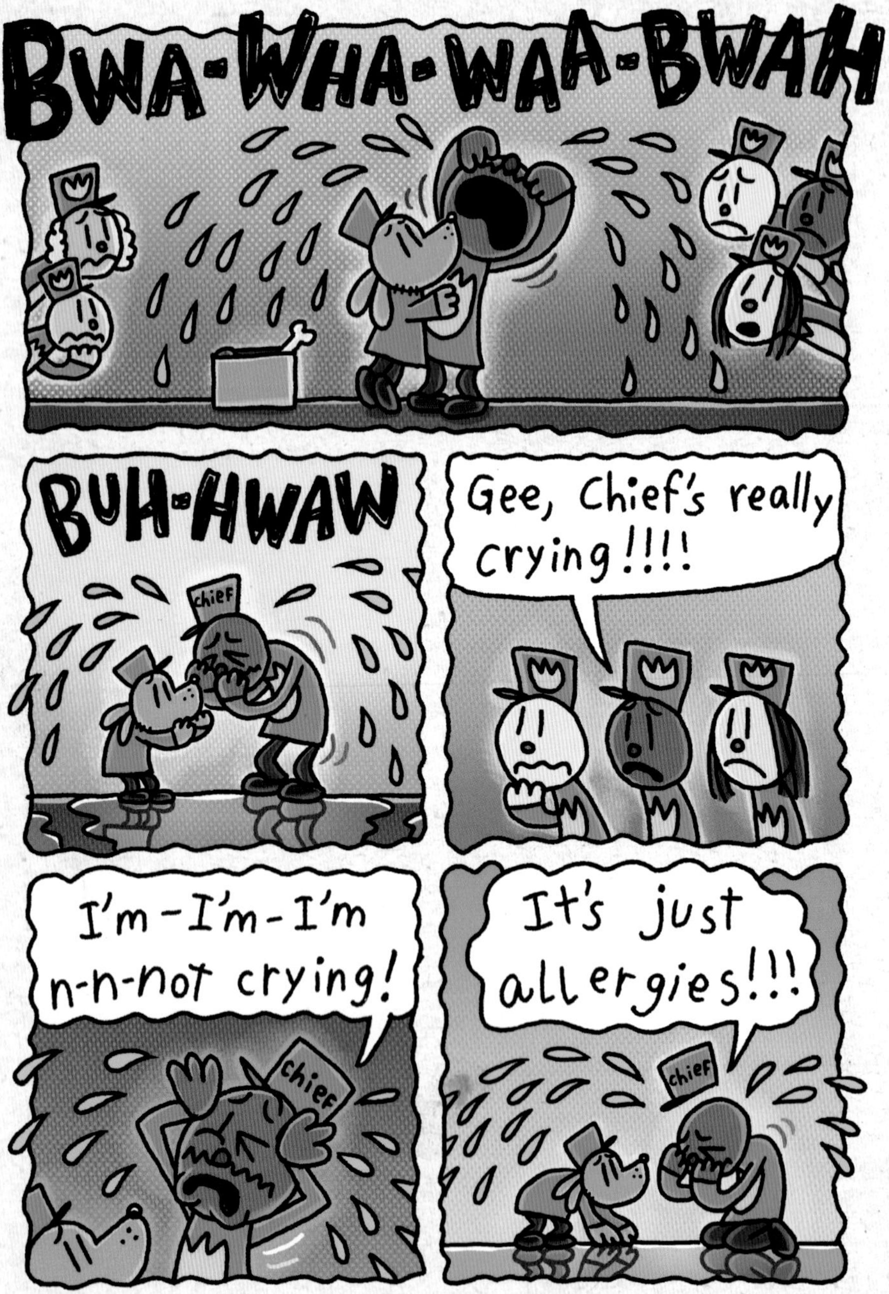
BWA-WHA-WAA-BWAH
BUH-HWAW
chief
Gee, Chief's really crying!!!!
I'm-I'm-I'm n-n-not crying!
chief
It's just allergies!!!
chief

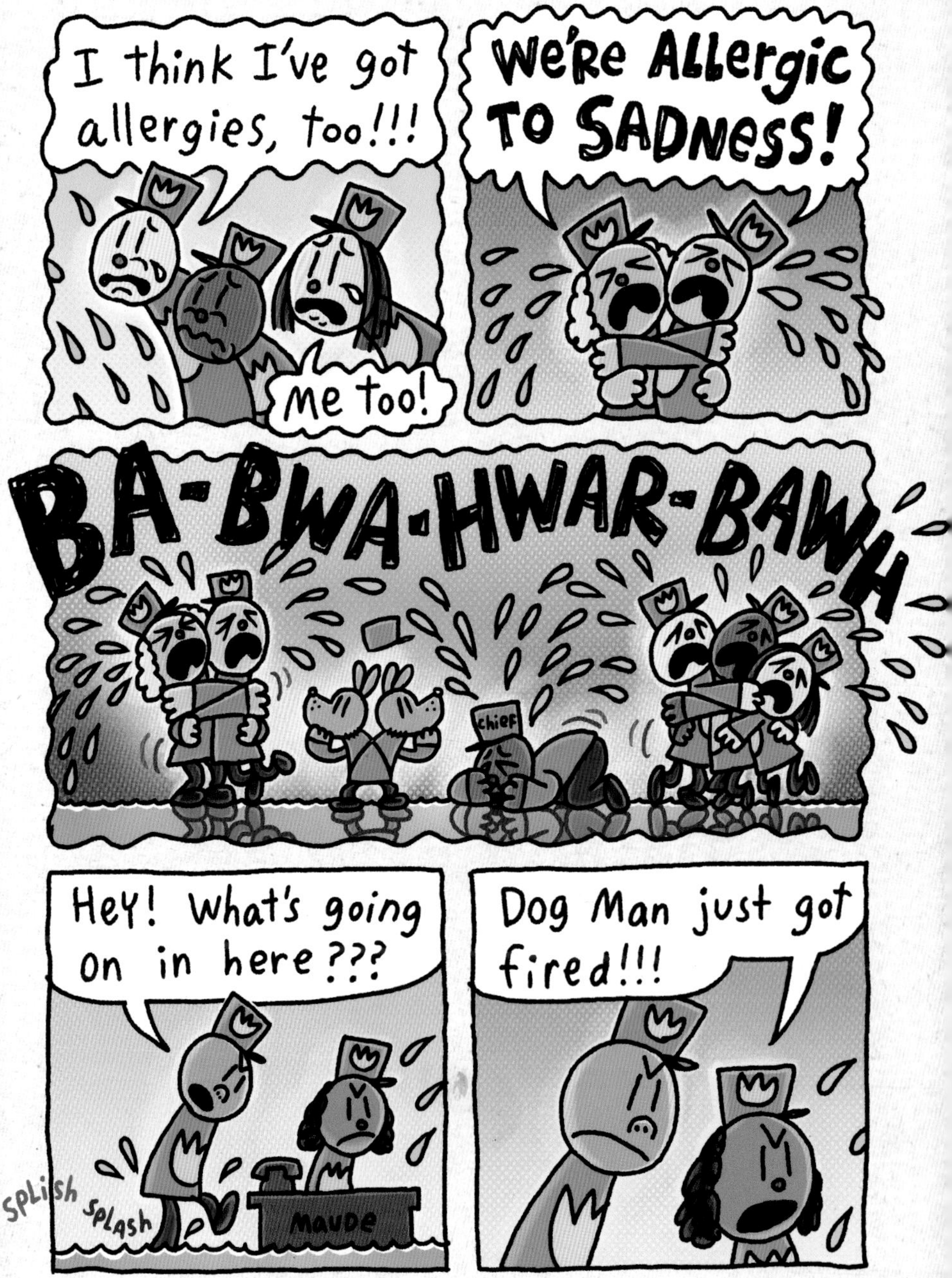
I think I've got allergies, too!!!
Me too!
We're ALLergic TO SADNESS!
BA-BWA-HWAR-BAWH
chief
Hey! What's going on in here???
SPLish SPLASH
MAUDE
Dog Man just got fired!!!

ish SPLASH SPlish SPLASH

42

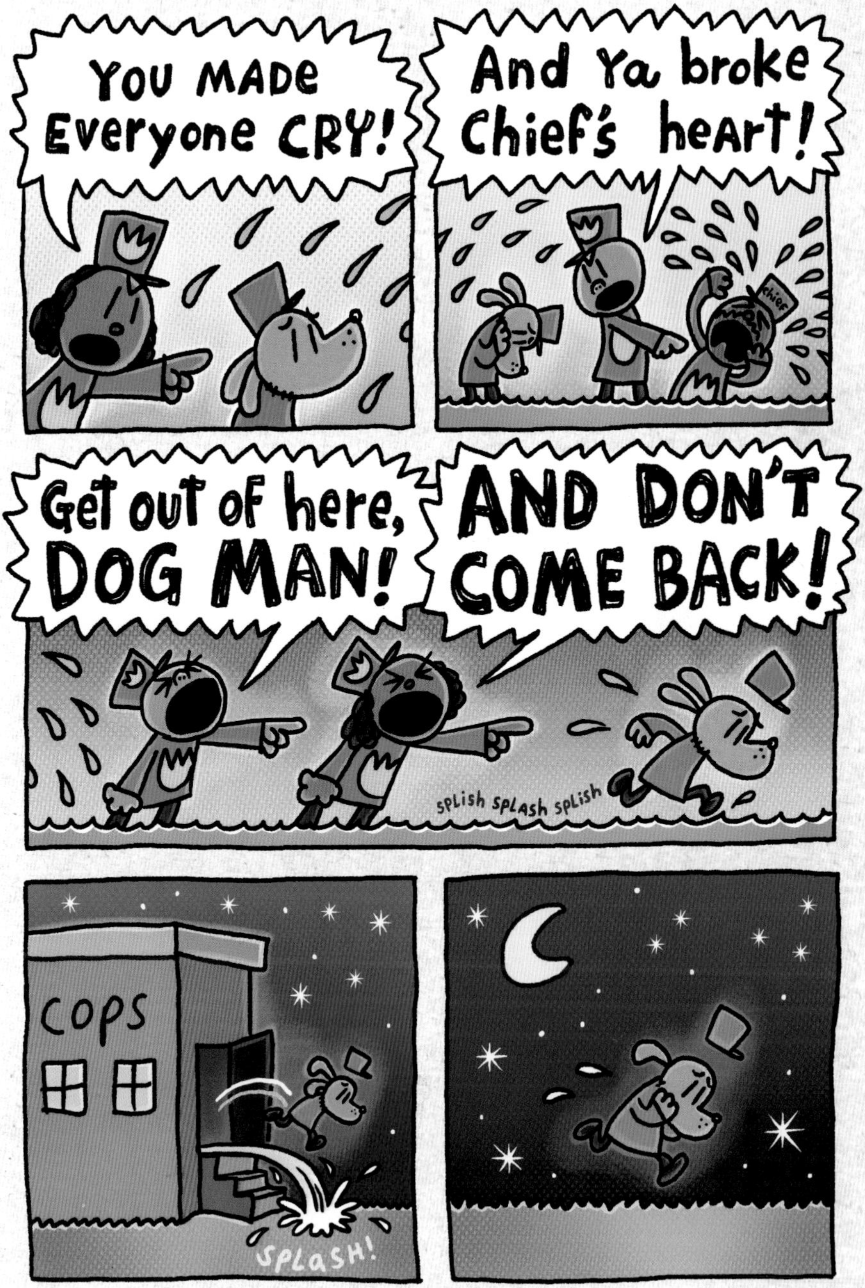
YOU MADE Everyone CRY!
And Ya broke Chief's heart!
Chief
Get out of here, DOG MAN!
AND DON'T COME BACK!
SPLish SPLASH SPLish
COPS
SPLASH!

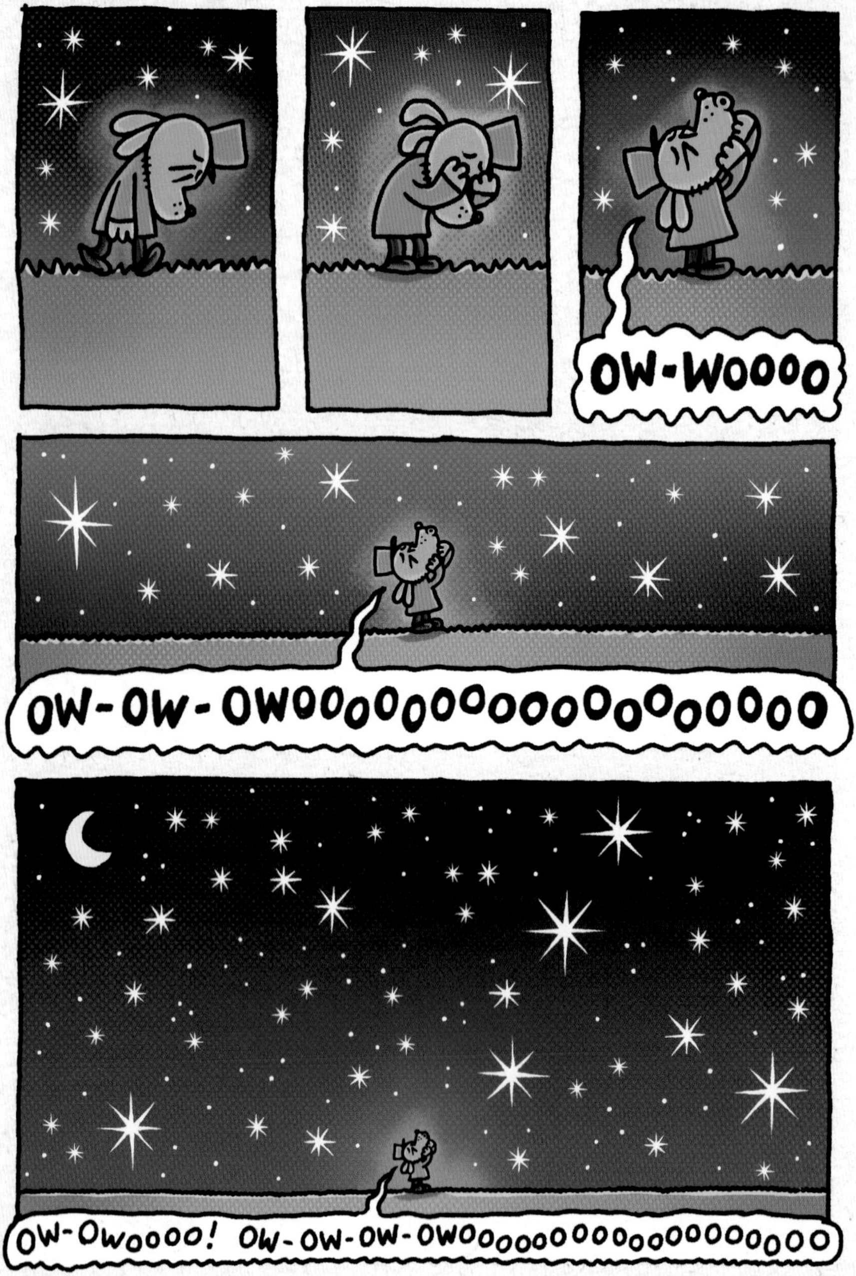
OW-WOOOO
OW-OW-OWOOOOOOOOOOOOOOOOOO
OW-OWOOOO! OW-OW-OW-OWOOOOOOOOOOOOOOOOO

CHAPTER 3

The Chapter That's Totally Not as Sad as The Last one

Meanwhile...

It's okay, 80-HD...

...You can make the tree red.

It's <u>our</u> story. We can color it any way we want!

Hey, Look! Dog Man is home from—

What's wrong, Dog Man?

FLIP FLOP FLIP FLOP FLIP F

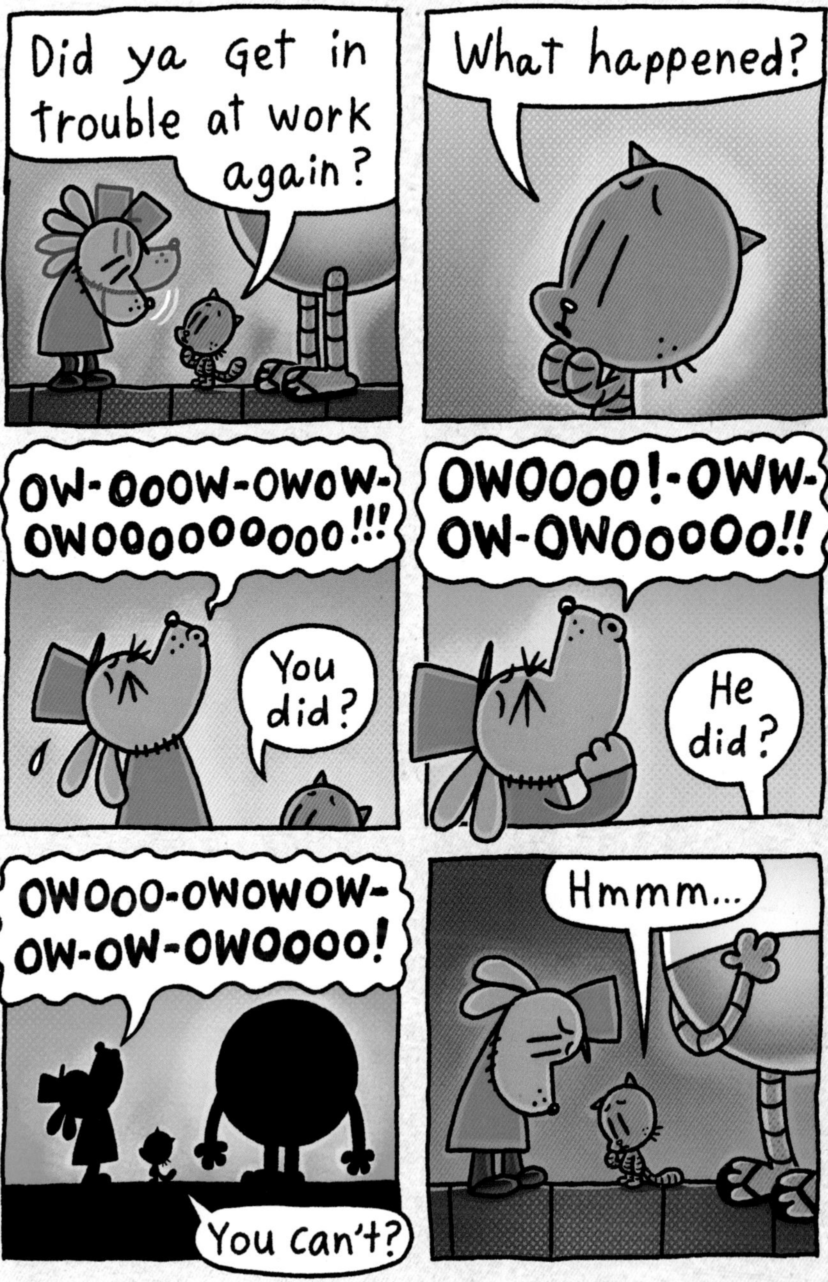
Did ya Get in trouble at work again?
What happened?
OW-OOOW-OWOW-OWOOOOOOOOOO!!!
You did?
OWOOOO!-OWW-OW-OWOOOOO!!
He did?
OWOOO-OWOWOW-OW-OW-OWOOOO!
You can't?
Hmmm...

I Got an idea!!!

We'll help ya get your job back!!!

FLIP FLOP

Don't worry about a thing!

Just come upstairs...

FLIP FLOP FLIP

...and lie down on your bed...

...and I'll read you a bedtime story!

48

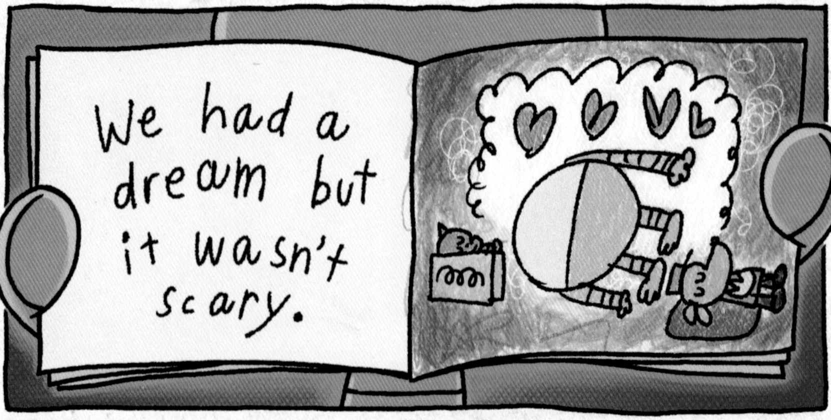
We had a dream but it wasn't scary.
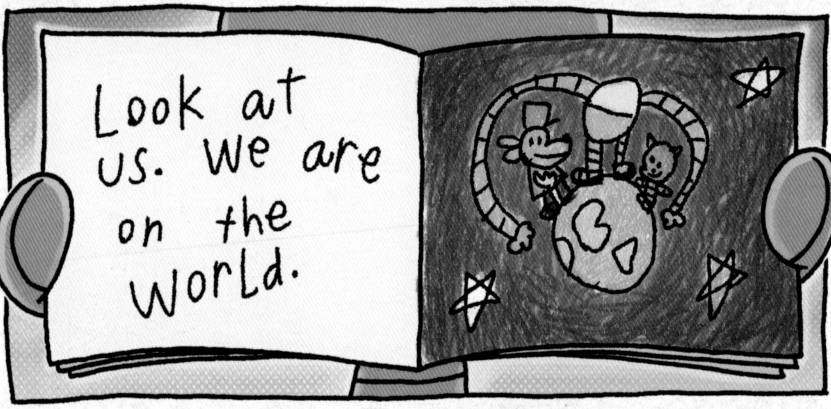
Look at us. We are on the World.
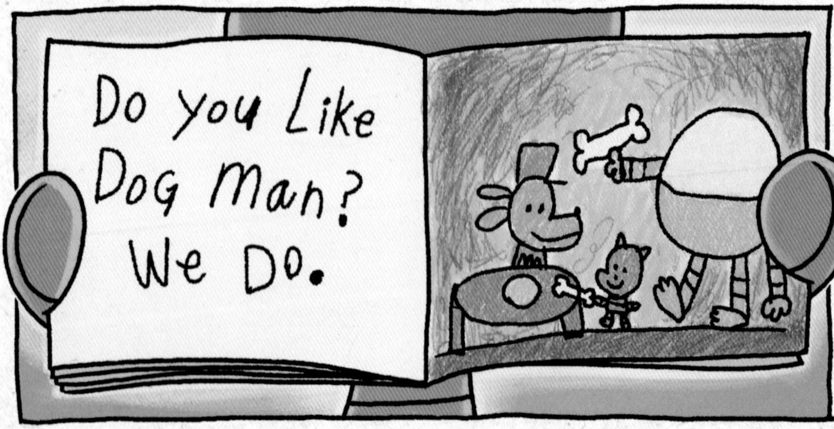
Do you Like Dog Man? We Do.

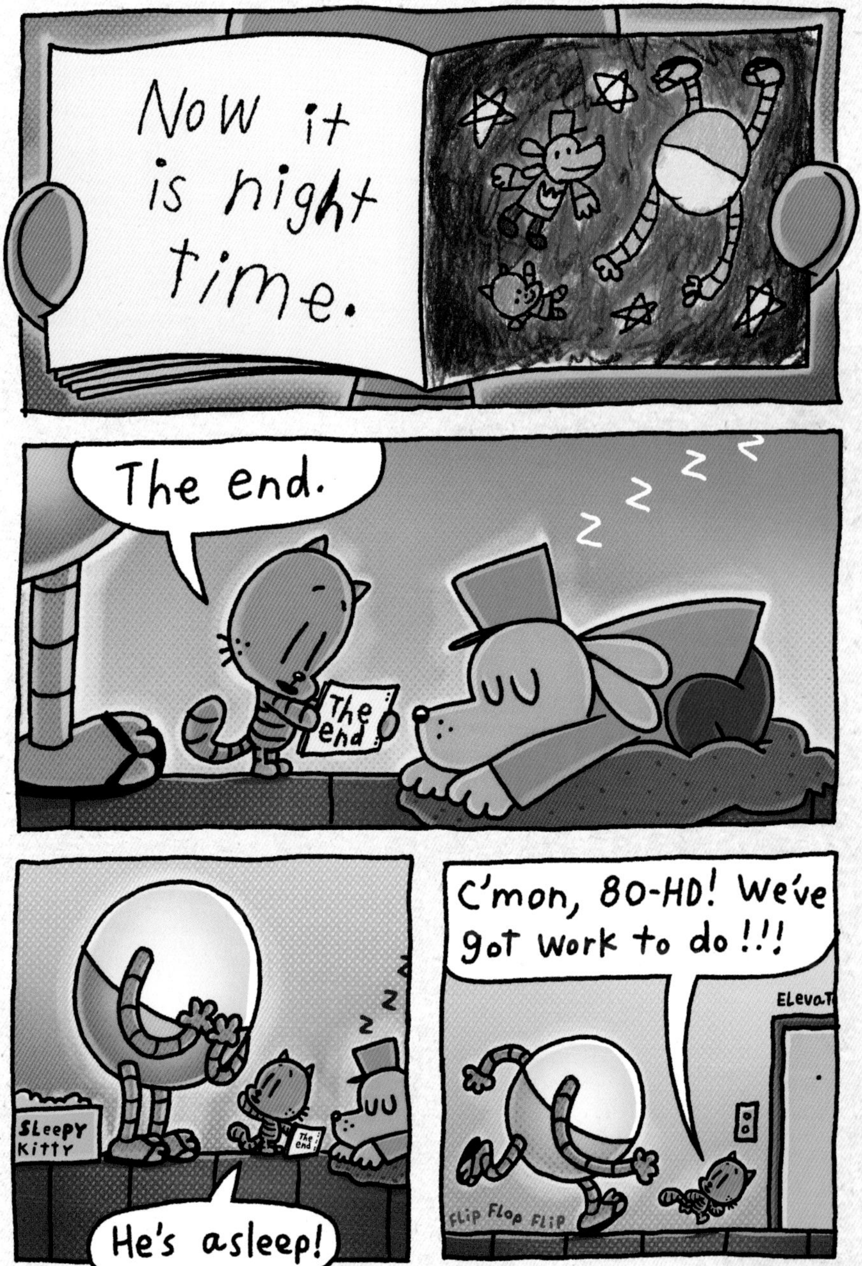
Now it is night time.
The end.
Z Z Z Z
The end
Z Z
SLeePY KITTY
The end
He's asleep!
C'mon, 80-HD! We've got work to do!!!
ELevaT
FLip FLop FLiP

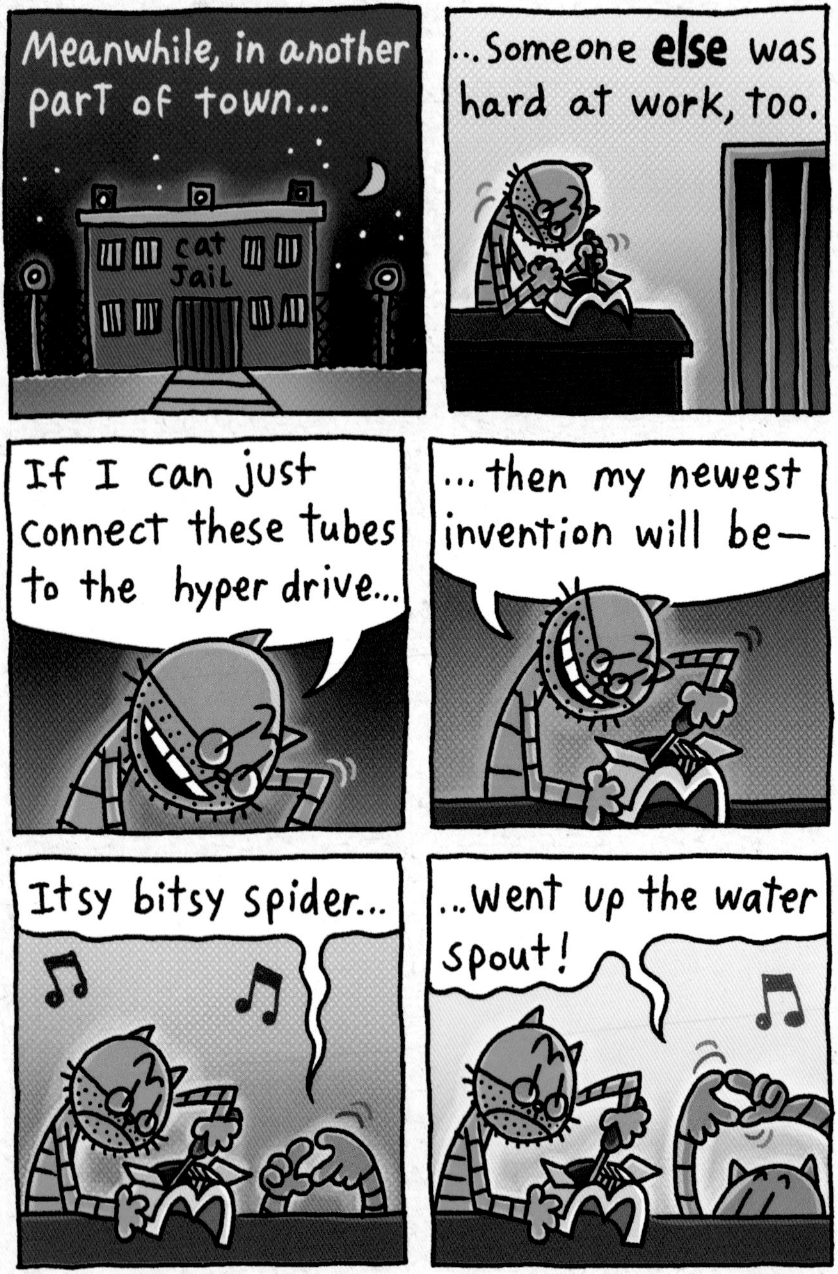
Meanwhile, in another part of town...
cat Jail
...Someone **else** was hard at work, too.
If I can just connect these tubes to the hyper drive...
...then my newest invention will be—
Itsy bitsy spider...
...went up the water spout!

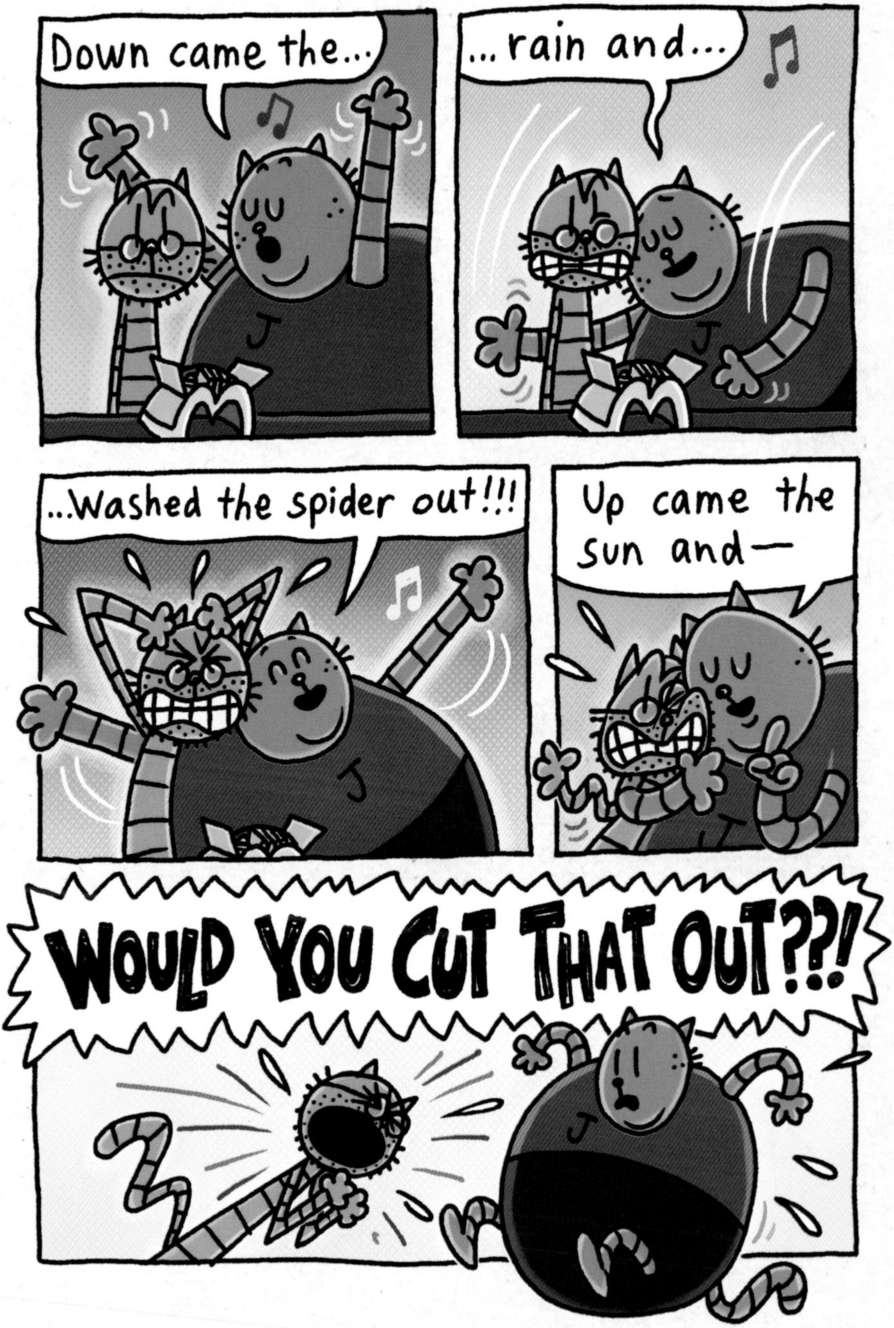
Down came the...
...rain and...
...Washed the spider out!!!
Up came the sun and—
WOULD YOU CUT THAT OUT??!

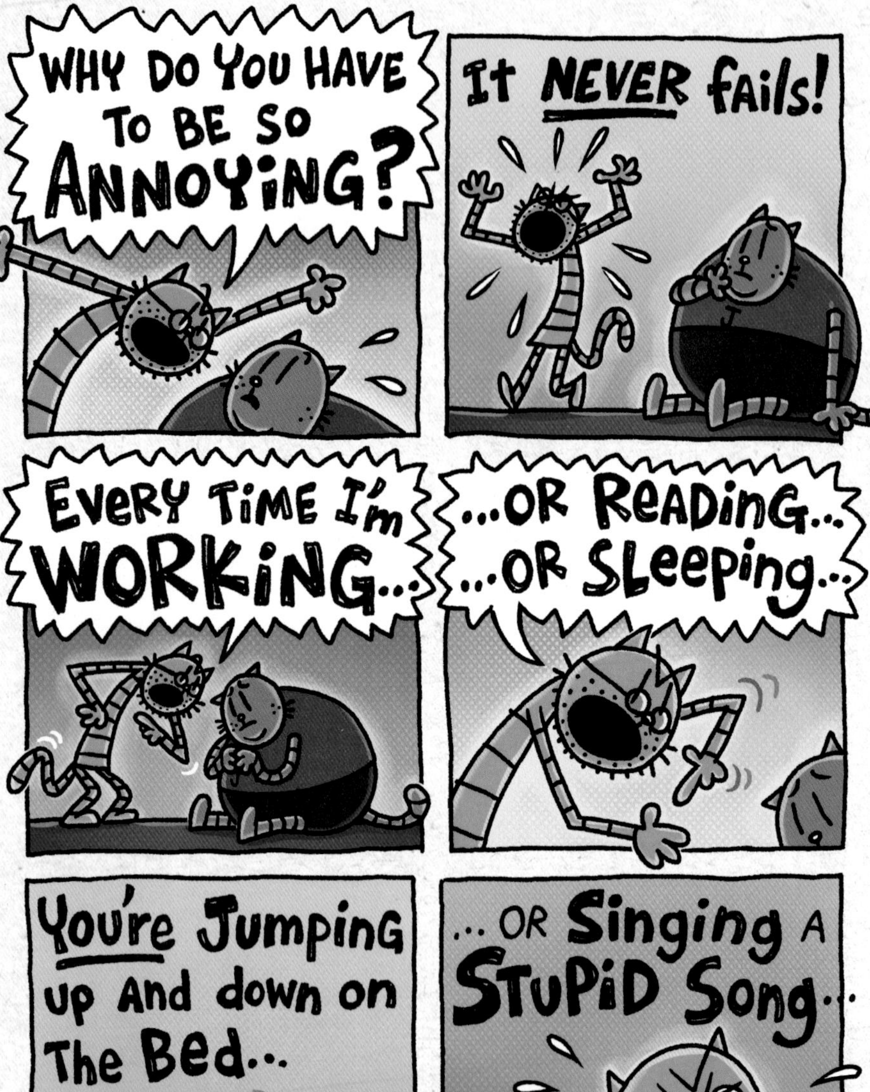
WHY DO YOU HAVE TO BE SO ANNOYING?
It NEVER fails!
EVERY TIME I'm WORKING...
...OR READING... ...OR SLEEPING...
You're Jumping up And down on The Bed...
... OR Singing A STUPID Song...

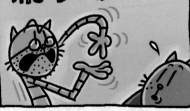

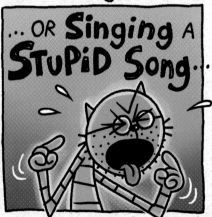

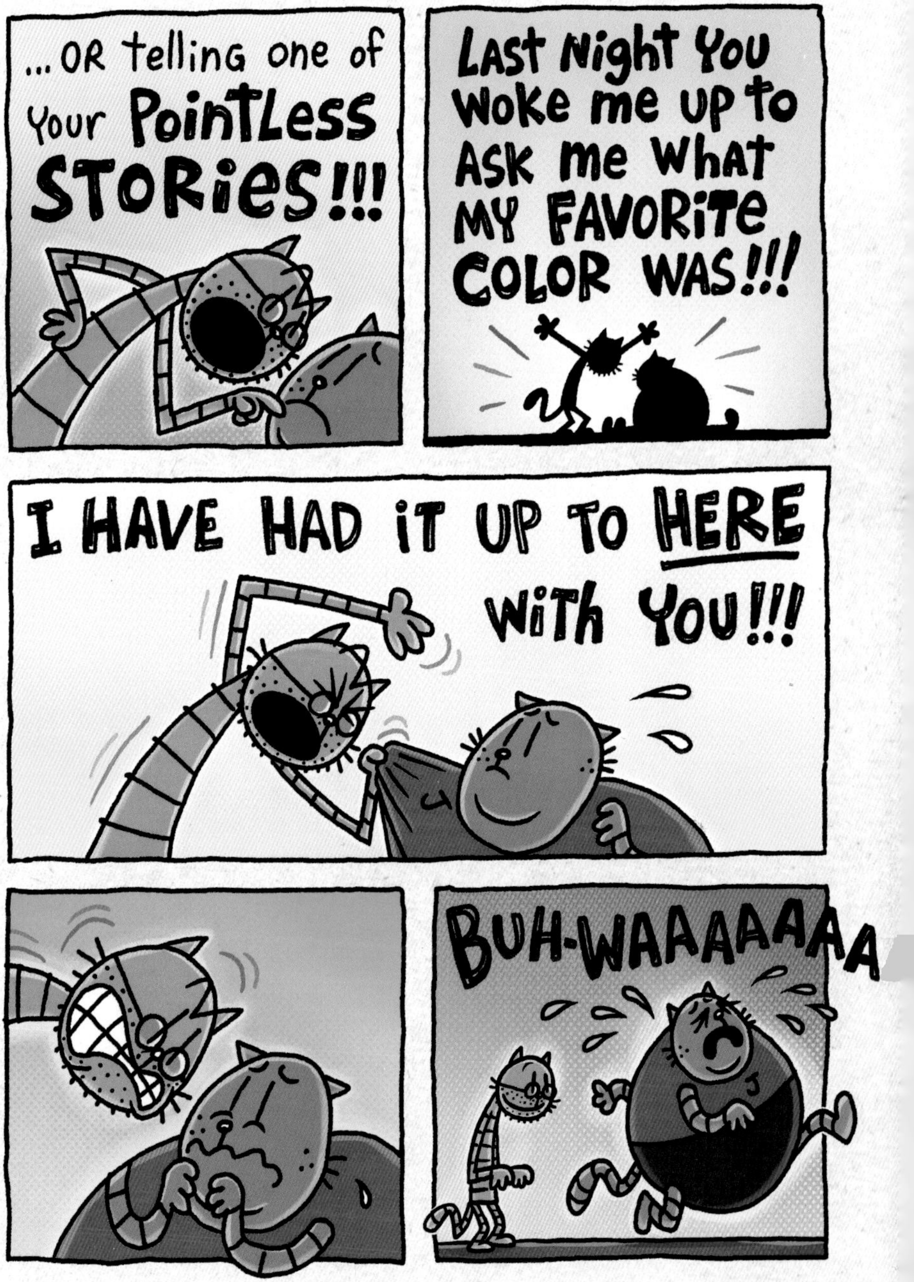
...OR telling one of your POINTLESS STORIES!!!
LAST Night YOU woke me up to ASK me WHAT MY FAVORITE COLOR WAS!!!
I HAVE HAD iT UP TO HERE with YOU!!!
BUH-WAAAAAAA

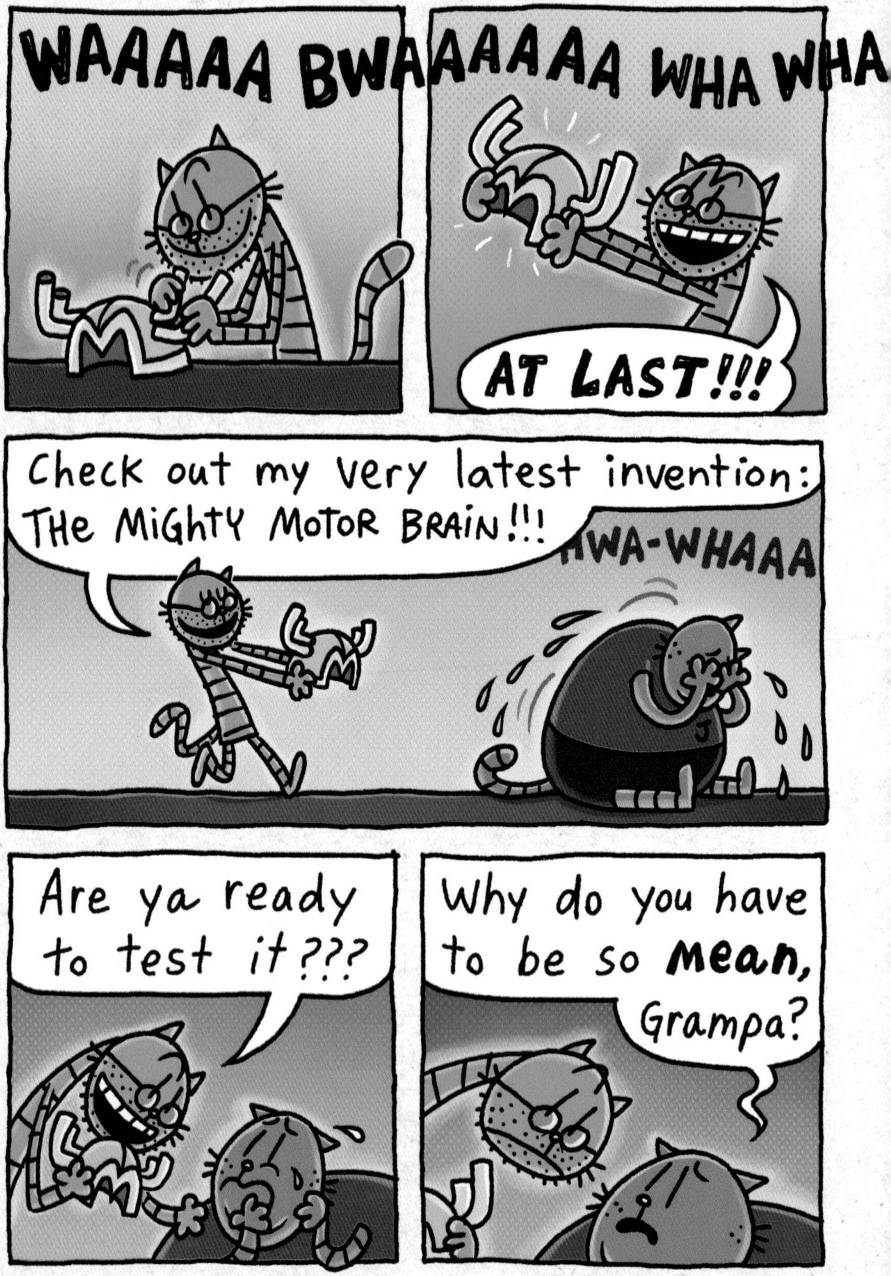
WAAAAA BWAAAAAAA WHA WHA
AT LAST!!!
Check out my very latest invention: THE MIGHTY MOTOR BRAIN!!!
HWA-WHAAA
Are ya ready to test it???
Why do you have to be so **mean,** Grampa?

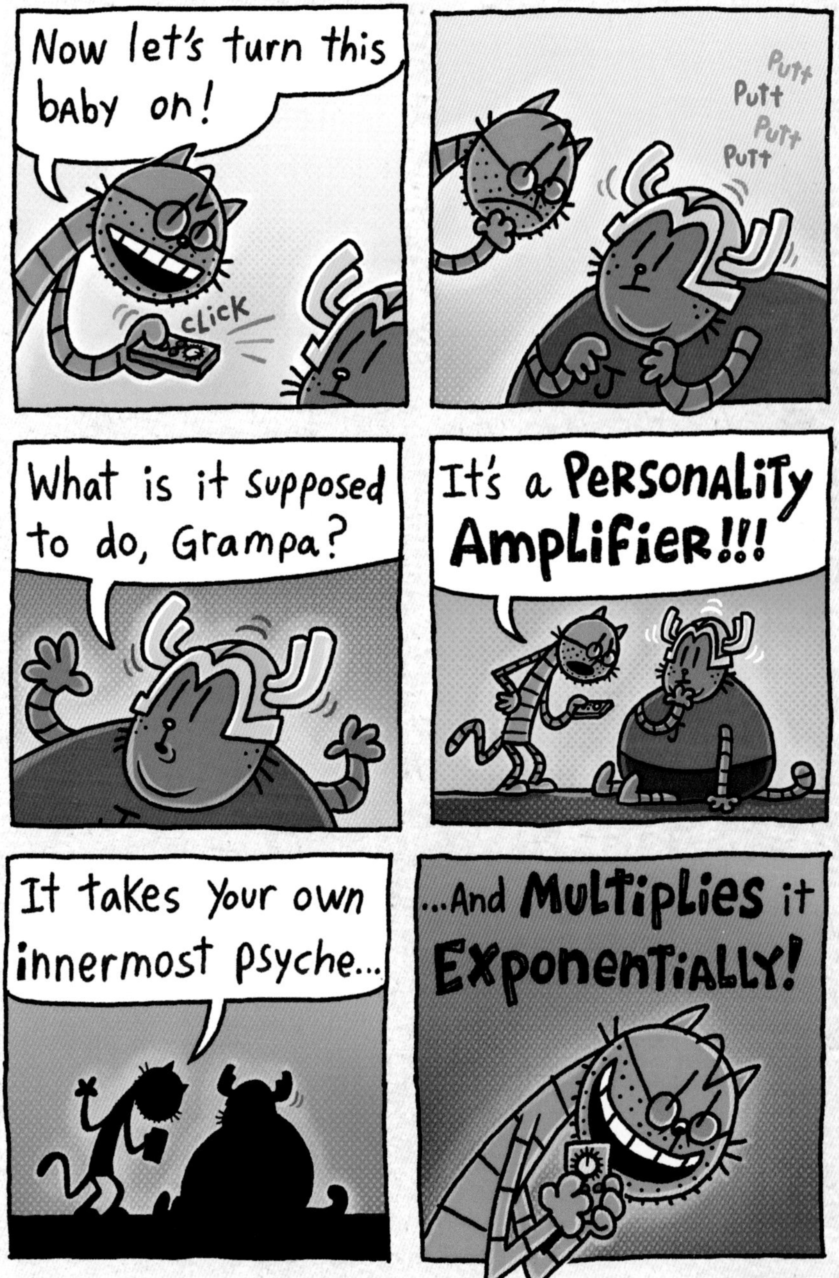
Now let's turn this baby on!
CLICK
PUTT
PUTT
PUTT
PUTT
What is it supposed to do, Grampa?
It's a PERSONALITY AMPLIFIER!!!
It takes your own innermost psyche...
...And MULTIPLIES it EXPONENTIALLY!

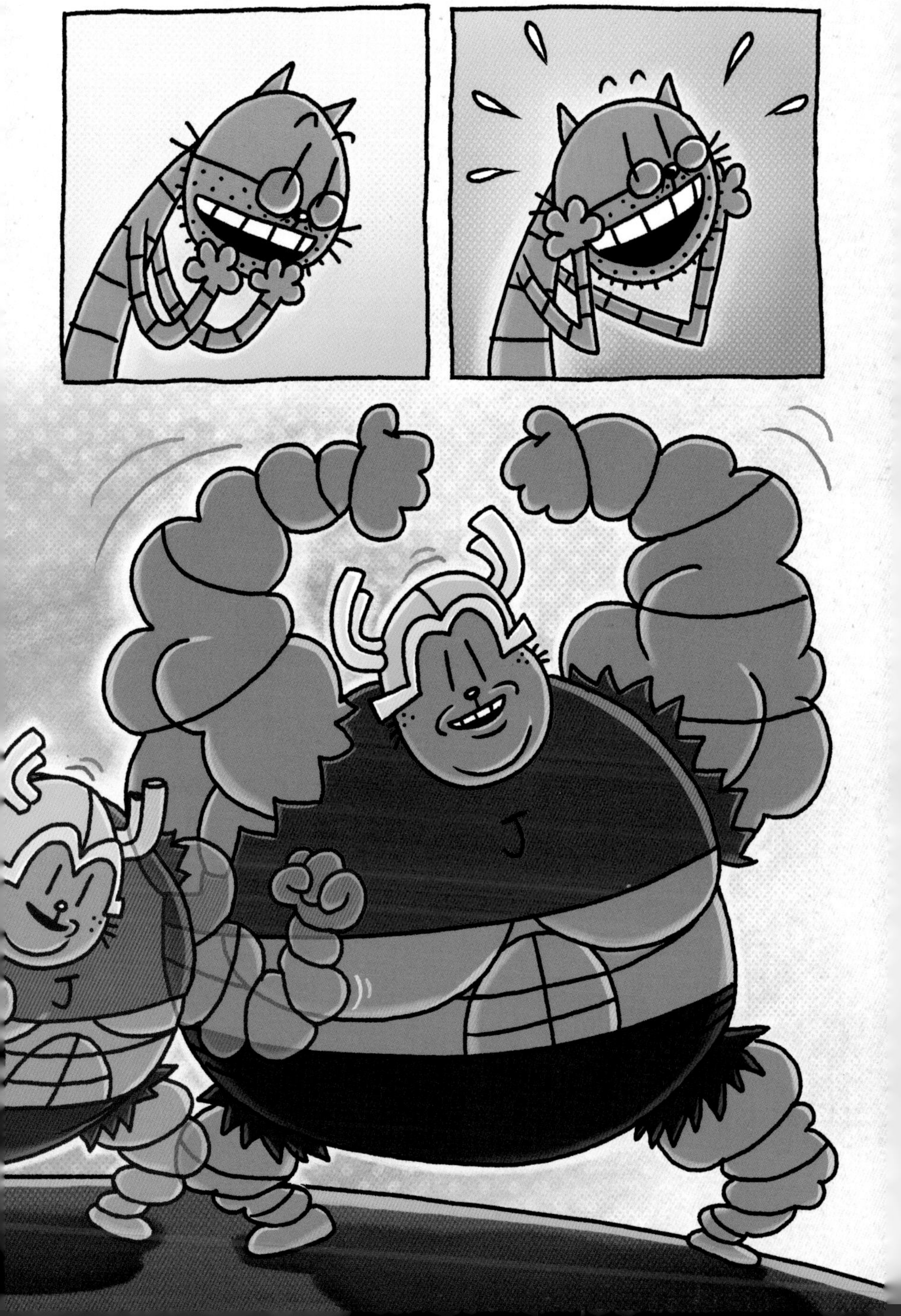

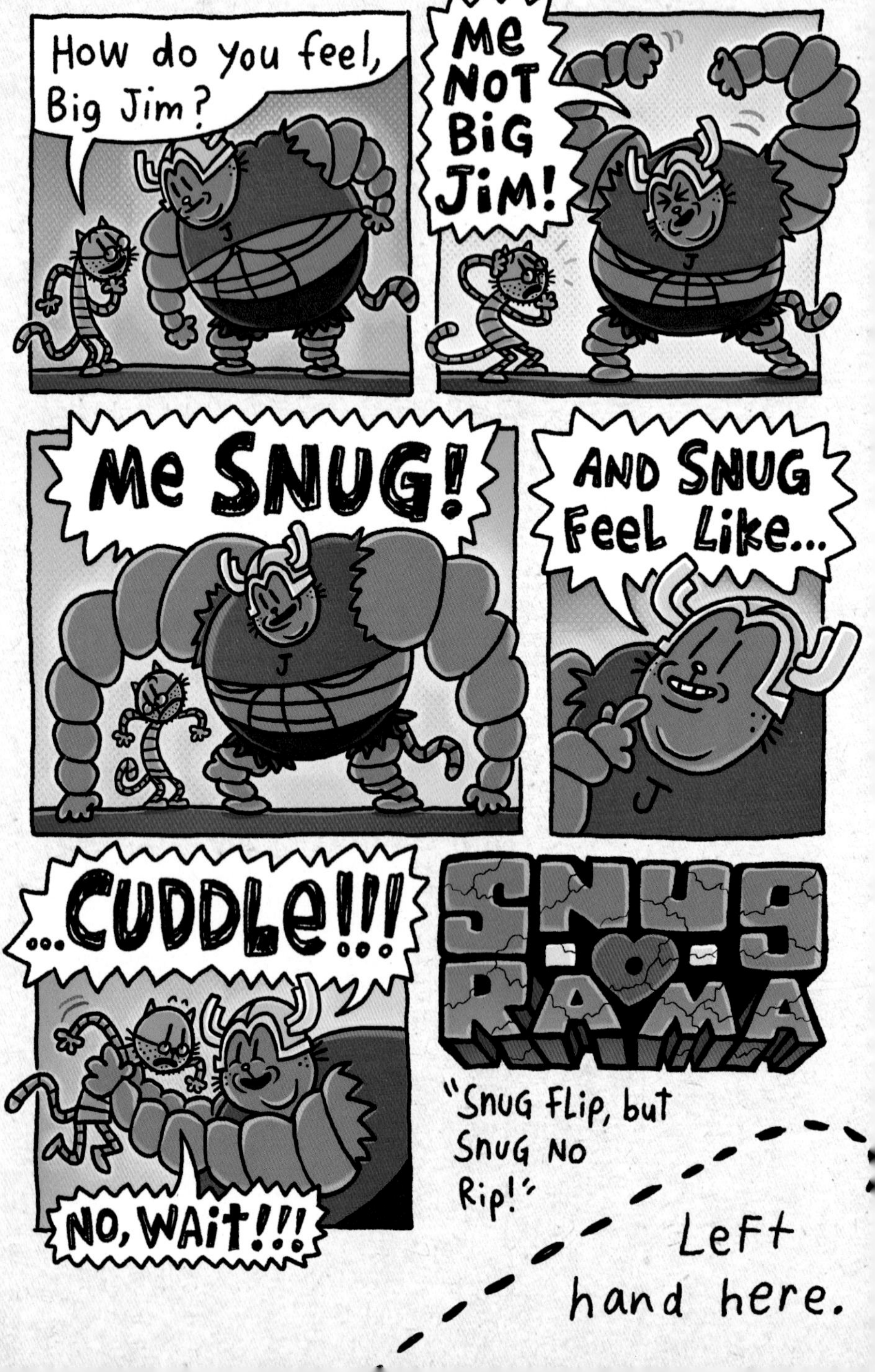
How do you feel, Big Jim?
Me NOT BIG JIM!
Me SNUG!
AND SNUG Feel Like...
...CUDDLE!!!
NO, WAIT!!!
SNUG-O-RAMA
"SNUG FLip, but SNUG NO Rip!"
Left hand here.

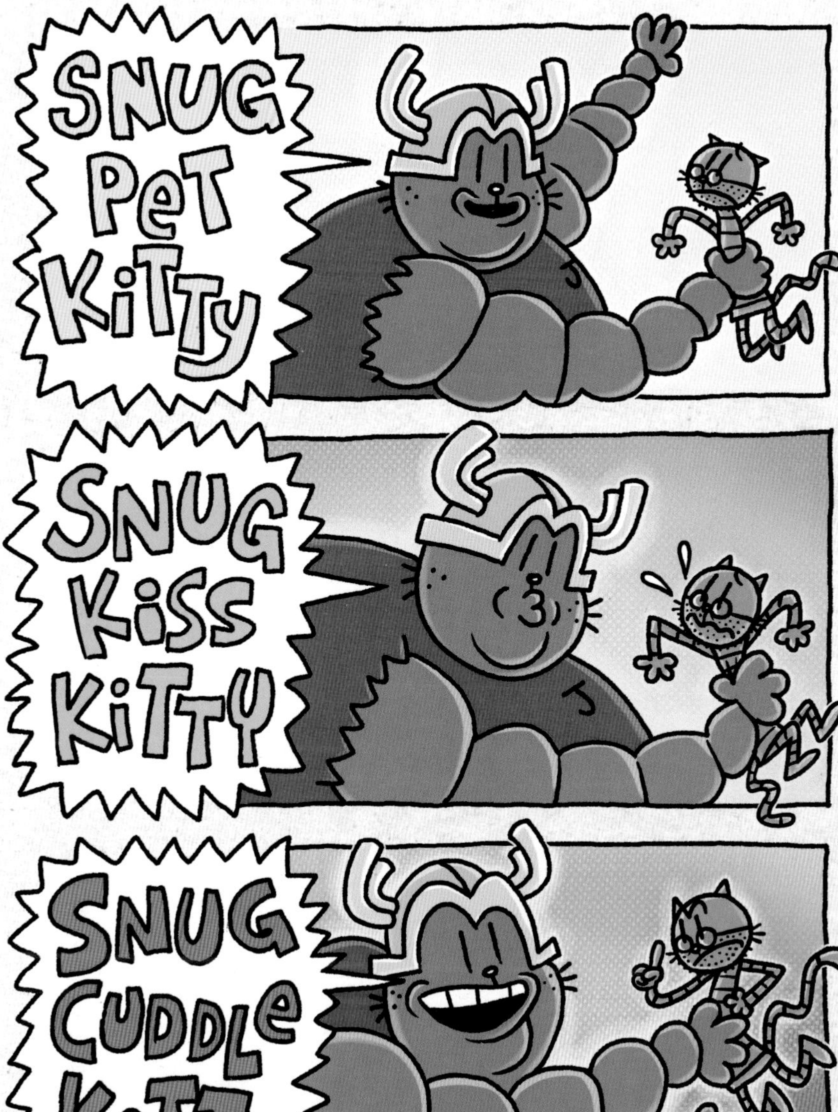
SNUG PET KITTY
SNUG KISS KITTY
SNUG CUDDLE KITTY

Right Thumb here.

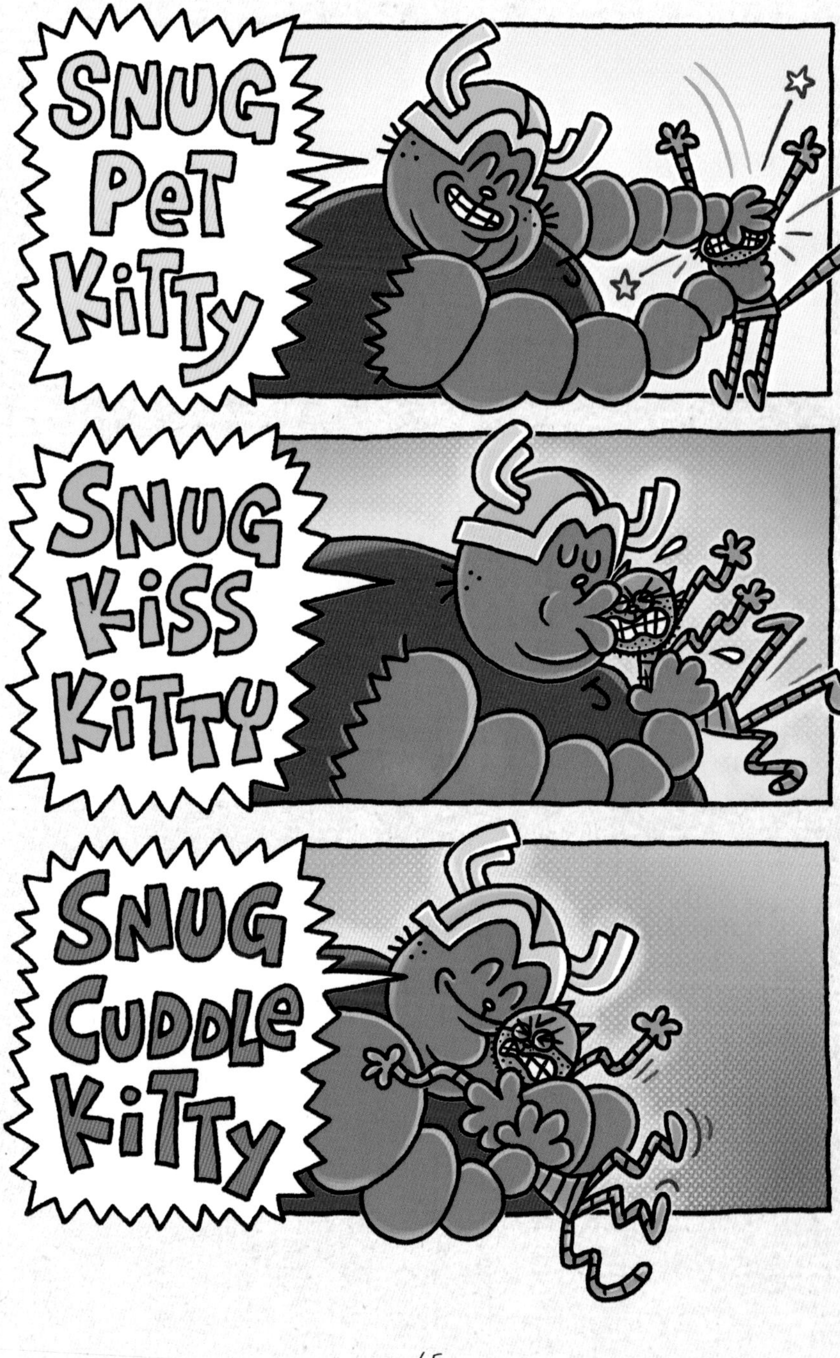
SNUG PET KITTY
SNUG KISS KITTY
SNUG CUDDLE KITTY

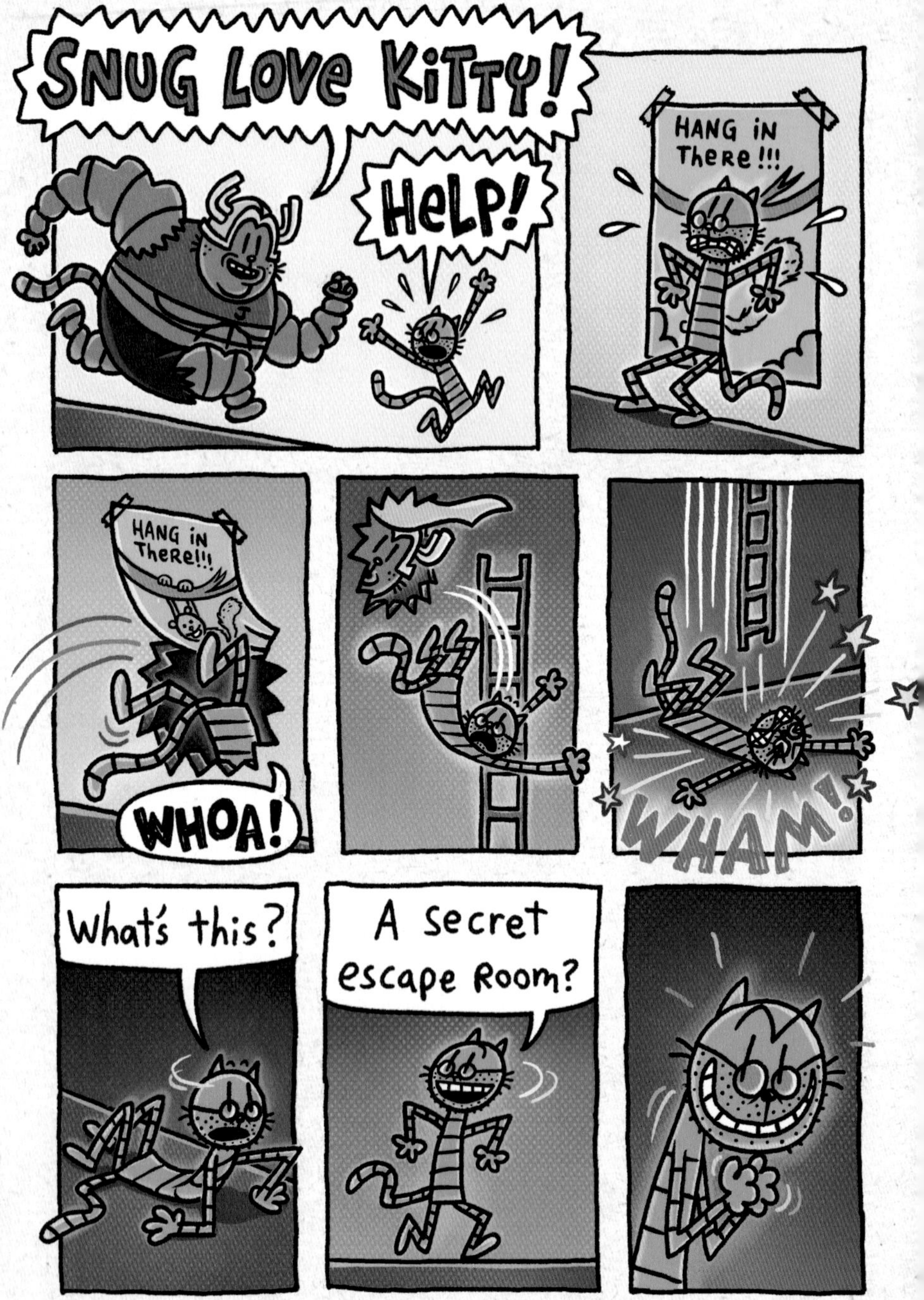

SNUG LOVE KITTY!
HELP!
HANG IN There!!!
HANG IN There!!!
WHOA!
WHAM!
What's this?
A secret escape Room?

CHAPTER 4

The Dog in The Hat

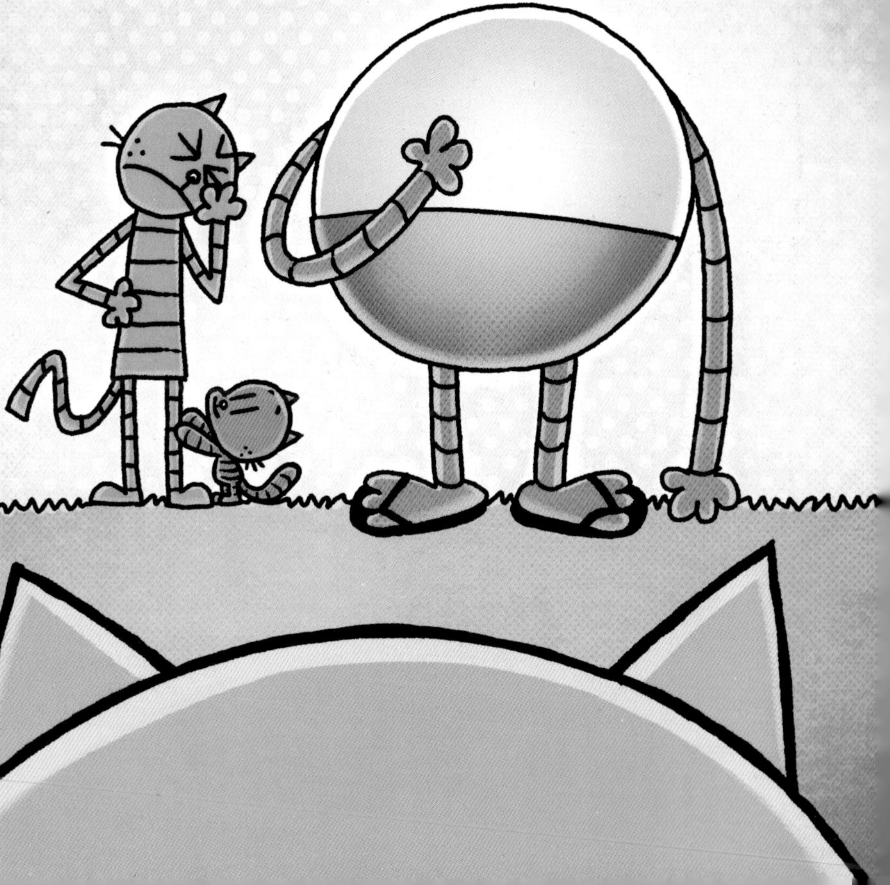

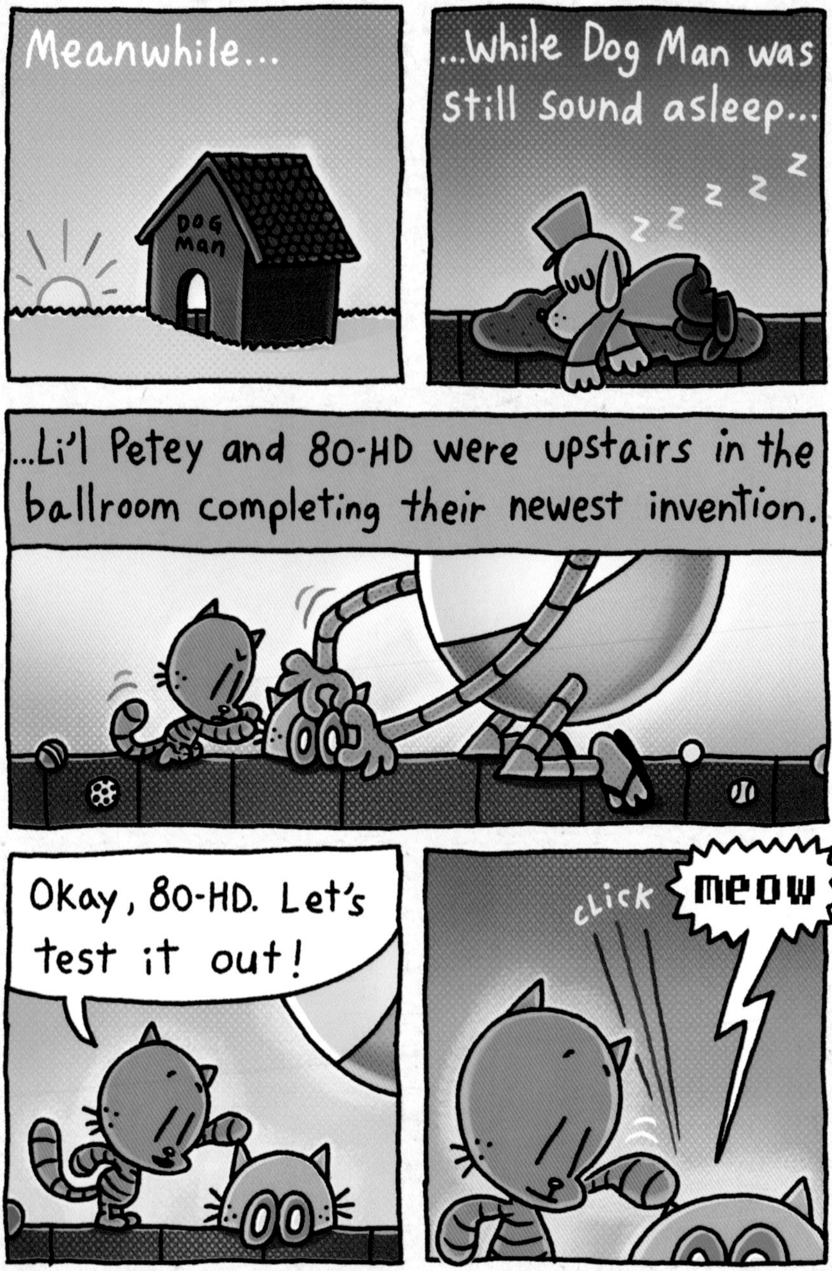
Meanwhile...
DOG Man
...While Dog Man was still sound asleep...
Z Z Z Z Z
...Li'l Petey and 80-HD were upstairs in the ballroom completing their newest invention.
Okay, 80-HD. Let's test it out!
CLICK
meow

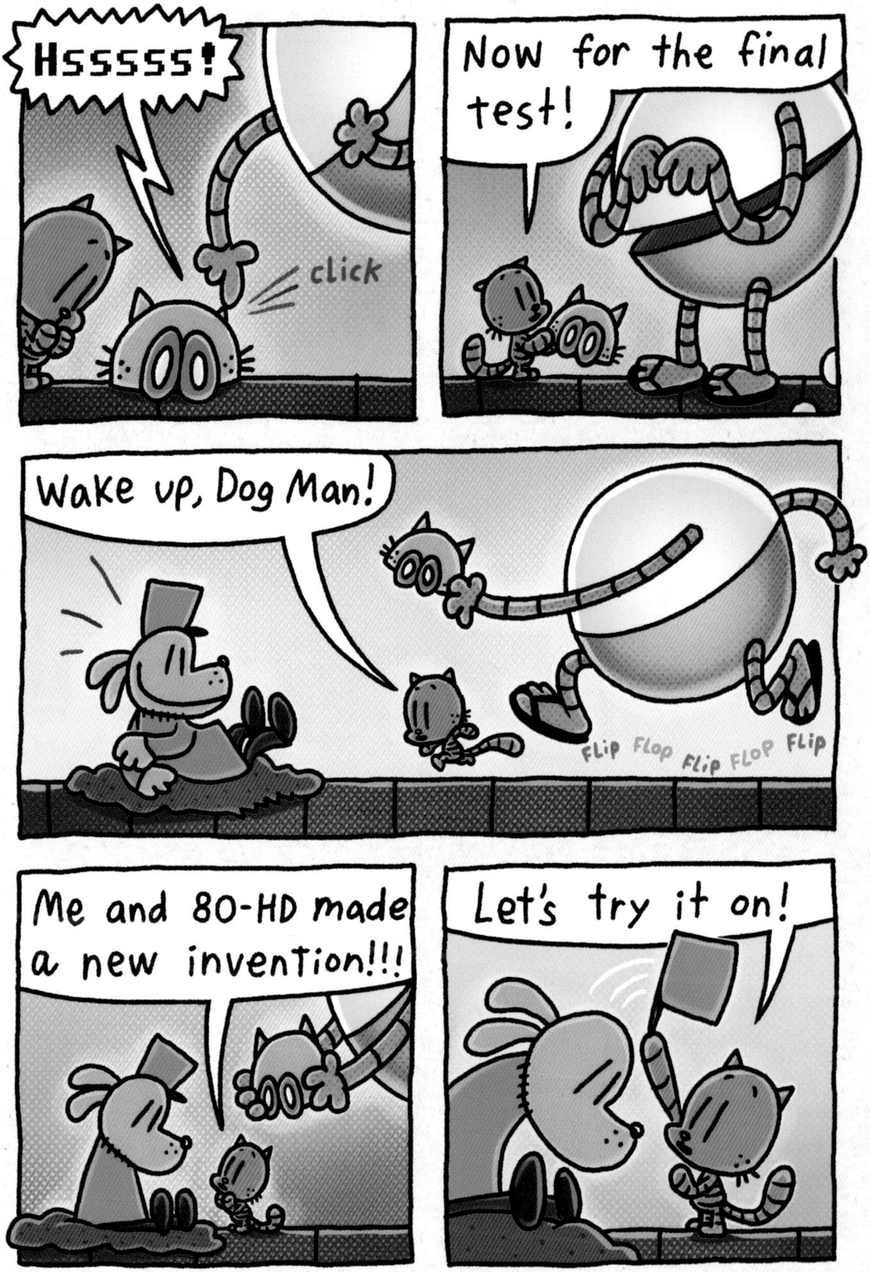
Hsssss!
click
Now for the final test!
Wake up, Dog Man!
FLip Flop FLip FLOP FLip
Me and 80-HD made a new invention!!!
Let's try it on!

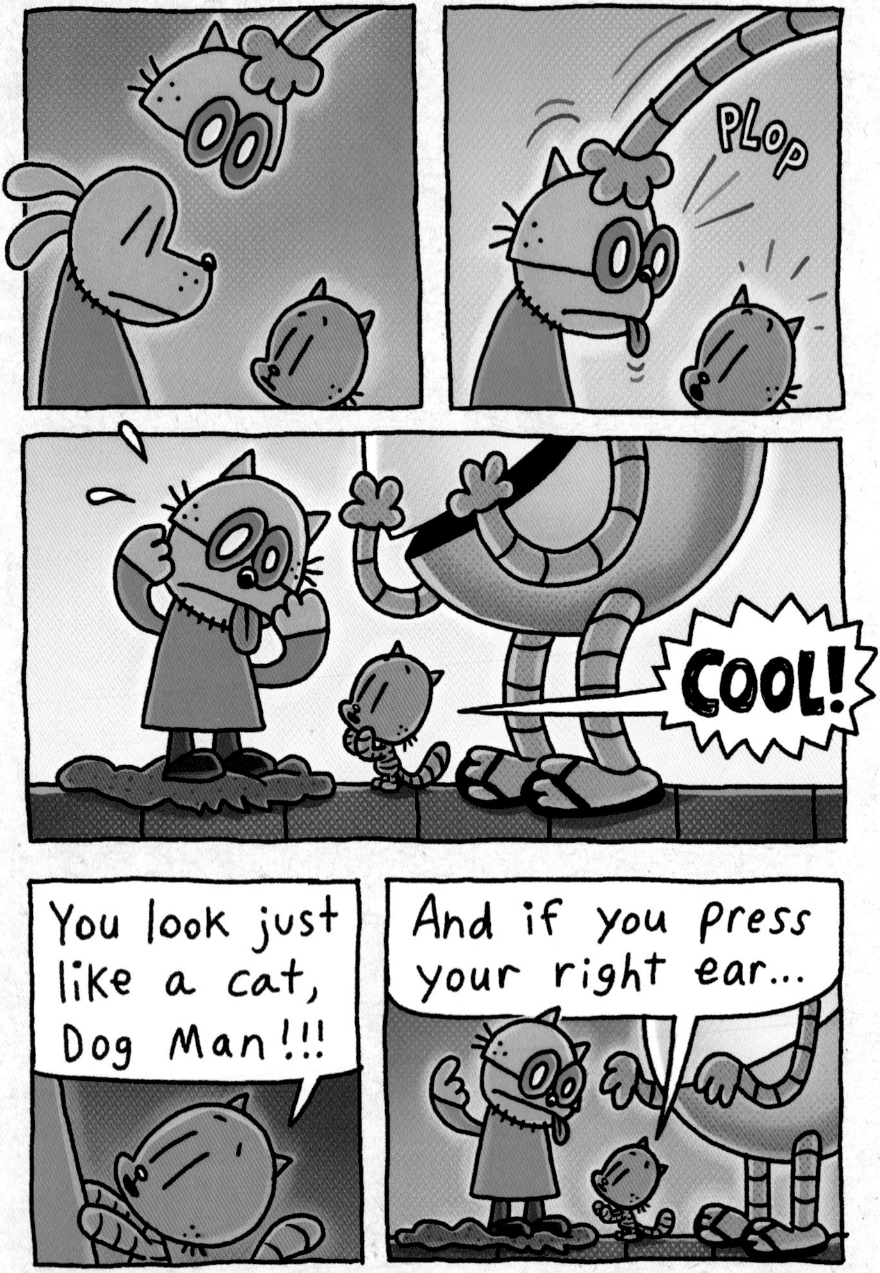
PLOP
COOL!
You look just like a cat, Dog Man!!!
And if you press your right ear...

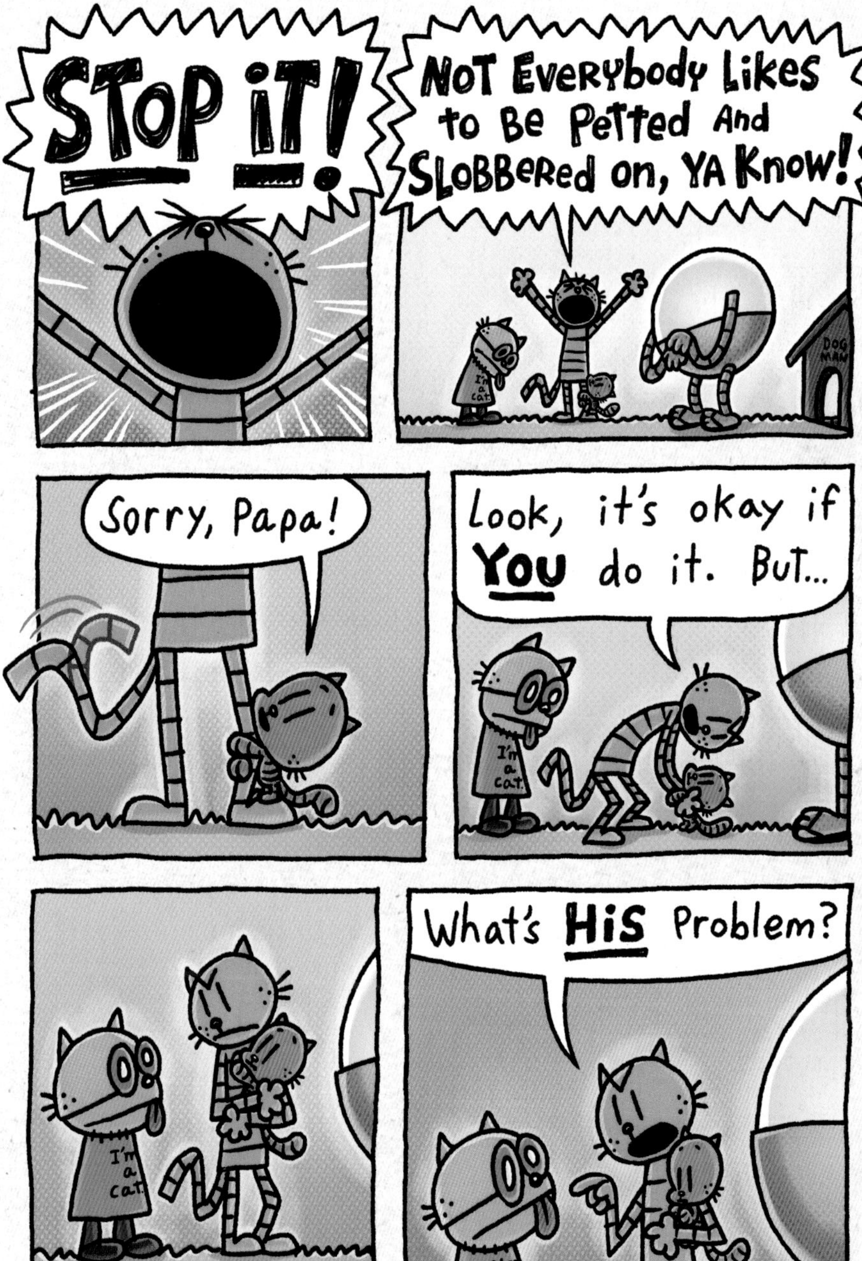
STOP IT!
NOT Everybody Likes to Be Petted And SLOBBERED on, YA Know!
DOG MAN
I'm a cat.
Sorry, Papa!
Look, it's okay if YOU do it. But...
I'm a cat.
I'm a cat.
What's HIS Problem?

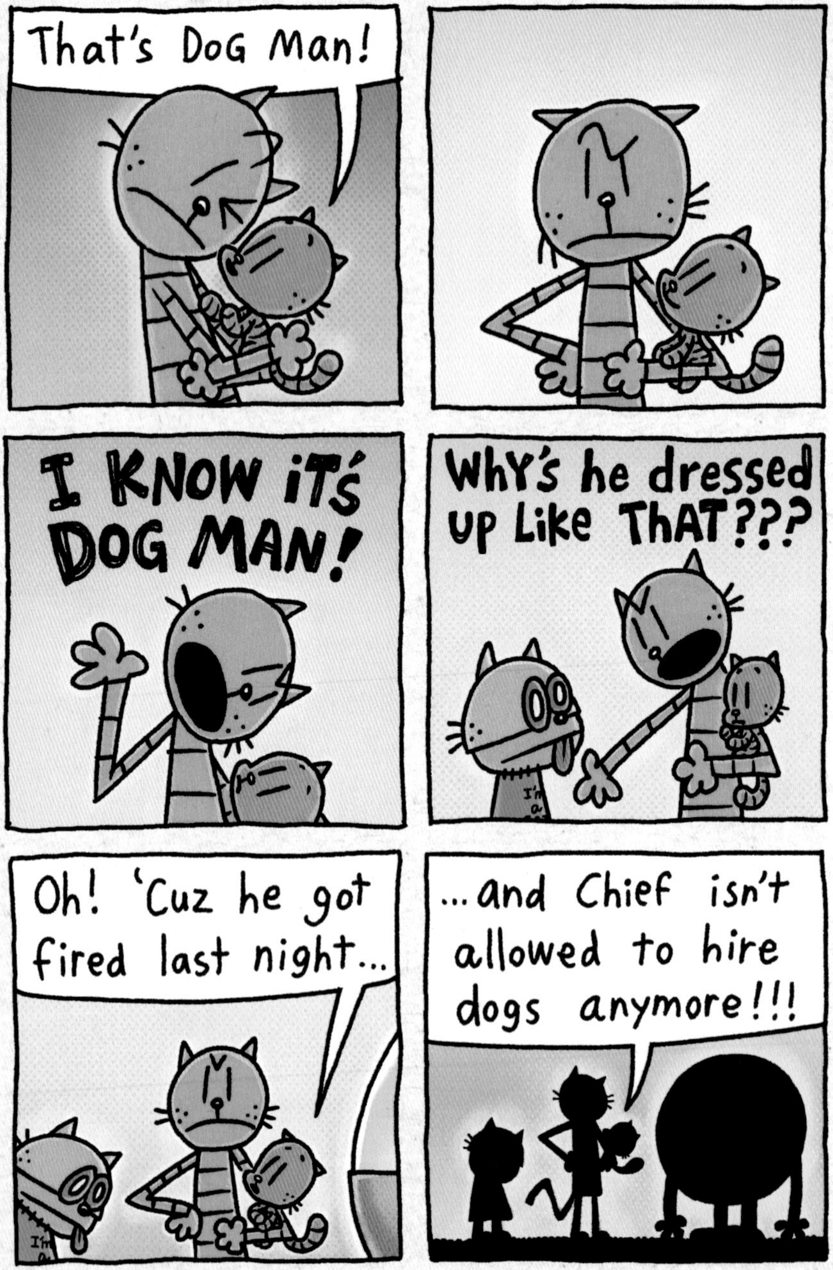
That's DoG Man!
I KNOW iT's DOG MAN!
WHY's he dressed up Like THAT???
Oh! 'Cuz he got fired last night...
...and Chief isn't allowed to hire dogs anymore!!!

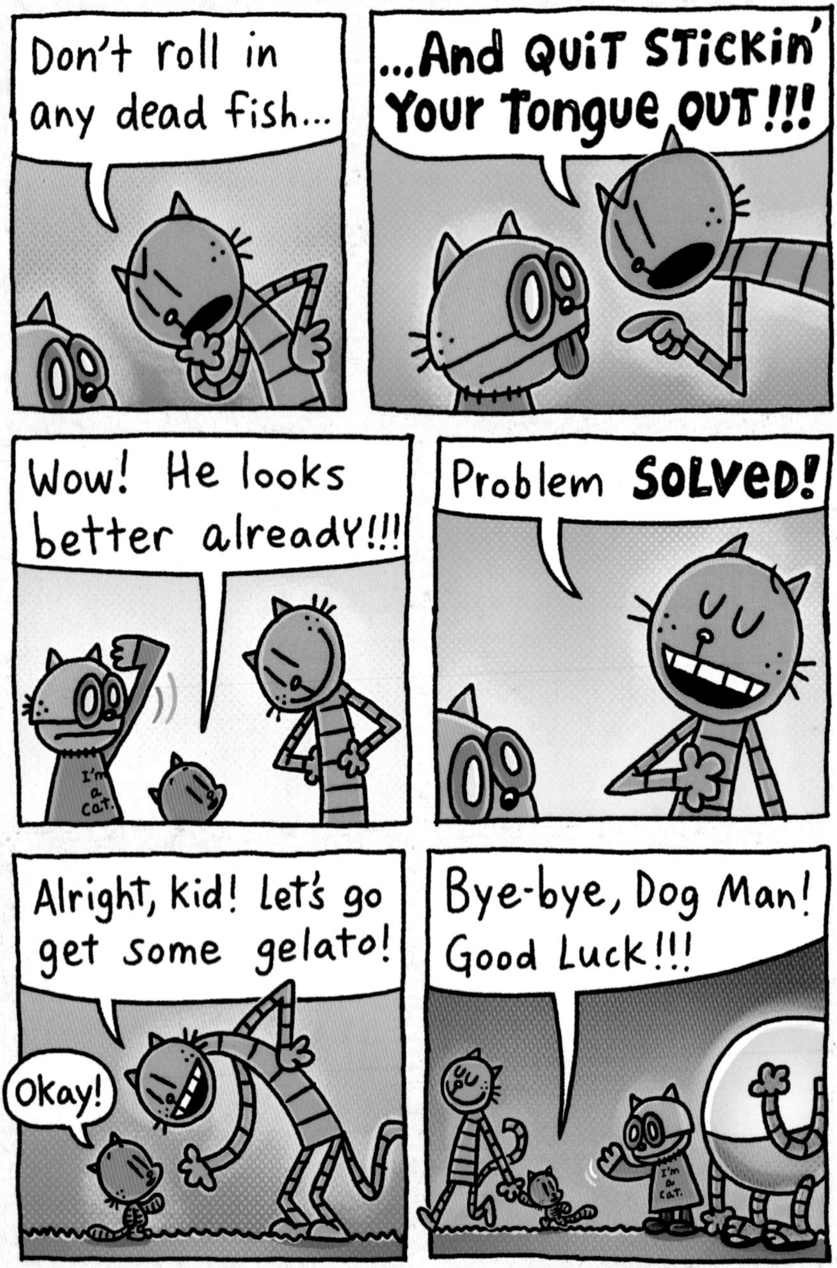
Don't roll in any dead fish...
...And QUIT STICKIN' YOUR TONGUE OUT!!!
Wow! He looks better already!!!
I'm a cat.
Problem SOLVED!
Alright, kid! Let's go get some gelato!
Okay!
Bye-bye, Dog Man! Good Luck!!!
I'm a cat.

CHAPTER 5

A Buncha Stuff That Happened Next

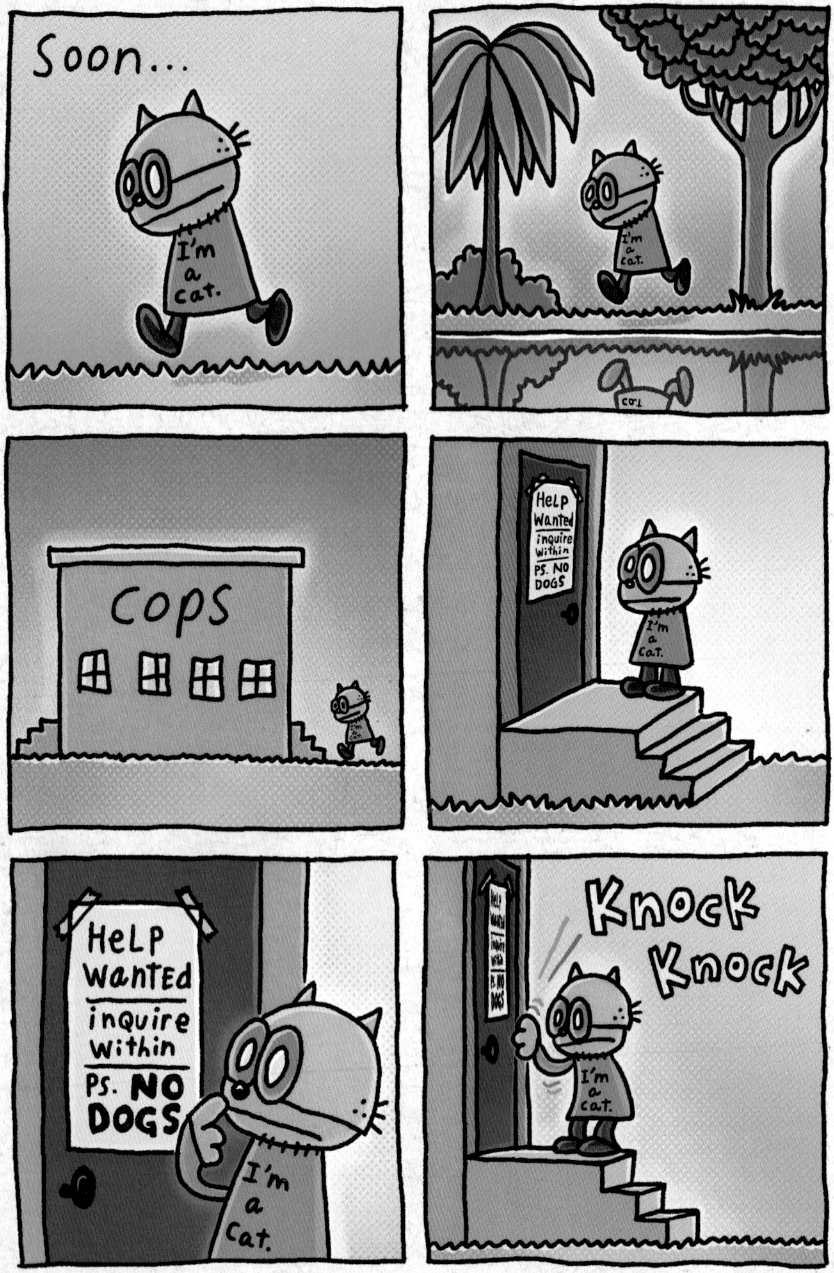

Soon...
I'm a cat.
I'm a cat.
COPS
HELP WANTED inquire within PS. NO DOGS
I'm a cat.
HELP WANTED inquire within PS. NO DOGS
I'm a cat.
Knock Knock
I'm a cat.

79

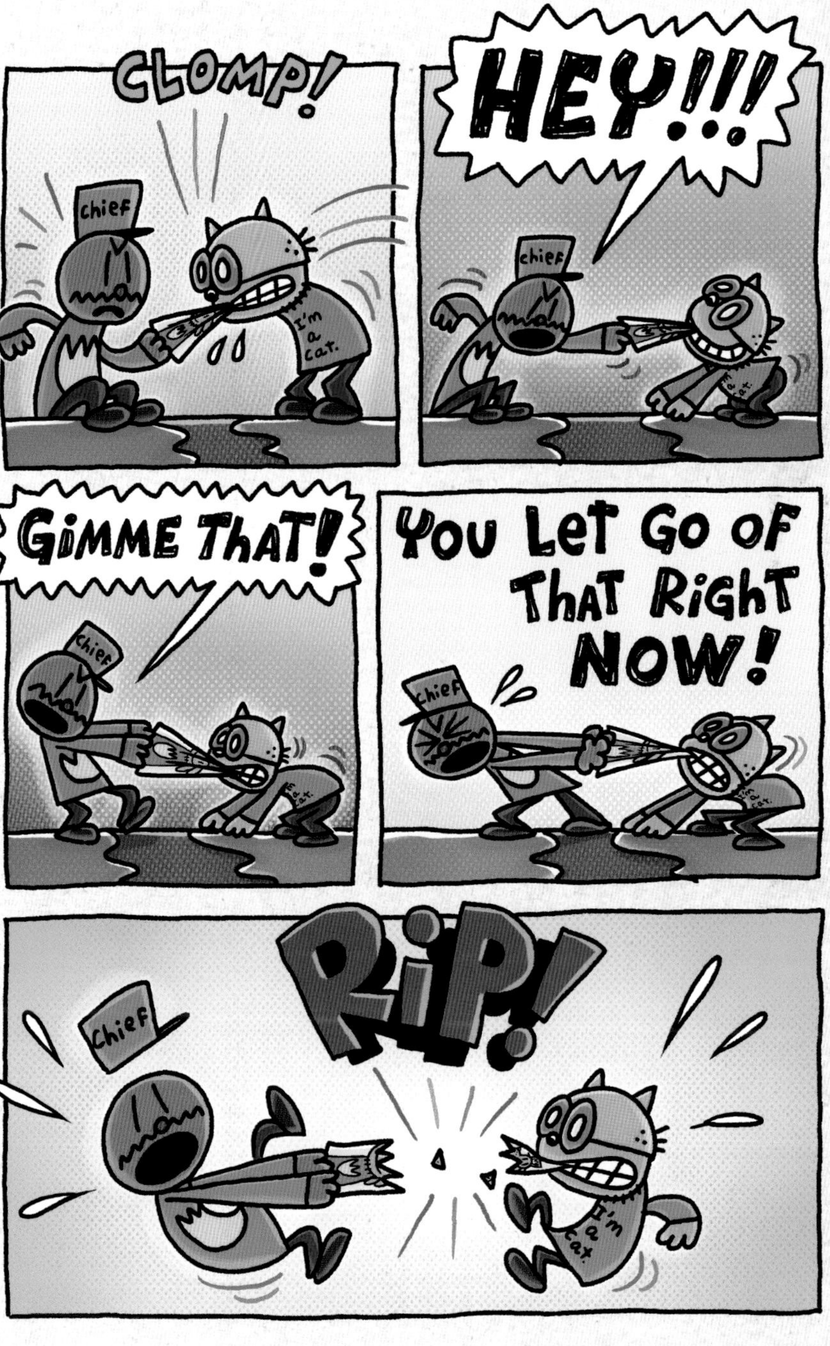
CLOMP!
chief
I'm a cat.
HEY!!!
GiMME ThAT!
YOU LeT GO OF ThAT RiGhT NOW!
RiP!

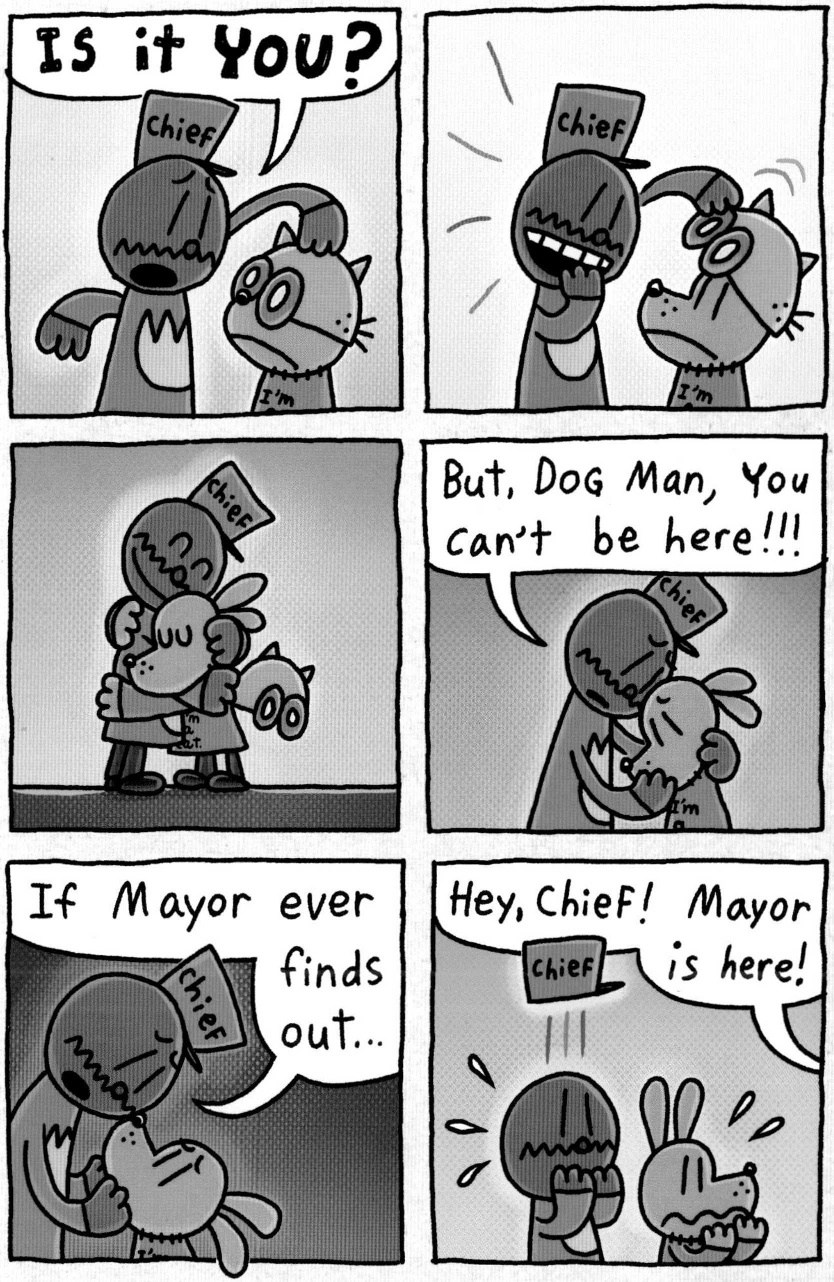
IS it YOU?
But, DOG Man, You can't be here!!!
If Mayor ever finds out...
Hey, ChieF! Mayor is here!

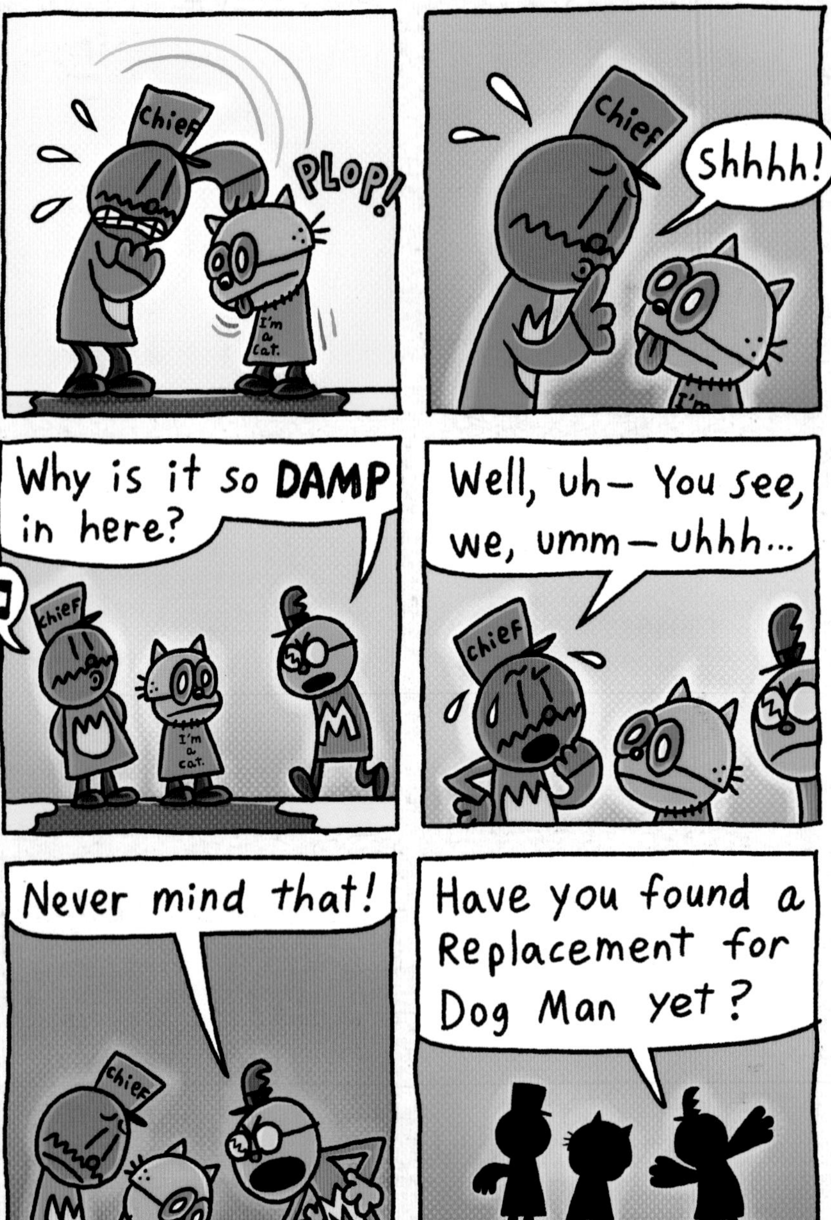
Chief
PLOP!
I'm a cat.
Chief
Shhhh!
Why is it so **DAMP** in here?
Chief
I'm a cat.
Well, uh– You see, we, umm–uhhh...
chief
Never mind that!
chief
Have you found a Replacement for Dog Man yet?

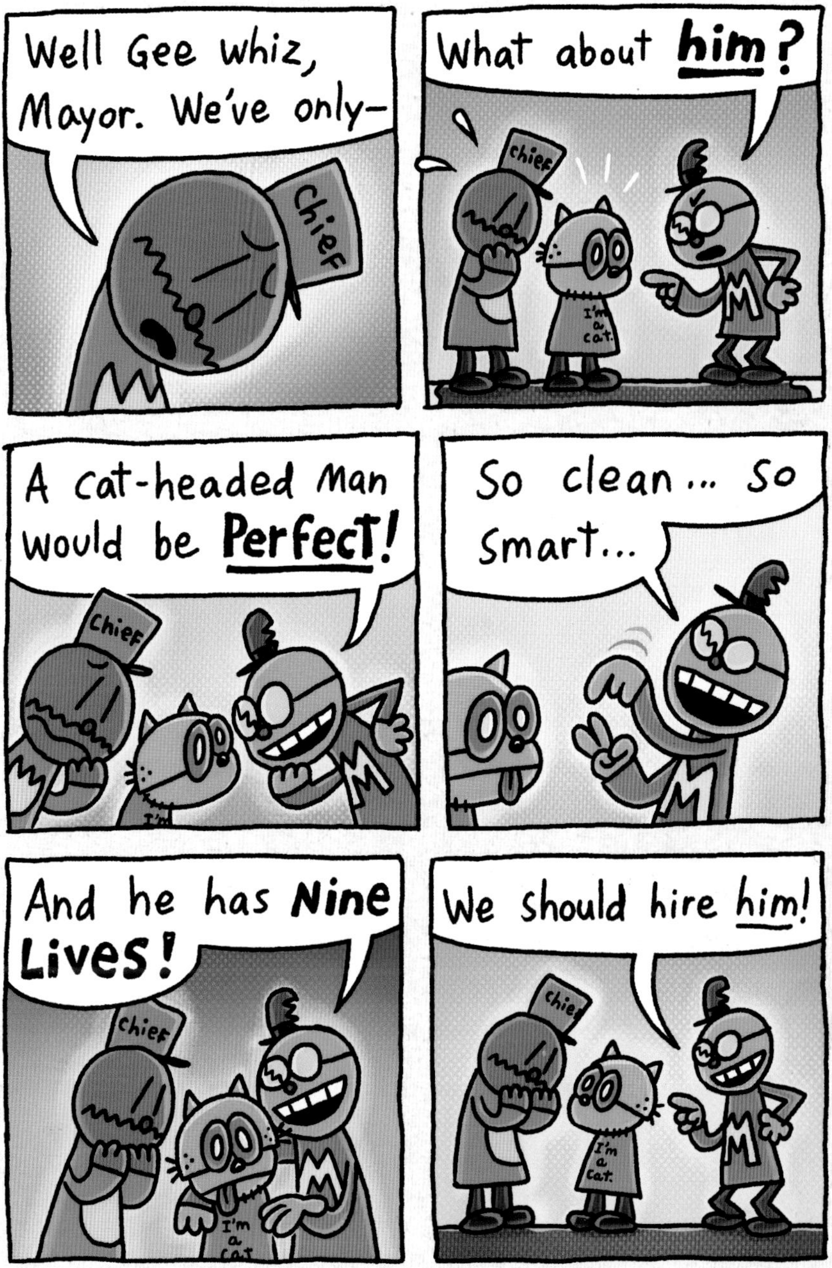
Well Gee whiz, Mayor. We've only–
What about him?
chief
I'm a cat.
M
A cat-headed man would be Perfect!
So clean... so smart...
And he has Nine Lives!
We should hire him!

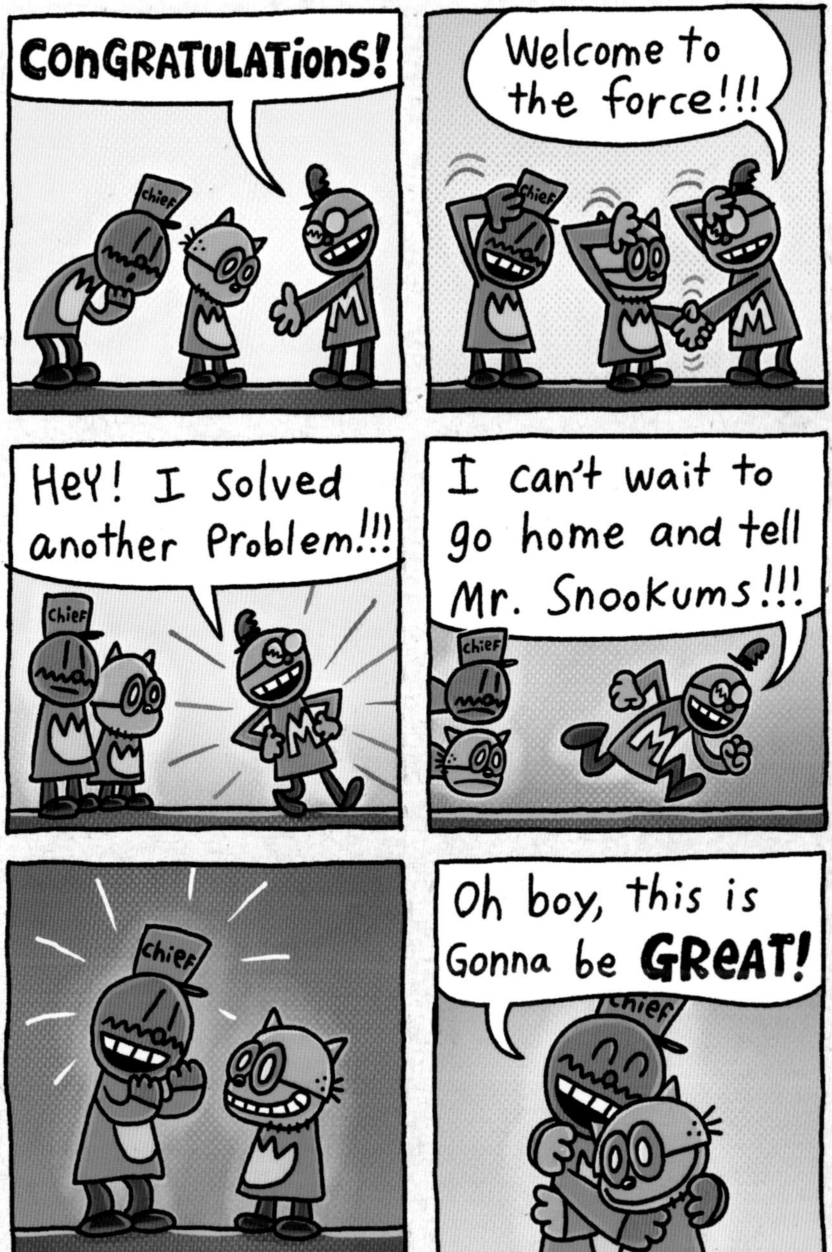
CONGRATULATIONS!
Welcome to the force!!!
Chief
Hey! I solved another Problem!!!
Chief
I can't wait to go home and tell Mr. Snookums!!!
Chief
Chief
Oh boy, this is Gonna be GREAT!
Chief

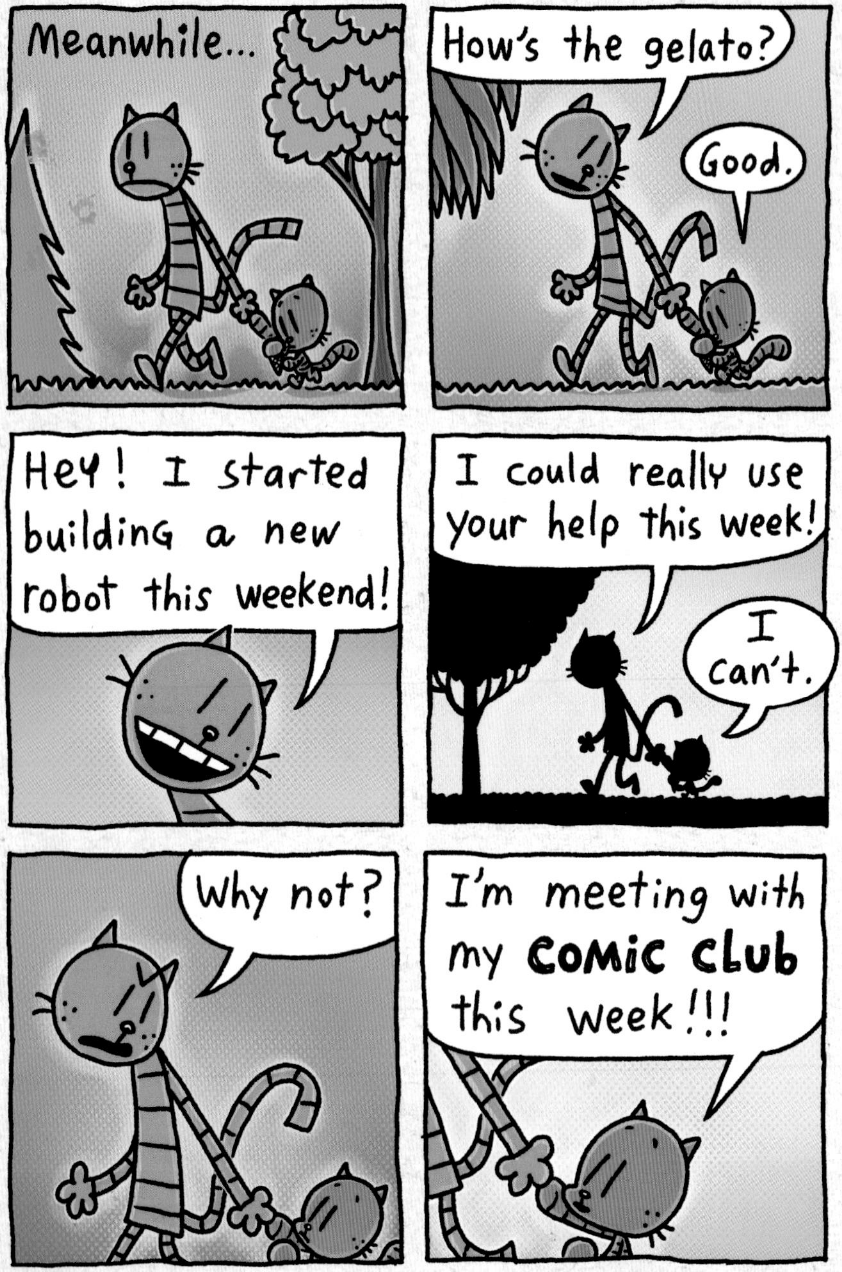
Meanwhile...
How's the gelato?
Good.
Hey! I started building a new robot this weekend!
I could really use your help this week!
I can't.
Why not?
I'm meeting with my **COMIC CLUB** this week!!!

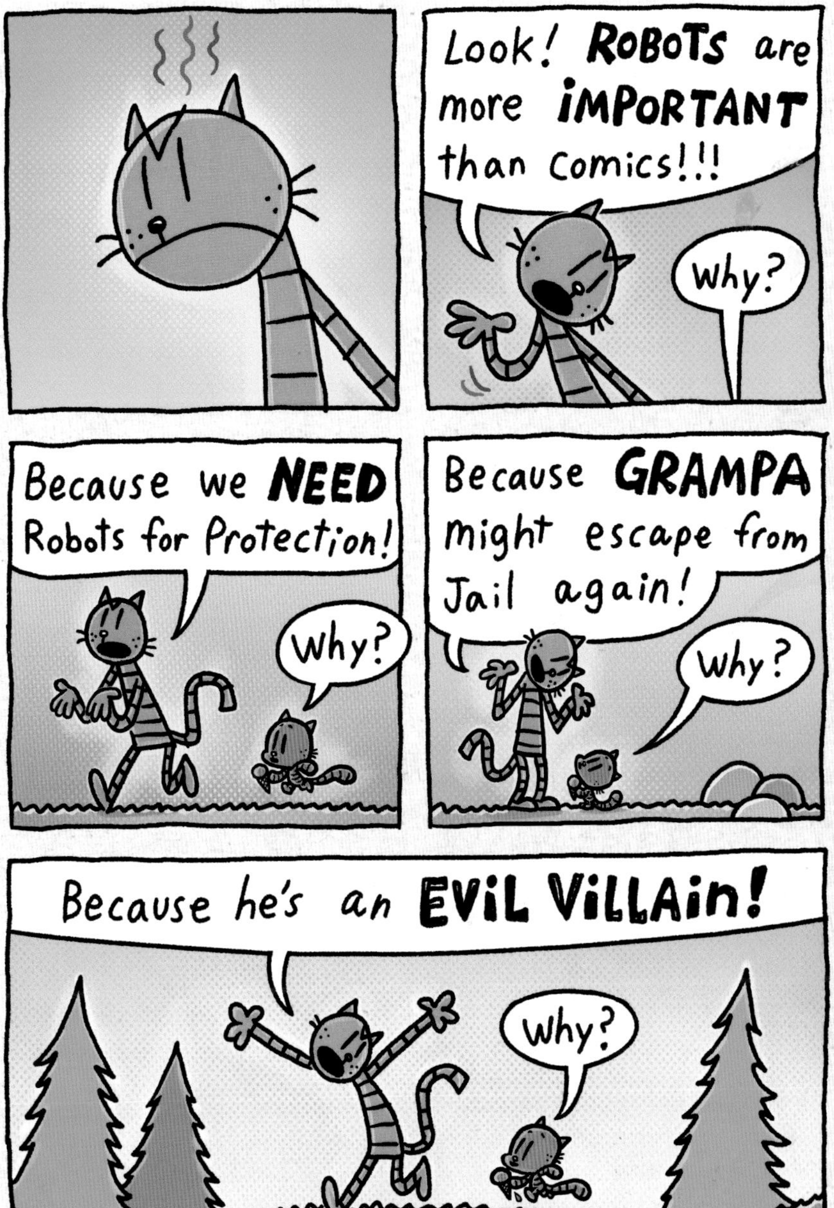
Look! ROBOTS are more IMPORTANT than comics!!!
Why?
Because we NEED Robots for Protection!
Why?
Because GRAMPA might escape from Jail again!
Why?
Because he's an EVIL VILLAIN!
Why?

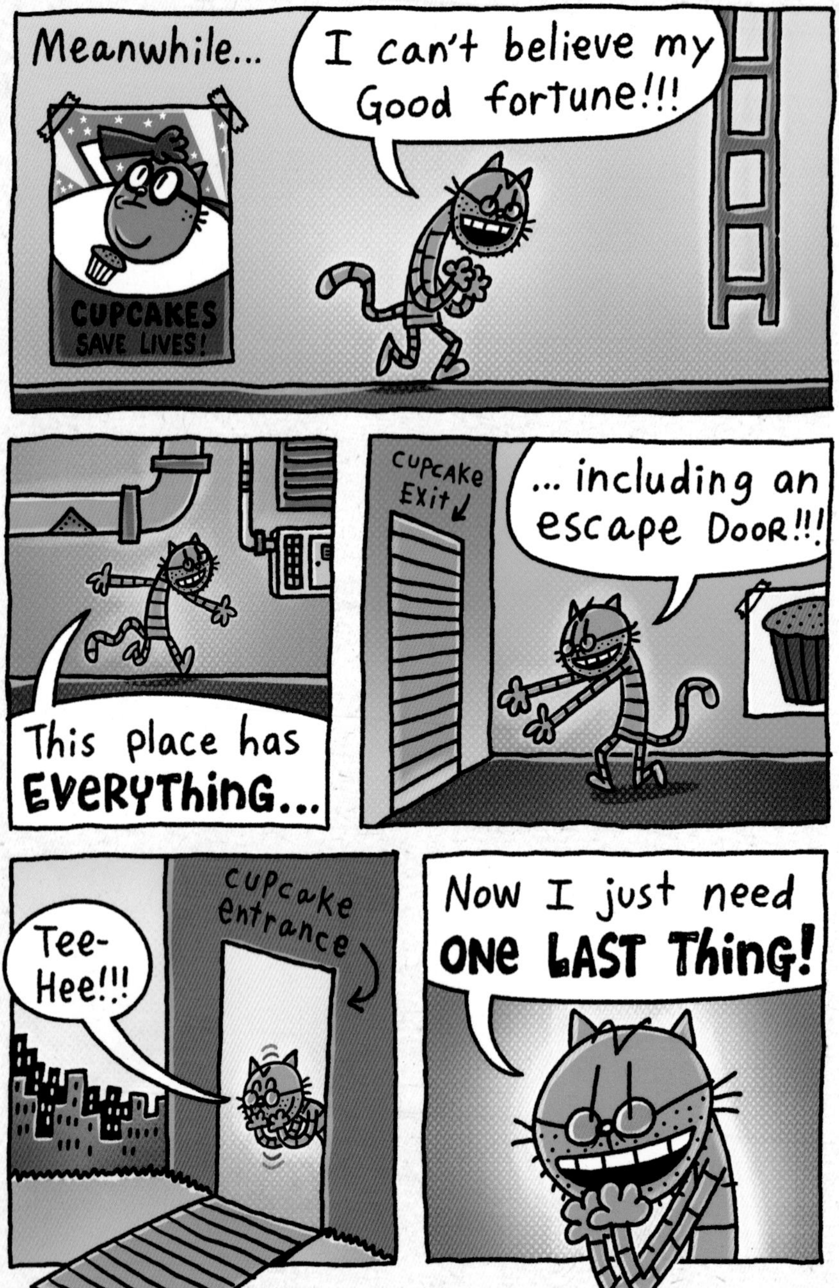
Meanwhile...
I can't believe my Good fortune!!!
CUPCAKES SAVE LIVES!
This place has EVERYThinG...
CUPCAKE EXIT
... including an escape DOOR!!!
Tee-Hee!!!
cupcake entrance
Now I just need ONE LAST Thing!

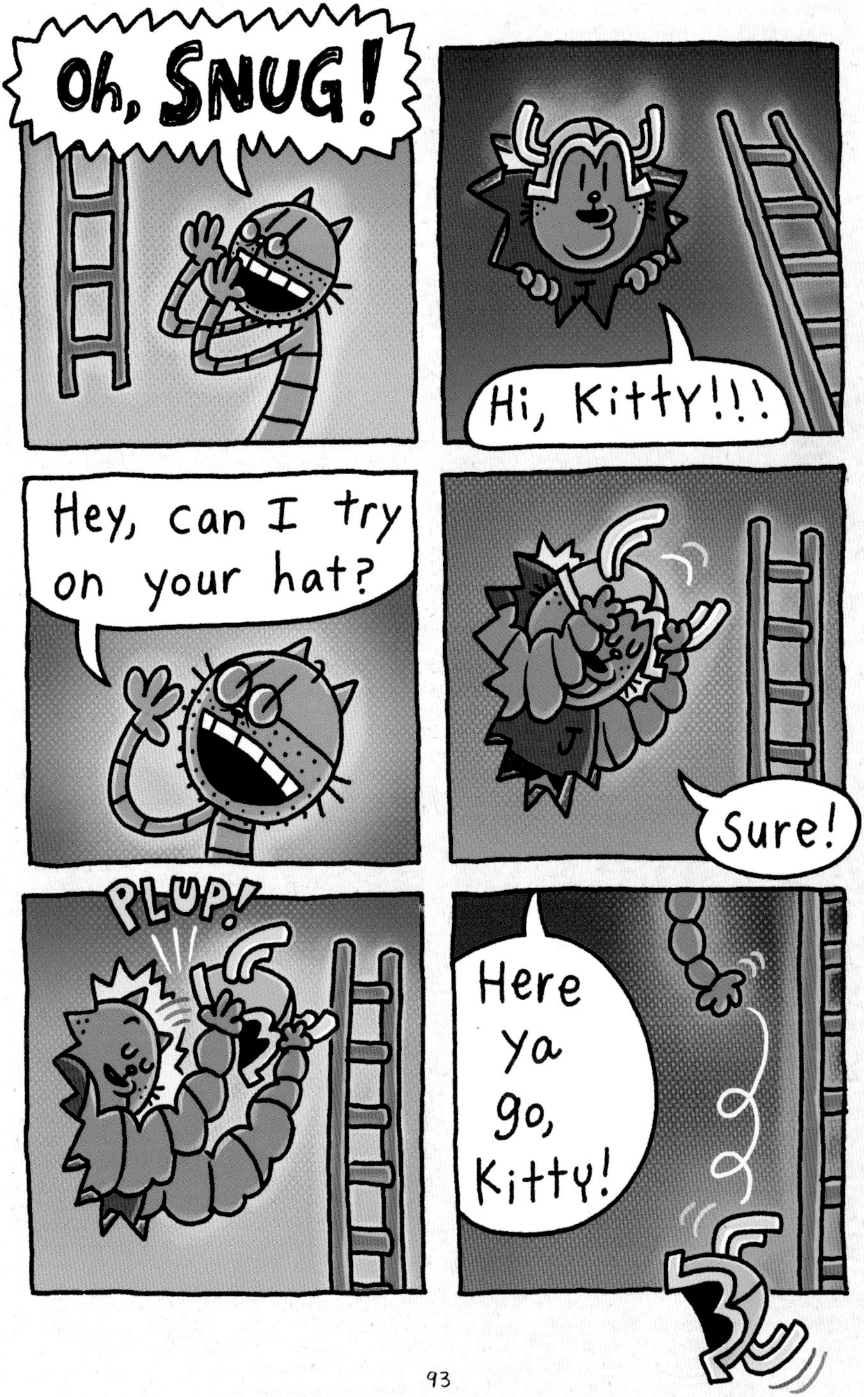
Oh, SNUG!
Hi, Kitty!!!
Hey, can I try on your hat?
Sure!
PLUP!
Here ya go, Kitty!

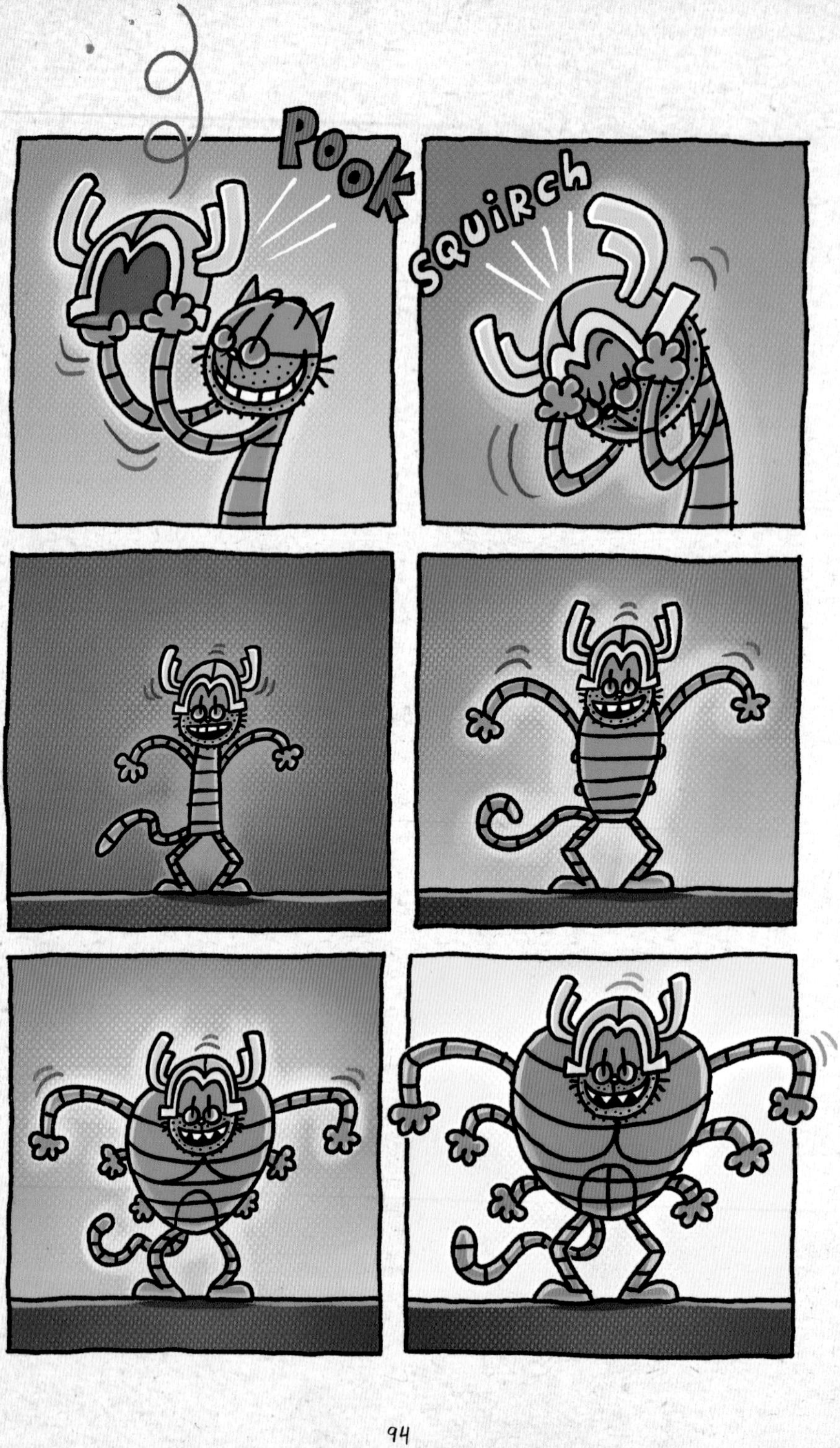
POOK
SQUIRCH

CHAPTER 6

THE INCORRIGIBLE
CRUD

By George Beard and Harold Hutchins

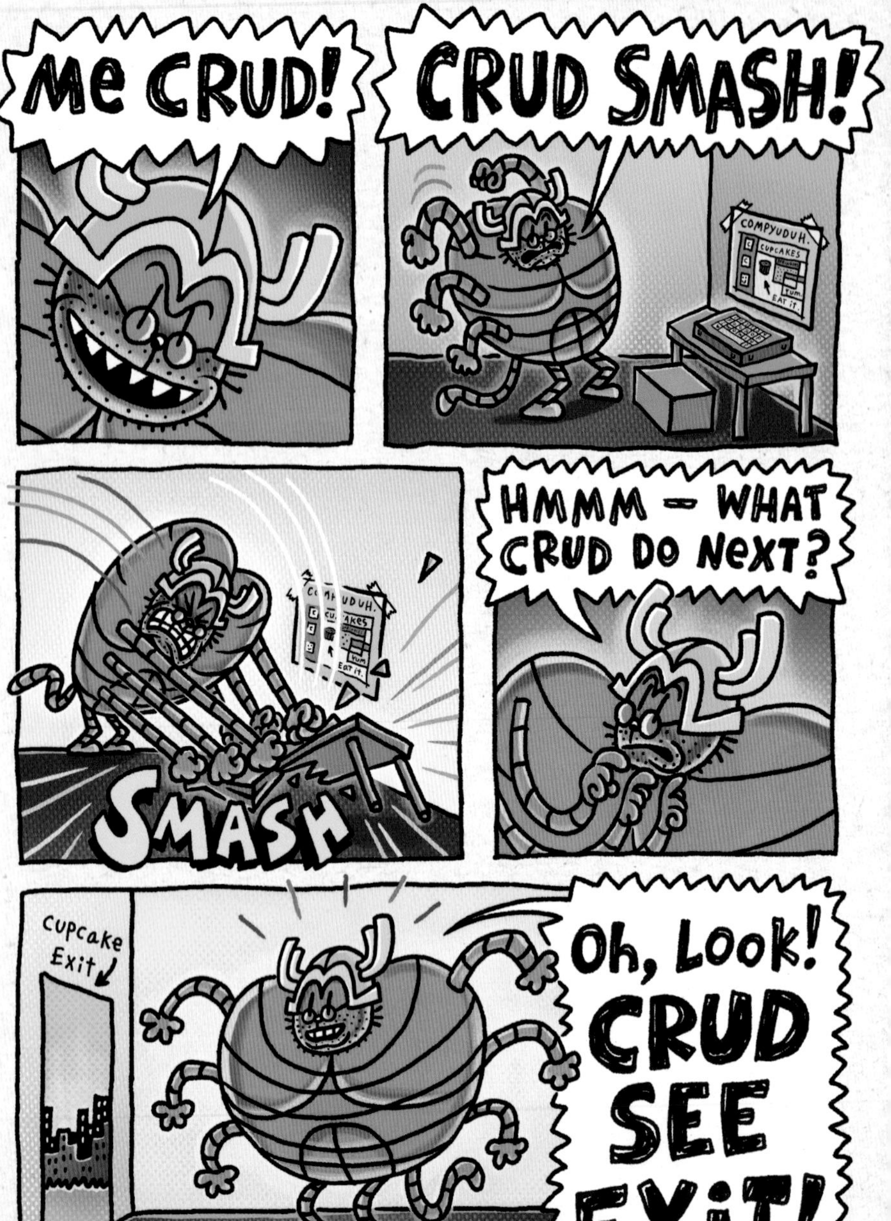
ME CRUD!
CRUD SMASH!
COMPYUDUH.
CUPCAKES
YUM.
EAT IT.
SMASH
HMMM — WHAT CRUD DO NEXT?
CUPCAKE EXIT
Oh, Look! CRUD SEE EXIT!

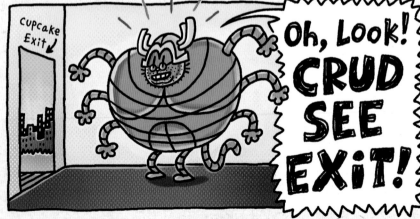

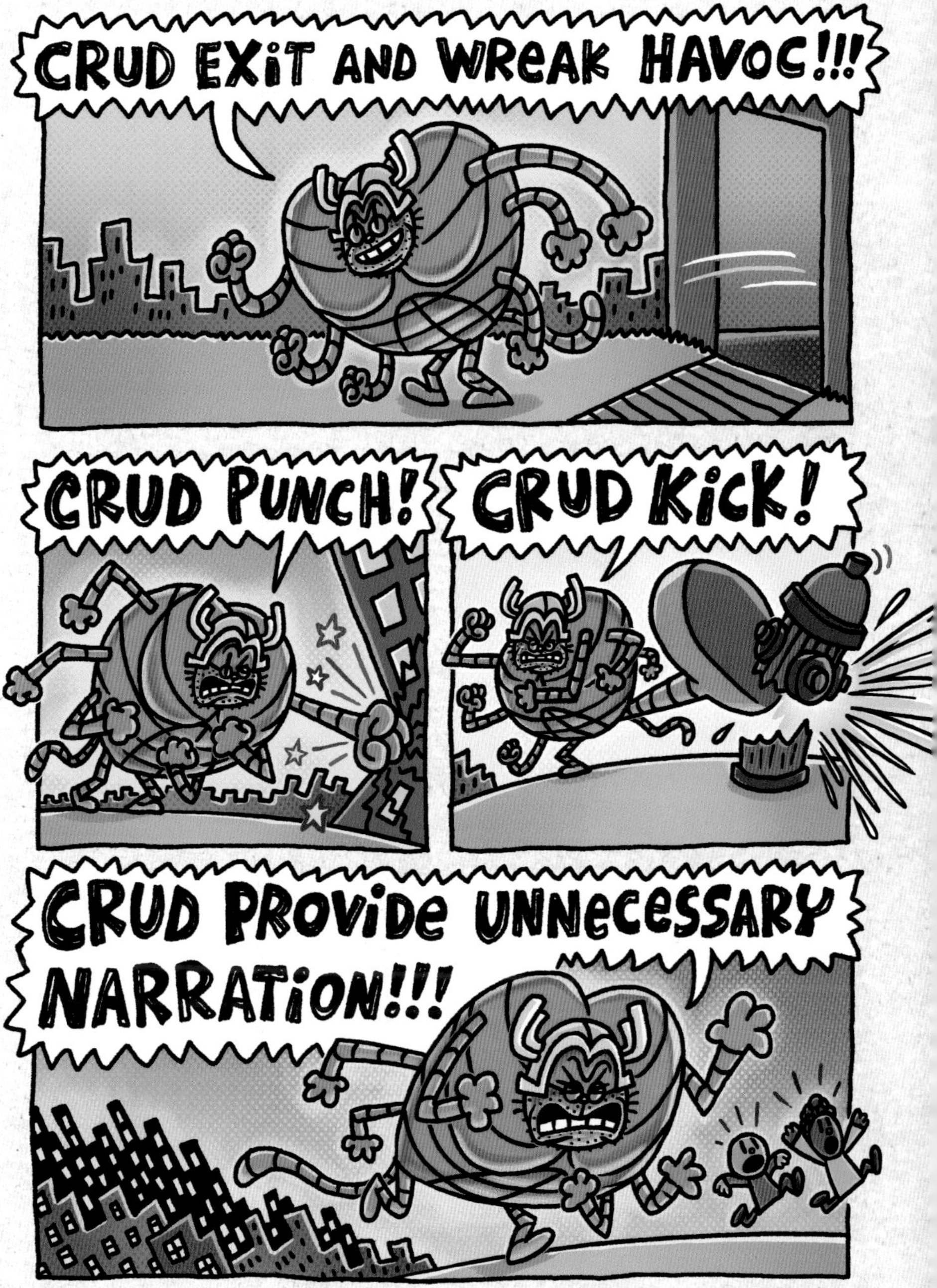
CRUD EXIT AND WREAK HAVOC!!!
CRUD PUNCH!
CRUD KICK!
CRUD PROVIDE UNNECESSARY NARRATION!!!

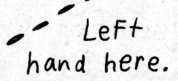

Left hand here.

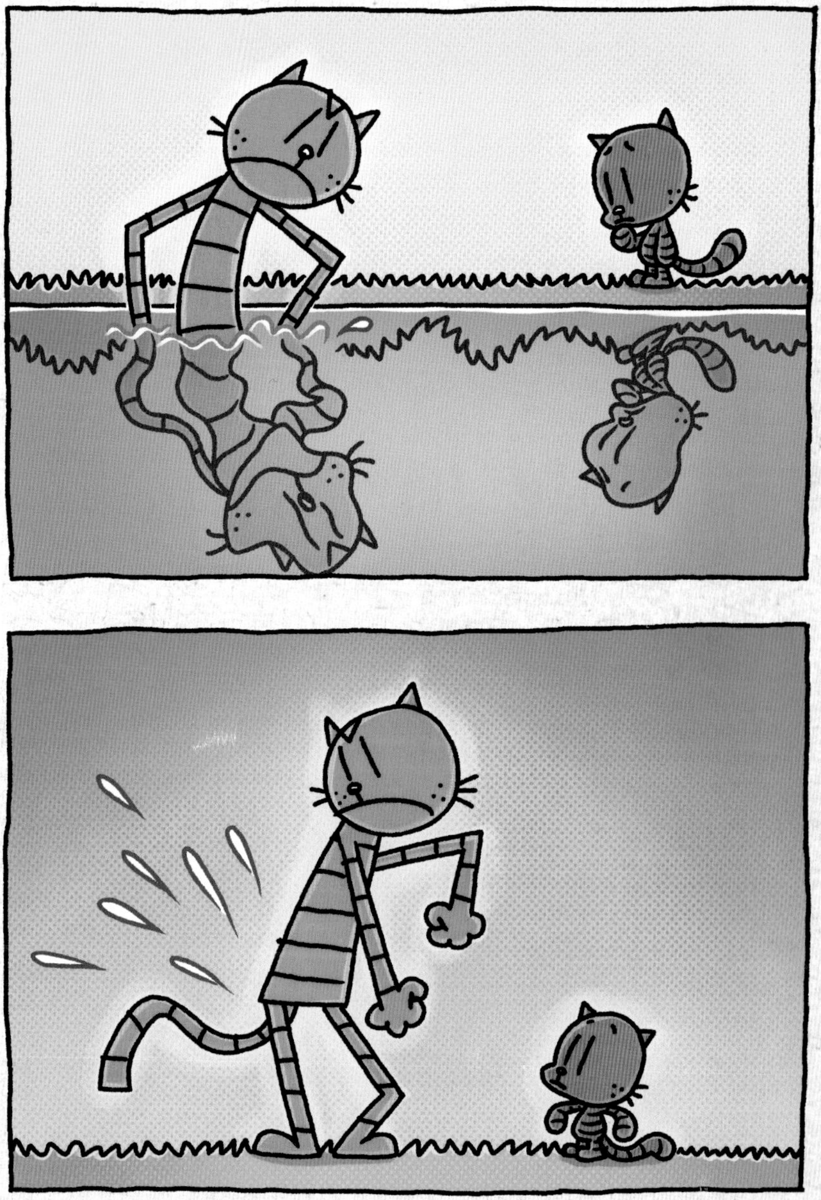

Right Thumb here.

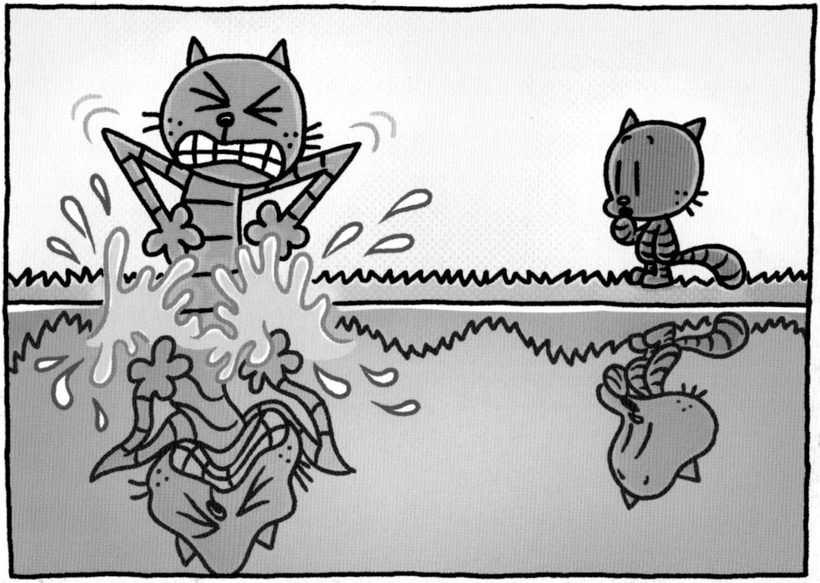

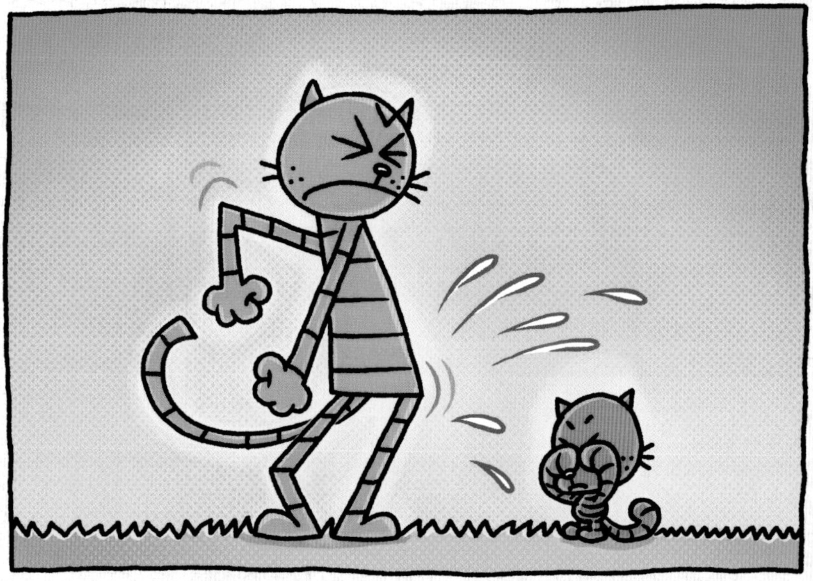

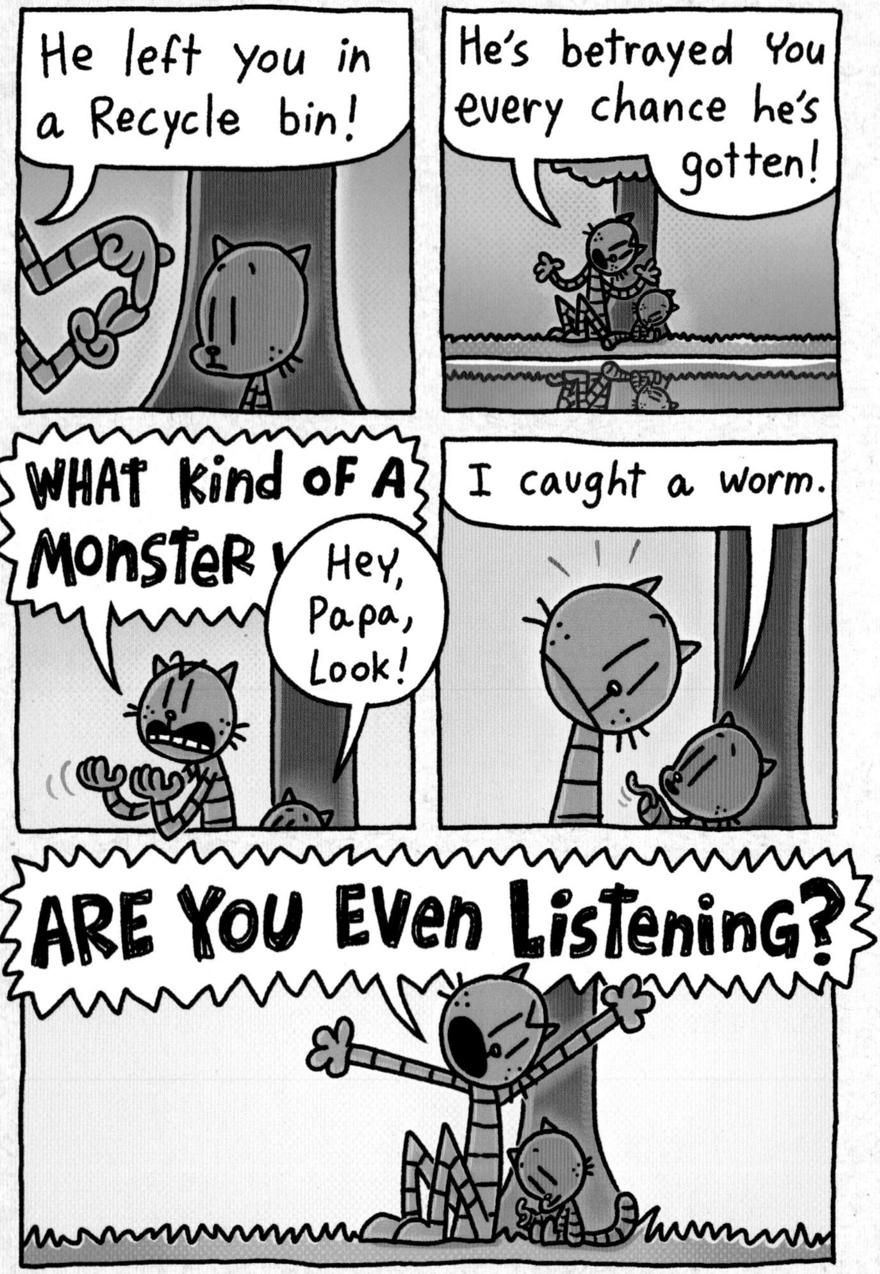
He left you in a Recycle bin!
He's betrayed You every chance he's gotten!
WHAT Kind OF A MONSTER
Hey, Papa, Look!
I caught a worm.
ARE YOU EVEN LISTENING?

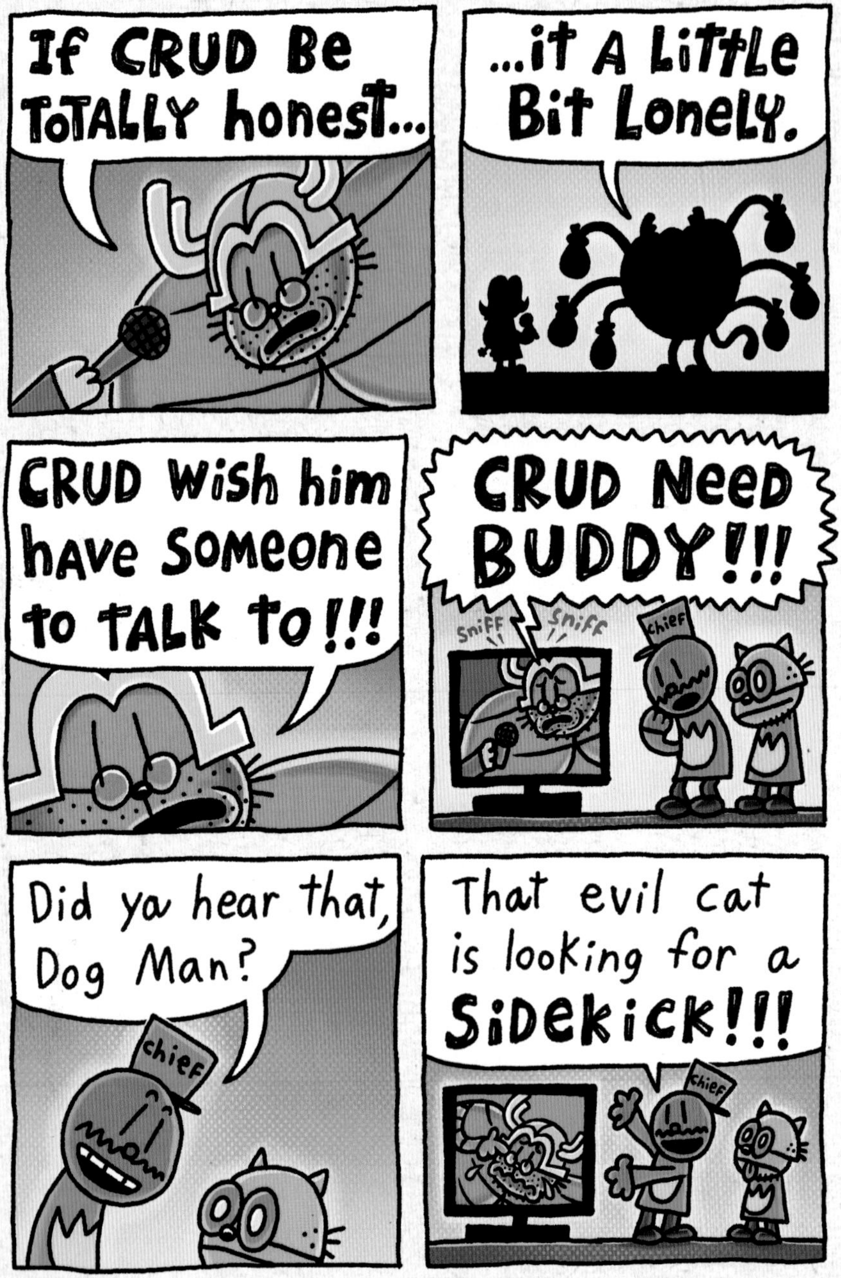
If CRUD Be TOTALLY honest...
...it A Little Bit Lonely.
CRUD Wish him have Someone to TALK to!!!
CRUD Need BUDDY!!!
Sniff
Sniff
chief
Did ya hear that, Dog Man?
chief
That evil cat is looking for a SiDEKiCK!!!
chief

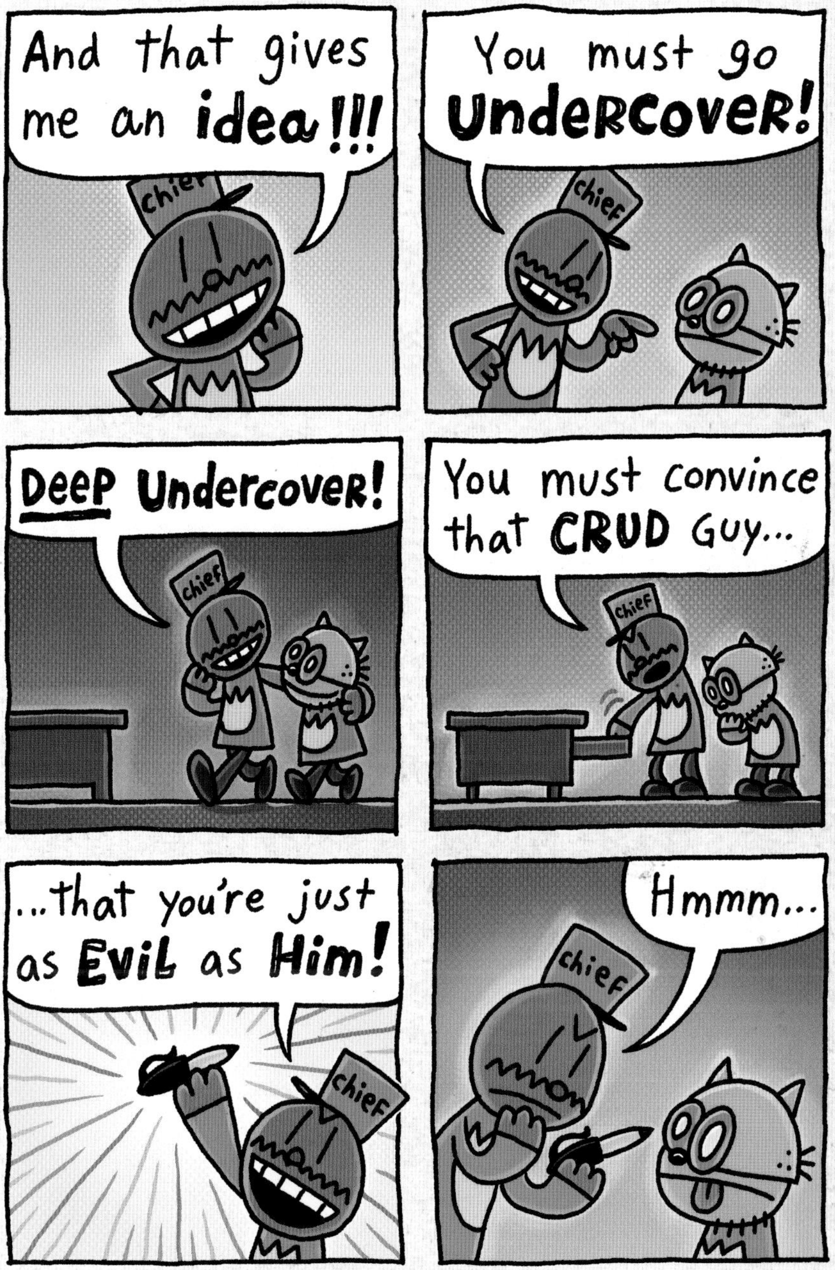
And that gives me an idea!!!
chief
You must go UNDERCOVER!
chief
DEEP Undercover!
chief
You must convince that CRUD Guy...
chief
...that you're just as EVIL as Him!
chief
Hmmm...
chief

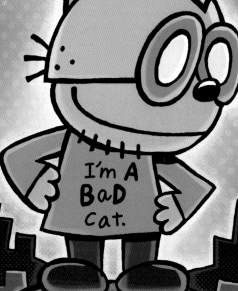

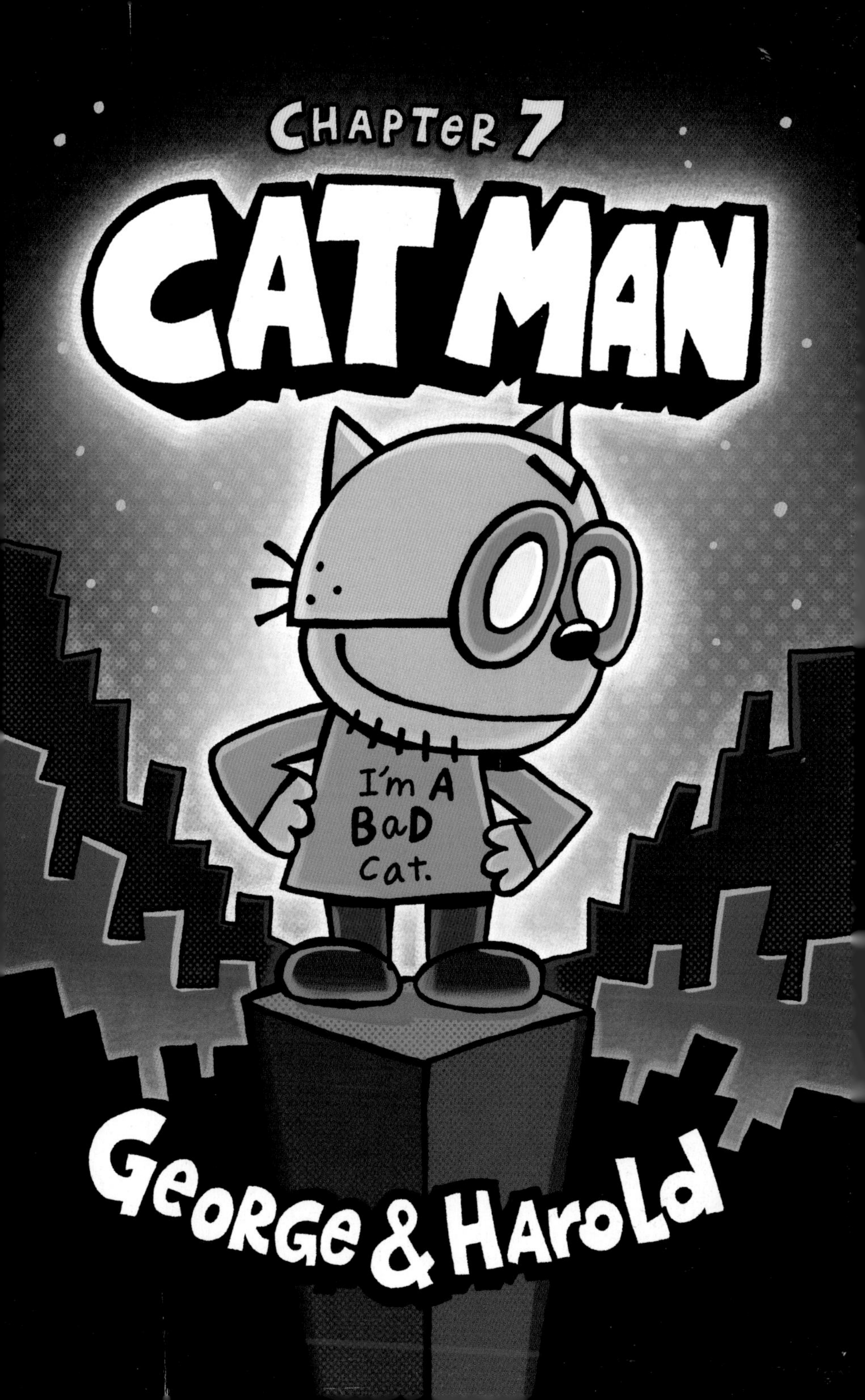
CHAPTER 7
CAT MAN
I'm A BaD Cat.
George & Harold

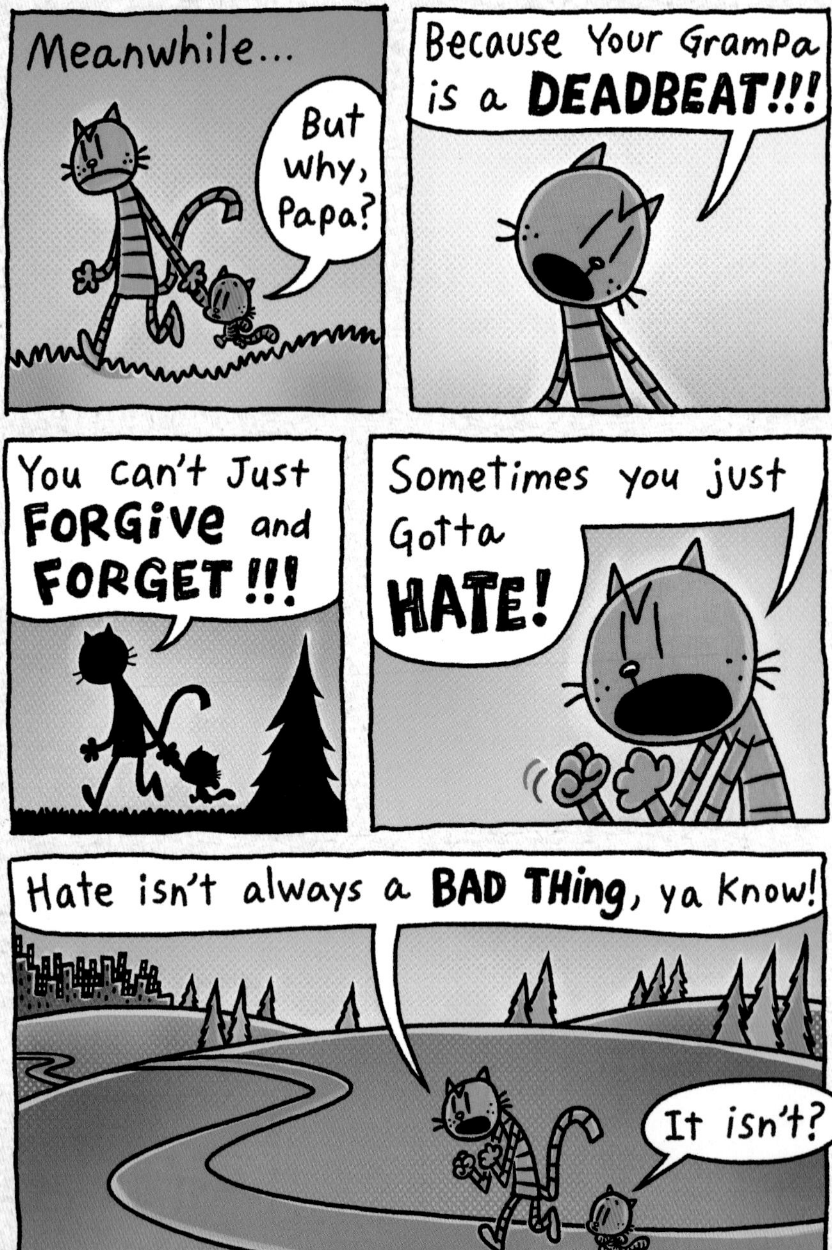

Meanwhile...
But why, Papa?
Because Your Grampa is a DEADBEAT!!!
You can't Just FORGive and FORGET!!!
Sometimes you just Gotta HATE!
Hate isn't always a BAD THing, ya Know!
It isn't?

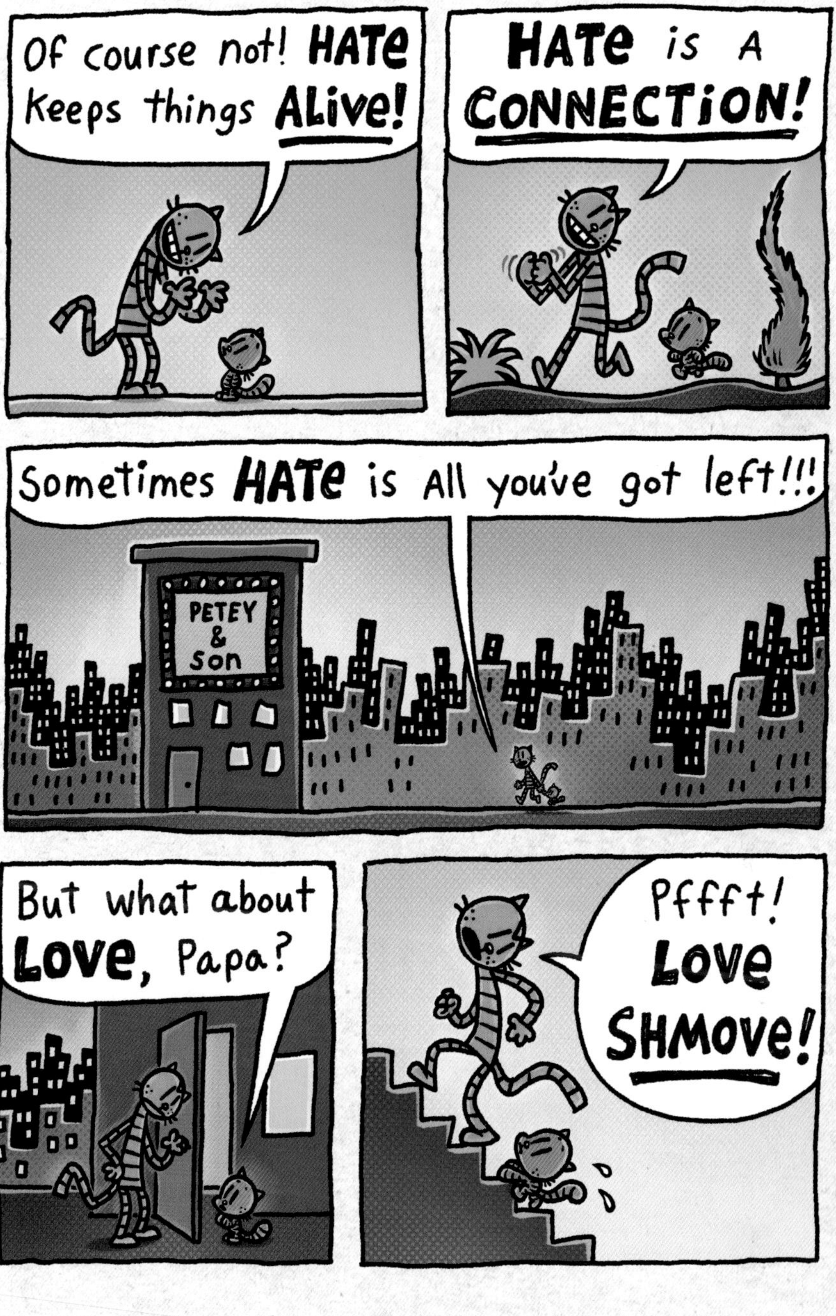
Of course not! HATE Keeps things ALive!
HATE is A CONNECTiON!
Sometimes HATE is All you've got left!!!
PETEY & Son
But what about Love, Papa?
Pffft! Love SHMove!

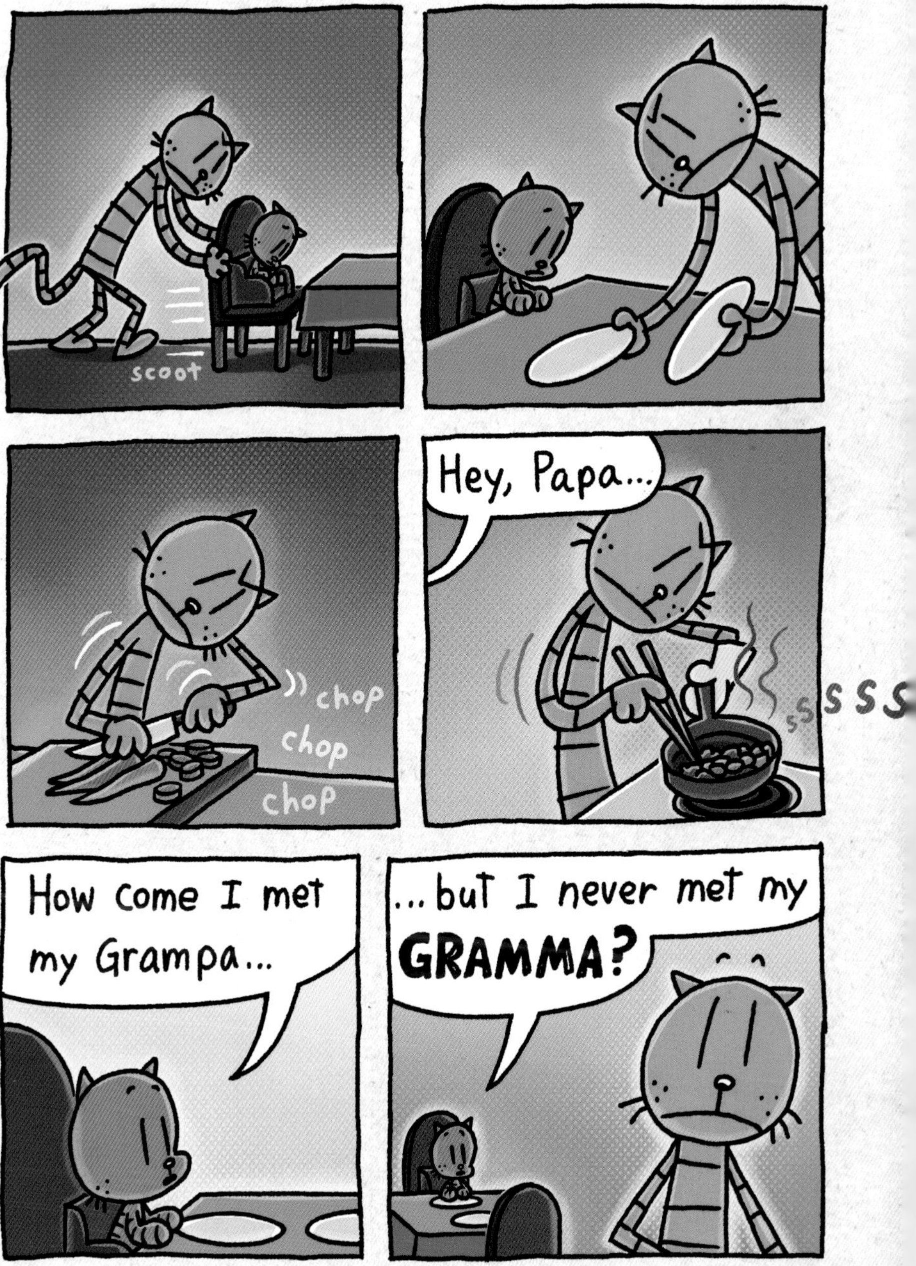
scoot
Hey, Papa...
chop
chop
chop
sSSSS
How come I met my Grampa...
...but I never met my GRAMMA?

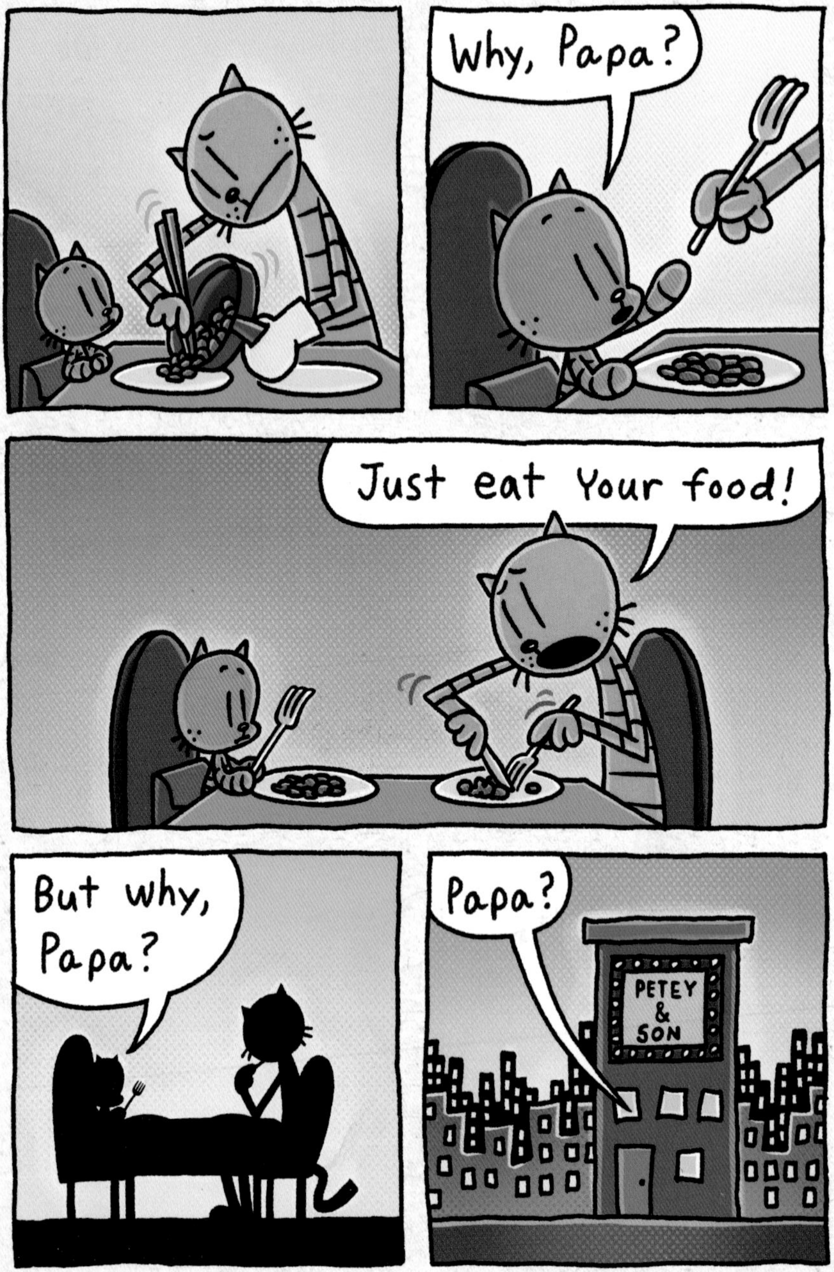
Why, Papa?
Just eat your food!
But why, Papa?
Papa?
PETEY & SON

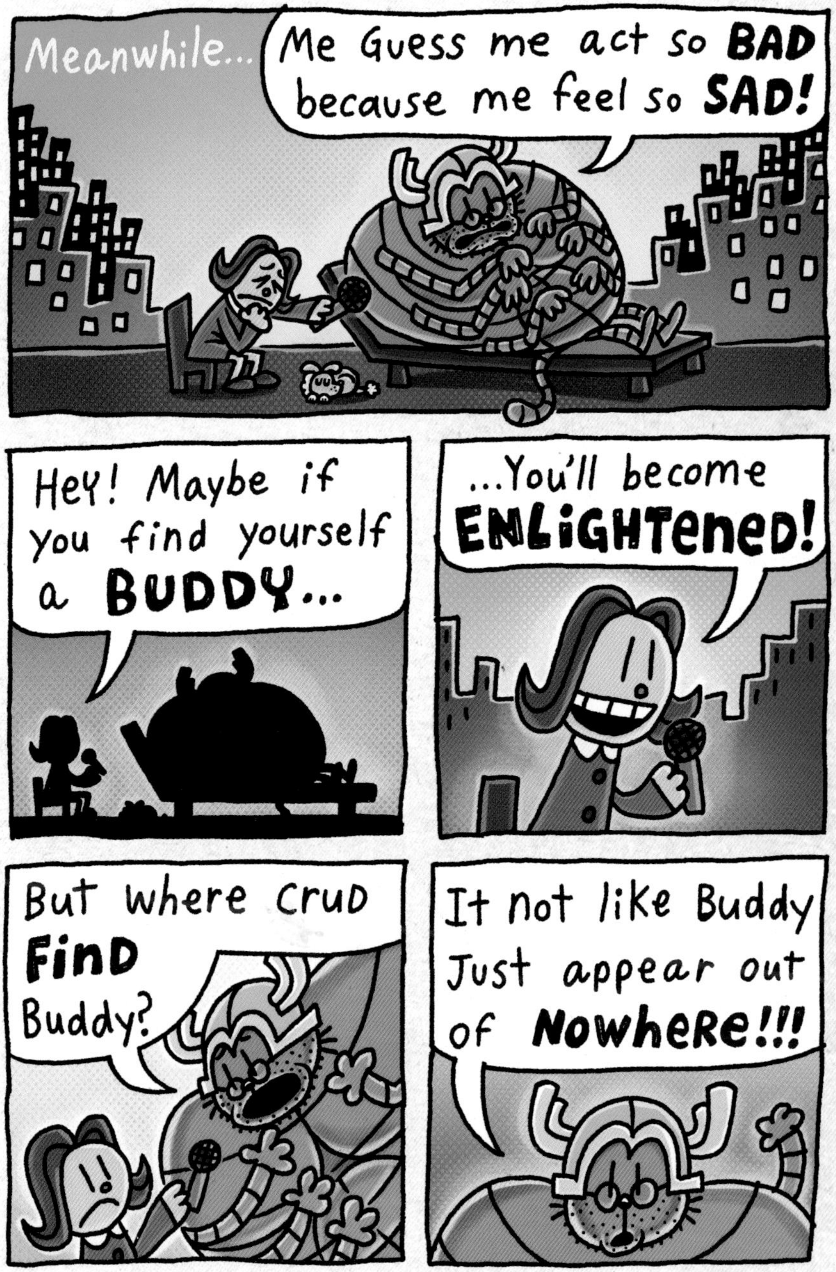
Meanwhile...
Me Guess me act so BAD because me feel so SAD!
Hey! Maybe if you find yourself a BUDDY...
...You'll become ENLIGHTENED!
But where Crud FIND Buddy?
It not like Buddy Just appear out of NOWHERE!!!

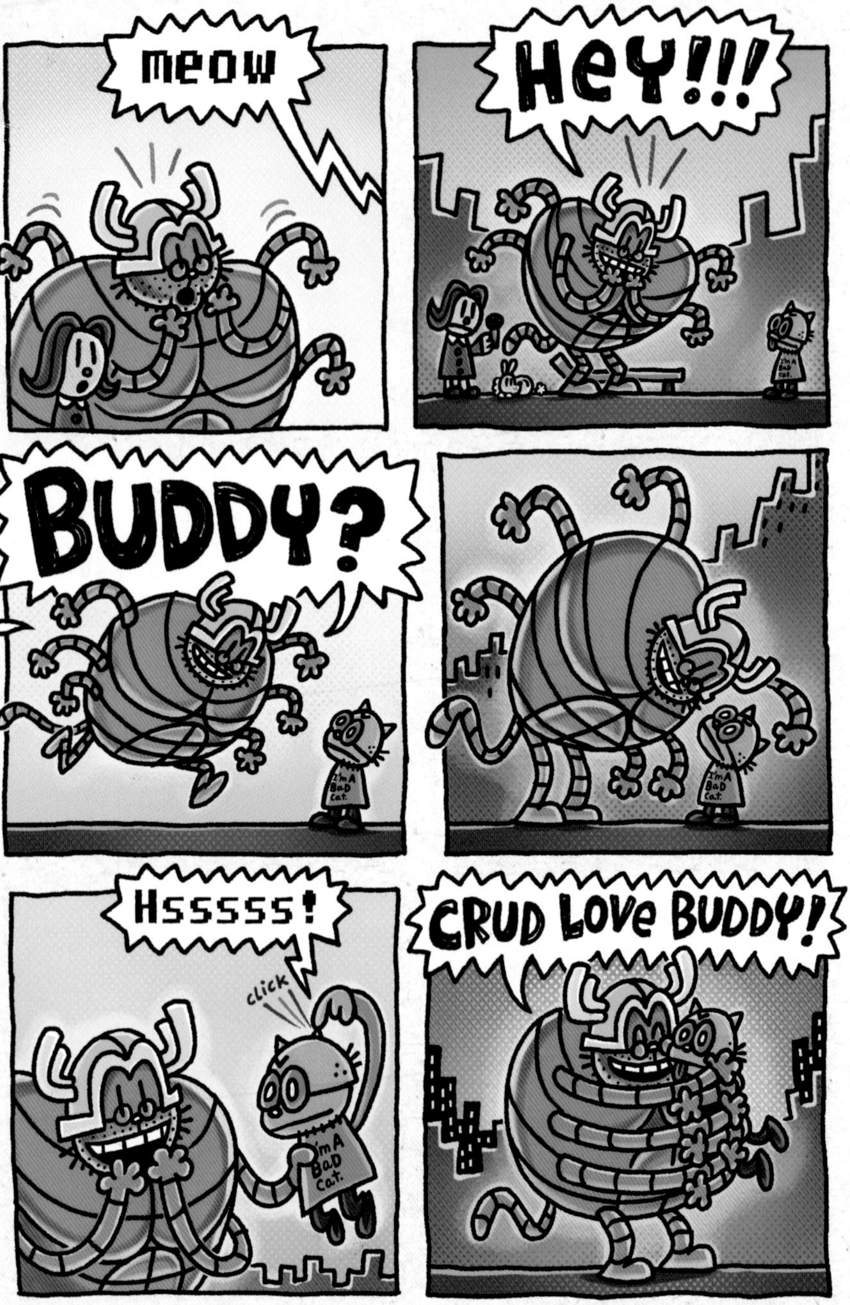
meow
HEY!!!
I'm A BaD Cat.
BUDDY?
I'm A BaD Cat.
I'm A BaD Cat.
Hsssss!
click
I'm A BaD Cat.
CRUD Love BUDDY!

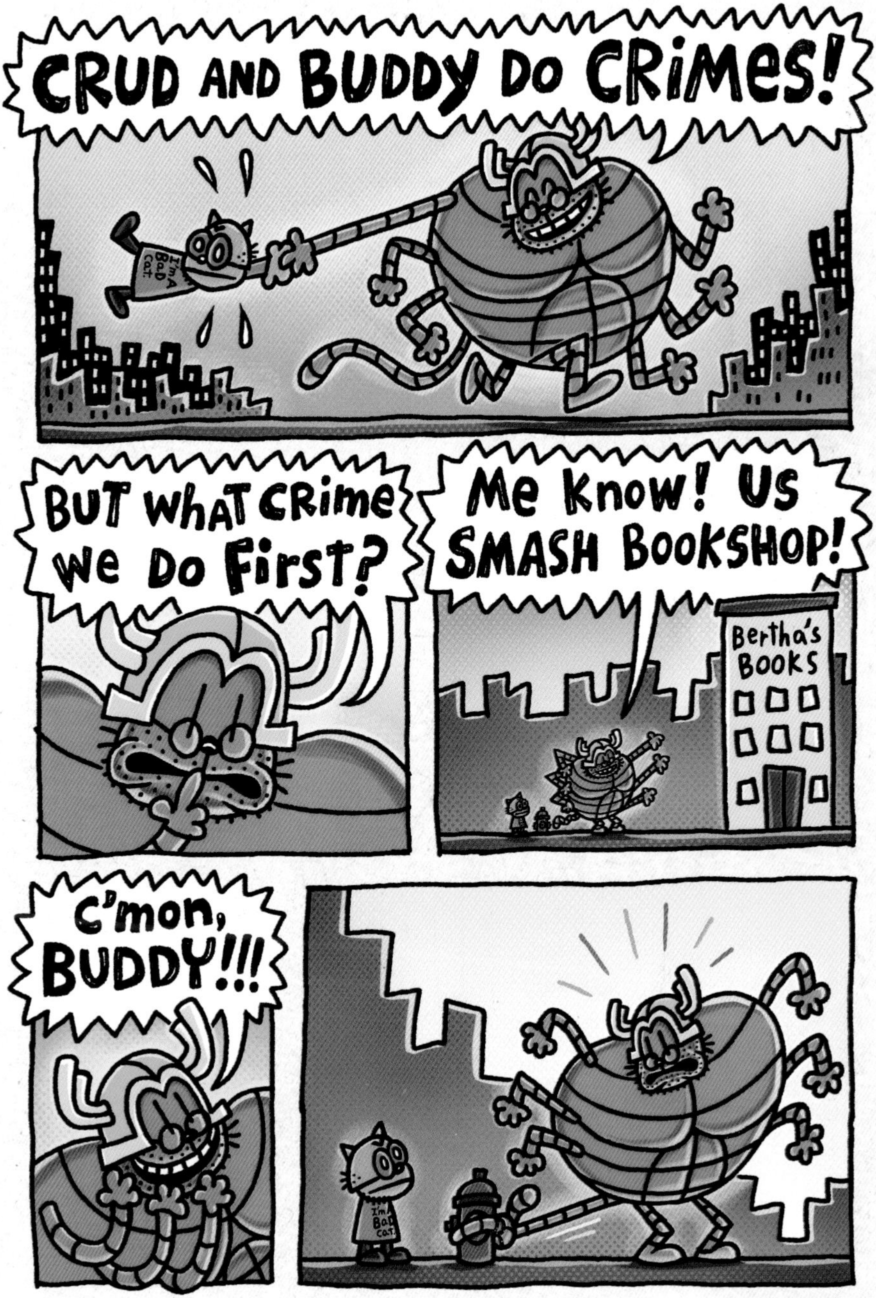
CRUD AND BUDDY DO CRIMES!
I'm A Bad Cat.
BUT WHAT CRIME we DO FIRST?
Me Know! US SMASH BOOKSHOP!
Bertha's BOOKS
C'mon, BUDDY!!!
I'm A Bad Cat.

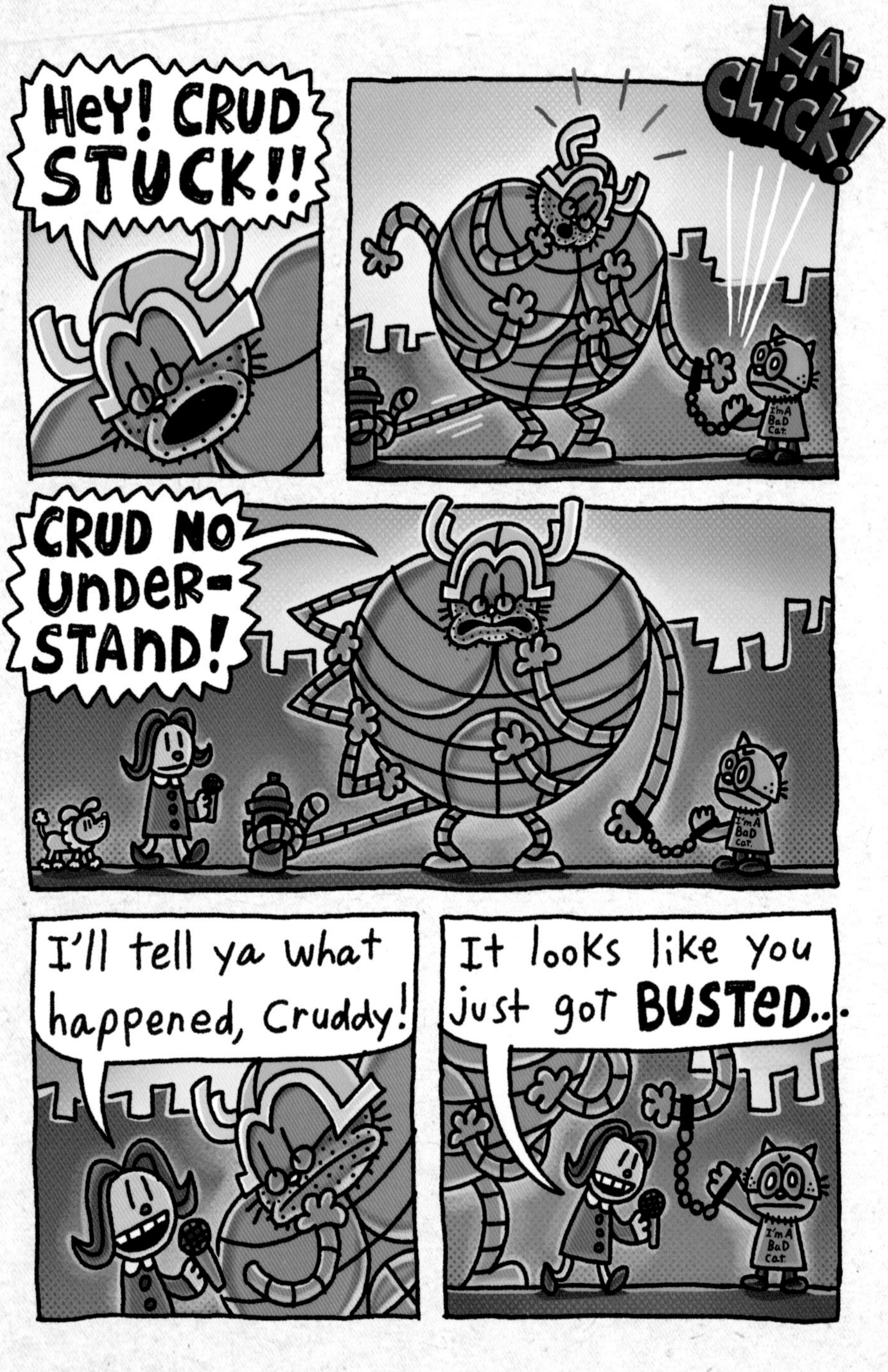
HEY! CRUD STUCK!!
KA-CLICK!
I'M A BAD CAT.
CRUD NO UNDER-STAND!
I'M A BAD CAT.
I'll tell ya what happened, Cruddy!
It looks like you just got BUSTED...
I'M A BAD CAT.

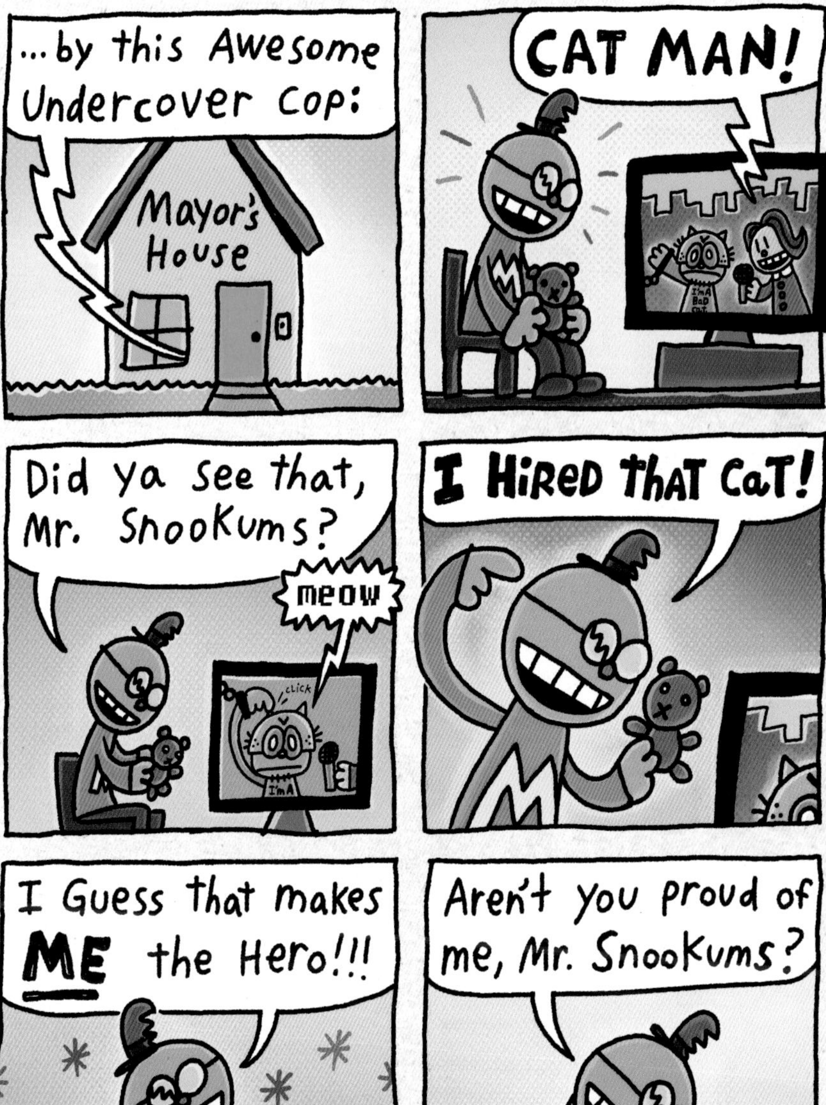
...by this Awesome Undercover Cop:
Mayor's House
CAT MAN!
Did ya see that, Mr. Snookums?
meow
CLICK
I'm A
I HIRED THAT CAT!
I Guess that makes ME the Hero!!!
Aren't you proud of me, Mr. Snookums?

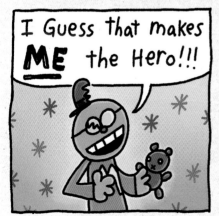

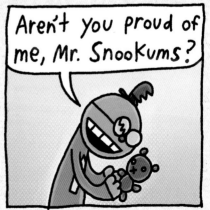

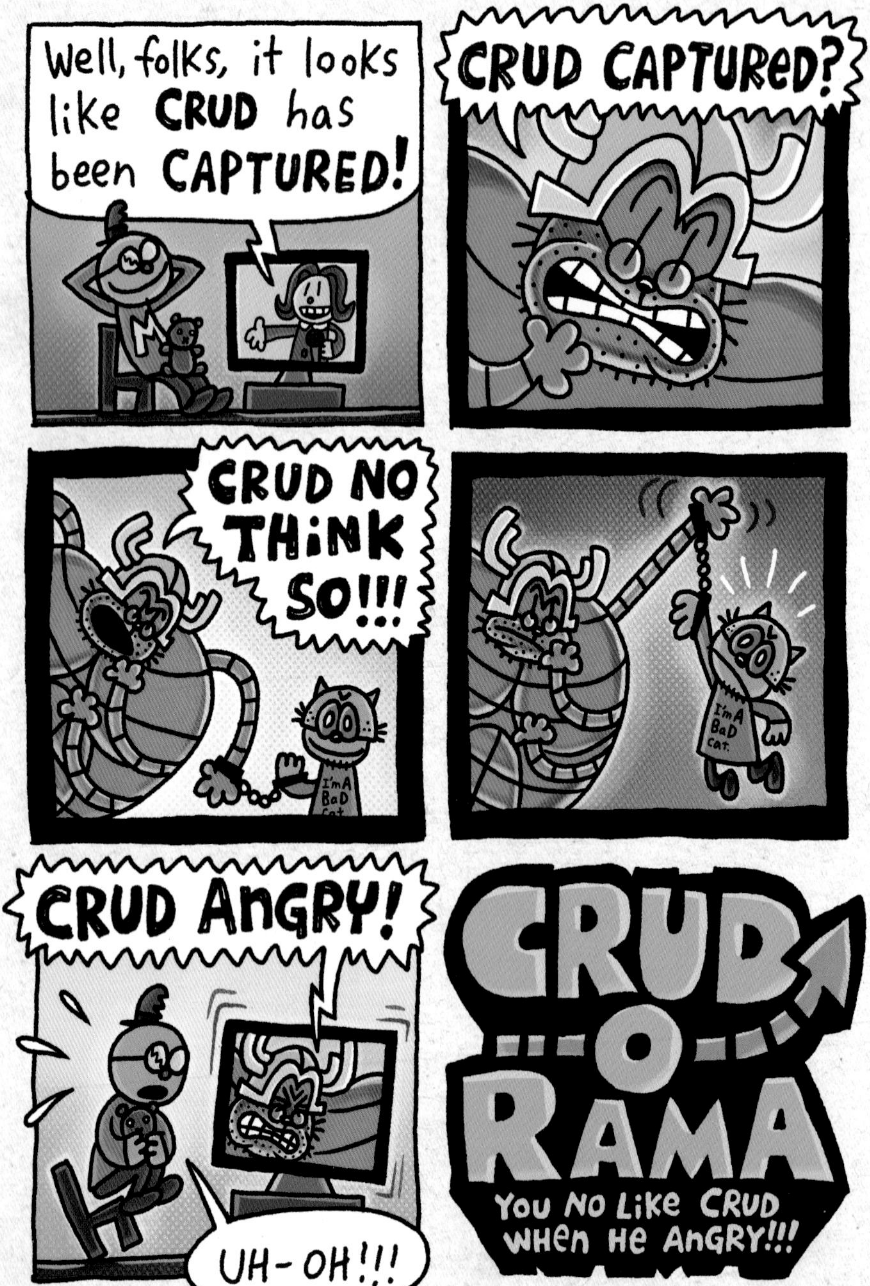
Well, folks, it looks like CRUD has been CAPTURED!
CRUD CAPTURED?
CRUD NO THINK SO!!!
I'm A BaD cat
I'm A BaD cat.
CRUD AnGRY!
UH-OH!!!
CRUD-O-RAMA
You No Like CRUD wHen He AnGRY!!!

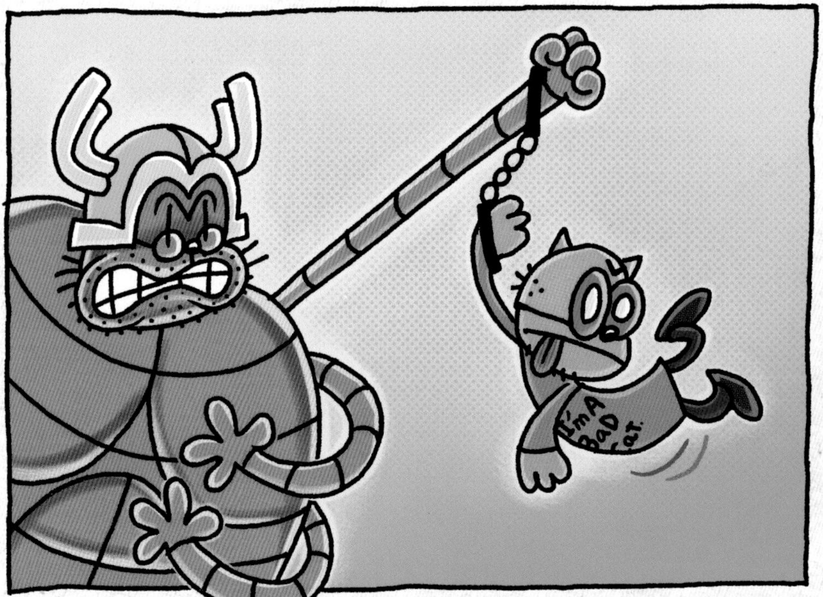
I'm A BAD CAT.

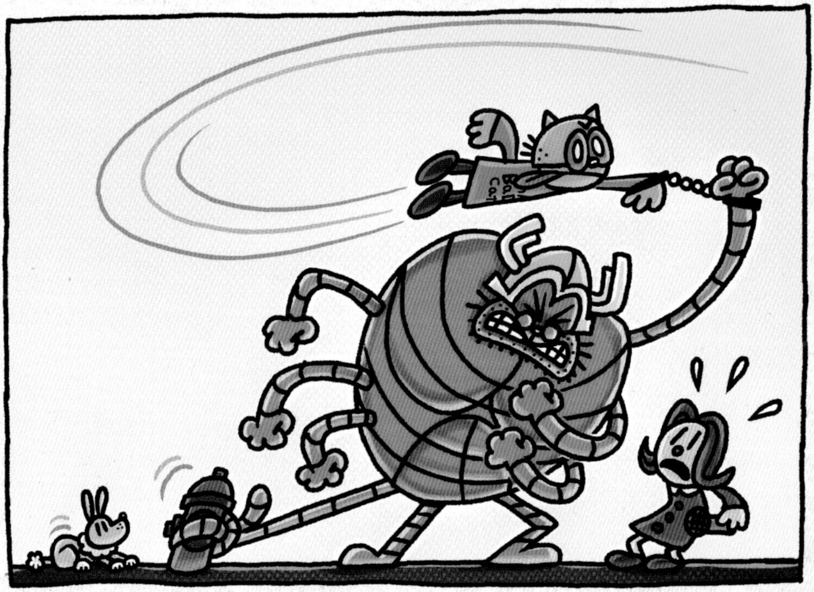

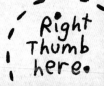

Right Thumb here.

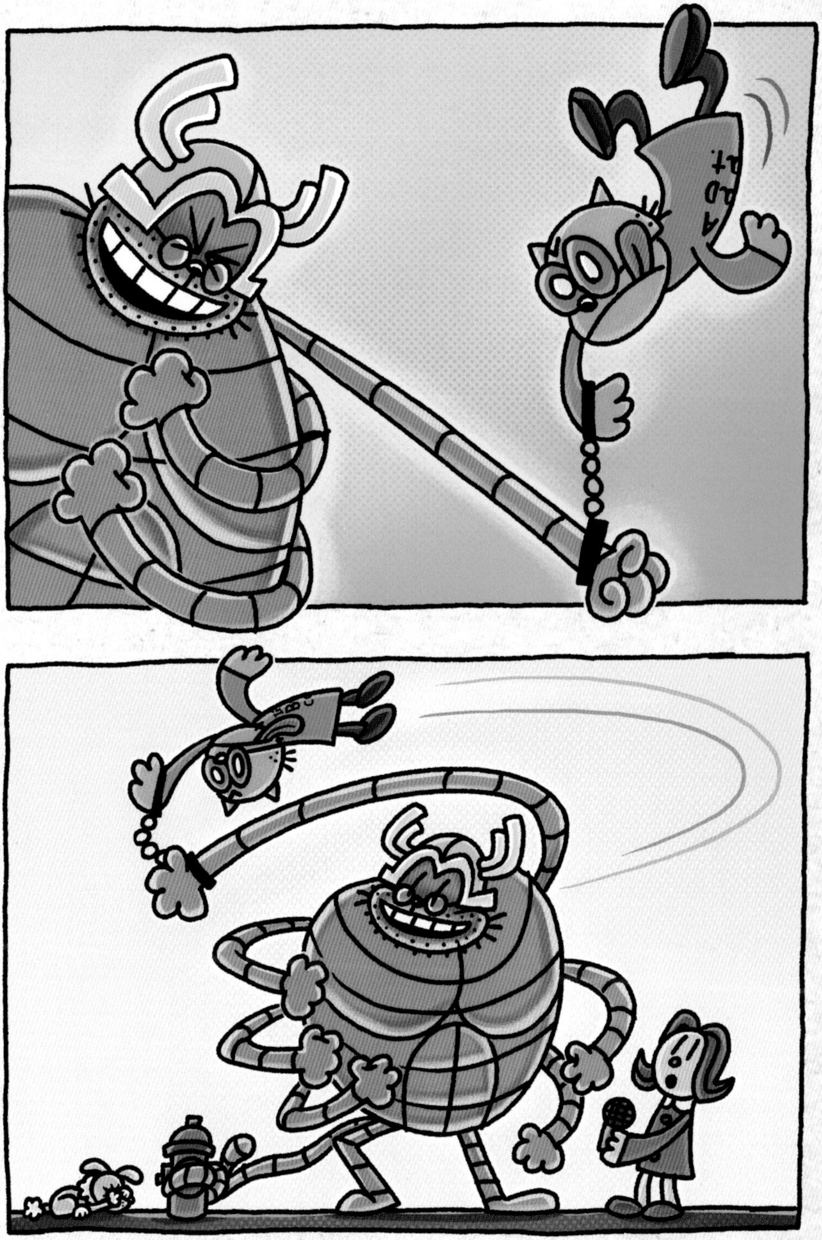

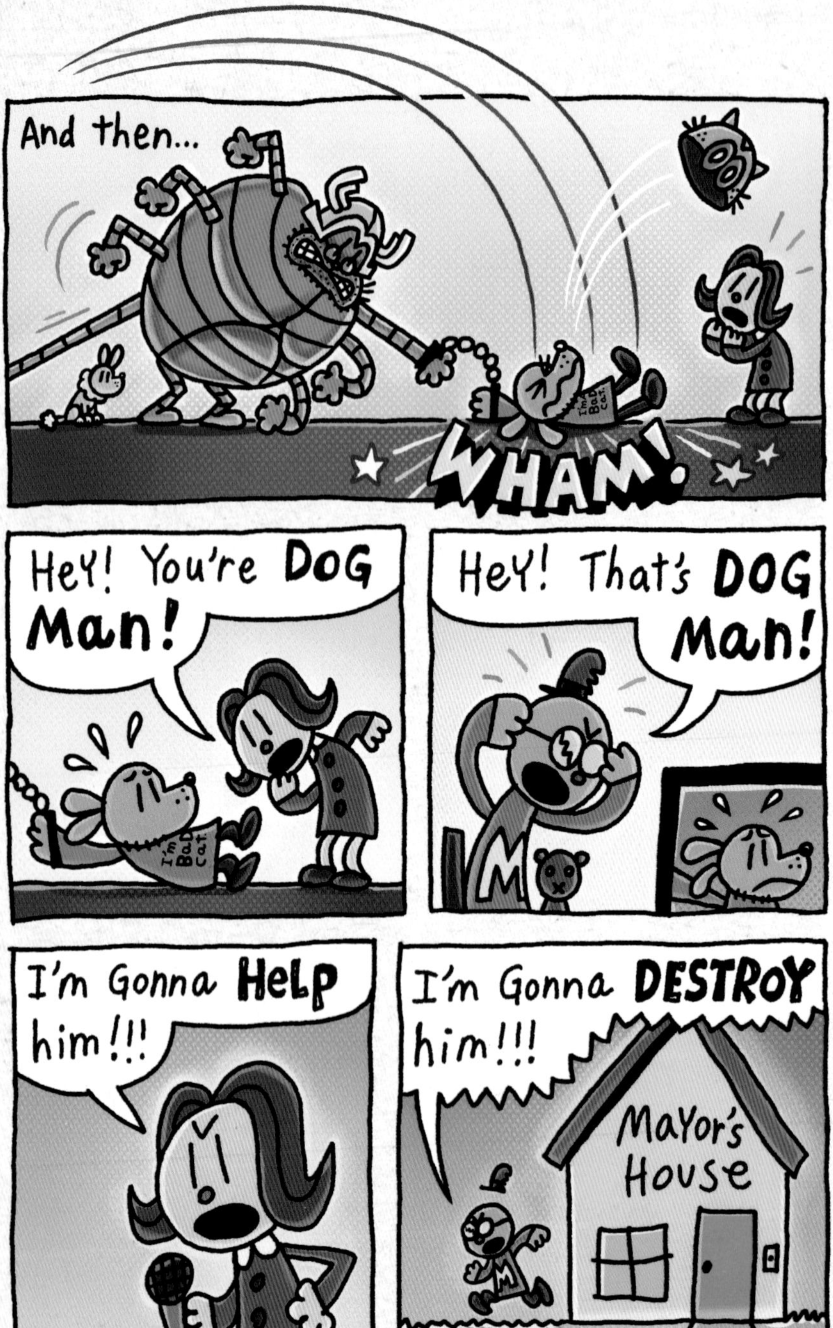
And then...
I'm BaD Cat.
WHAM!
Hey! You're DOG Man!
I'm BaD Cat.
Hey! That's DOG Man!
M
I'm Gonna HELP him!!!
I'm Gonna DESTROY him!!!
Mayor's House
M

CHAPTER 8

BIG FIGHT

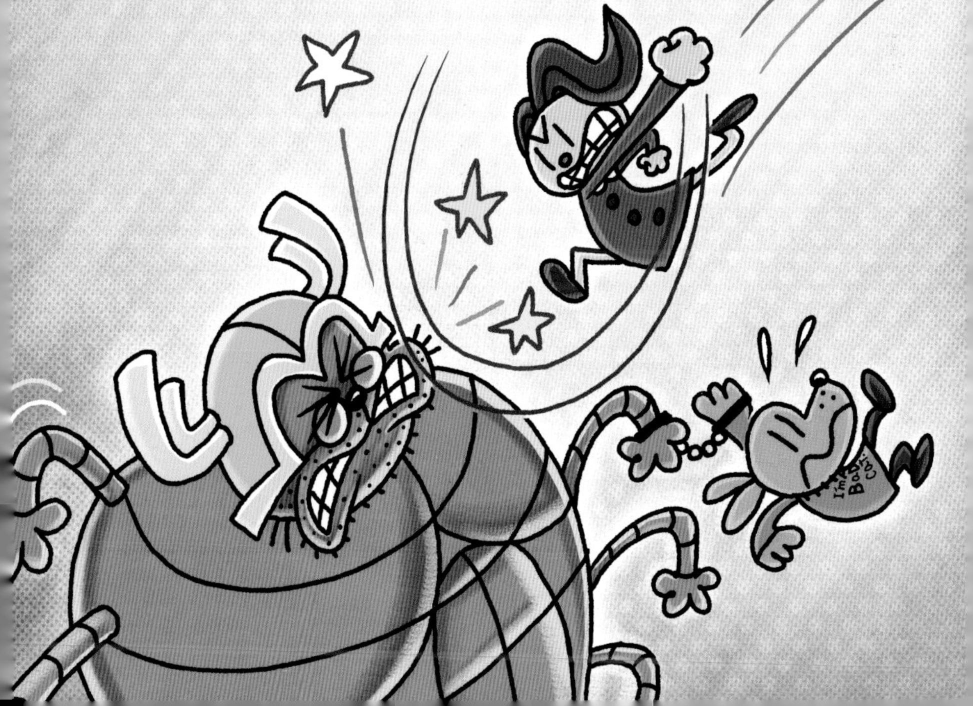

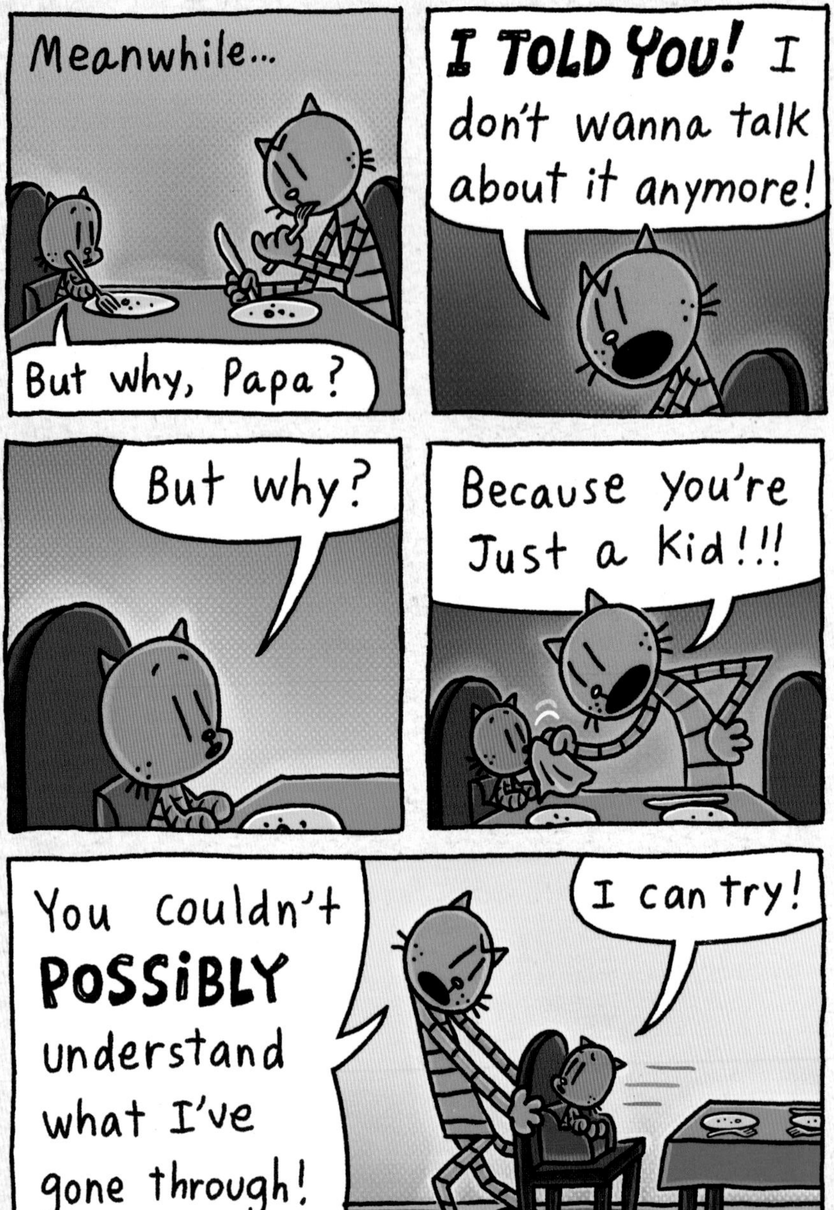
Meanwhile...
But why, Papa?
I TOLD YOU! I don't wanna talk about it anymore!
But why?
Because you're Just a Kid!!!
You couldn't POSSIBLY understand what I've gone through!
I can try!

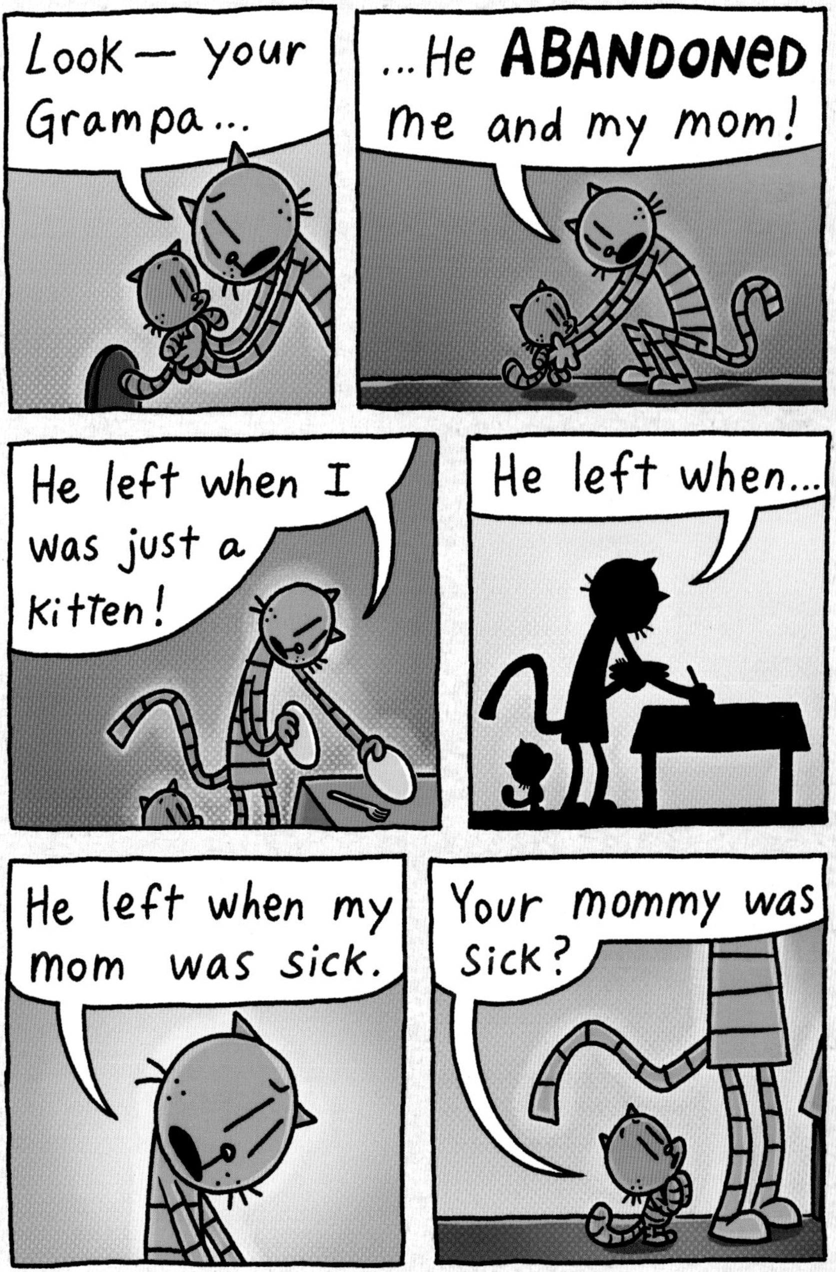
Look— your Grampa...
...He ABANDONED me and my mom!
He left when I was just a kitten!
He left when...
He left when my mom was sick.
Your mommy was sick?

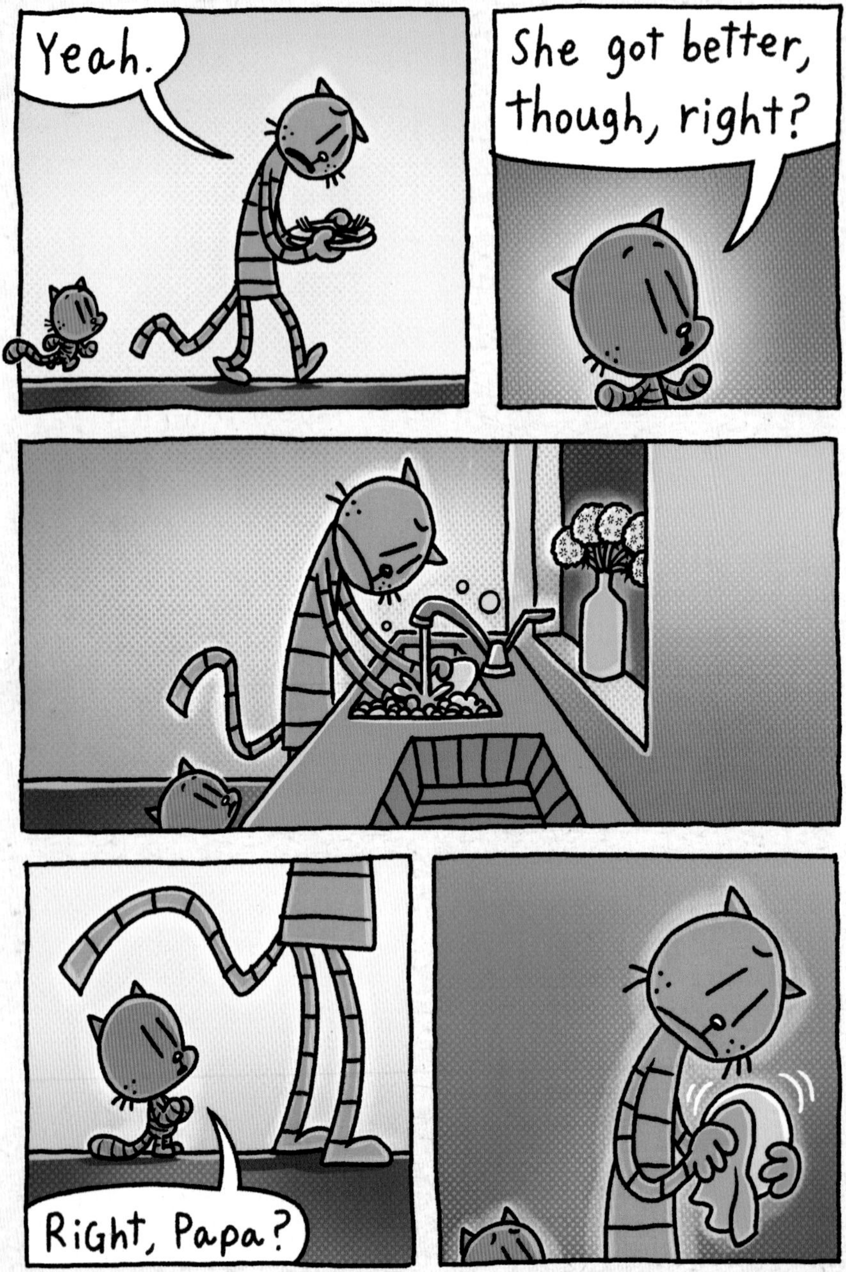
Yeah.
She got better, though, right?
Right, Papa?

Look, Kid...

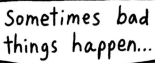

Sometimes bad things happen...

...and you just can't **FORGIVE**...

...and you can't **FORGET!**

Sometimes all you've got left is **HATE!**

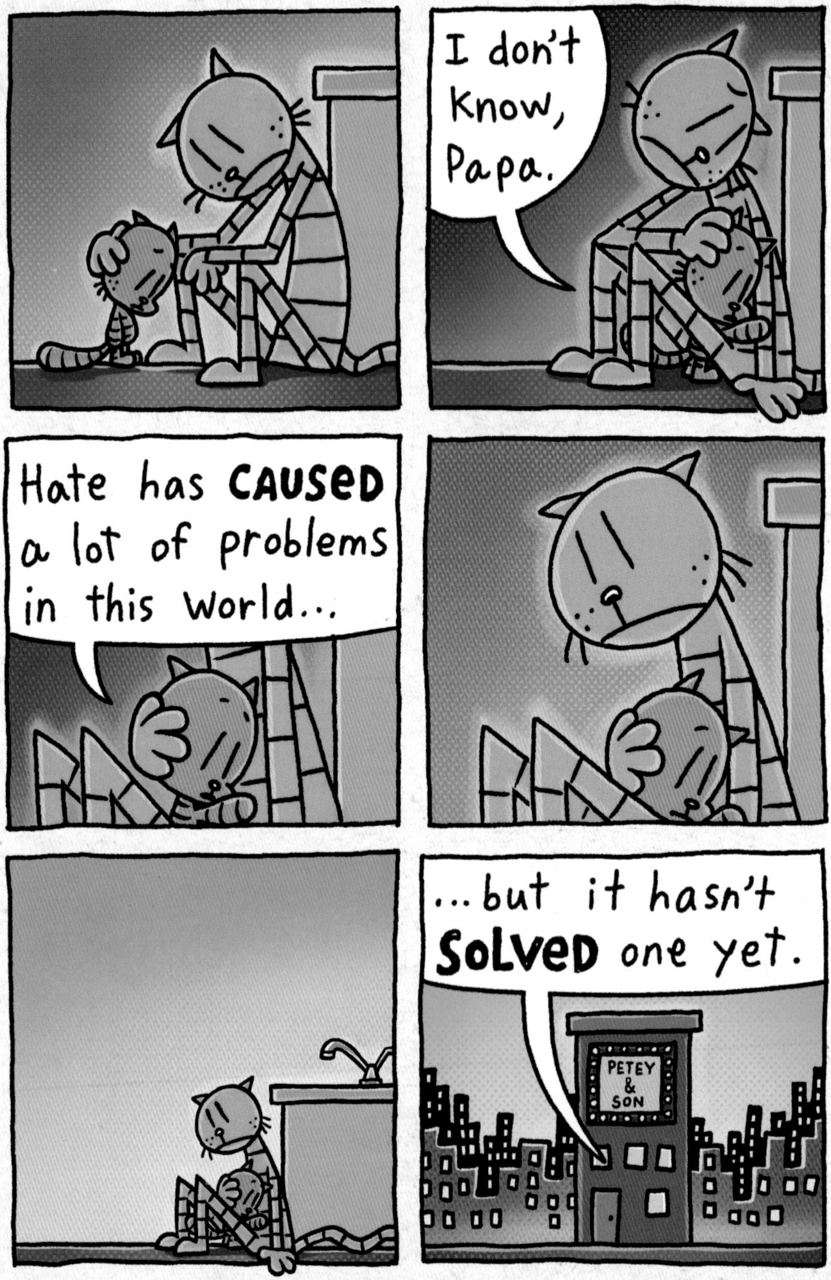
I don't Know, Papa.
Hate has CAUSED a lot of problems in this World...
...but it hasn't SOLVED one yet.
PETEY & SON

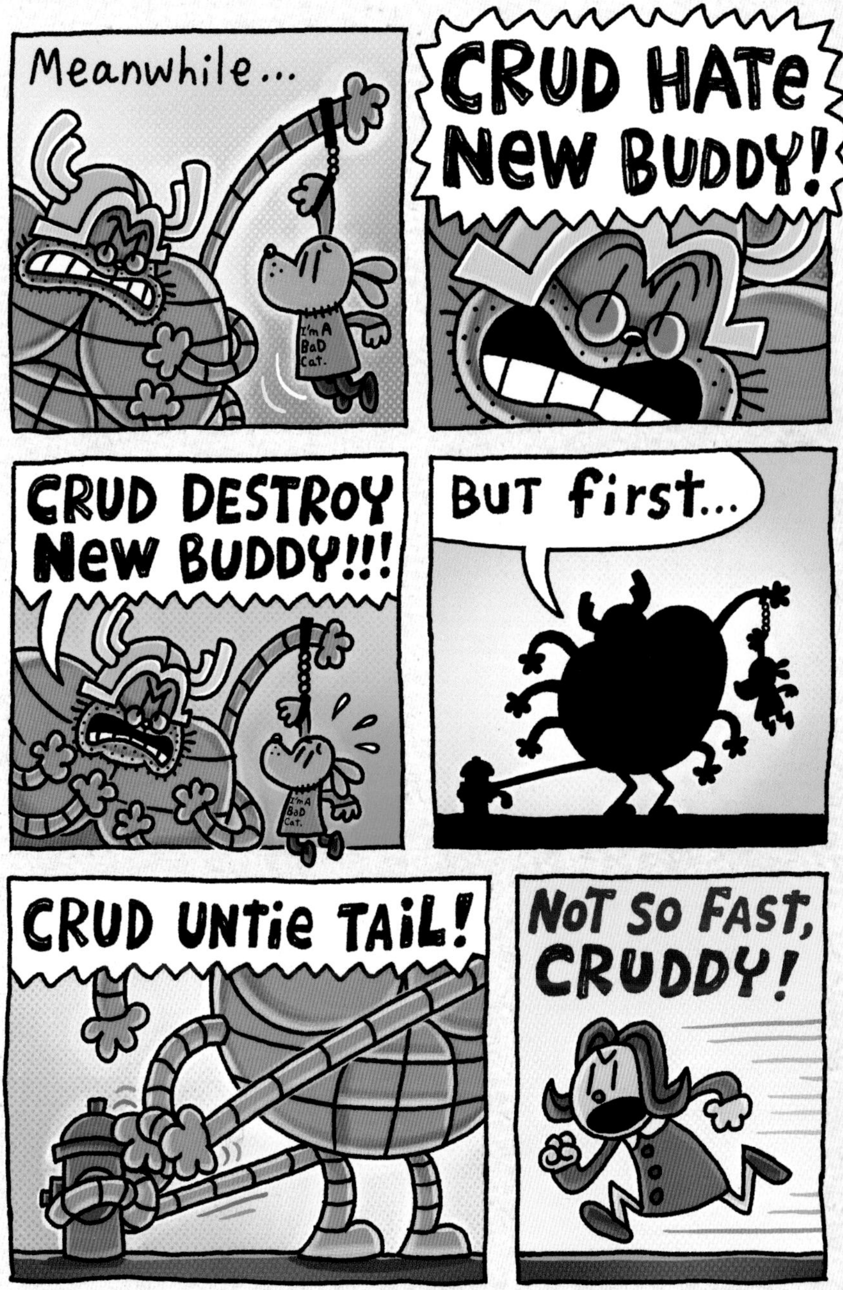
Meanwhile...
I'm A BaD Cat.
CRUD HATe New BUDDY!
CRUD DESTROY New BUDDY!!!
I'm A BaD Cat.
BUT first...
CRUD UNTie TAIL!
NOT SO FAST, CRUDDY!

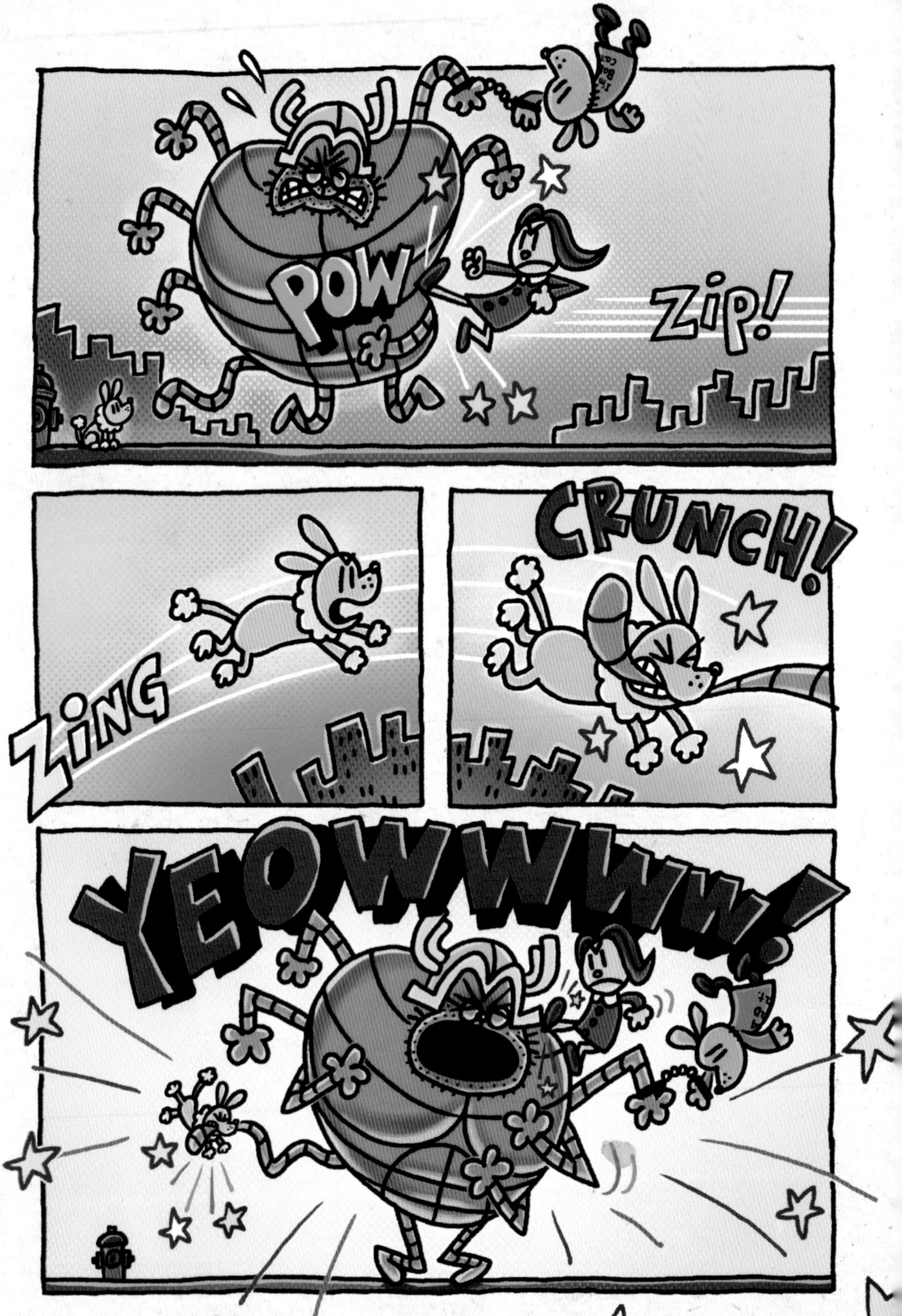
POW
ZIP!
ZING
CRUNCH!
YEOWWWWW!

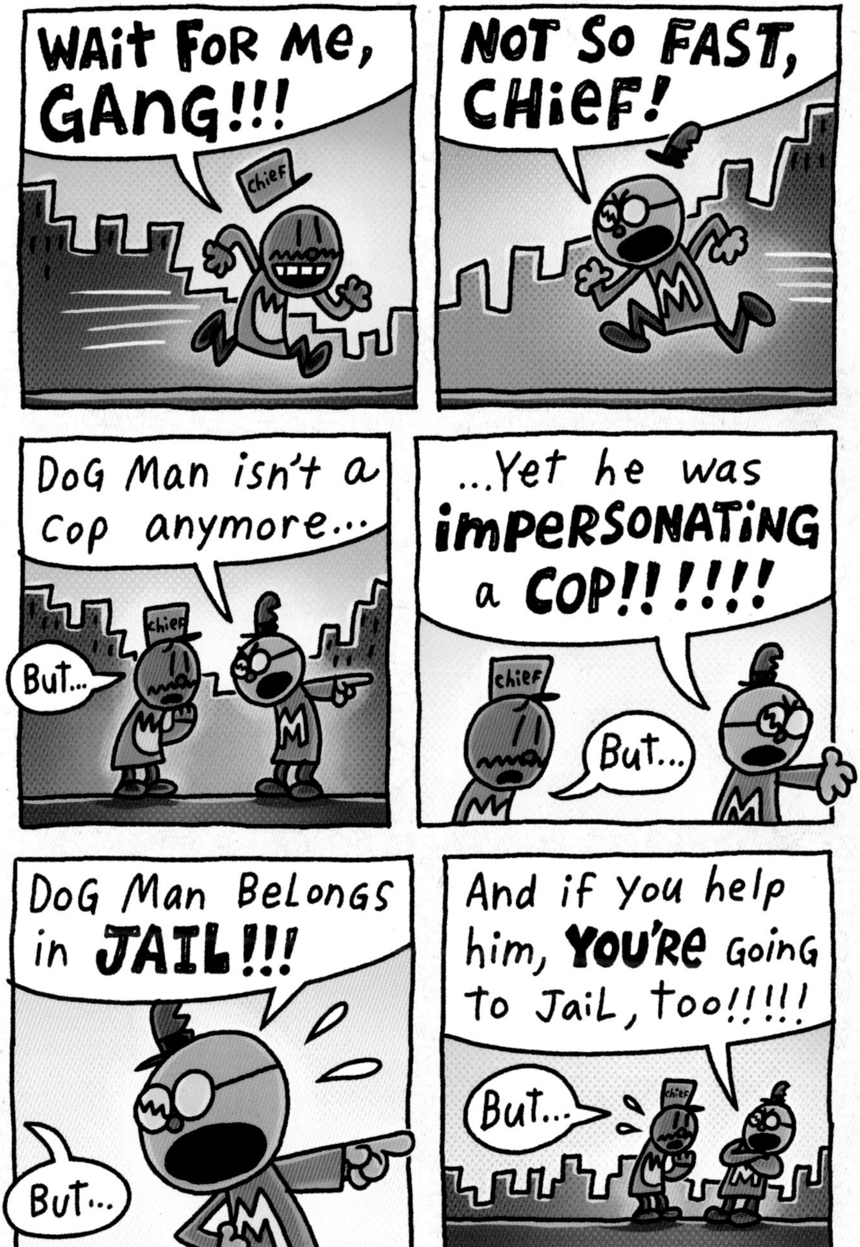
WAIT FOR ME, GANG!!!
CHIEF
NOT SO FAST, CHIEF!
DOG Man isn't a cop anymore...
But...
CHIEF
...Yet he was IMPERSONATING a COP!!!!!!
CHIEF
But...
DOG Man BELONGS in JAIL!!!
But...
And if you help him, YOU'RE GOING to JAIL, too!!!!!
But...
CHIEF

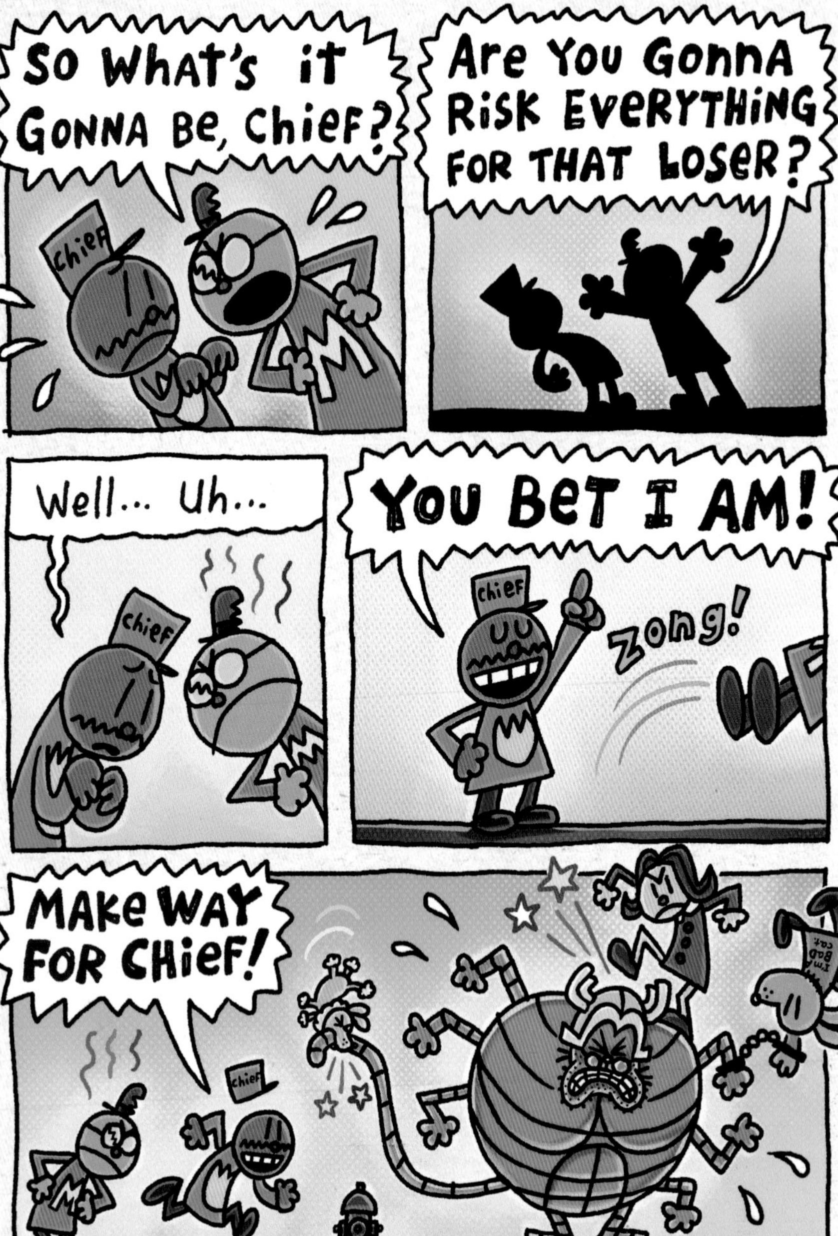
SO WHAT'S IT GONNA BE, CHIEF?
ARE YOU GONNA RISK EVERYTHING FOR THAT LOSER?
chief
Well... Uh...
chief
YOU BET I AM!
chief
ZONG!
MAKE WAY FOR CHIEF!
chief
I'm a Bad cat.

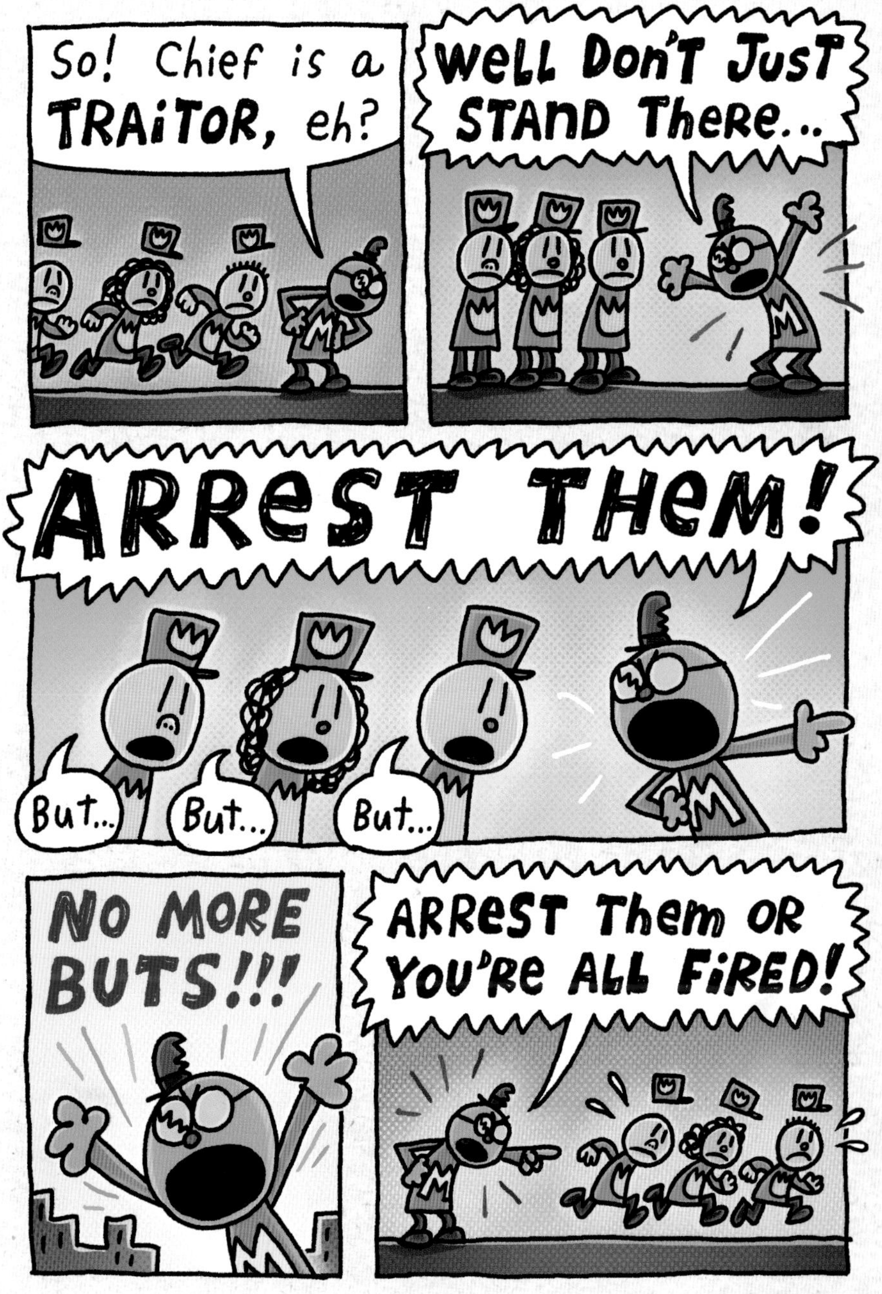
So! Chief is a TRAITOR, eh?
WELL DON'T JUST STAND There...
ARREST THEM!
But...
But...
But...
NO MORE BUTS!!!
ARREST Them OR YOU'RE ALL FIRED!

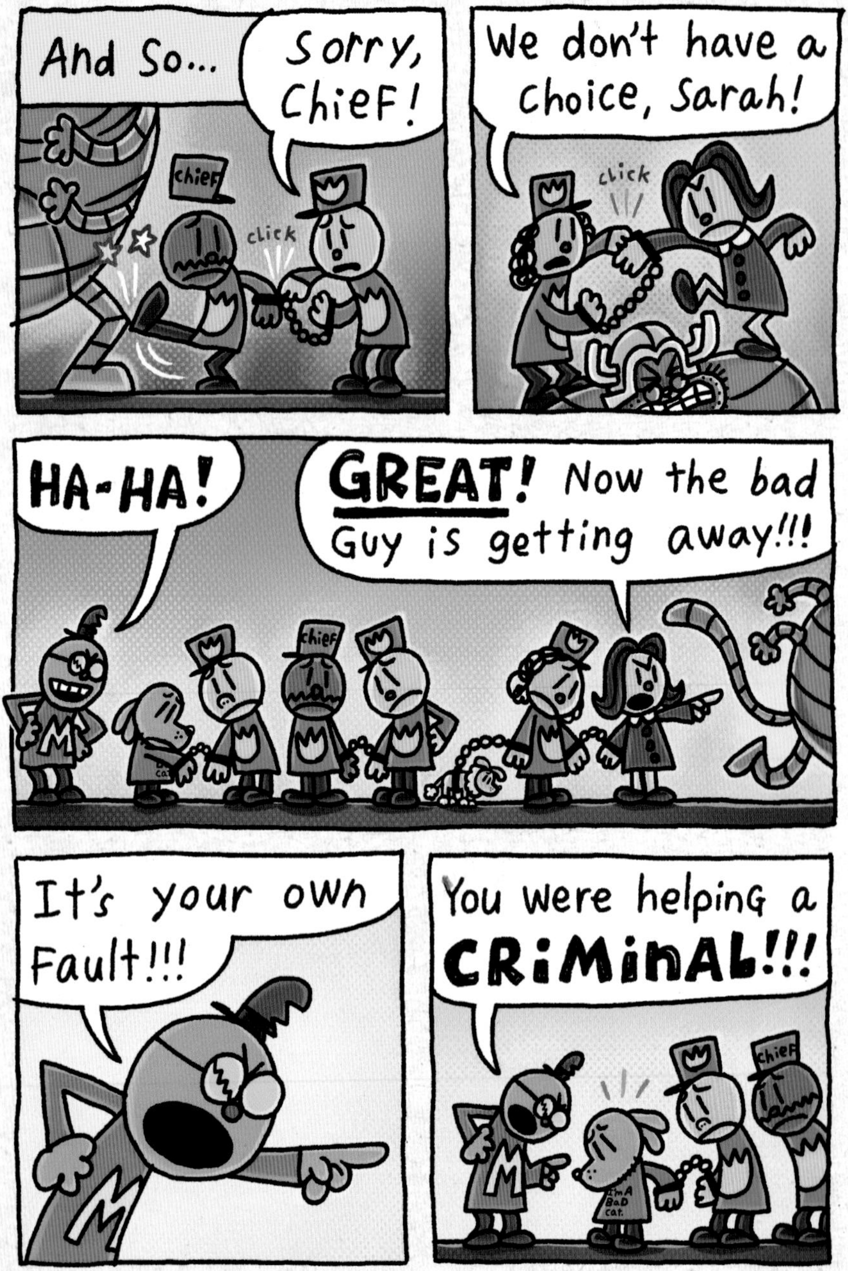
And So...
Sorry, Chief!
chief
click
We don't have a choice, Sarah!
click
HA-HA!
GREAT! Now the bad Guy is getting away!!!
chief
It's your own Fault!!!
You were helping a CRiMinAL!!!
I'm A BaD cat.
chief

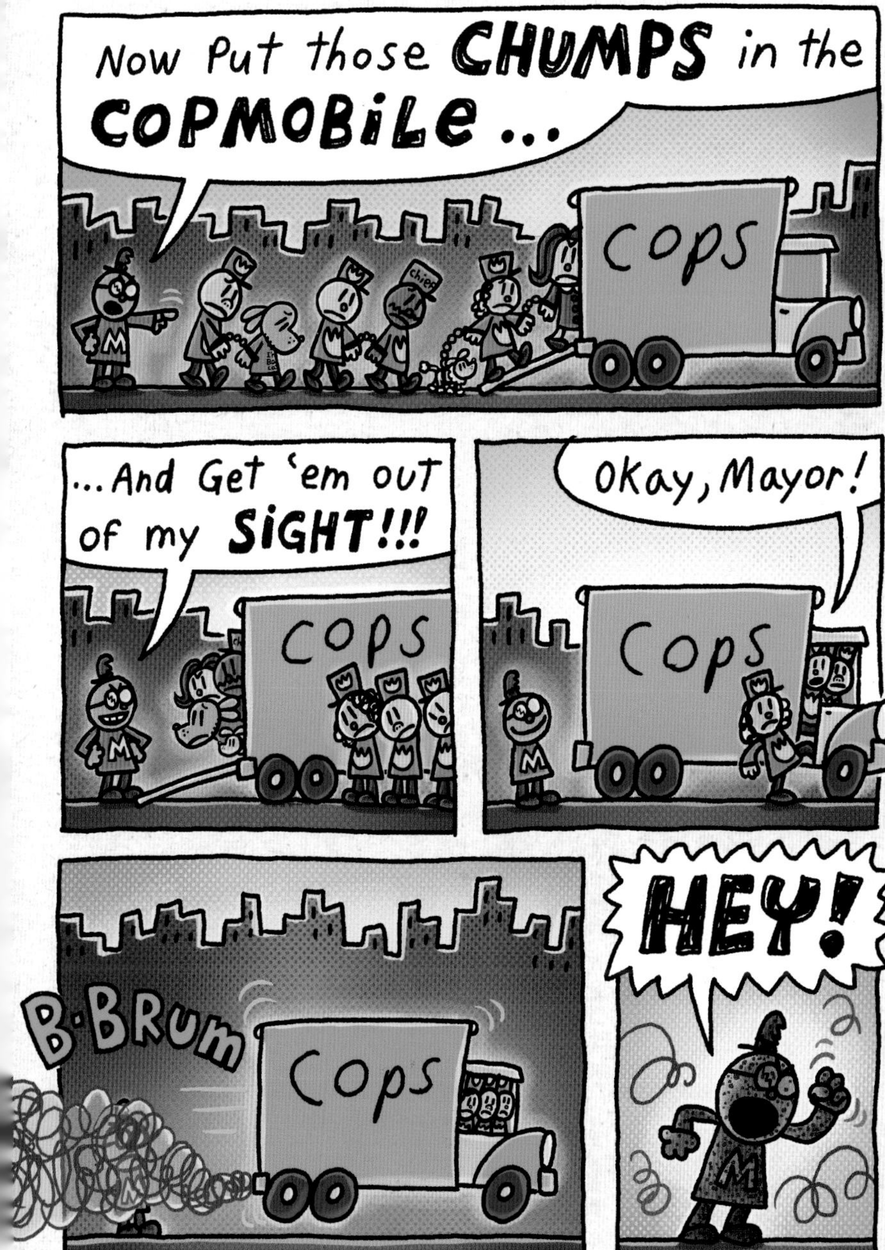
Now Put those CHUMPS in the COPMOBiLe...
COPS
...And Get 'em out of my SiGHT!!!
COPS
Okay, Mayor!
COPS
B-BRUM
COPS
HEY!

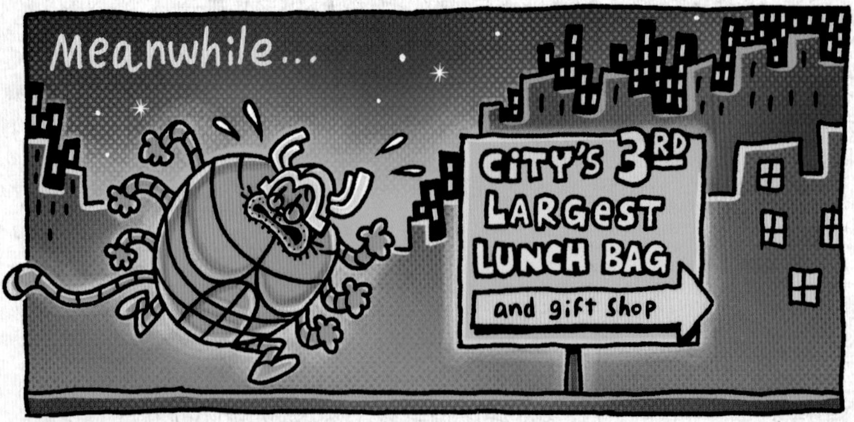
Meanwhile...
CiTY'S 3RD LARGEST LUNCH BAG
and gift Shop

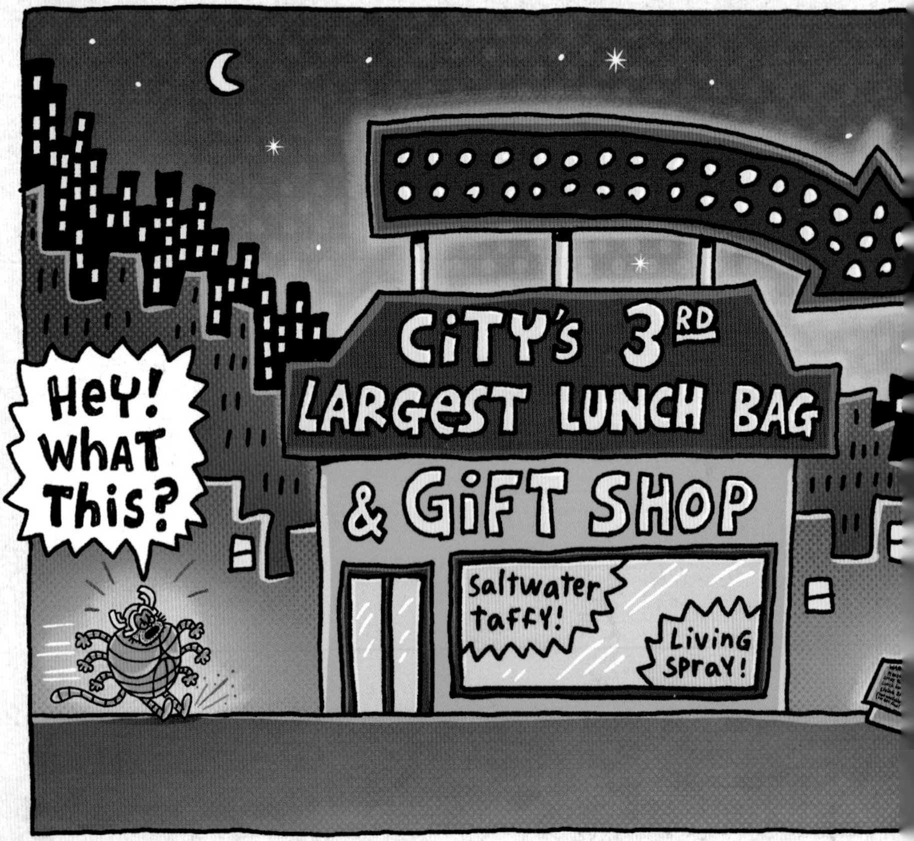
Hey! WHAT This?
CiTY'S 3RD LARGEST LUNCH BAG
& GiFT SHOP
Saltwater taffy!
Living Spray!

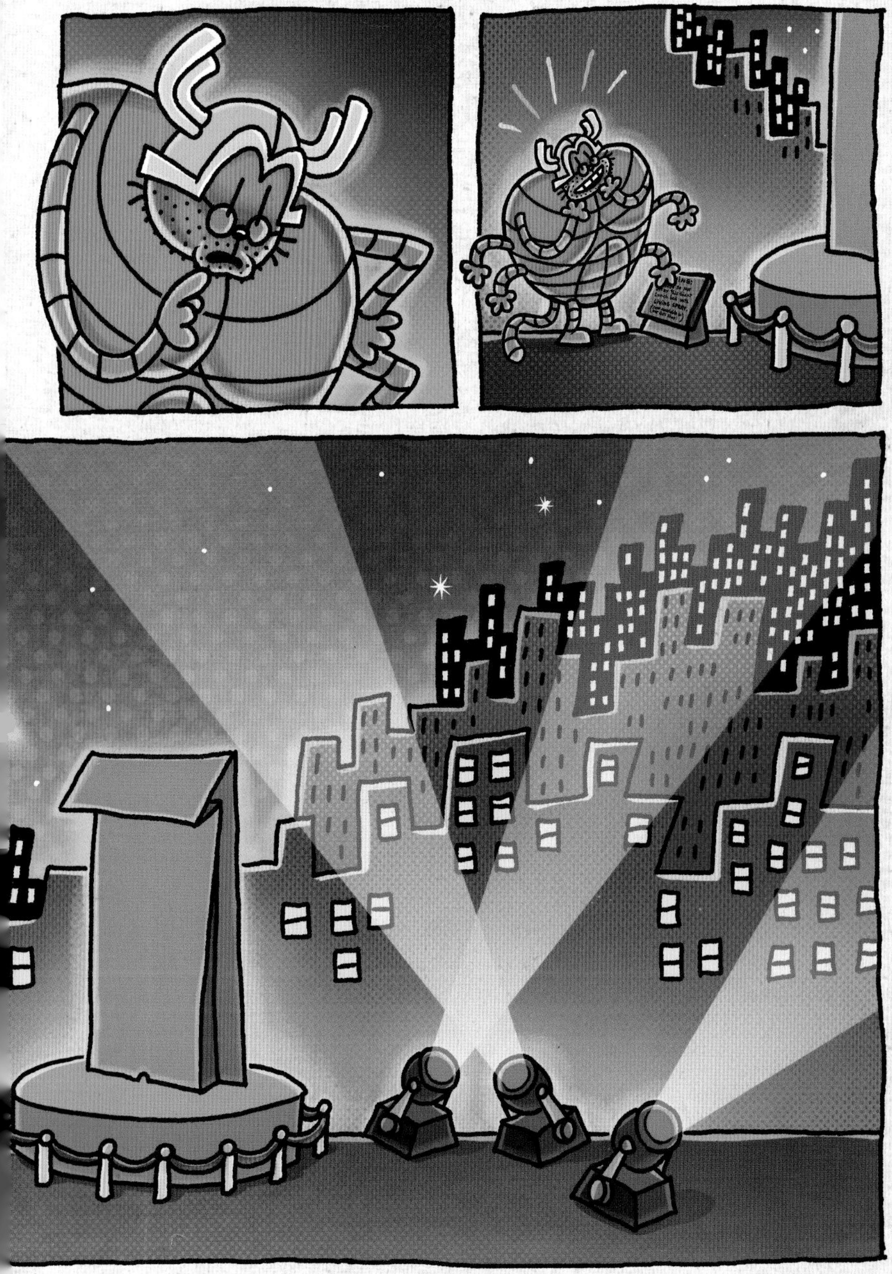
LIVING SPRAY.

Chapter 9

The Lunch Bag of Motor Brain

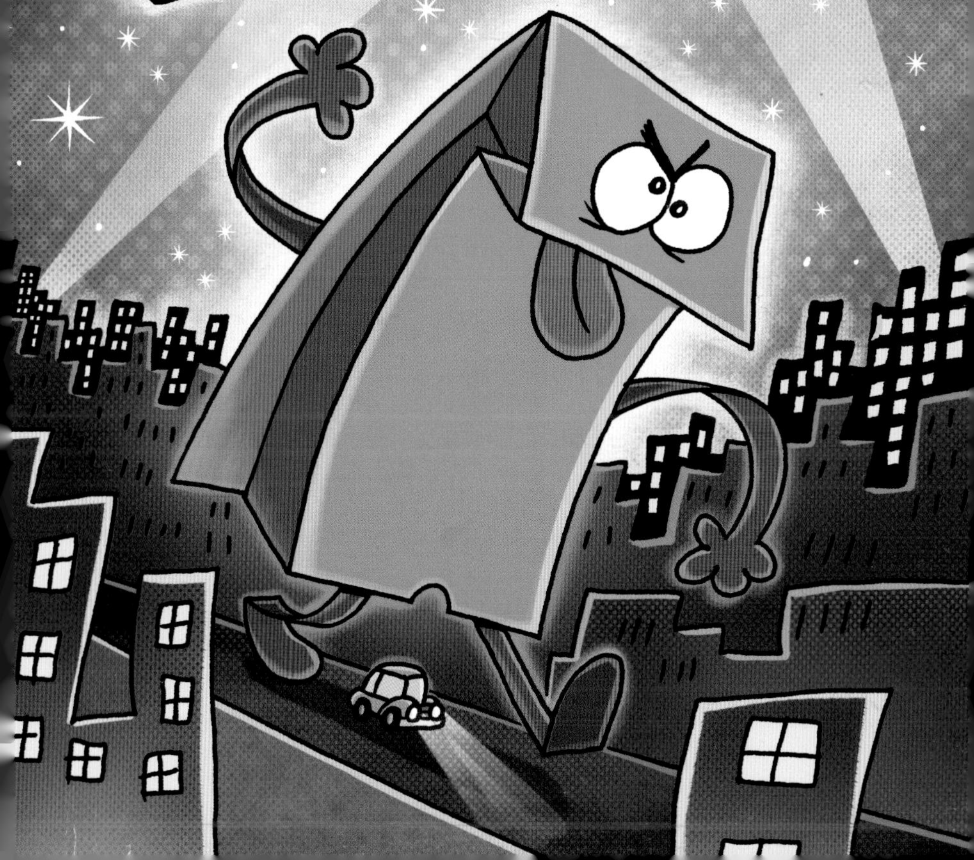

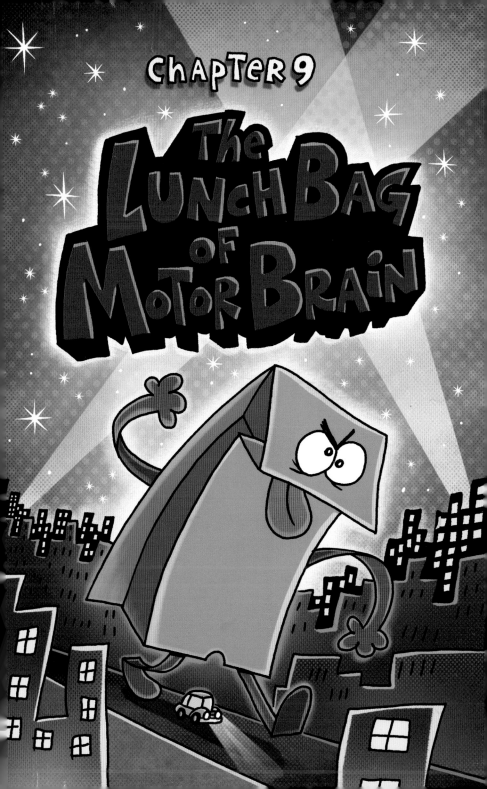

Left hand here.

CRUD READ LABEL CAREFULLY

CRUD SHAKE CAN VIGOROUSLY

CRUD SPRAY BAG THOROUGHLY

Right Thumb here.

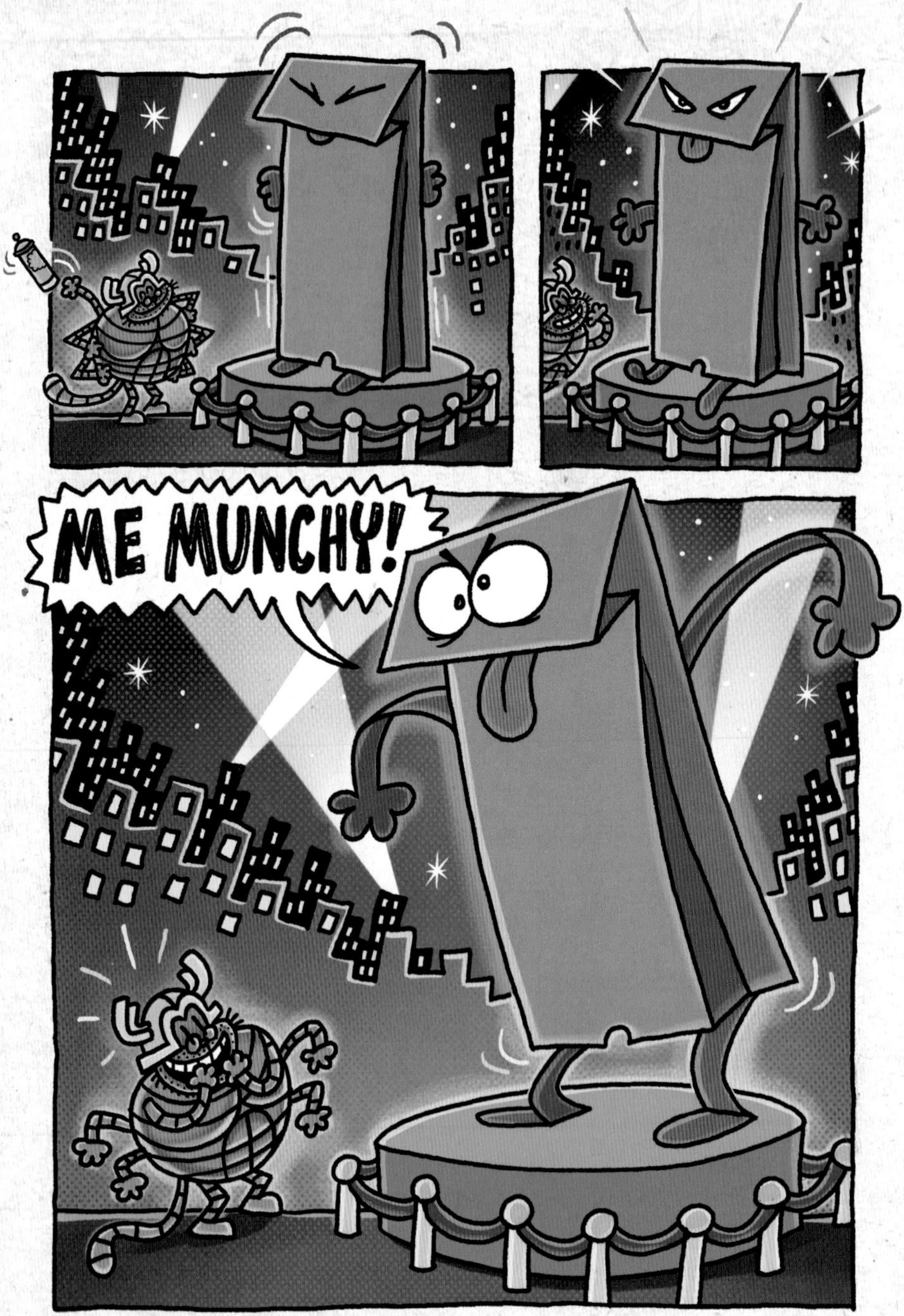
ME MUNCHY!

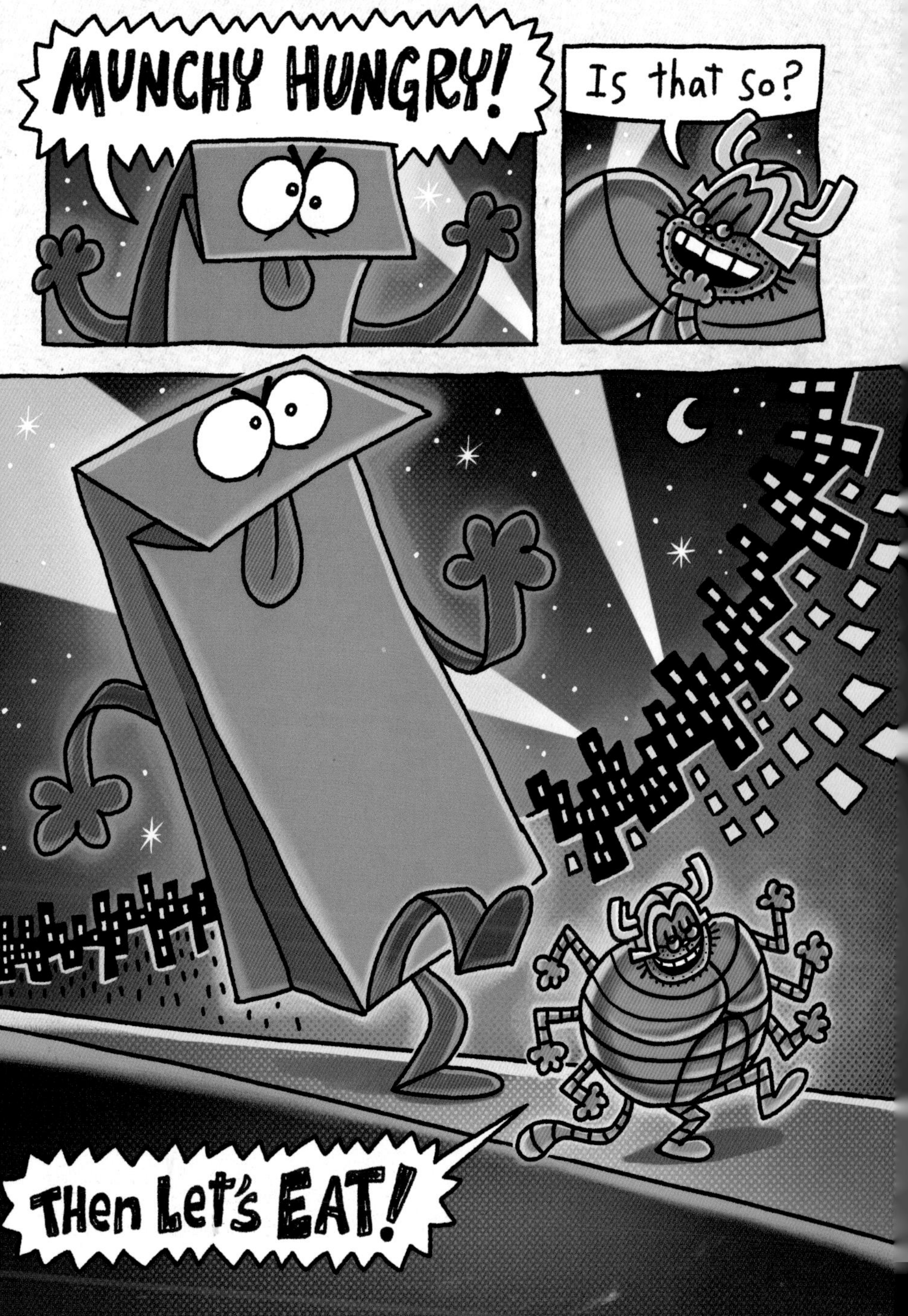
MUNCHY HUNGRY!
Is that so?
Then Let's EAT!

SLUUUUURP!

KLONK

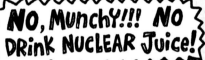

NO, MUNCHY!!! NO DRINK NUCLEAR JUICE!

Bob's NUCLEAR POWER PLANT

GET BELLYACHE!!!

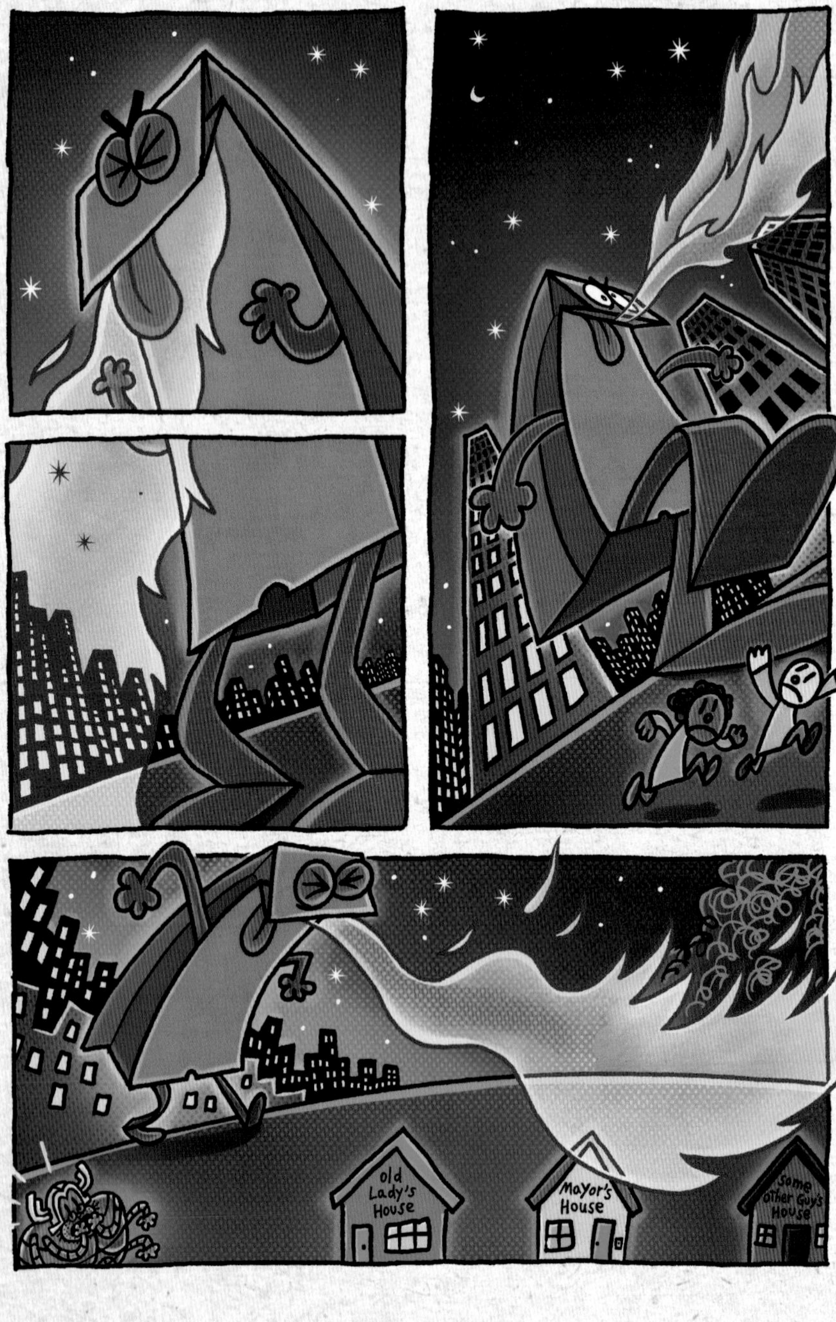
Old Lady's House
Mayor's House
Some other Guy's House

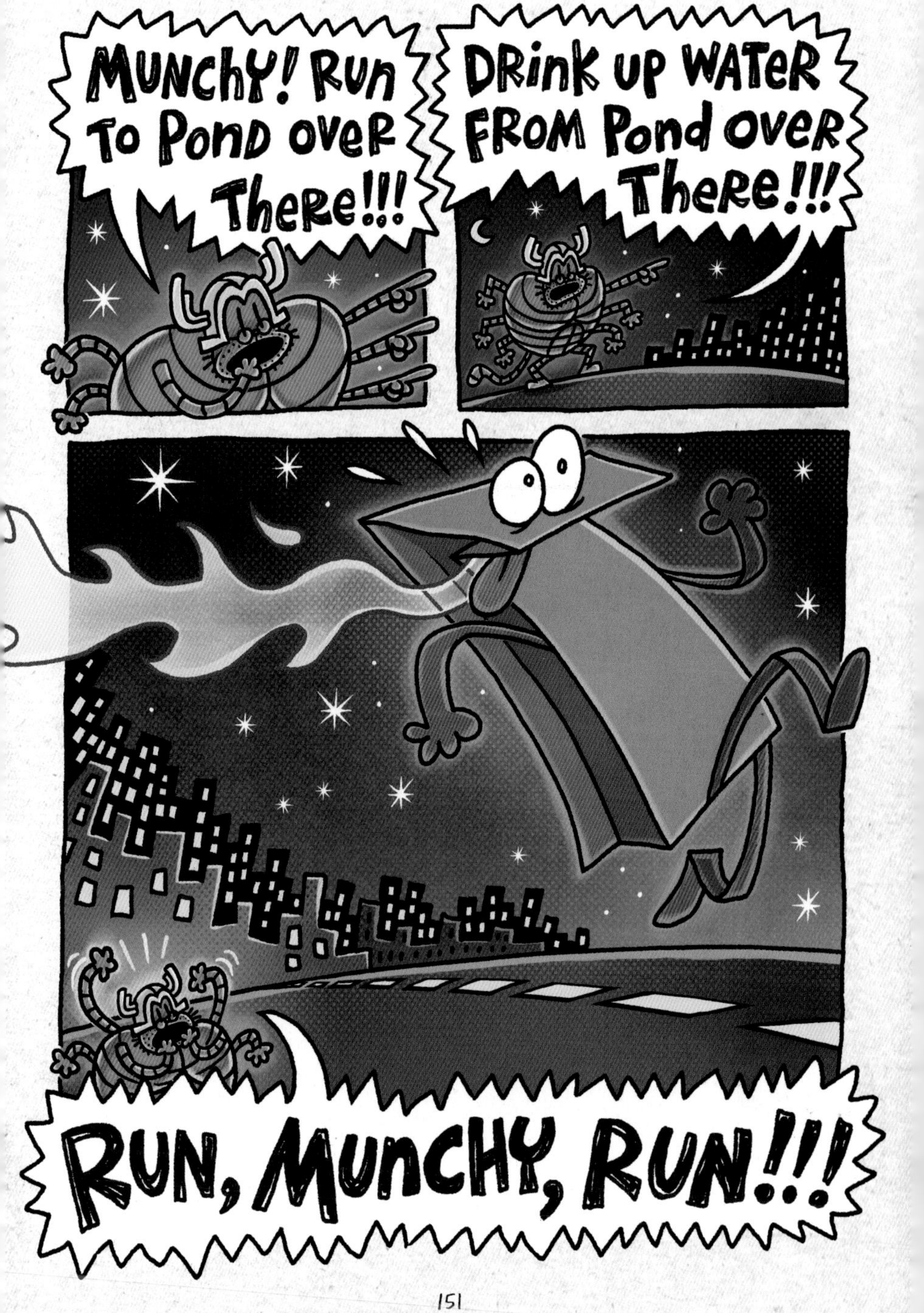
MUNCHY! RUN TO POND OVER THERE!!!
DRINK UP WATER FROM POND OVER THERE!!!
RUN, MUNCHY, RUN!!!

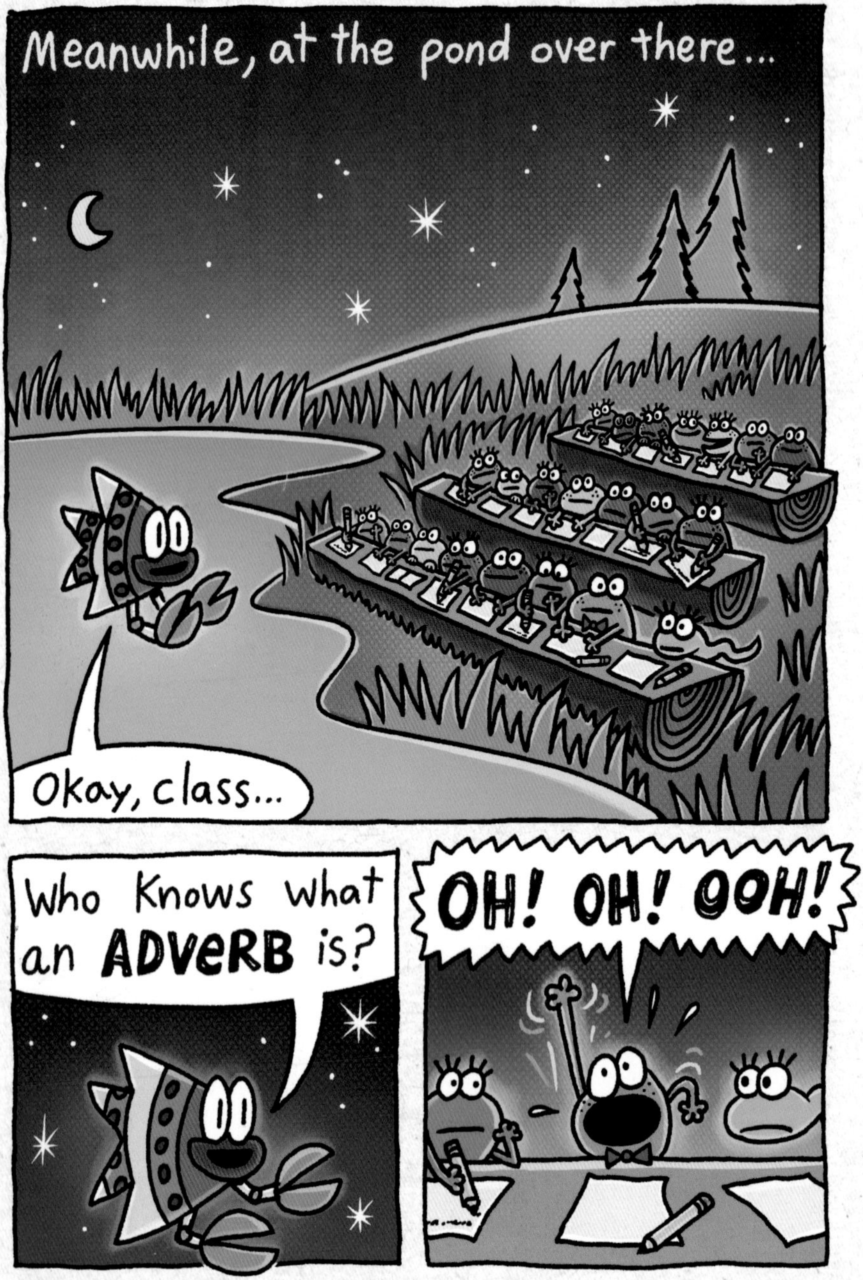
Meanwhile, at the pond over there...
Okay, class...
Who knows what an ADVERB is?
OH! OH! OOH!

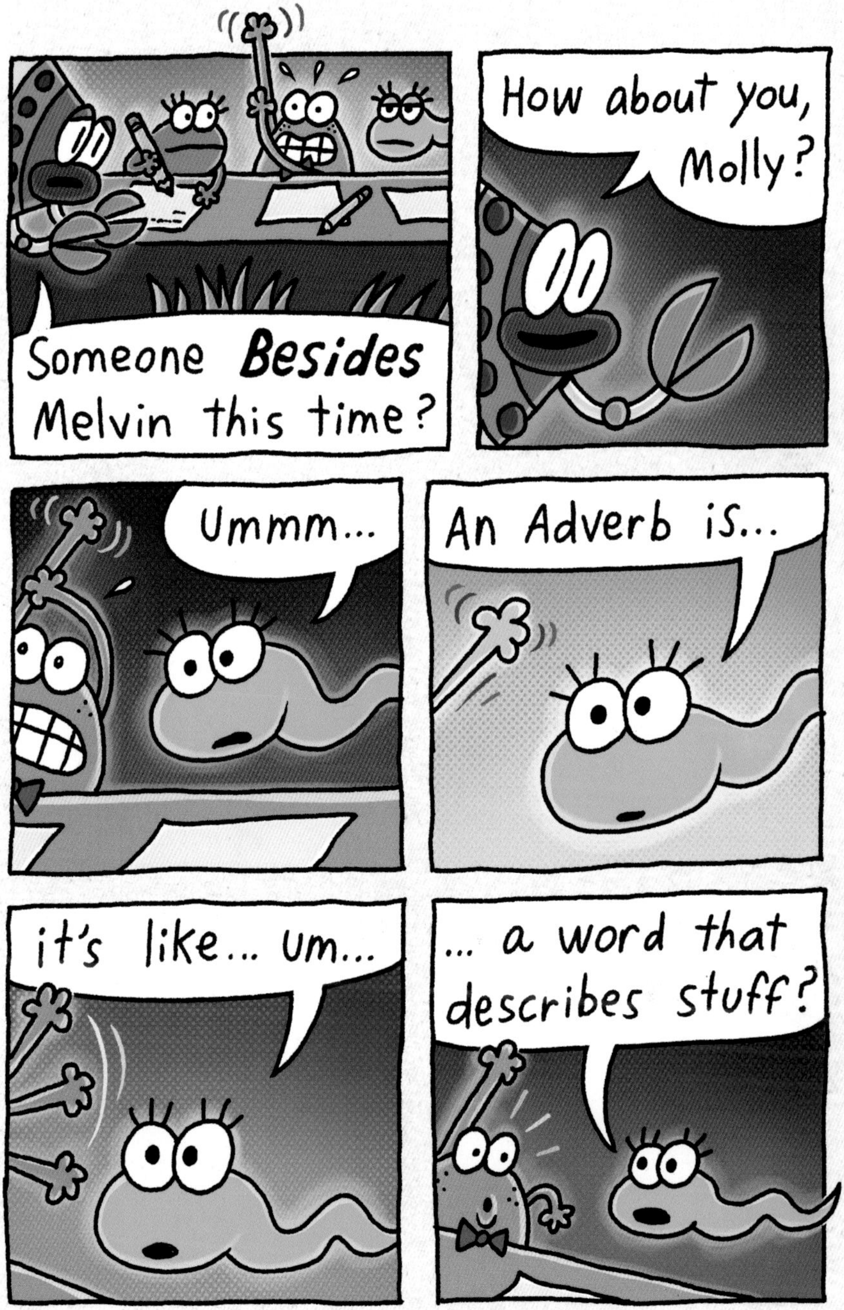
Someone Besides Melvin this time?
How about you, Molly?
Ummm...
An Adverb is...
it's like... um...
... a word that describes stuff?

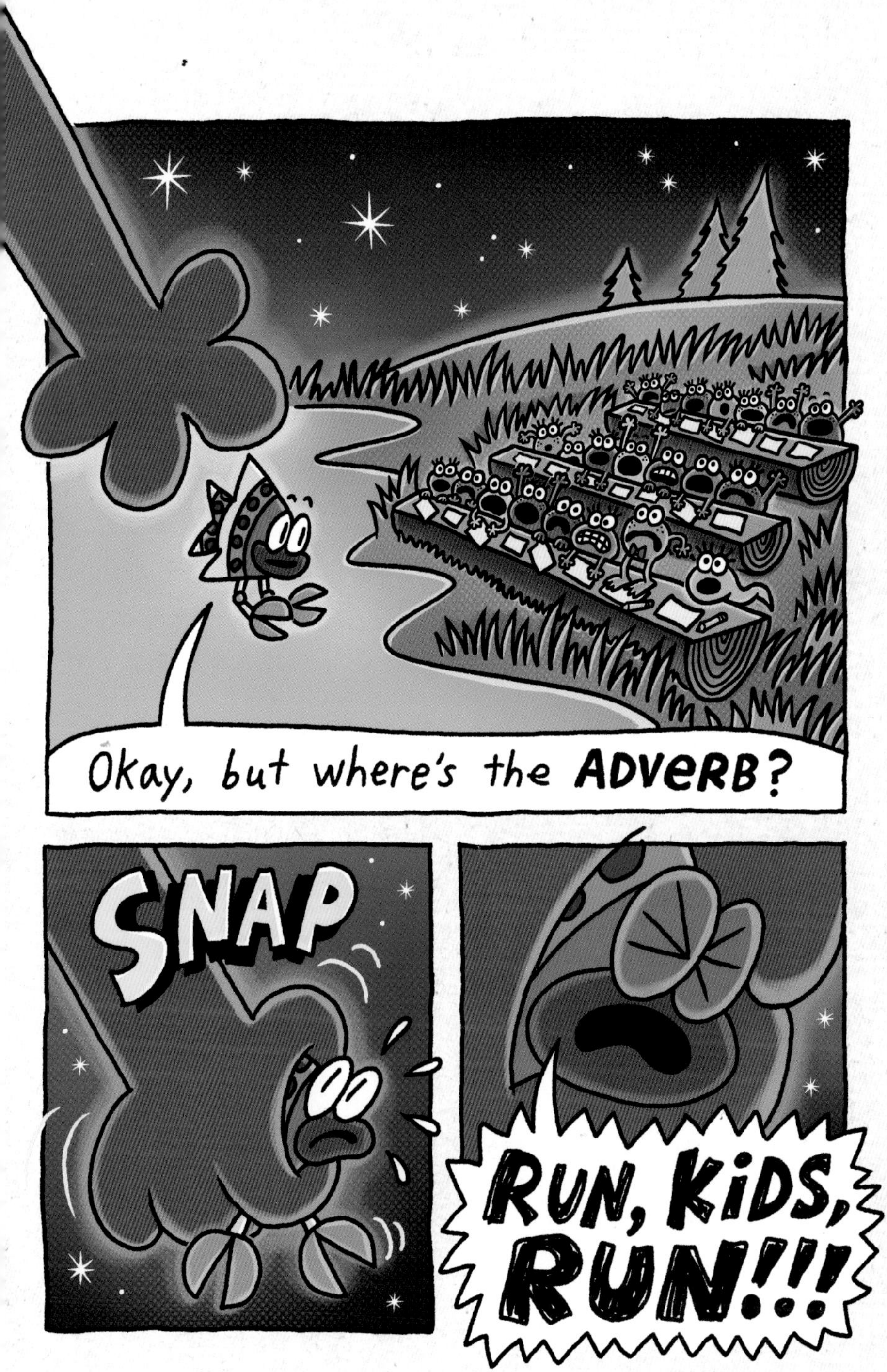
Okay, but where's the ADVERB?
SNAP
RUN, KIDS, RUN!!!

CHAPTER 10
80-HD POWER

Meanwhile...

Well, folks...

...it Looks Like we are all **DOOMED!**

...**CRUD** is on the Loose...

...**MUNCHY** is **ATTACKING**...

...And the **GOOD GUYS** Are heading to **JAIL!**

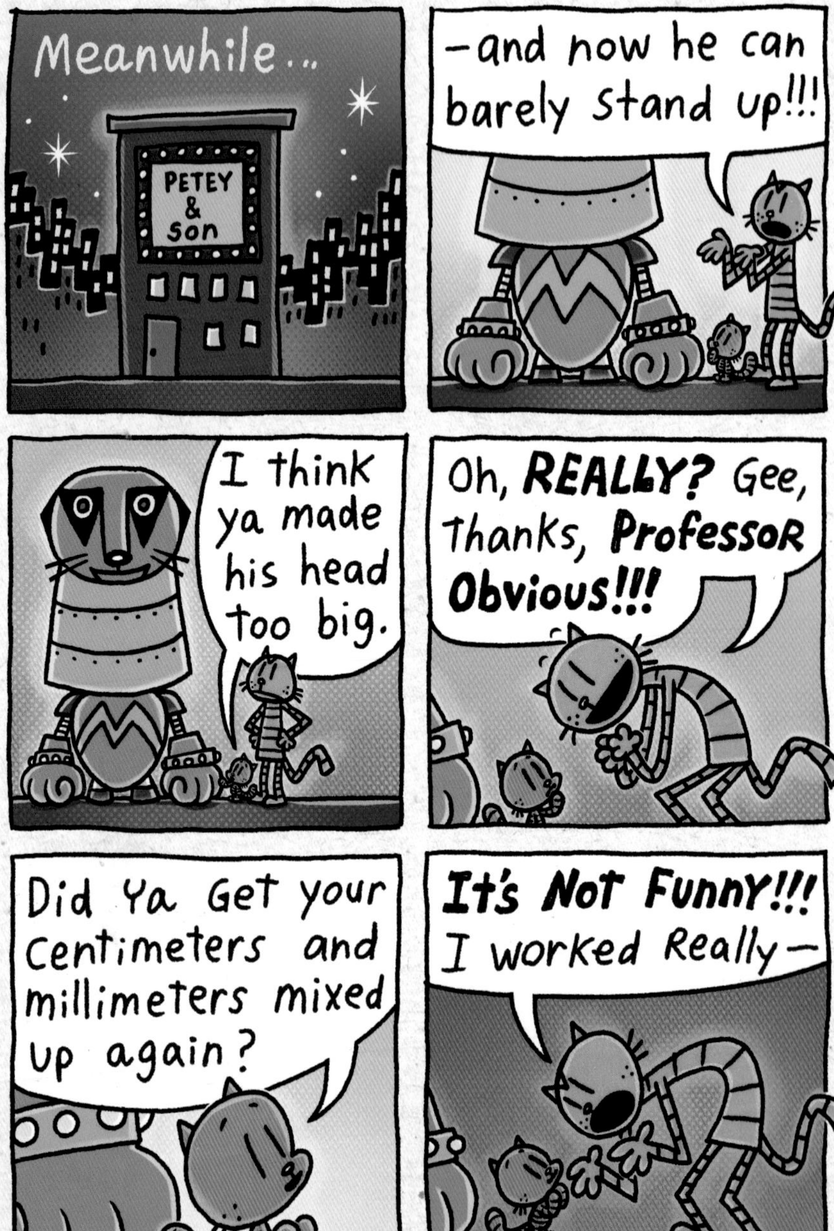
Meanwhile...
PETEY & SON
–and now he can barely stand up!!!
I think ya made his head too big.
Oh, REALLY? Gee, Thanks, Professor Obvious!!!
Did Ya Get your centimeters and millimeters mixed up again?
It's Not Funny!!! I worked Really–

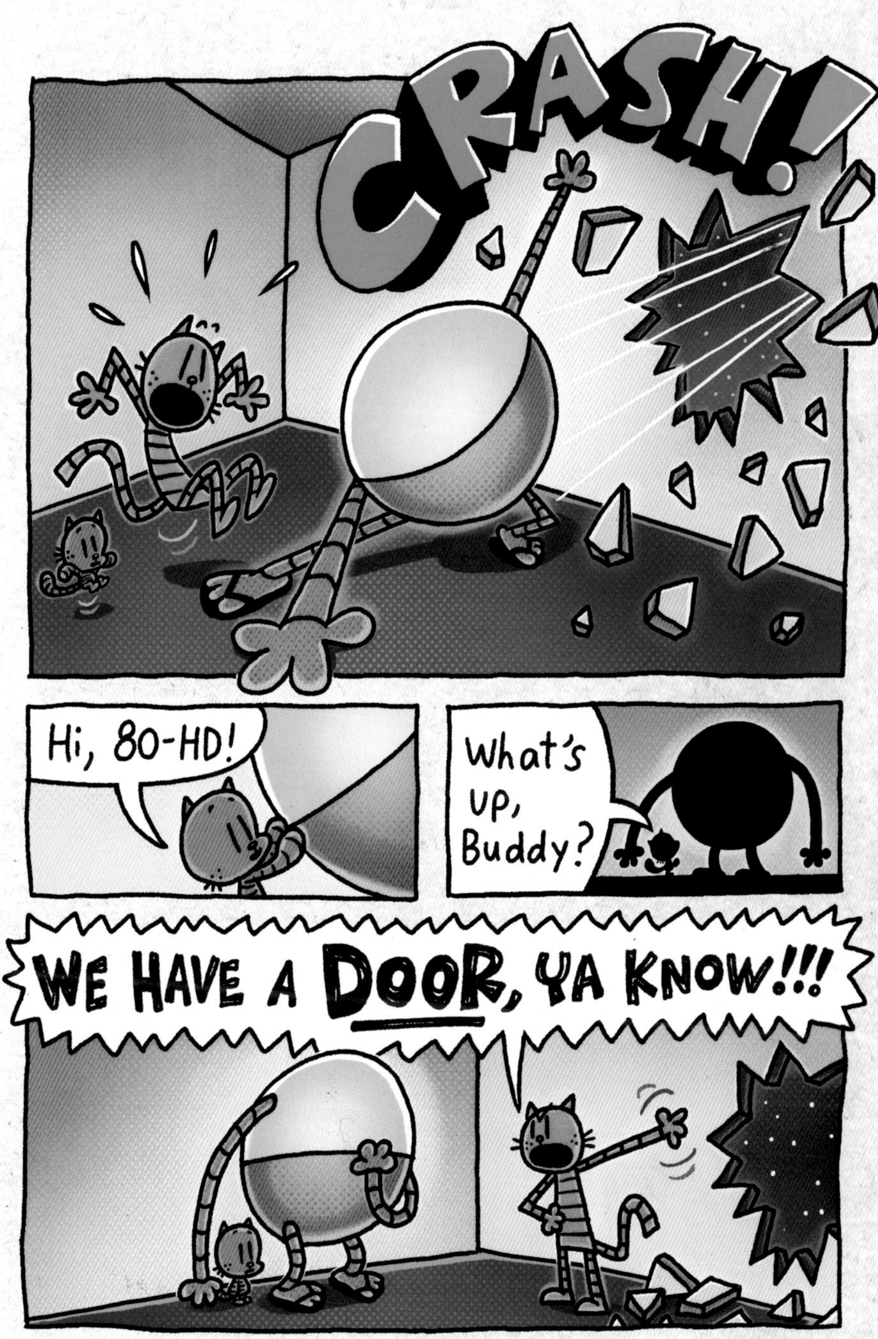
CRASH!
Hi, 80-HD!
What's up, Buddy?
WE HAVE A DOOR, YA KNOW!!!

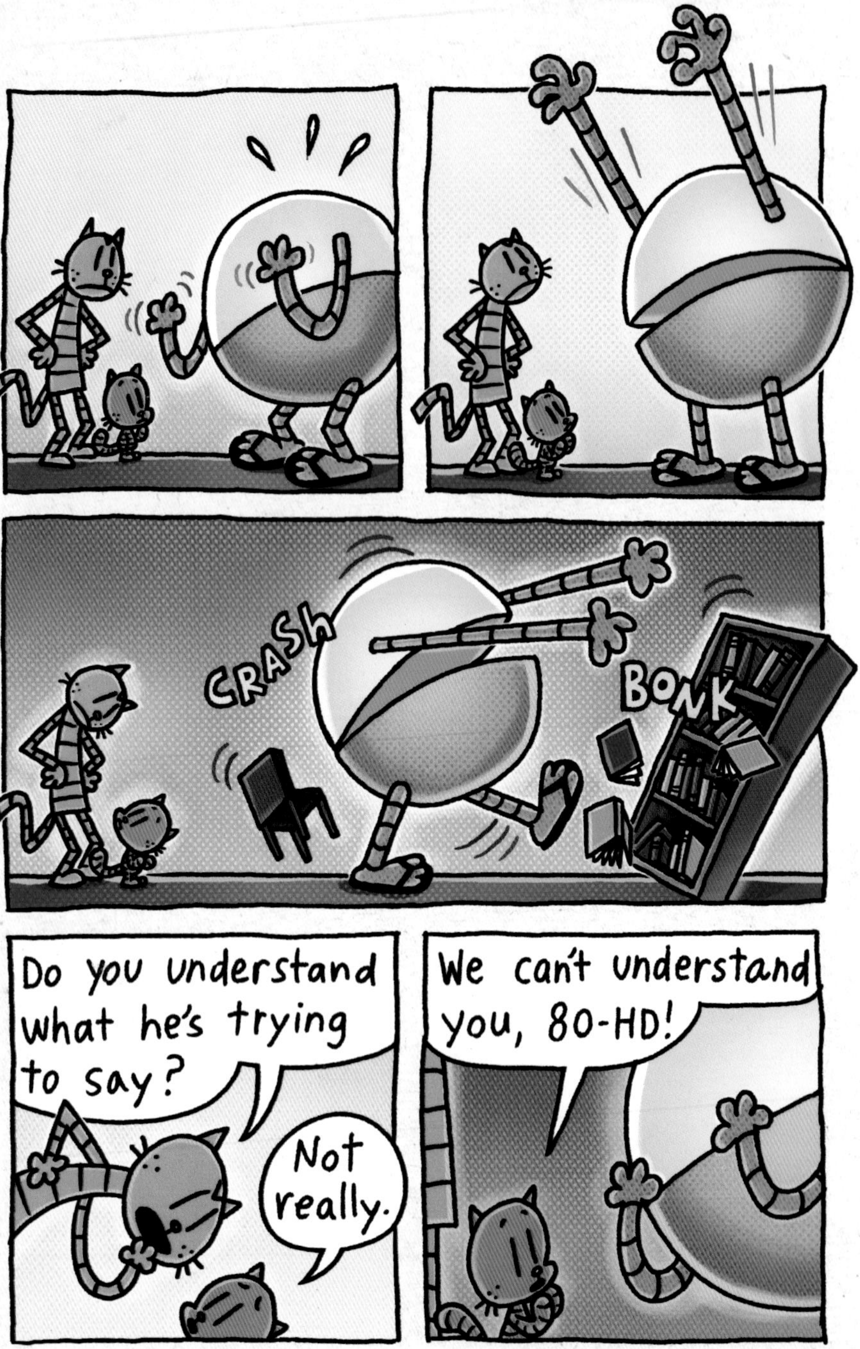
CRASH
BONK
Do you understand what he's trying to say?
Not really.
We can't understand you, 80-HD!

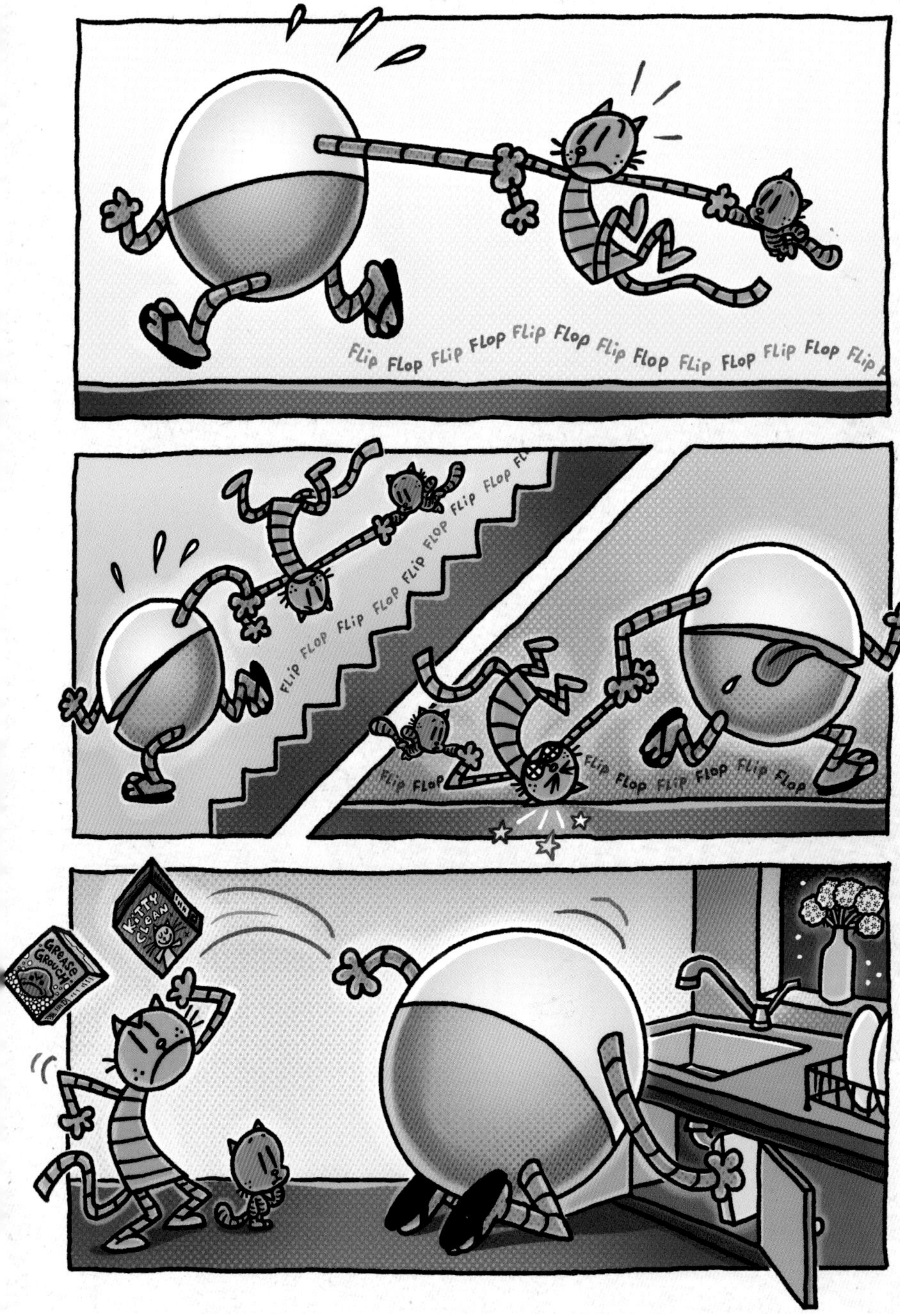
FLip FLop FLip FLop FLip FLop FLip FLop FLip FLop FLip FLop FLip
FLip FLop FLip FLop FLip FLop FLip FLop FLip FLop
FLip FLop
FLip FLop FLip FLop FLip FLop
GREASE GROUCH
KiTTY CLEAN

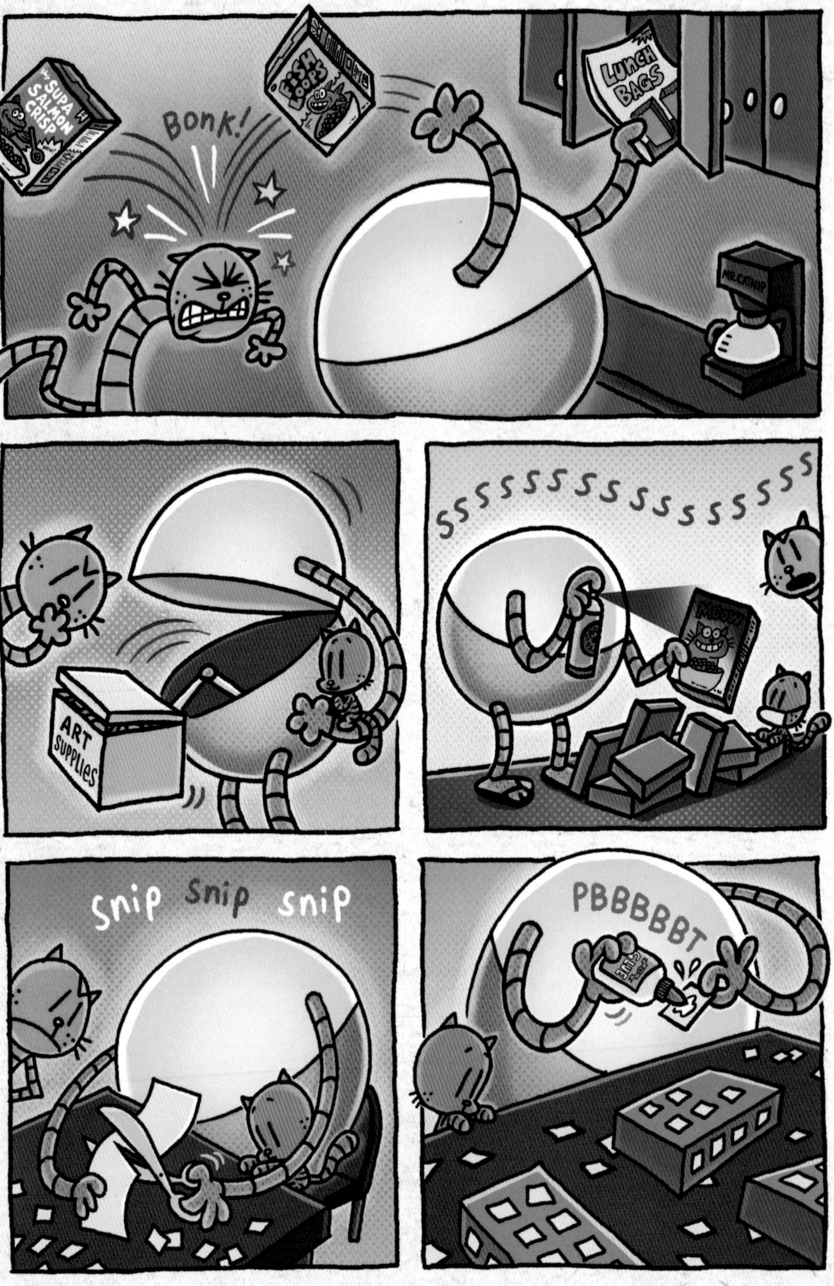
SUPA SALMON CRISP
BONK!
FISH LOOPS
LUNCH BAGS
MR.CATNIP
ART SUPPLIES
SSSSSSSSSSSSSSSSS
MEOWY
snip snip snip
PBBBBBT
GLUE

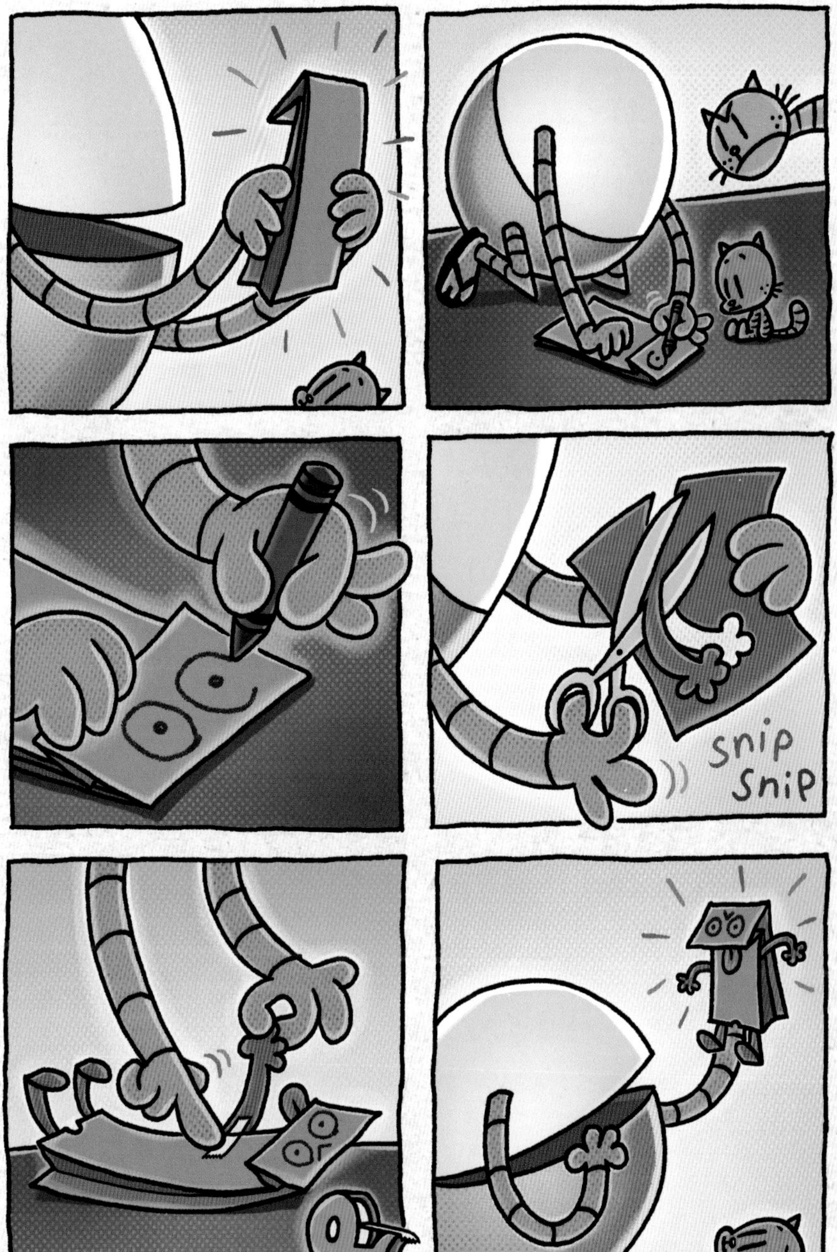
snip
snip

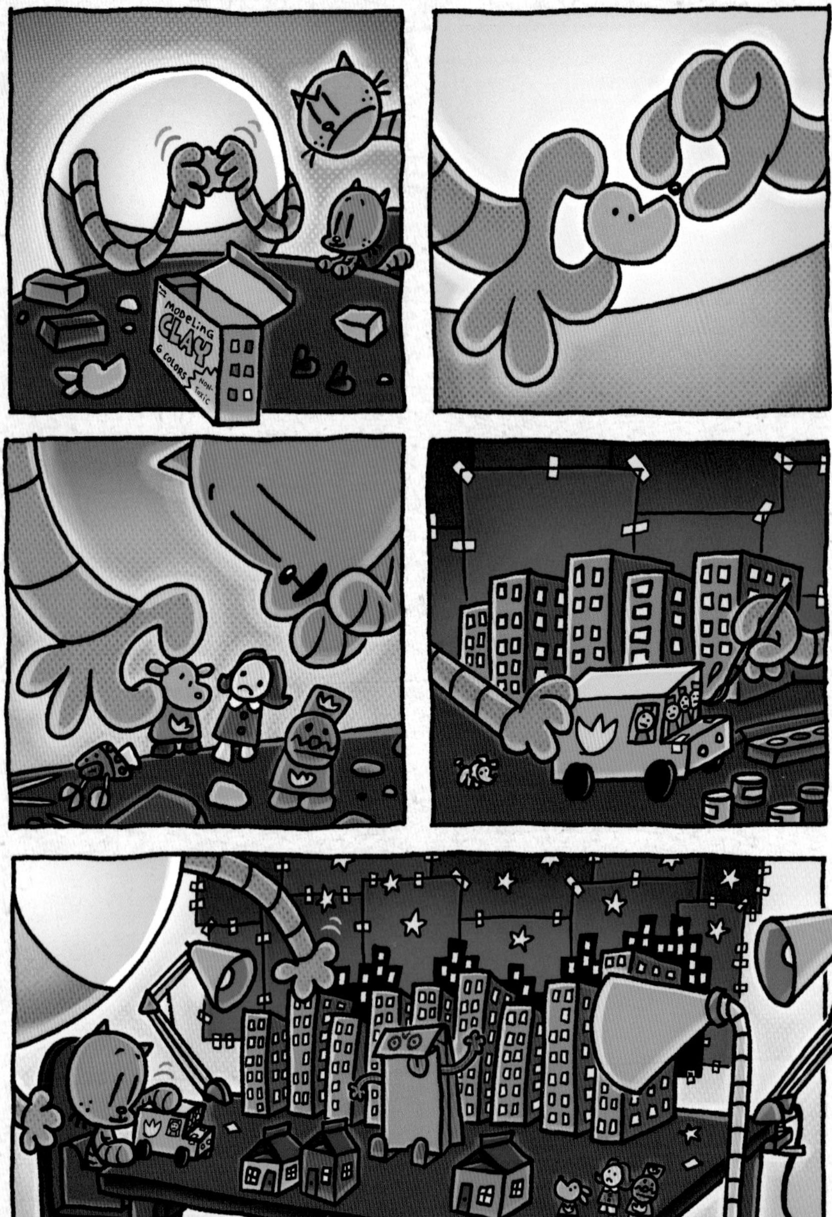
MODELING CLAY
6 COLORS
NON-TOXIC

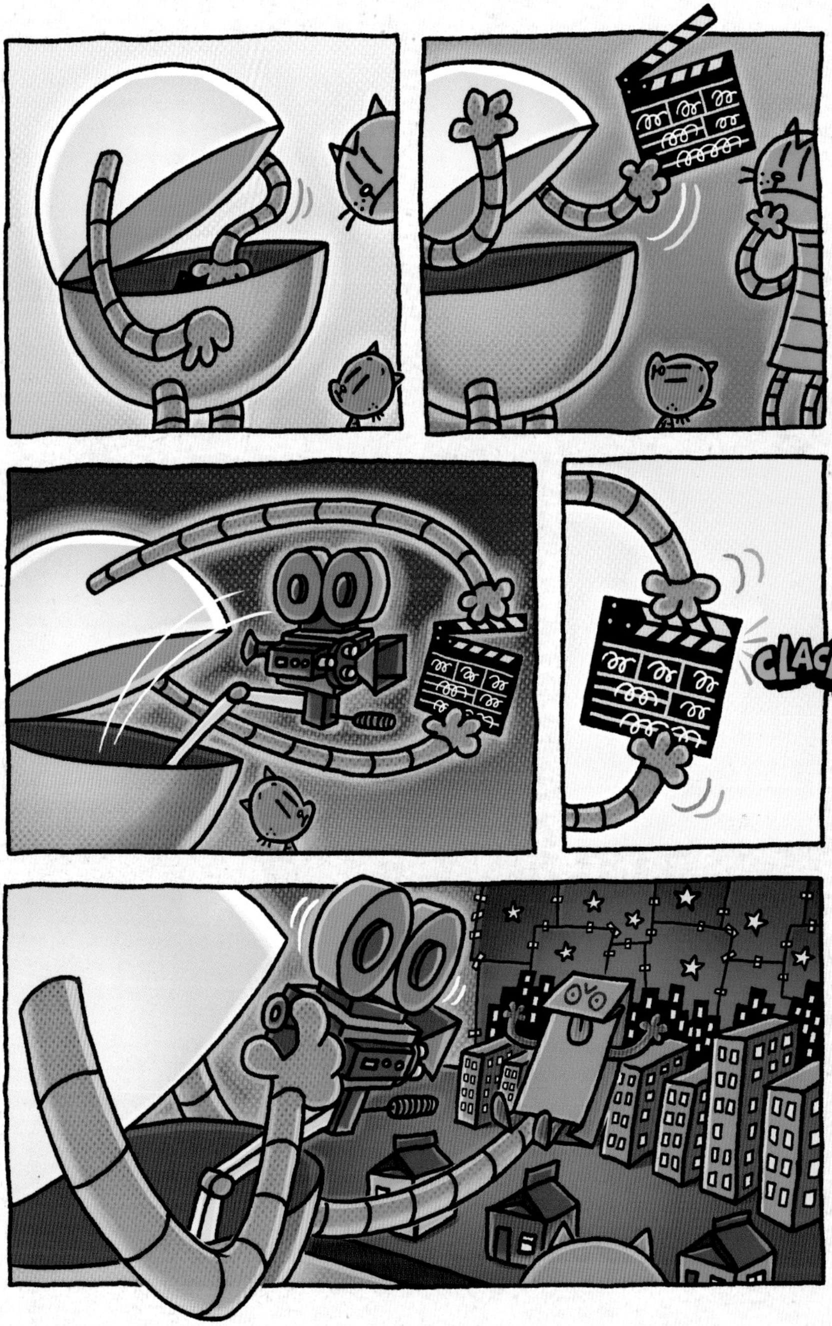
CLACK!

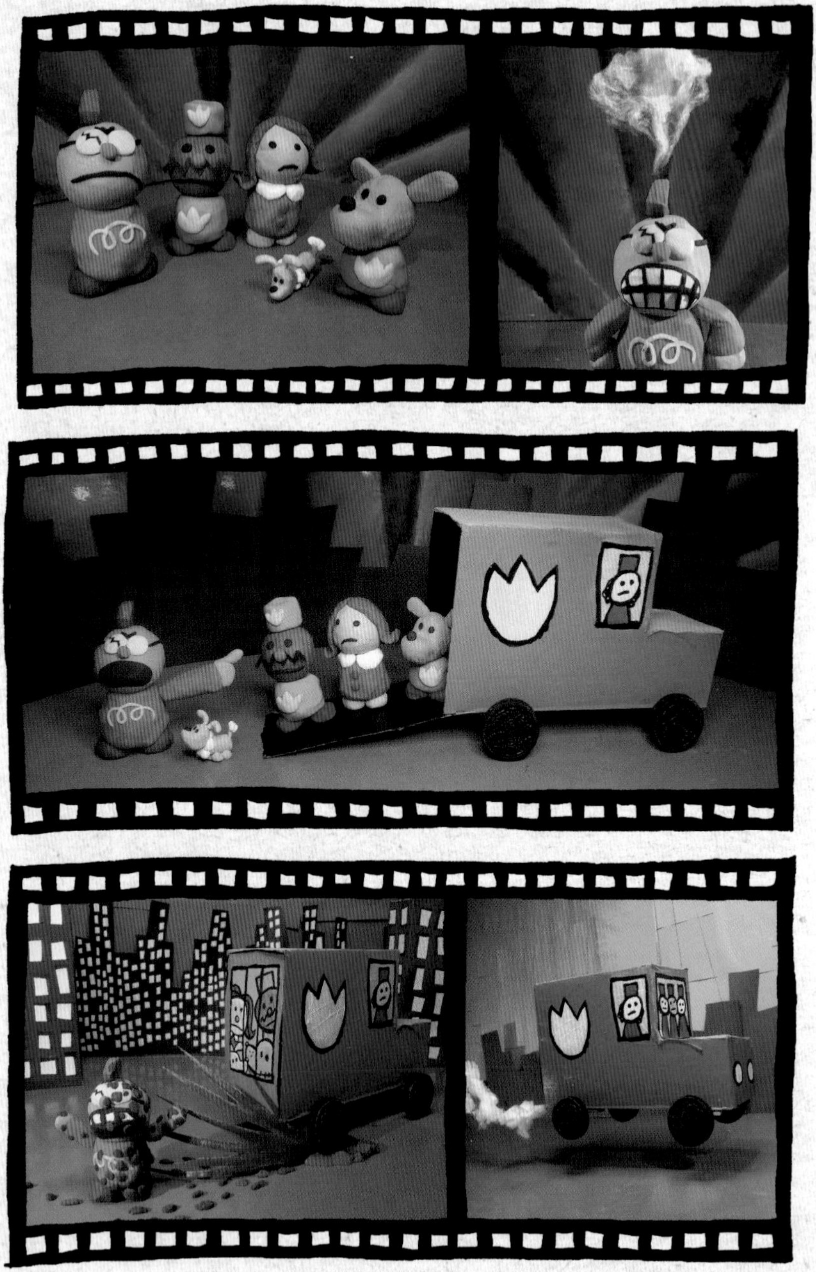

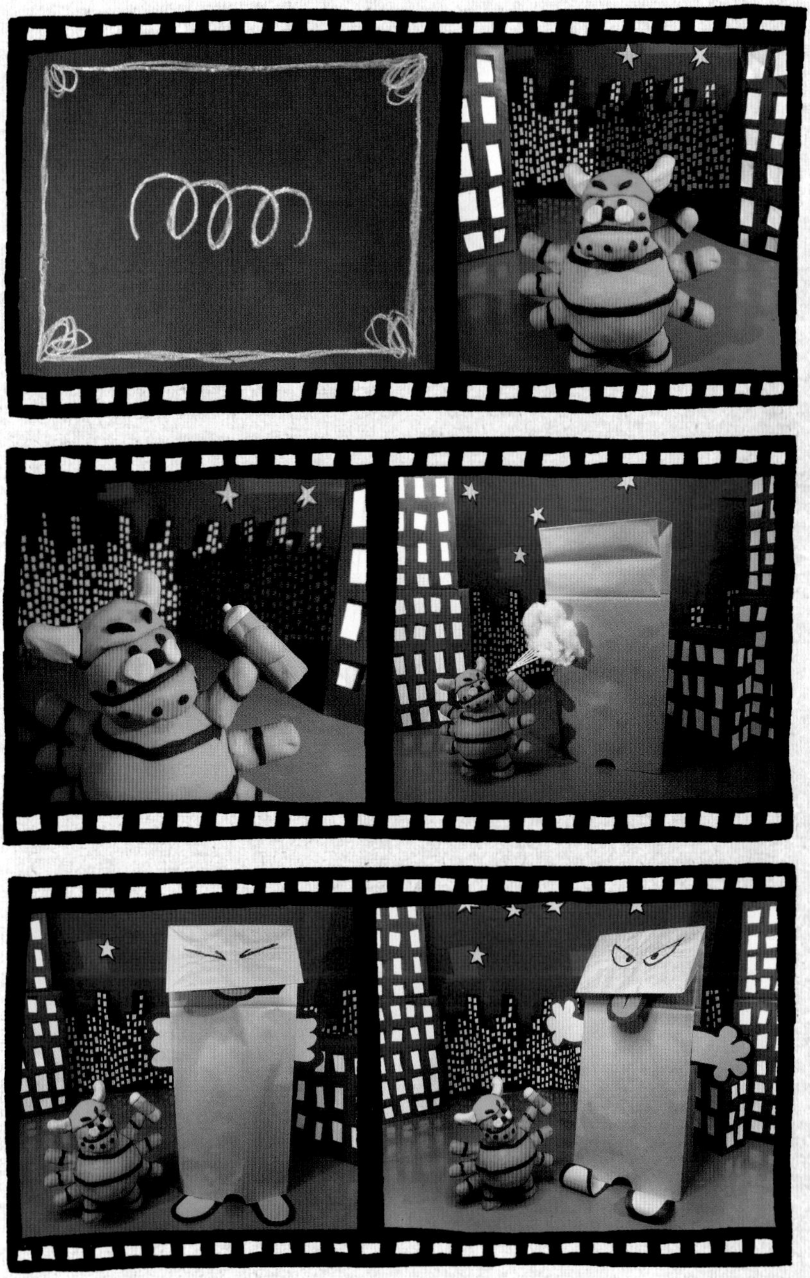

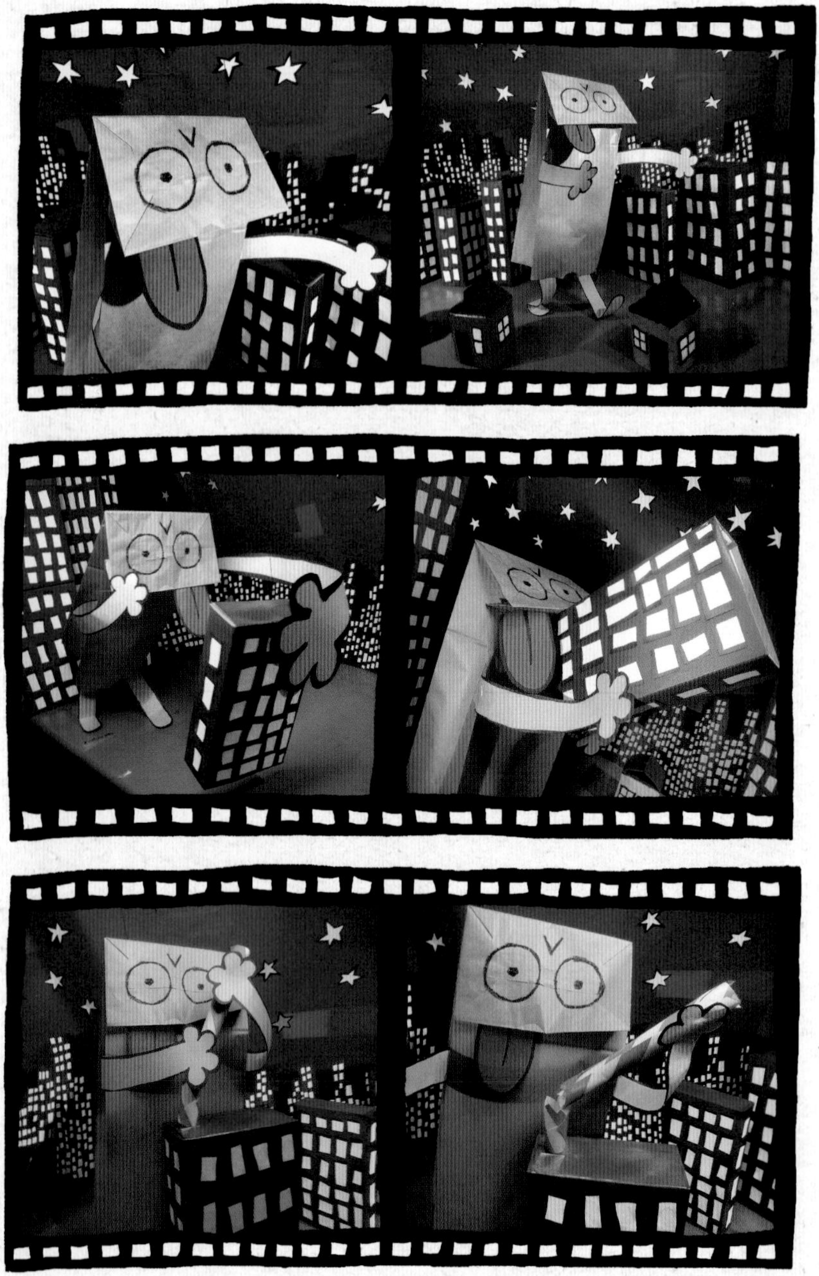

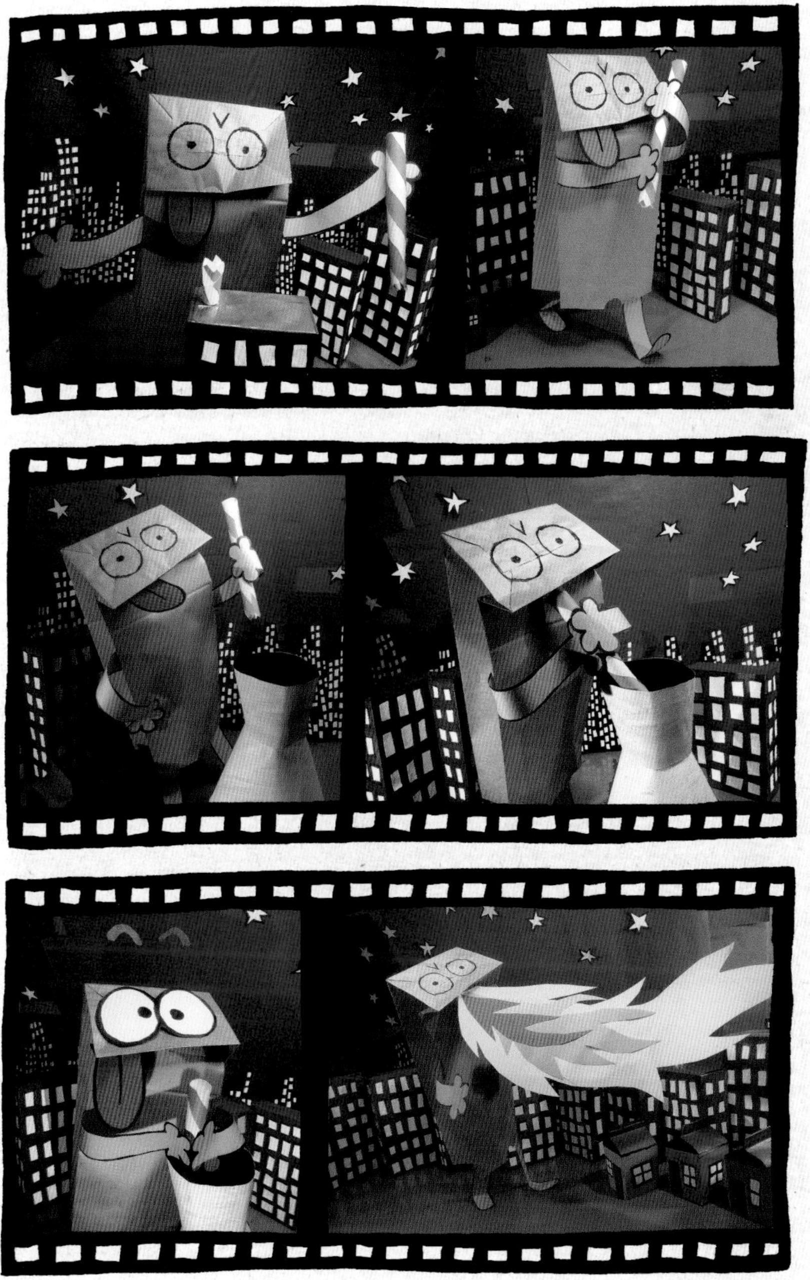

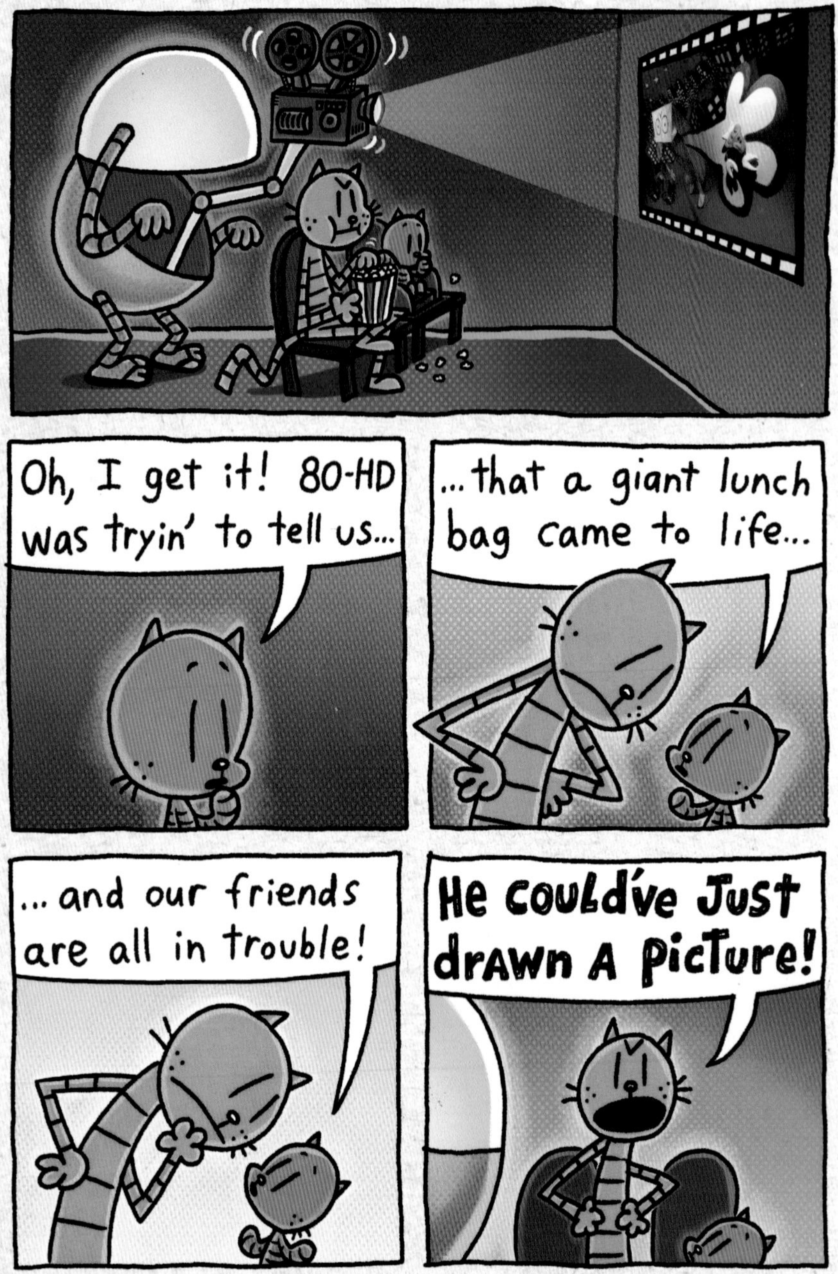
Oh, I get it! 80-HD was tryin' to tell us...
...that a giant lunch bag came to life...
...and our friends are all in trouble!
He could've just drawn a picture!

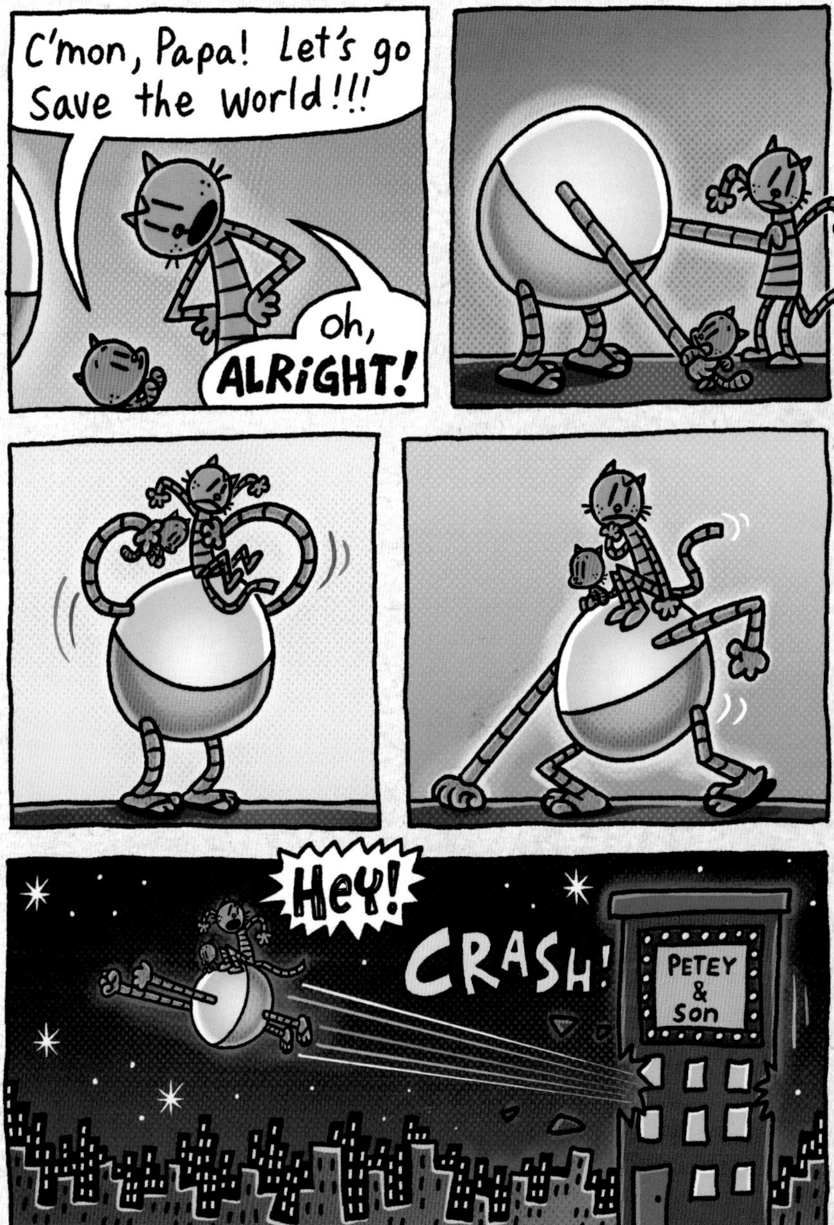
C'mon, Papa! Let's go Save the World!!!
oh, ALRIGHT!
HEY!
CRASH!
PETEY & Son

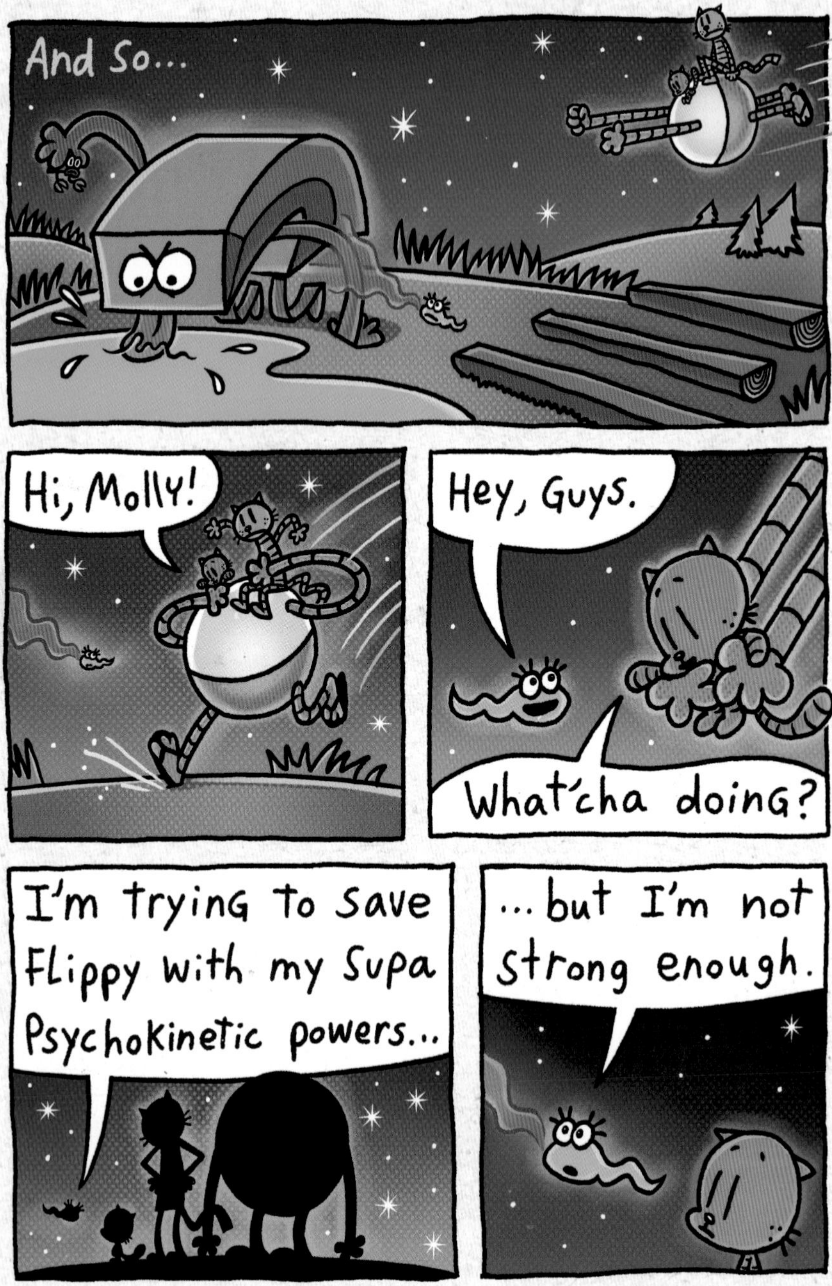
And so...
Hi, Molly!
Hey, Guys.
What'cha doing?
I'm trying to save Flippy with my Supa Psychokinetic powers...
...but I'm not strong enough.

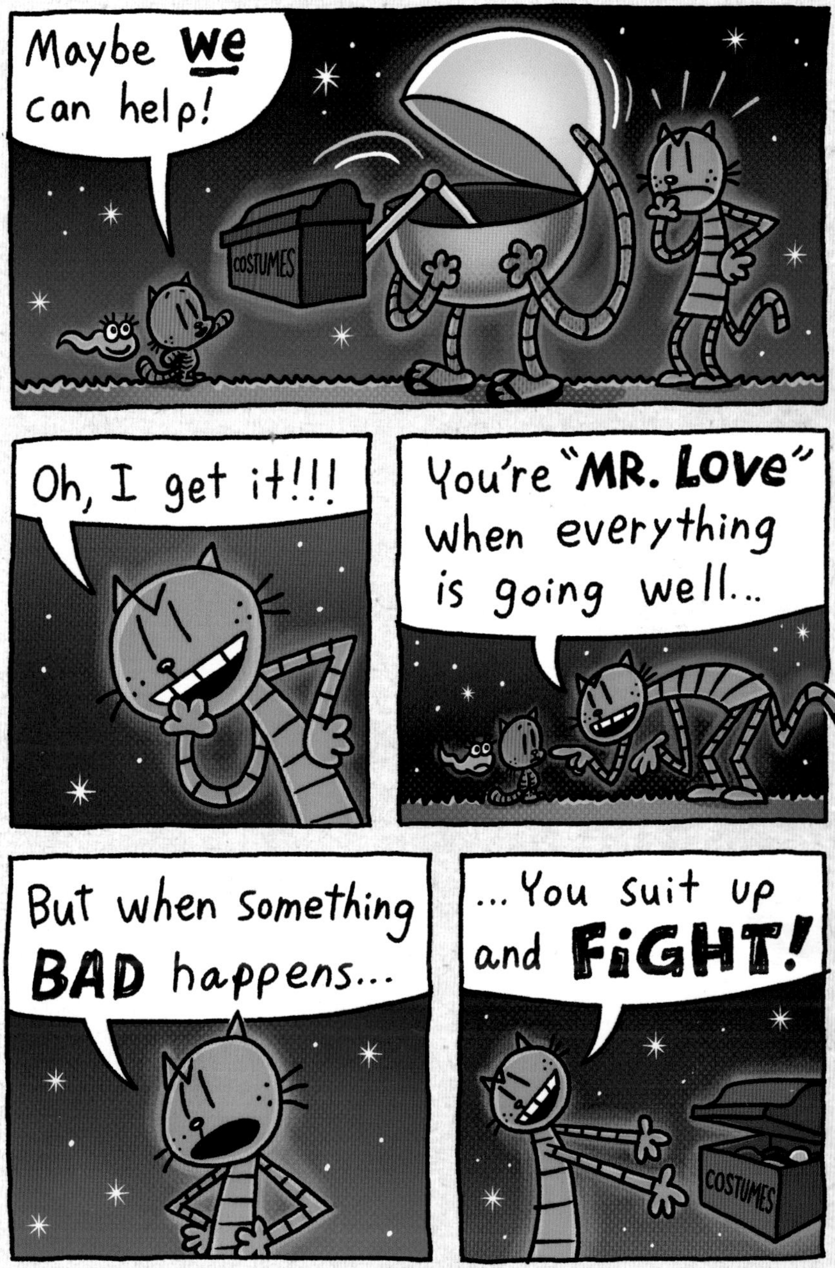

Maybe WE can help!
COSTUMES
Oh, I get it!!!
You're "MR. LOVE" when everything is going well...
But when something BAD happens...
...You suit up and FiGHT!
COSTUMES

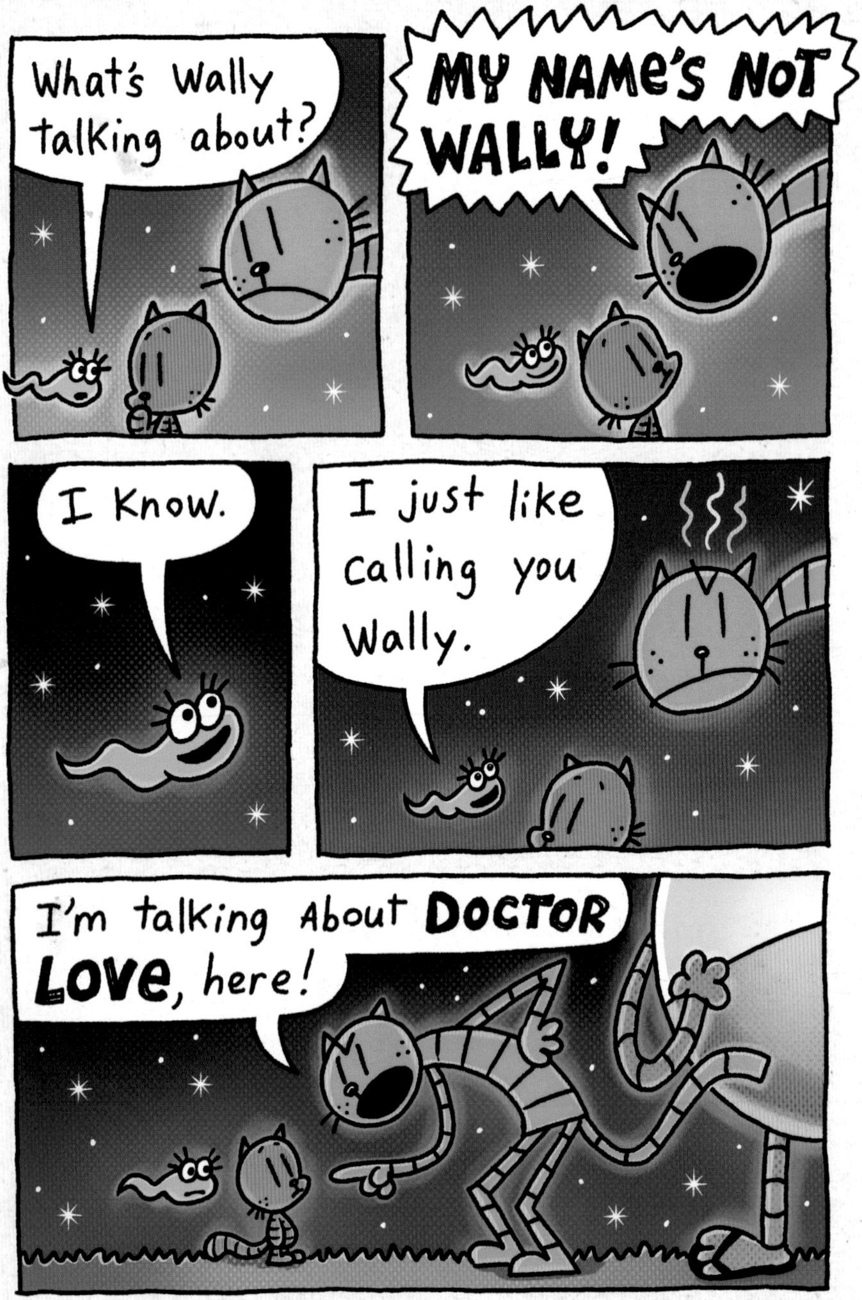
What's Wally talking about?
MY NAME'S NOT WALLY!
I know.
I just like calling you Wally.
I'm talking about DOCTOR LOVE, here!

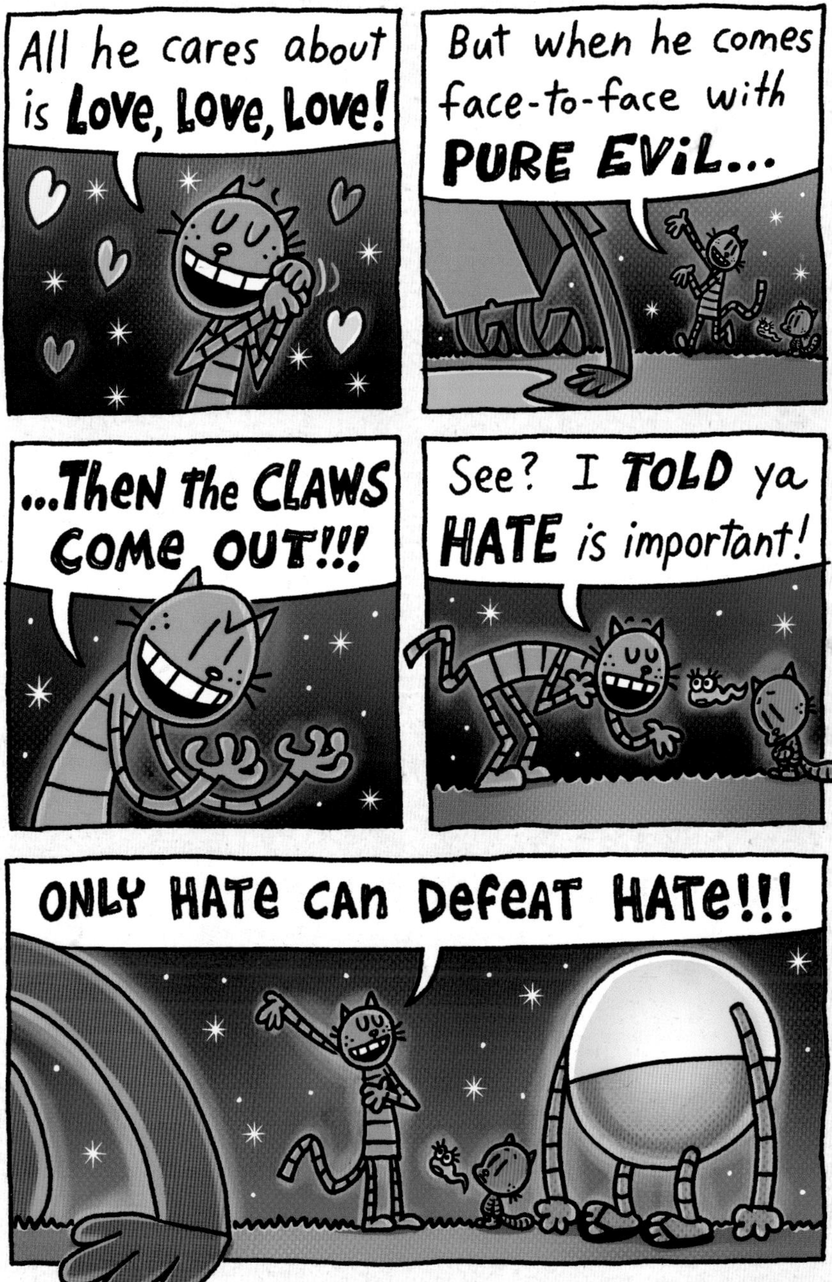
All he cares about is Love, Love, Love!
But when he comes face-to-face with PURE EVIL...
...Then the CLAWS COME OUT!!!
See? I TOLD ya HATE is important!
ONLY HATE CAN DEFEAT HATE!!!

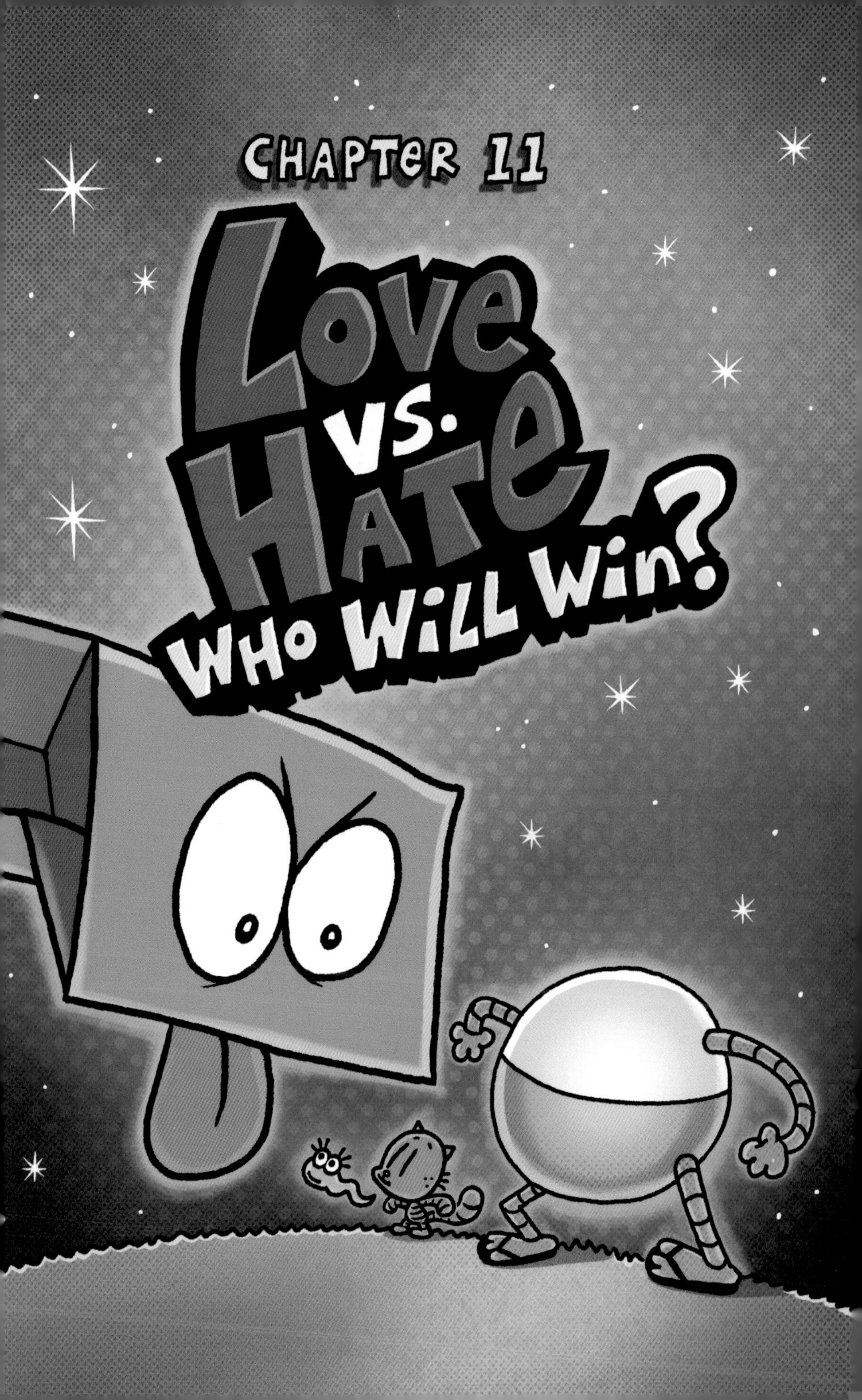
CHAPTER 11
Love vs. Hate
Who Will Win?

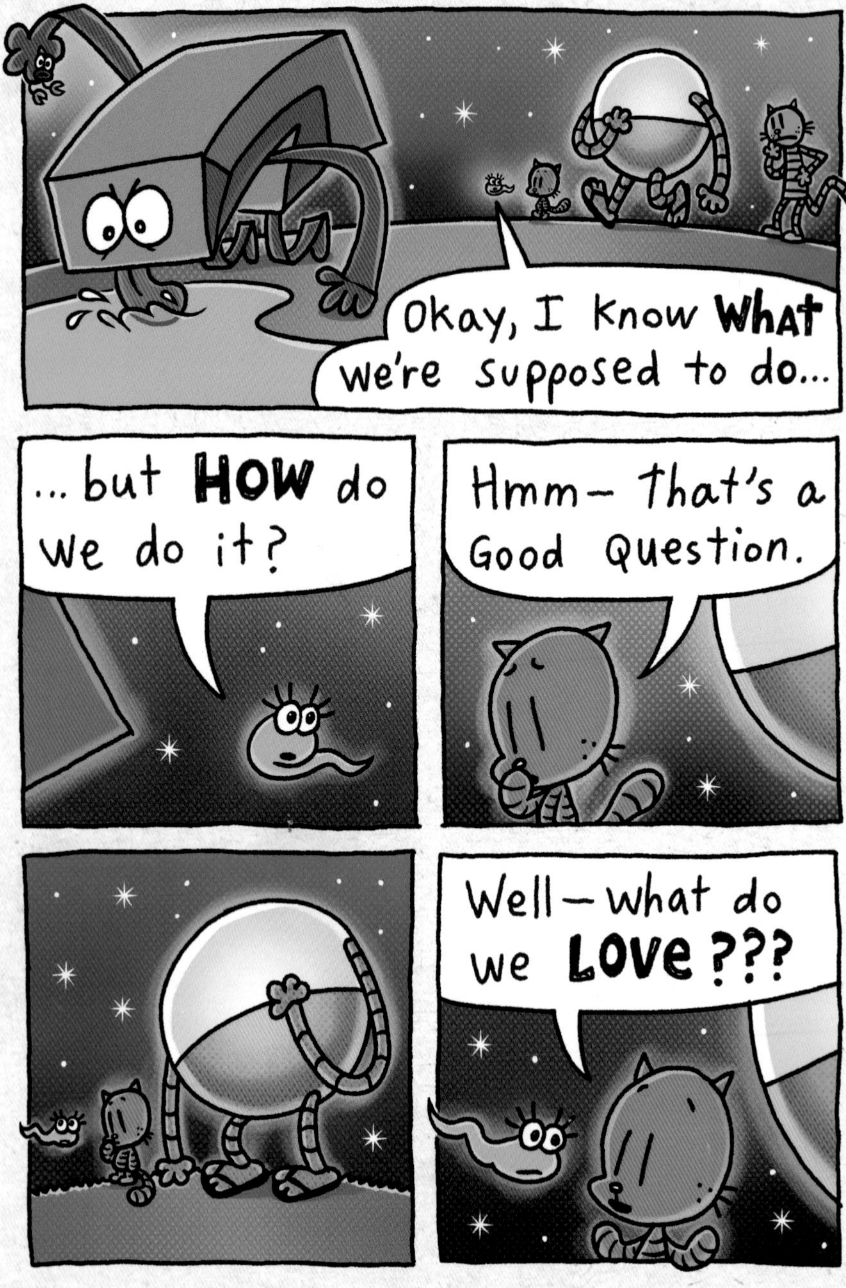
Okay, I know WHAT we're supposed to do...
...but HOW do we do it?
Hmm– That's a Good Question.
Well–what do we LOVE???

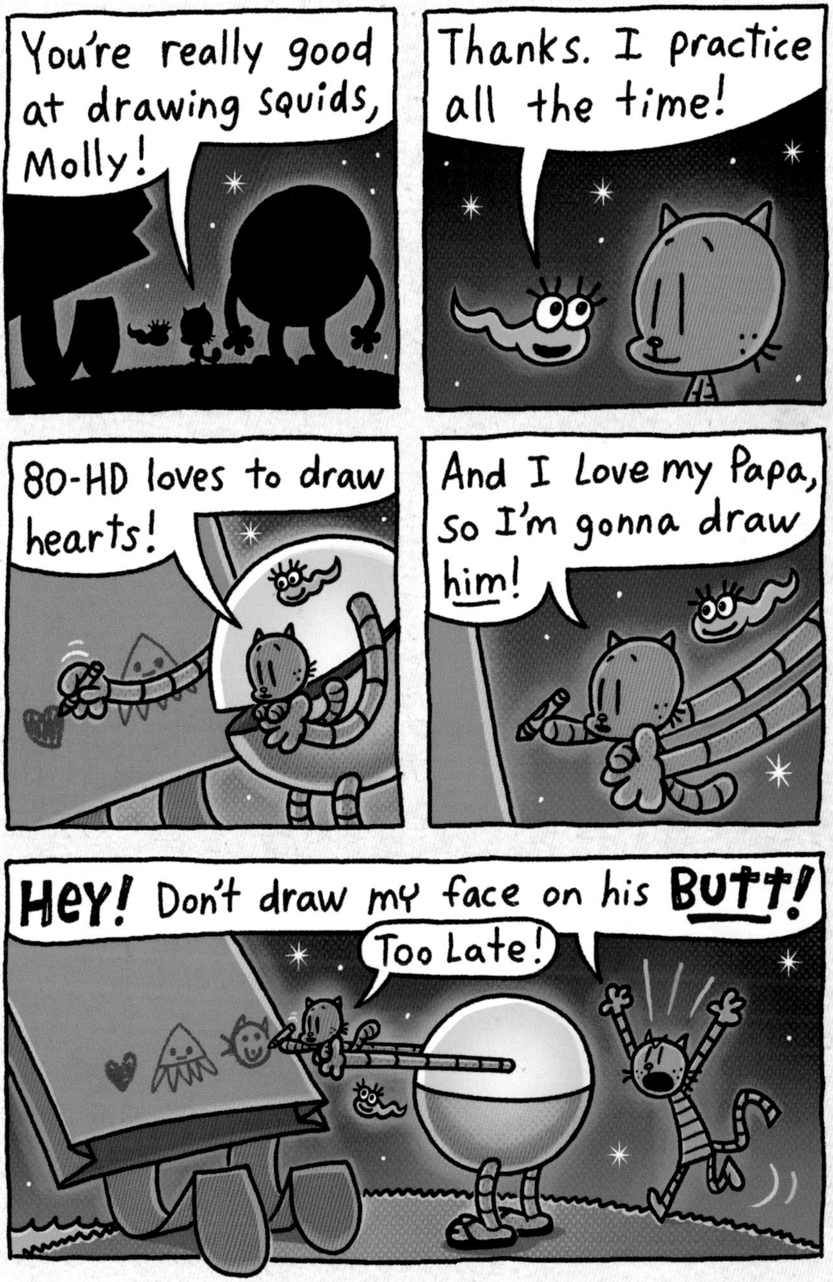
You're really good at drawing squids, Molly!
Thanks. I practice all the time!
80-HD loves to draw hearts!
And I Love my Papa, so I'm gonna draw him!
HEY! Don't draw my face on his BUTT!
Too Late!

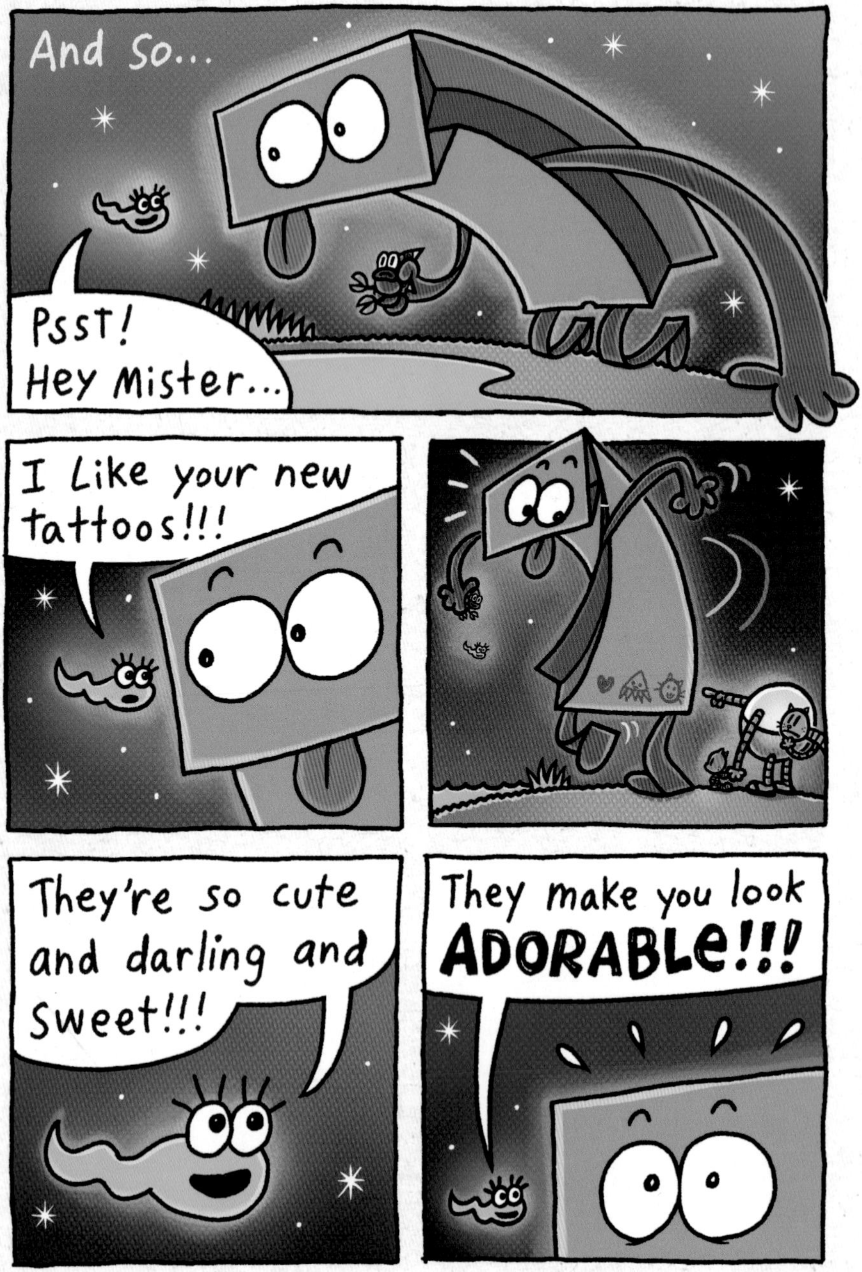
And so...
Psst!
Hey Mister...
I like your new tattoos!!!
They're so cute and darling and sweet!!!
They make you look ADORABLE!!!

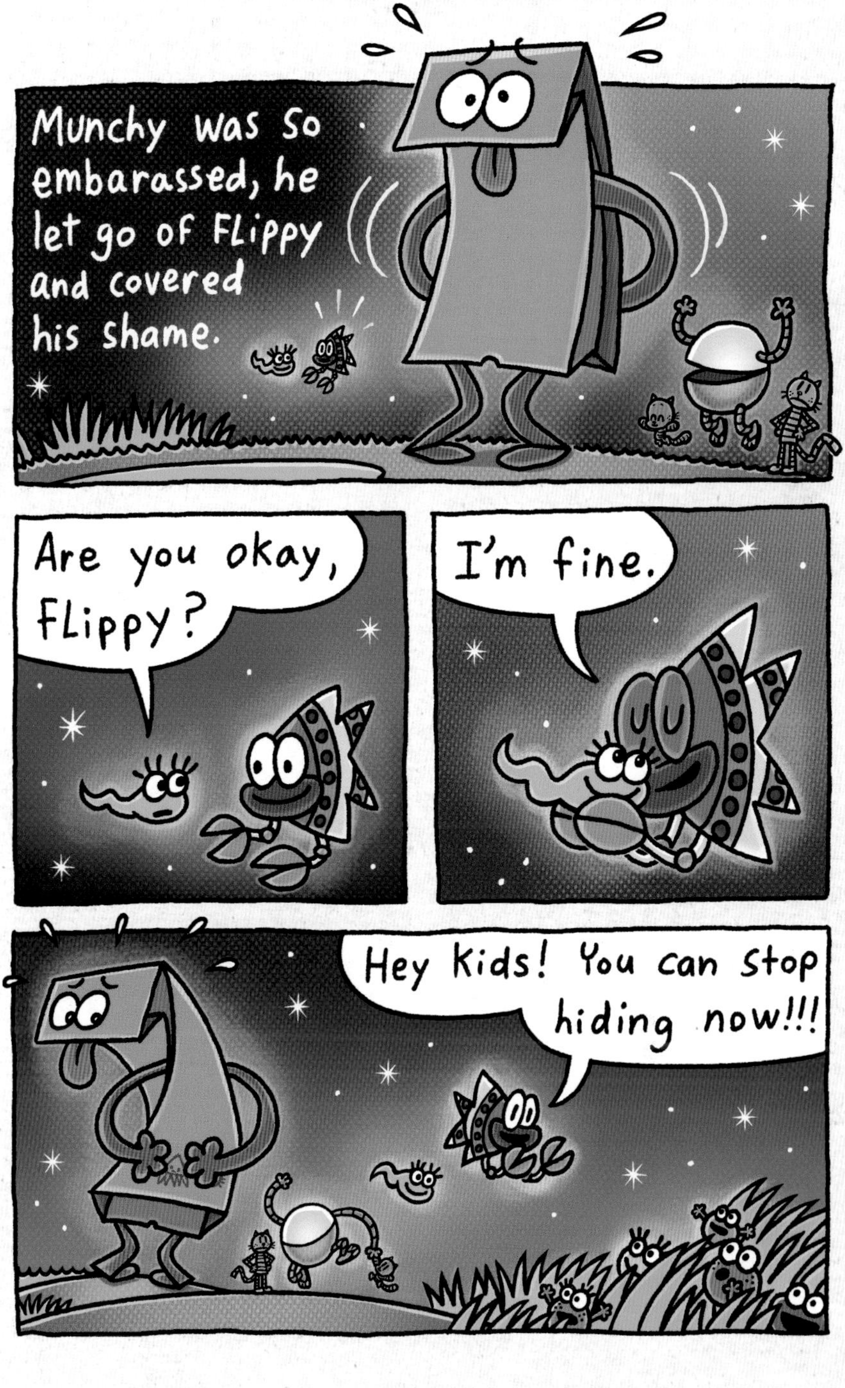
Munchy was so embarassed, he let go of Flippy and covered his shame.
Are you okay, Flippy?
I'm fine.
Hey kids! You can stop hiding now!!!

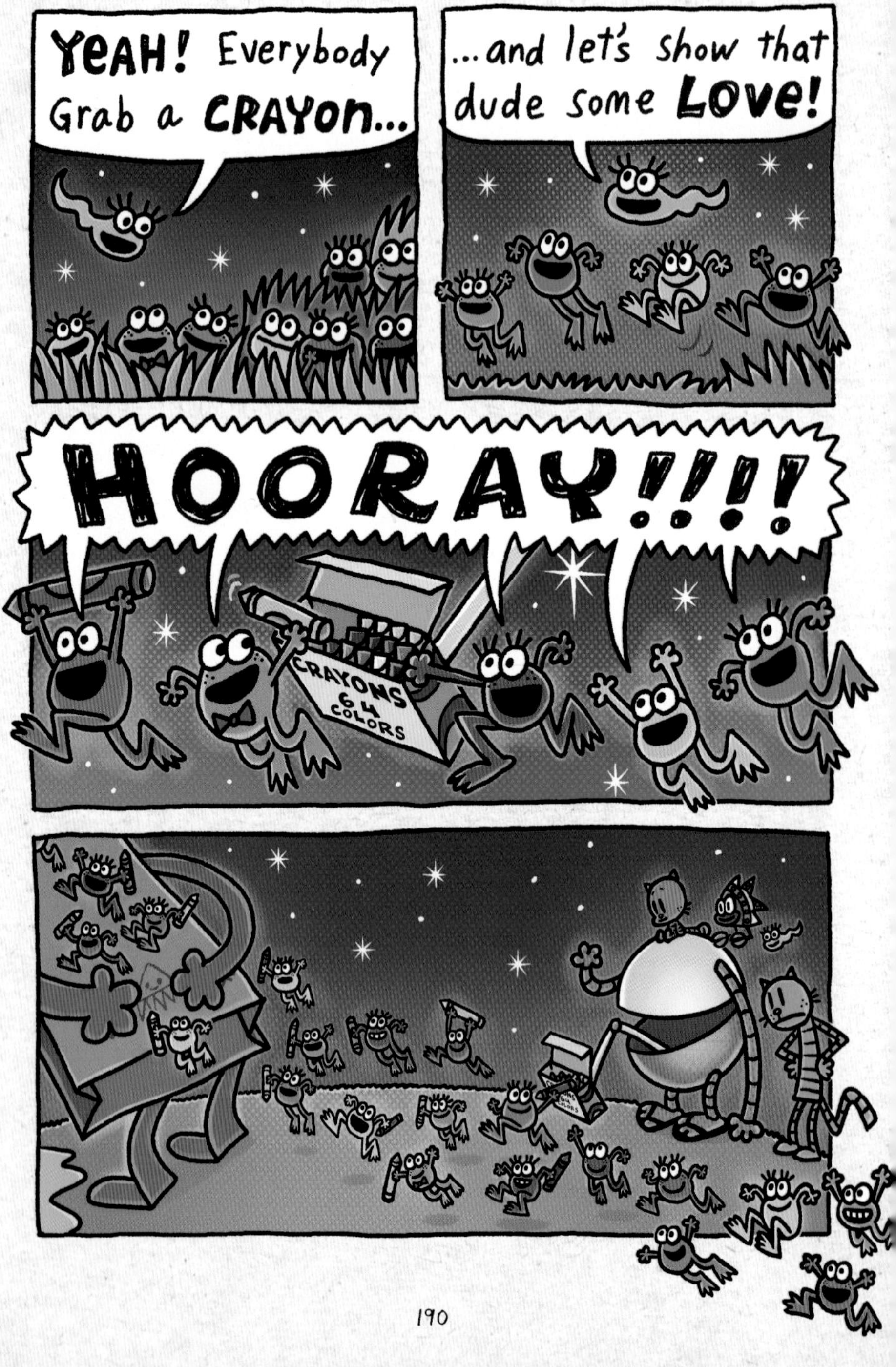
YEAH! Everybody Grab a CRAYON...
...and let's show that dude some LOVE!
HOORAY!!!!
CRAYONS 64 COLORS

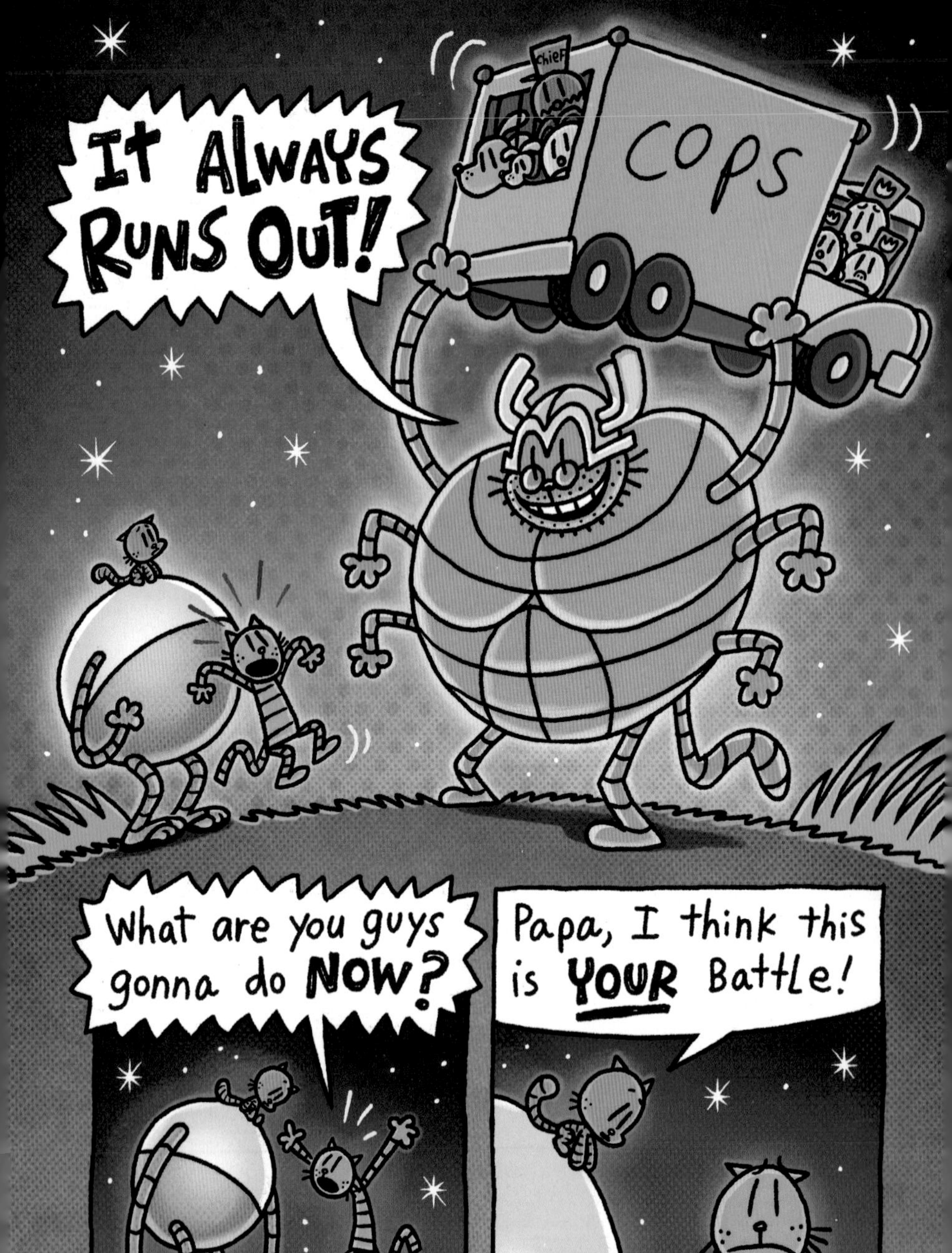

Chief
COPS
IT ALWAYS RUNS OUT!
What are you guys gonna do NOW?
Papa, I think this is YOUR Battle!

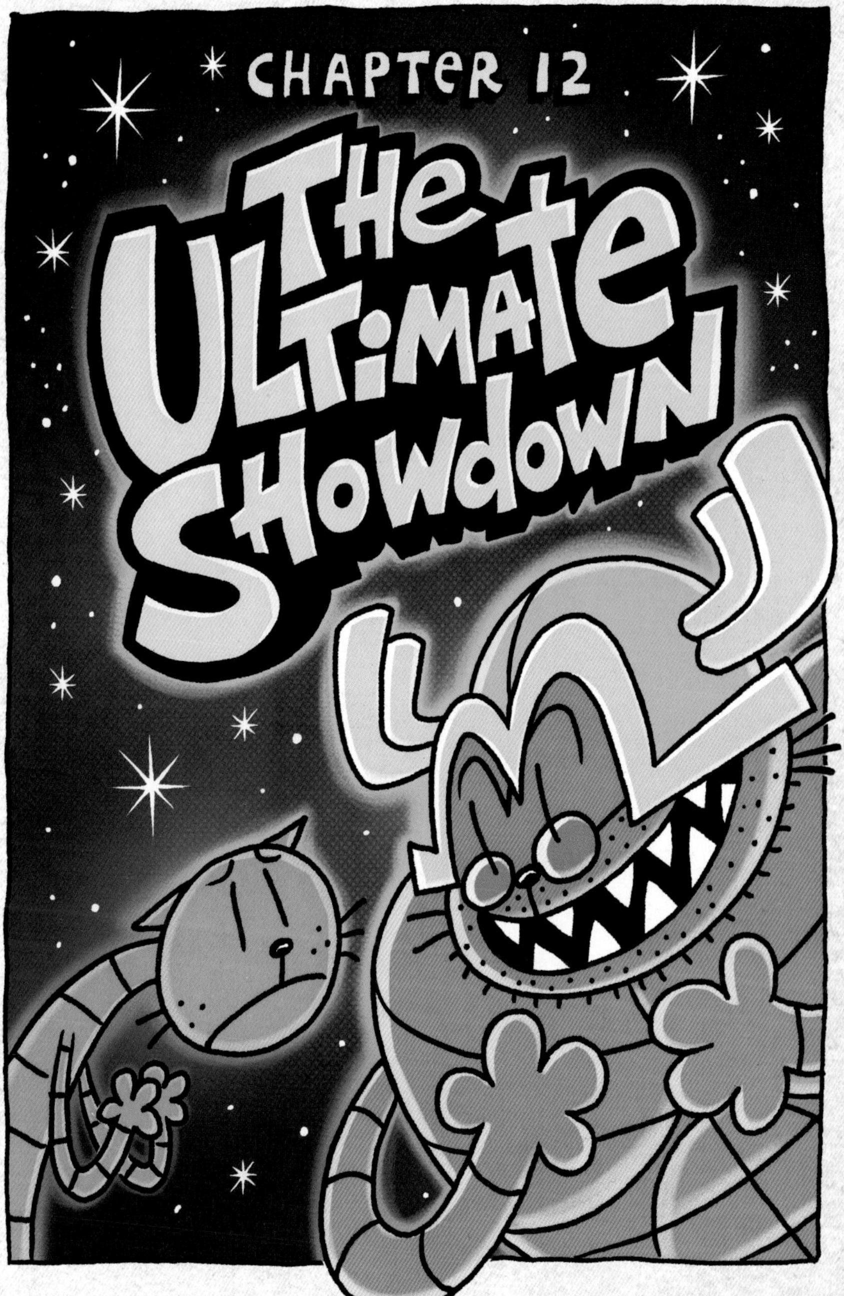
CHAPTER 12
THE ULTIMATE SHOWDOWN

Technically, they're not really **MY** friends!

Me GOT YOUR FRIENDS, PETEY!

Oh. So YOU WON'T MIND if Me DOES...

...THiS!!!

OH, NO!!!

Let's Roll, FLippY!

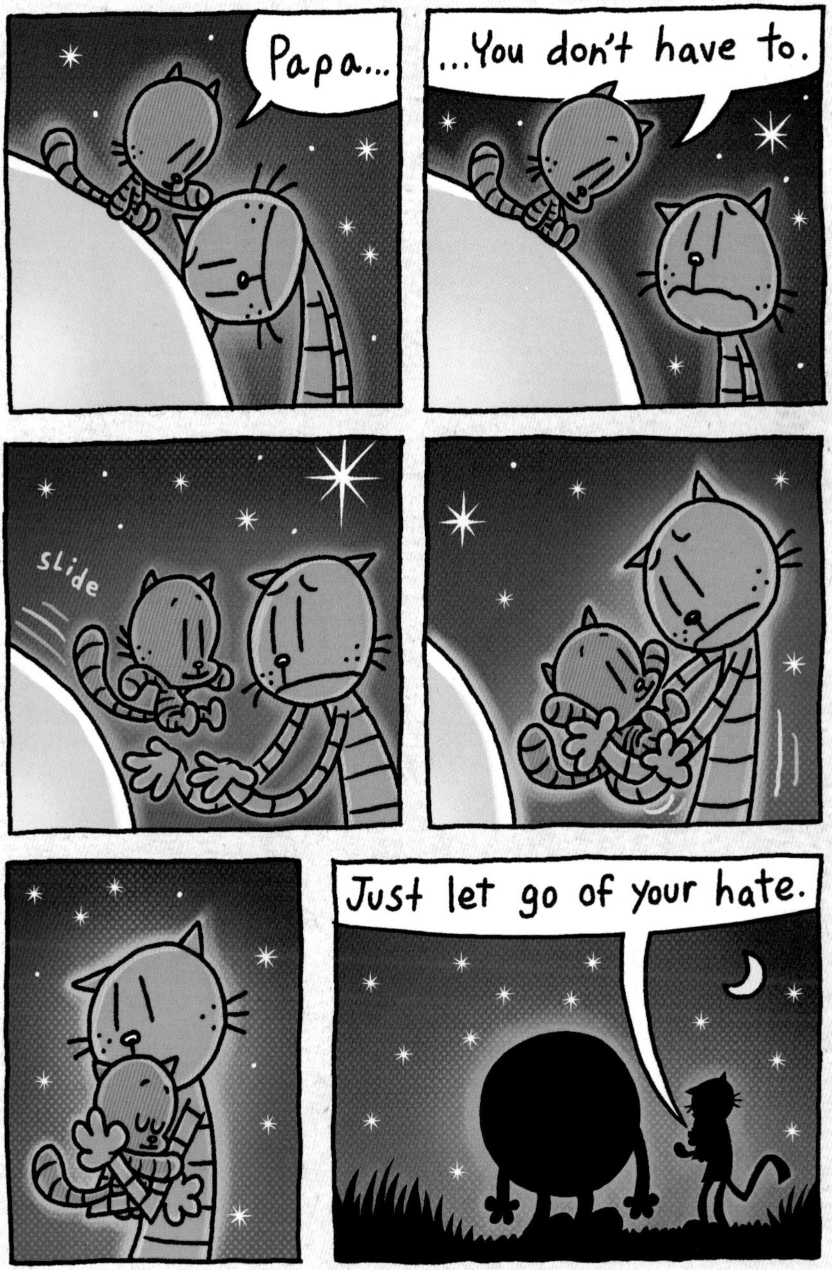

Papa...
...You don't have to.
slide
Just let go of your hate.

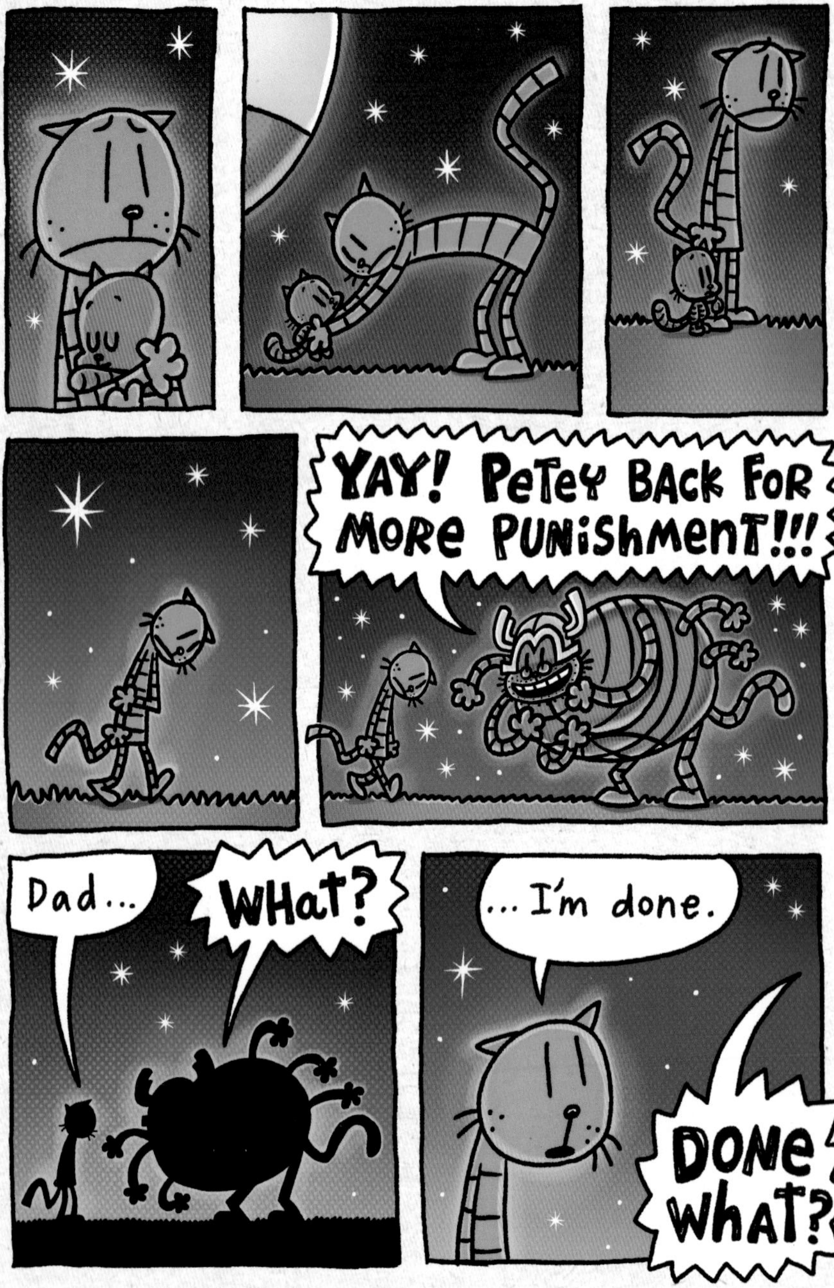
YAY! PETEY BACK FOR MORE PUNISHMENT!!!
Dad...
WHAT?
...I'm done.
DONE WHAT?

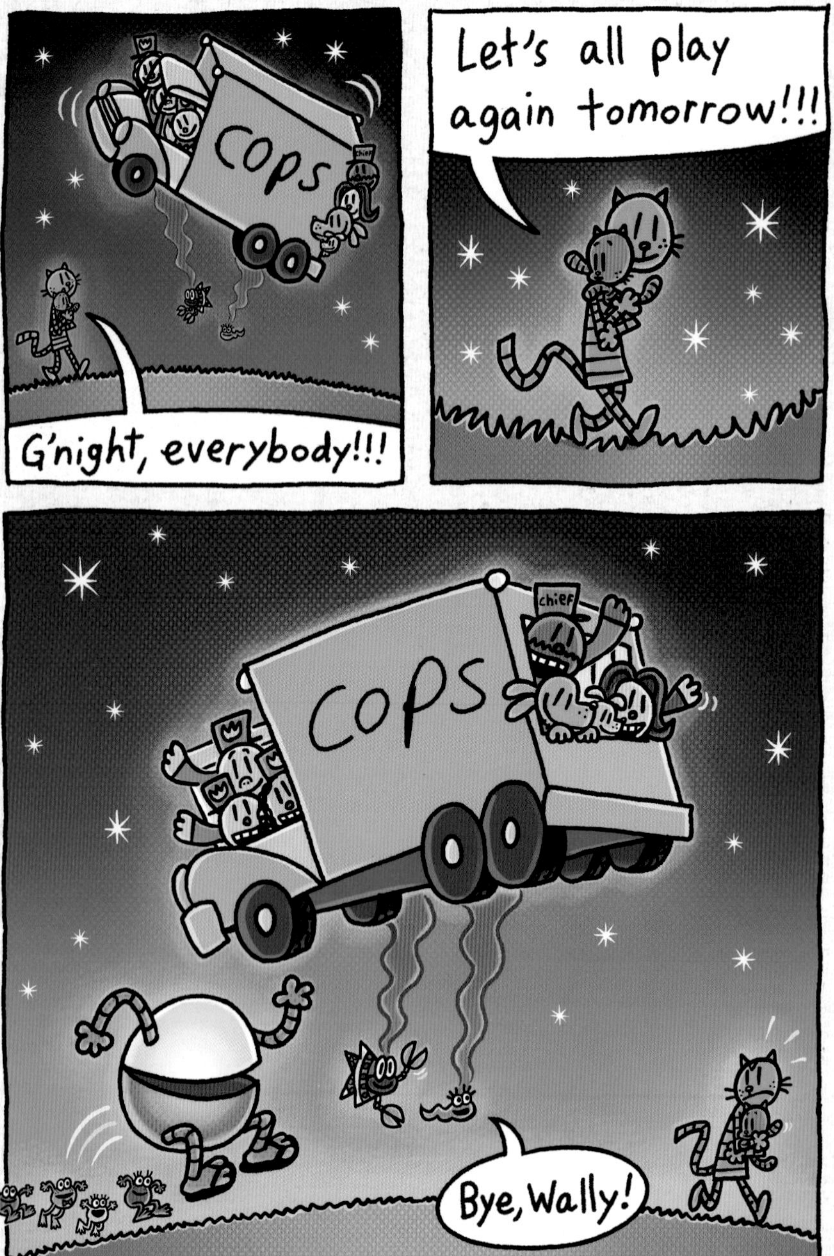
G'night, everybody!!!
Let's all play again tomorrow!!!
COPS
chief
COPS
Bye, Wally!

CHAPTER 13

THREE Endings

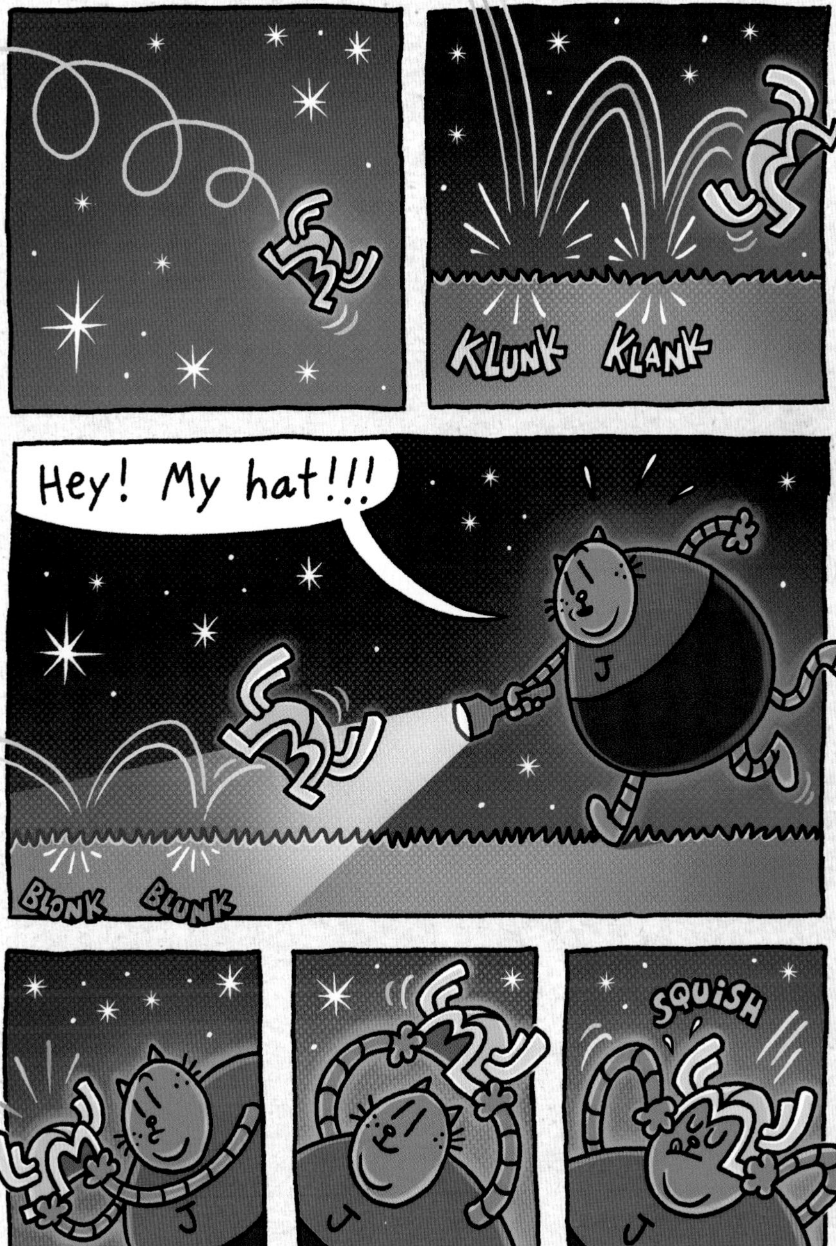
KLUNK
KLANK
Hey! My hat!!!
BLONK
BLUNK
SQUISH

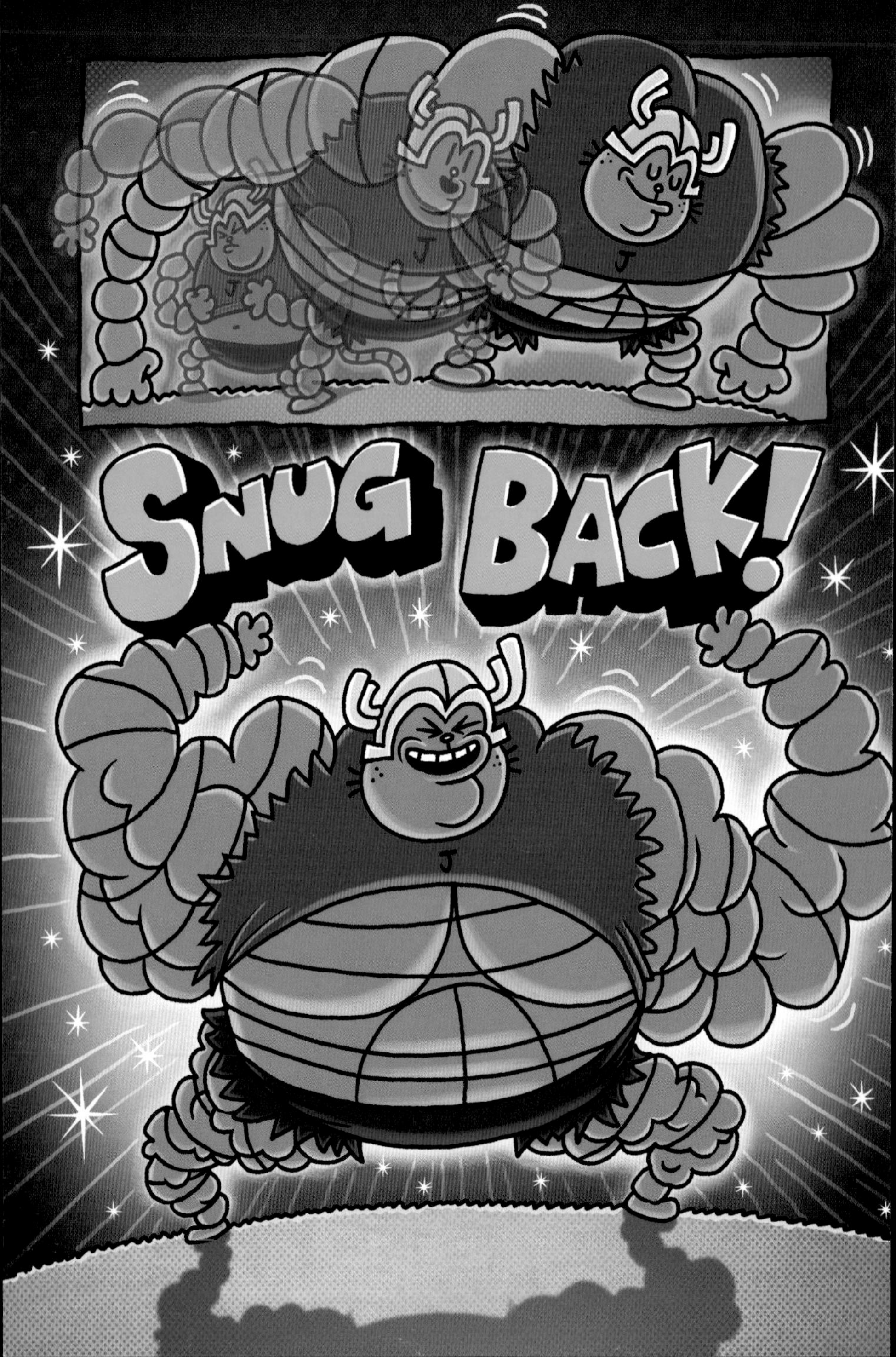
SNUG BACK!

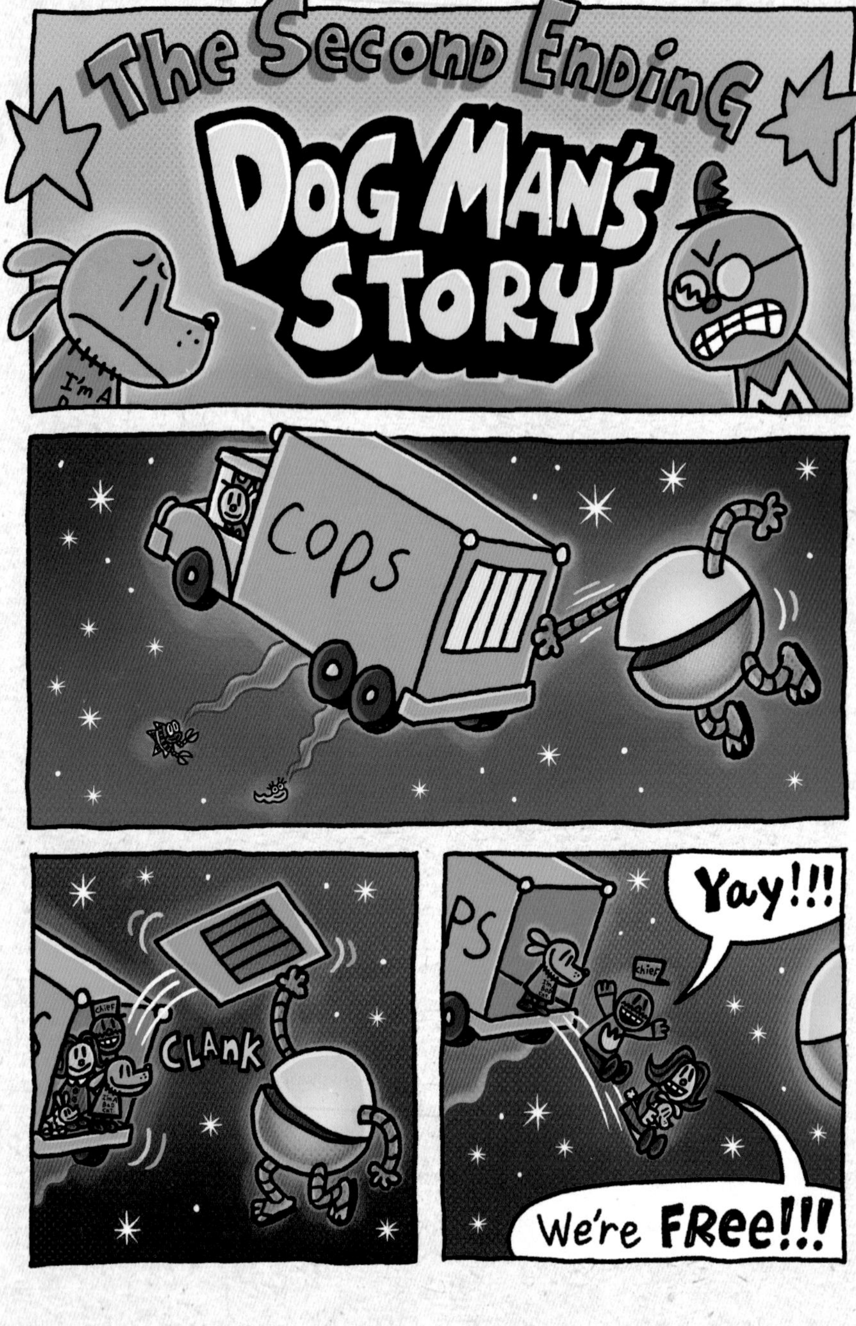
The Second Ending
Dog Man's Story
COPS
CLANK
Yay!!!
We're FREE!!!

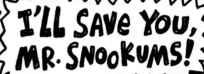

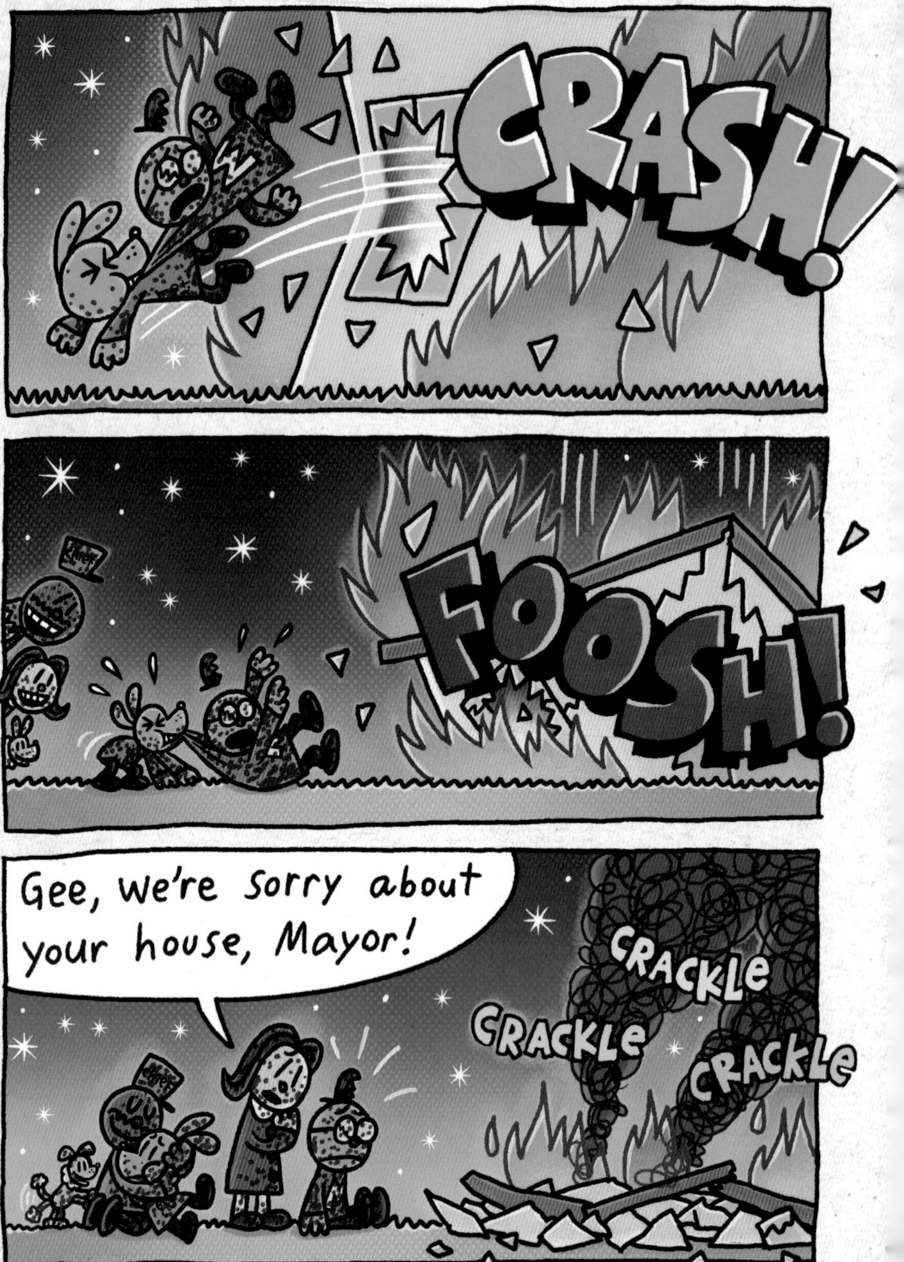
CRASH!
FOOSH!
Gee, we're sorry about your house, Mayor!
CRACKLE
CRACKLE
CRACKLE

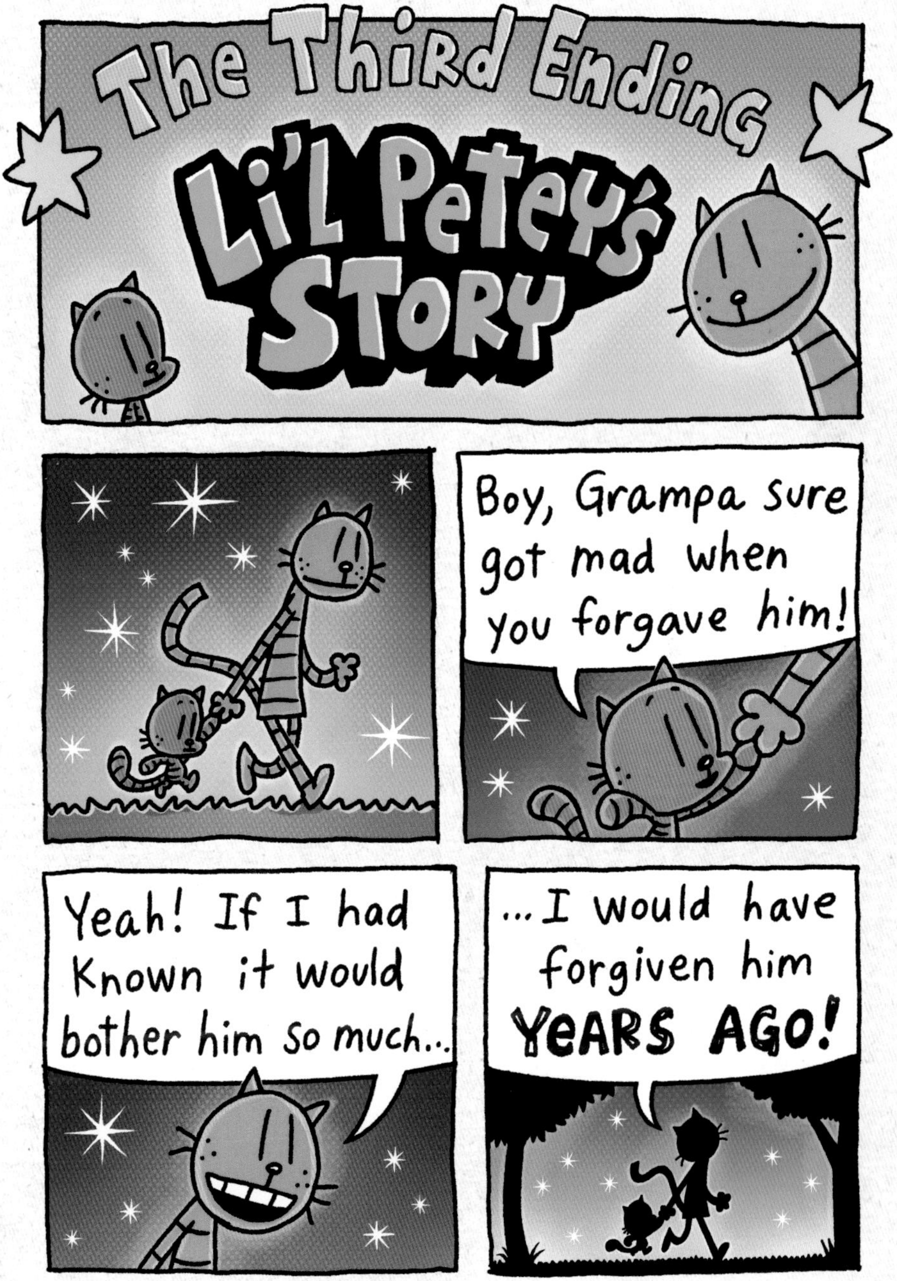
The Third Ending
Li'L Petey's STORY
Boy, Grampa sure got mad when you forgave him!
Yeah! If I had Known it would bother him so much...
...I would have forgiven him YEARS AGO!

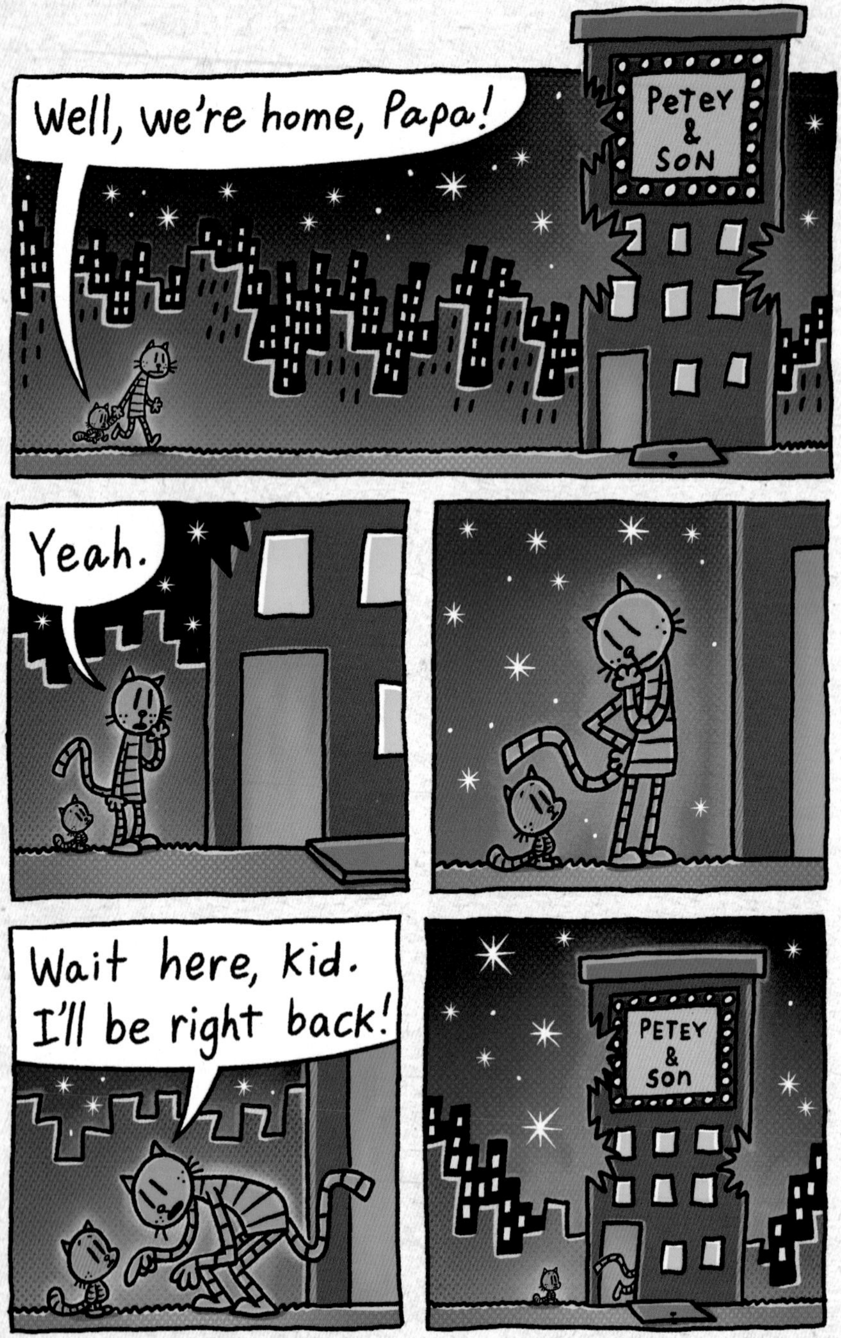
Well, we're home, Papa!
PETEY & SON
Yeah.
Wait here, kid. I'll be right back!
PETEY & SON

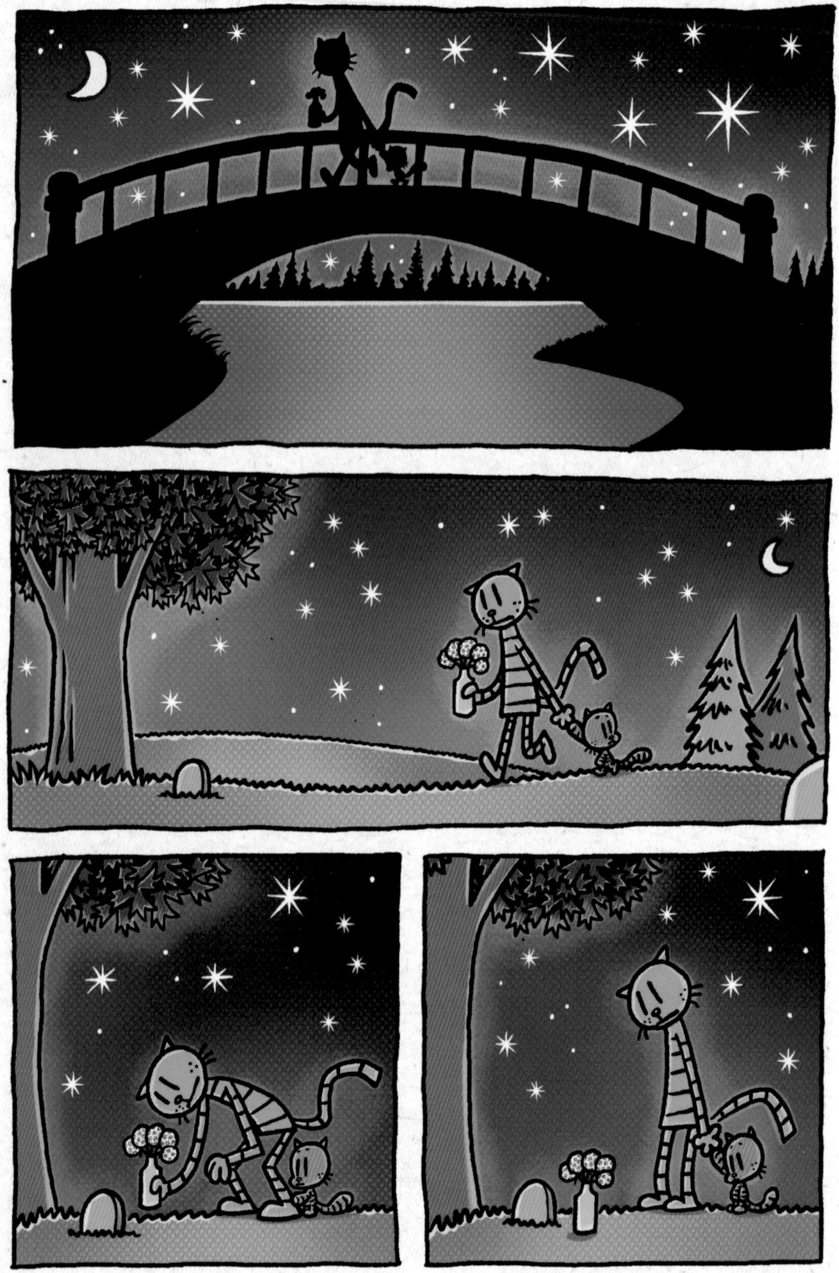

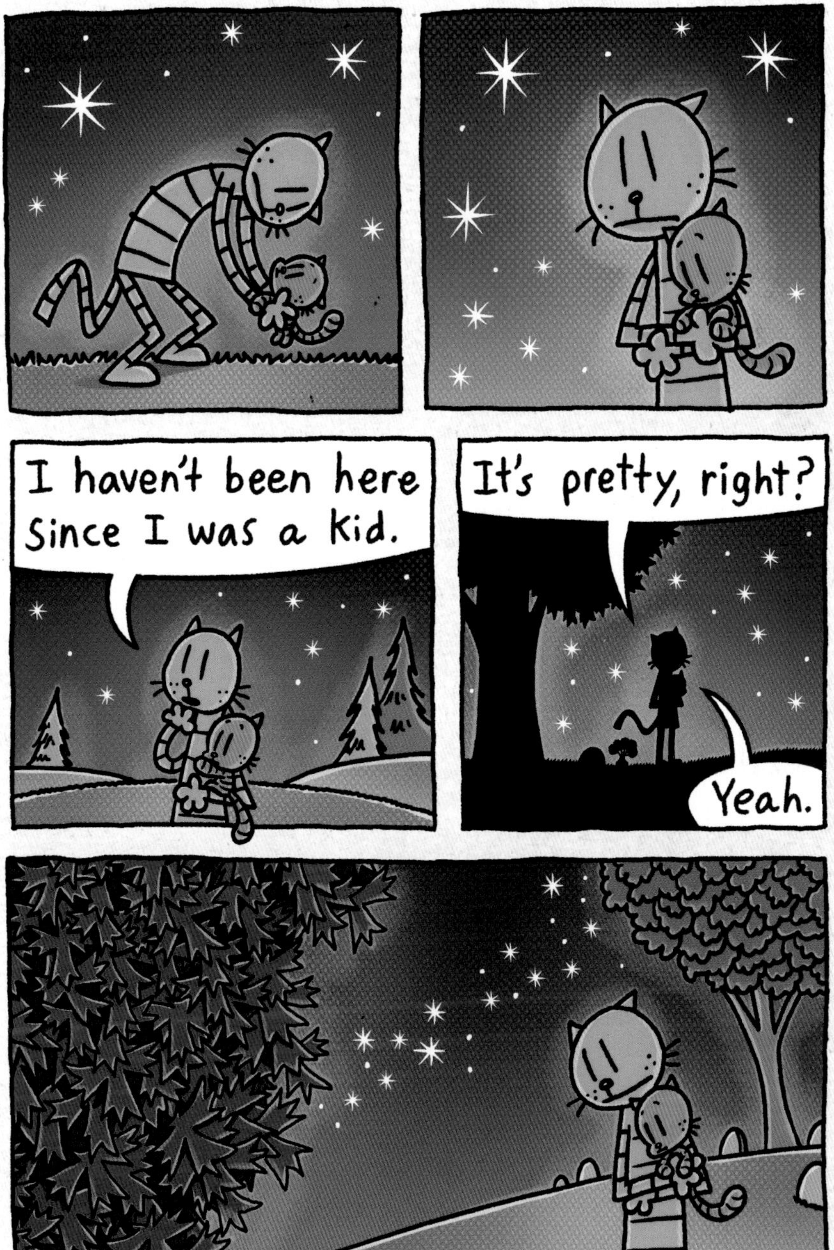
I haven't been here since I was a kid.
It's pretty, right?
Yeah.

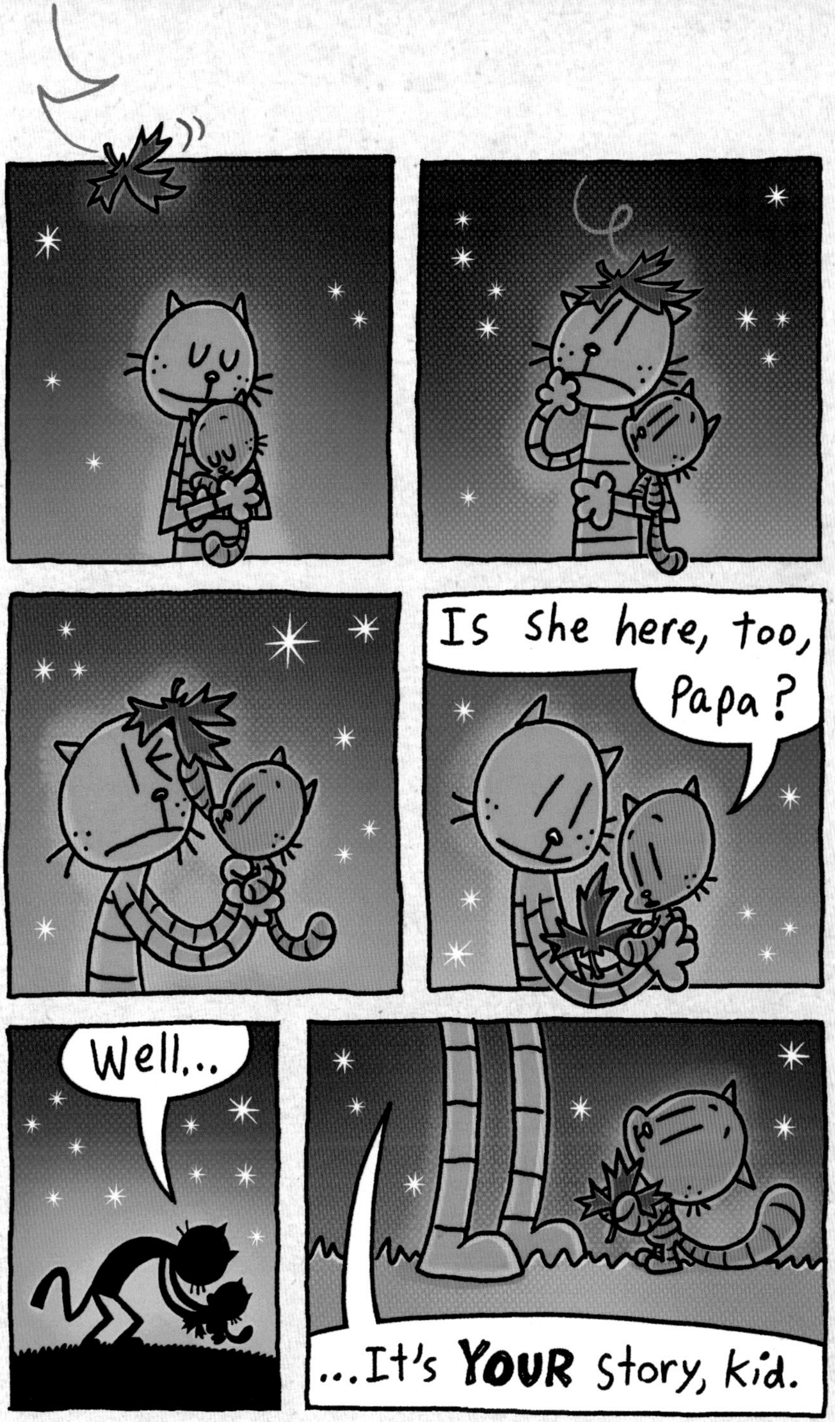
Is she here, too, Papa?
Well...
...It's YOUR story, kid.

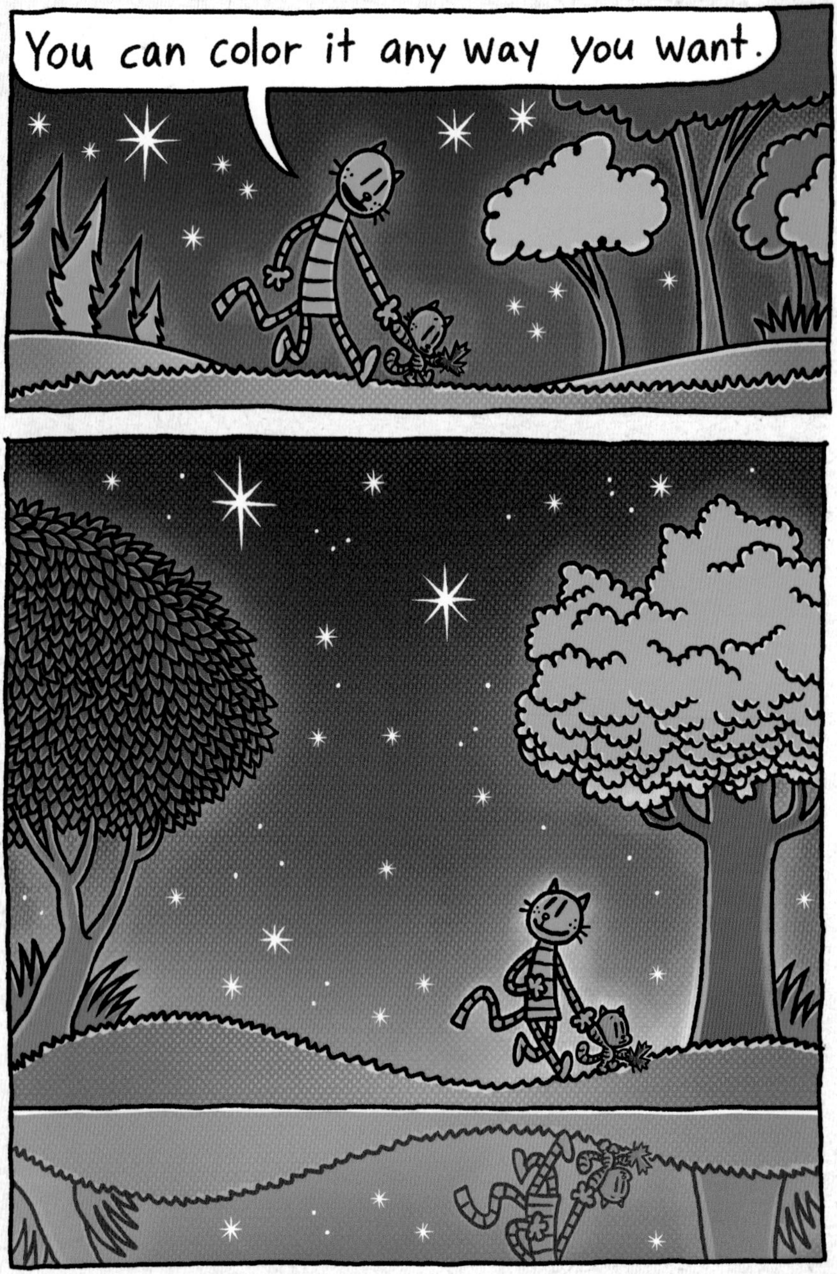
You can color it any way you want.

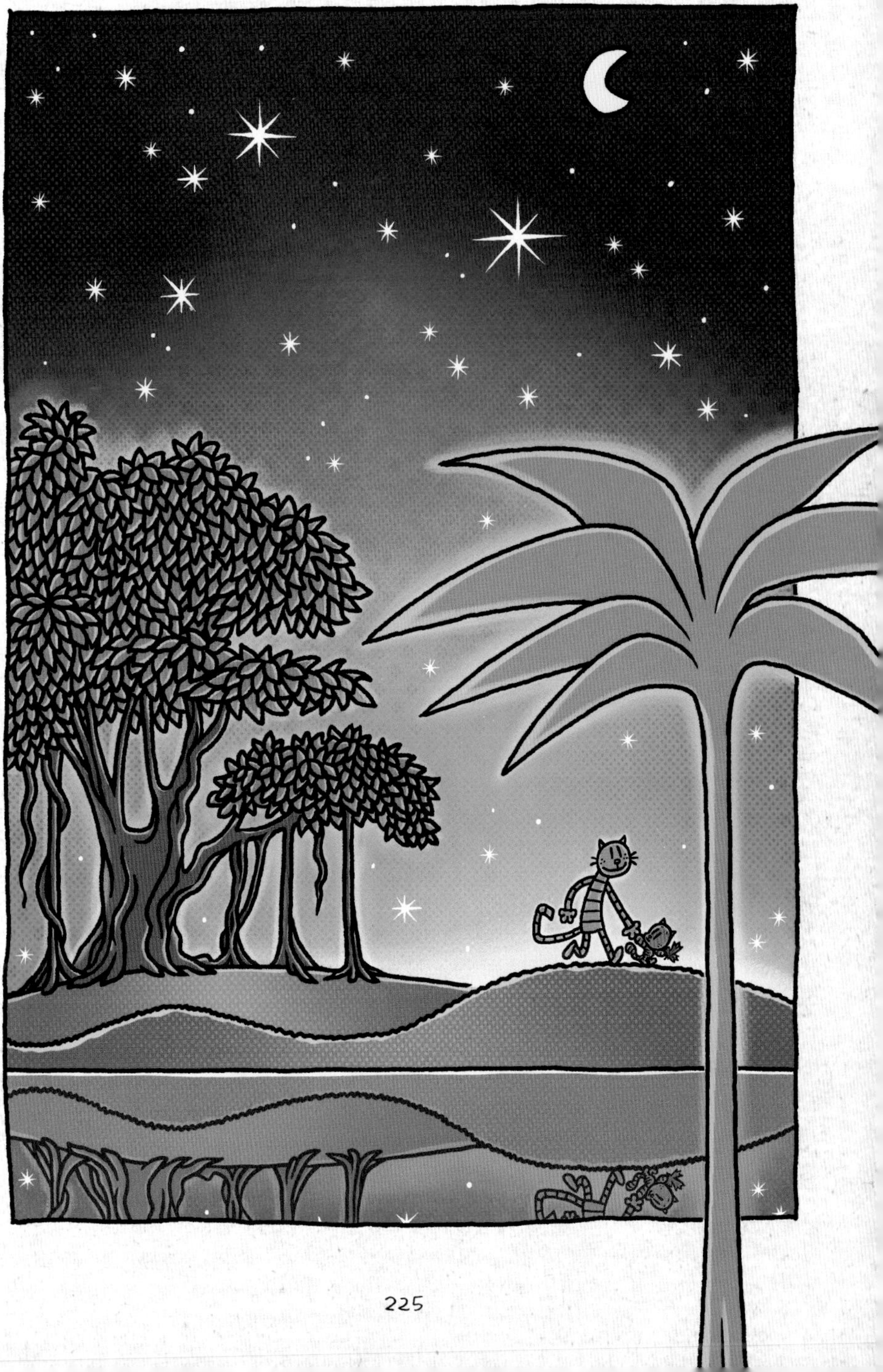

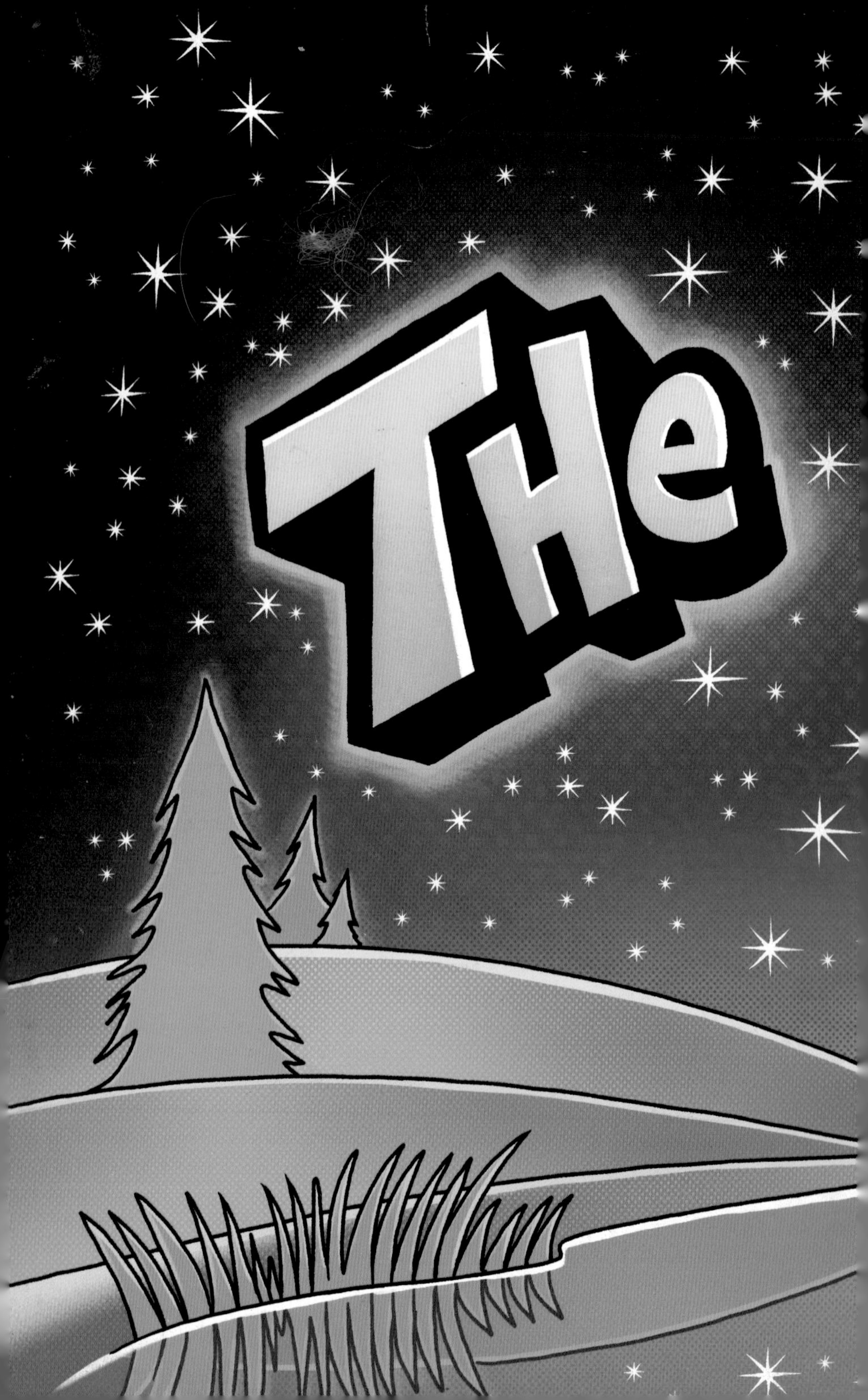
THE

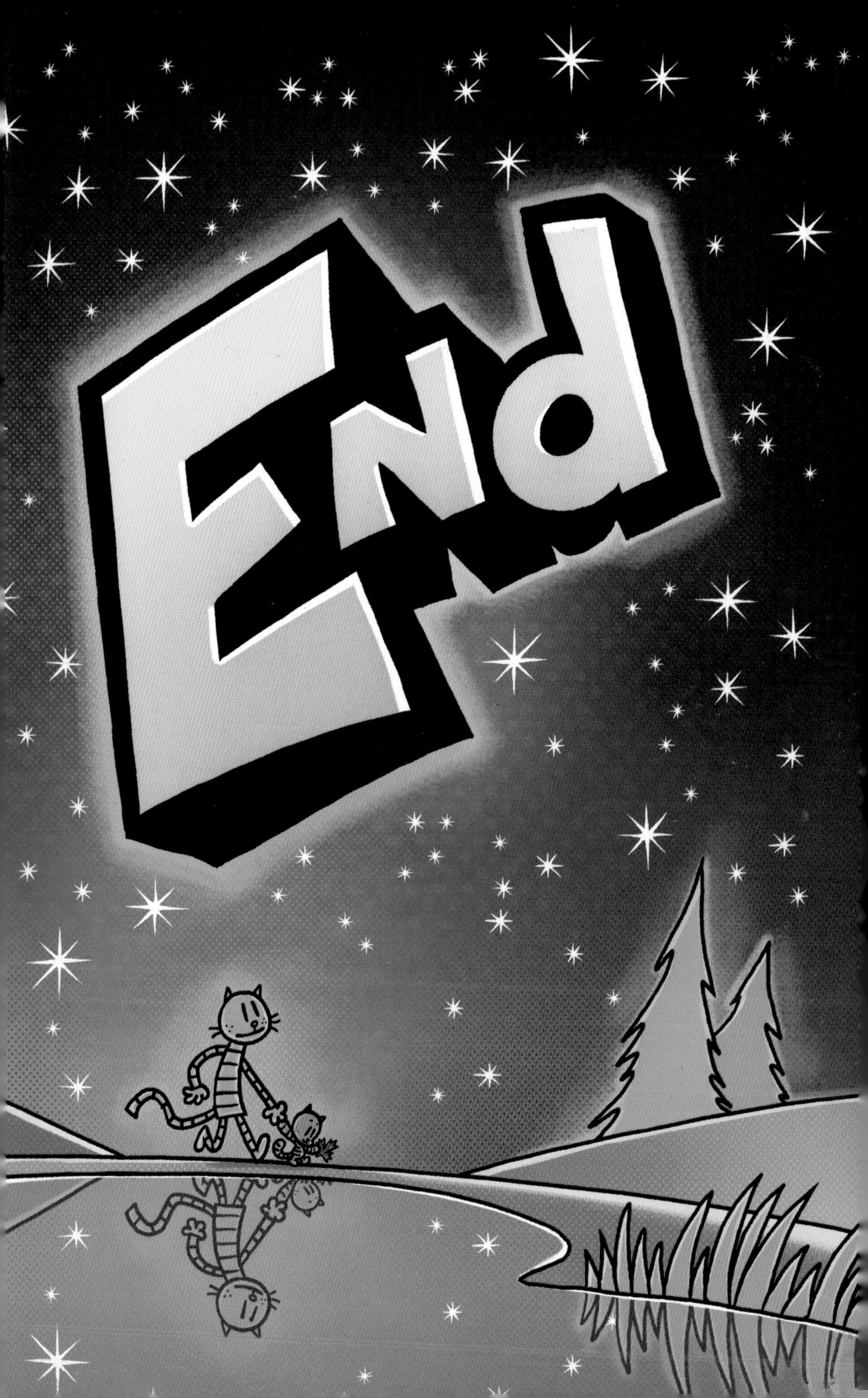
End

NOTES

by George and Harold

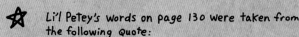

⭐ Li'l Petey's words on page 130 were taken from the following Quote:

> "Hate, it has caused a lot of problems
> in this world,
> but has not solved one yet."
>
> —Maya Angelou

⭐ Chapter 12 was based on this precept:

> "Resentment is like drinking poison
> and waiting for the other person to die."
>
> —Carrie Fisher

⭐ Part 3 of the final chapter was inspired by this poem:

> Do not stand at my grave and weep,
> I am not there. I do not sleep.
> I am a thousand winds that blow,
> I am the softly falling snow.
> I am the gentle showers of rain,
> I am the fields of ripening grain.
> I am in the morning hush,
> I am in the graceful rush
> Of beautiful birds in circling flight.
> I am the starshine of the night.
> I am in the flowers that bloom,
> I am in a quiet room.
> I am in the birds that sing.
> I am in each lovely thing.
> Do not stand at my grave and cry.
> I am not there — I did not die.
>
> — Mary Elizabeth Frye

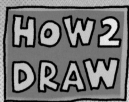

HOW 2 DRAW CAT MAN

in **21** Ridiculously Easy Steps!!!

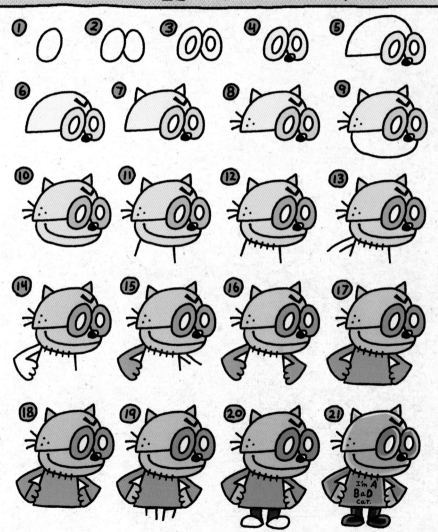

HOW 2 DRAW MeLvin The FROG
in 17 Ridiculously easy steps!

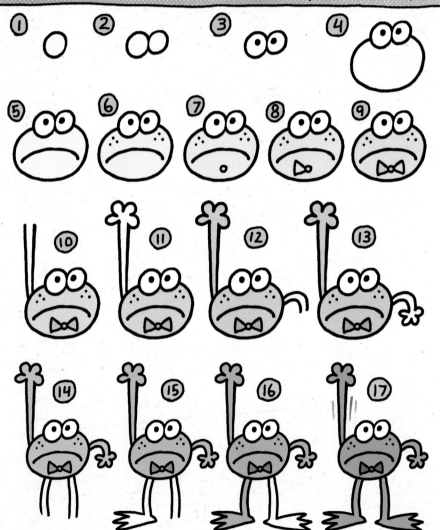

SARAH

in 18 Ridiculously Easy Steps!!!

MUNCHY The Lunch BAG

in 4 Ridiculously easy steps!

Step 1:

Get Supplies:
- ⭐ Lunch bag
- ⭐ Pencil
- ⭐ Tape

⭐ Construction paper ⭐ Scissors

⭐ Crayons / markers / Colored Pencils

STEP 2:
Draw and cut out the arms, Legs, eyes + tongue.

FREE Printable / CoLorabLe template available at: Scholastic.com / catKidcomicclub

232

STEP 3:

Assemble as shown using tape or glue or paste.

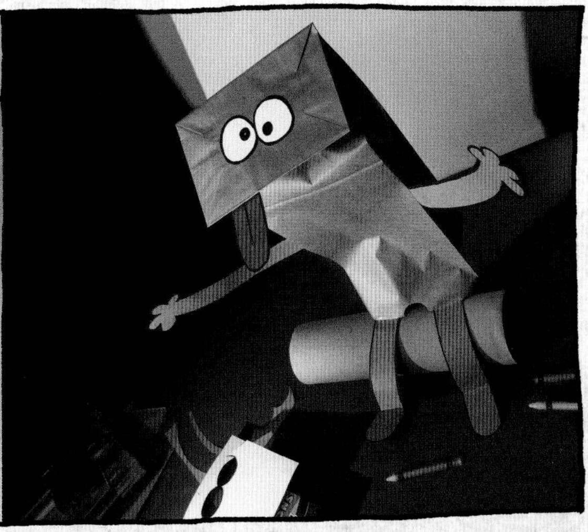

STEP 4:

Take away his evil powers by filling him up with all the people and things you **LOVE!**

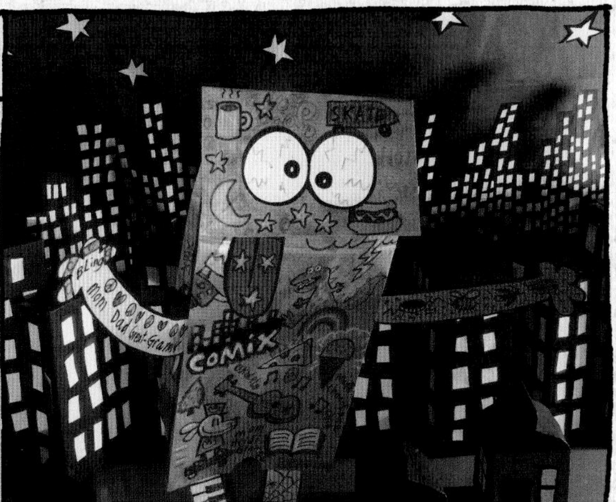
COMIX

Use pencils, crayons, paint, or whatever!!!

WRITE... DRAW... BE CREATIVE!

How 2 Draw The Insuppressible Snug

in 34 Ridiculously easy steps!

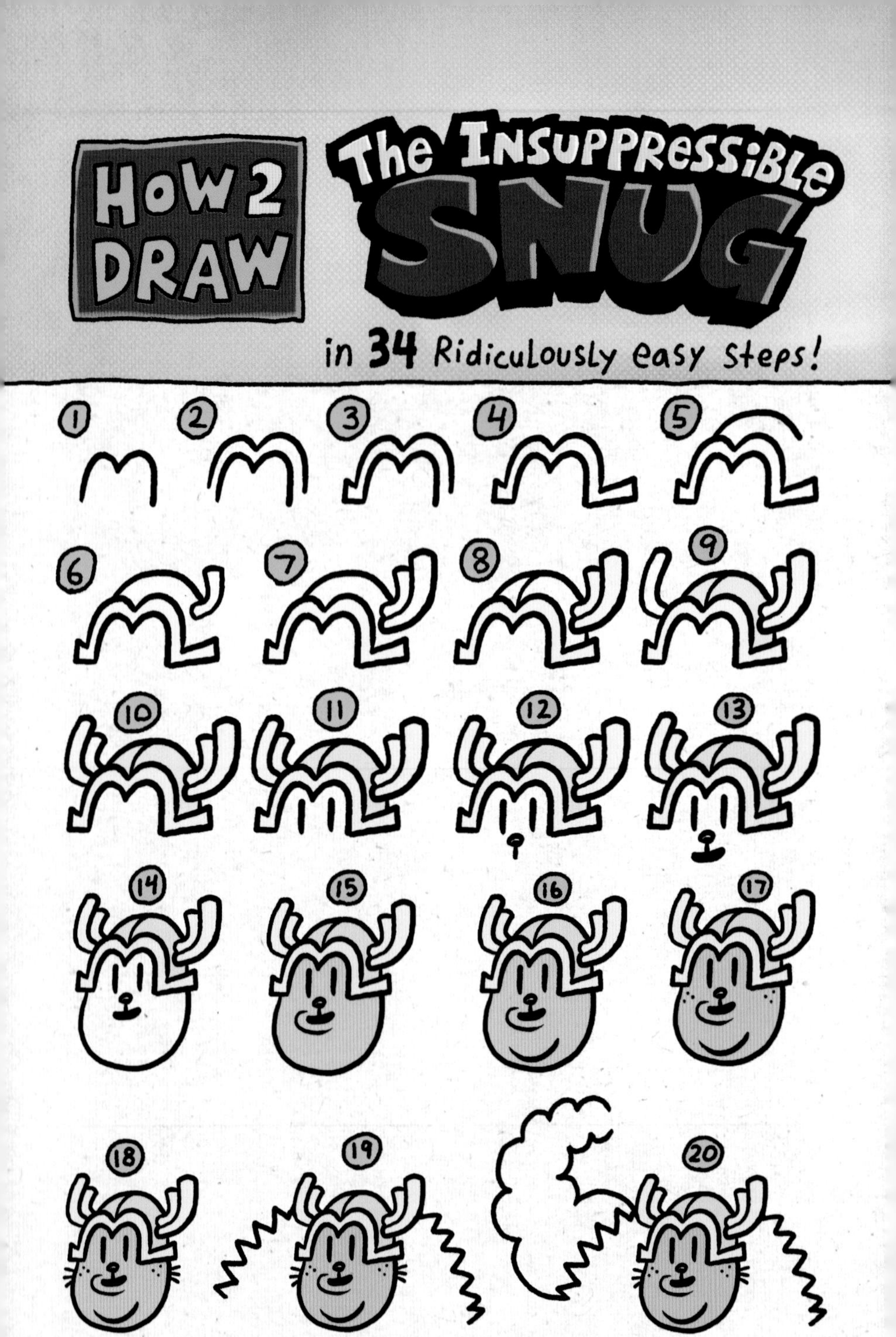

1
2
3
4
5
6
7
8
9
10
11
12
13
14
15
16
17
18
19
20

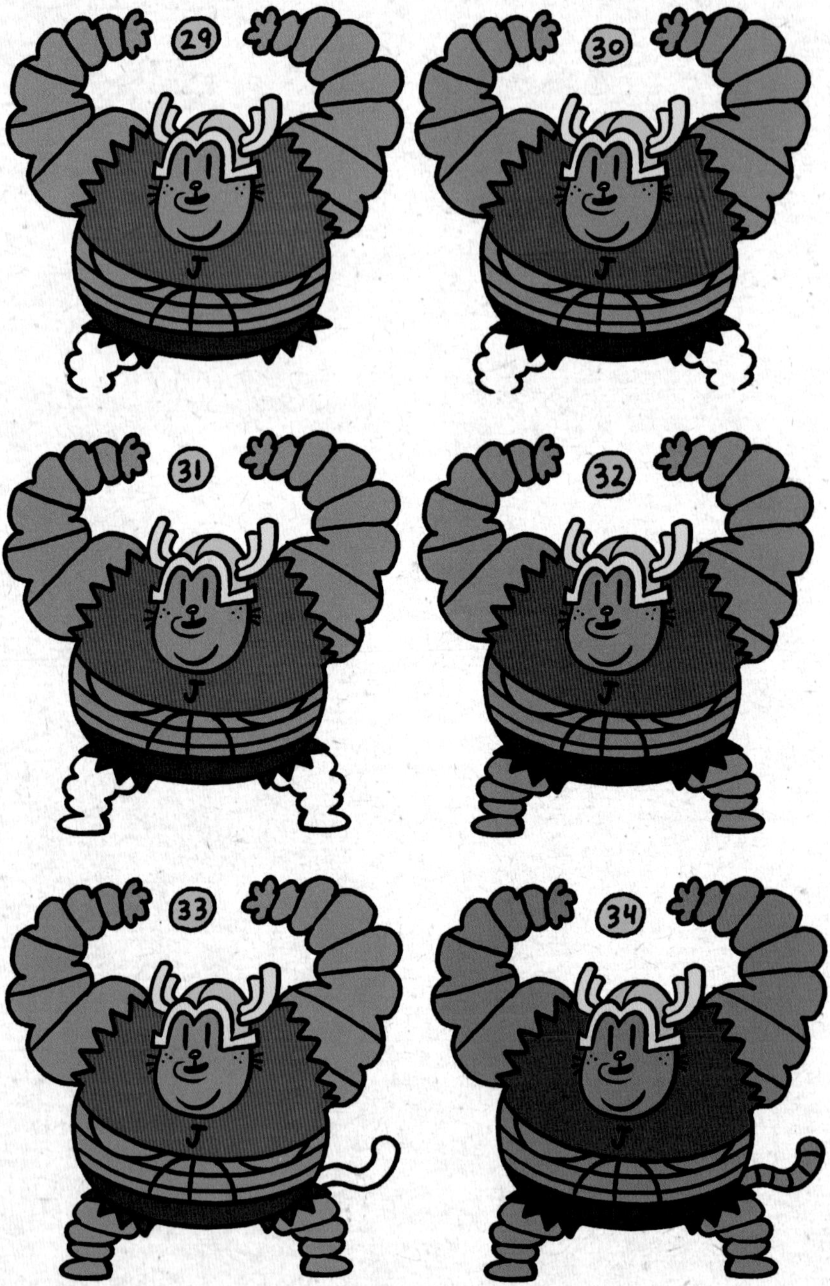
29
30
31
32
33
34

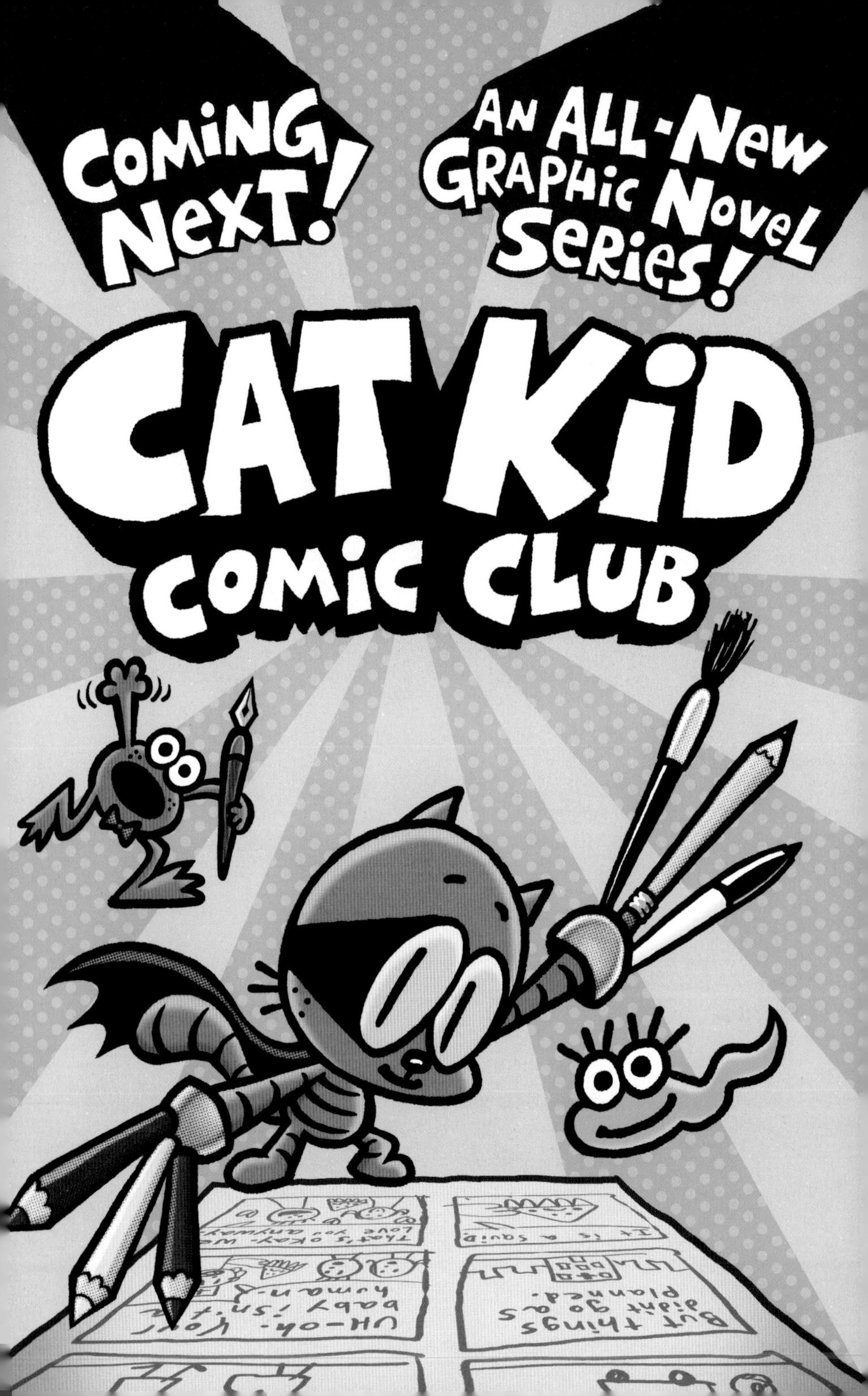
COMING NEXT!
AN ALL-NEW GRAPHIC NOVEL SERIES!
CAT KID COMIC CLUB
It is a squid.
But things didn't go as planned.

GET READING W

ITH DAV PILKEY!

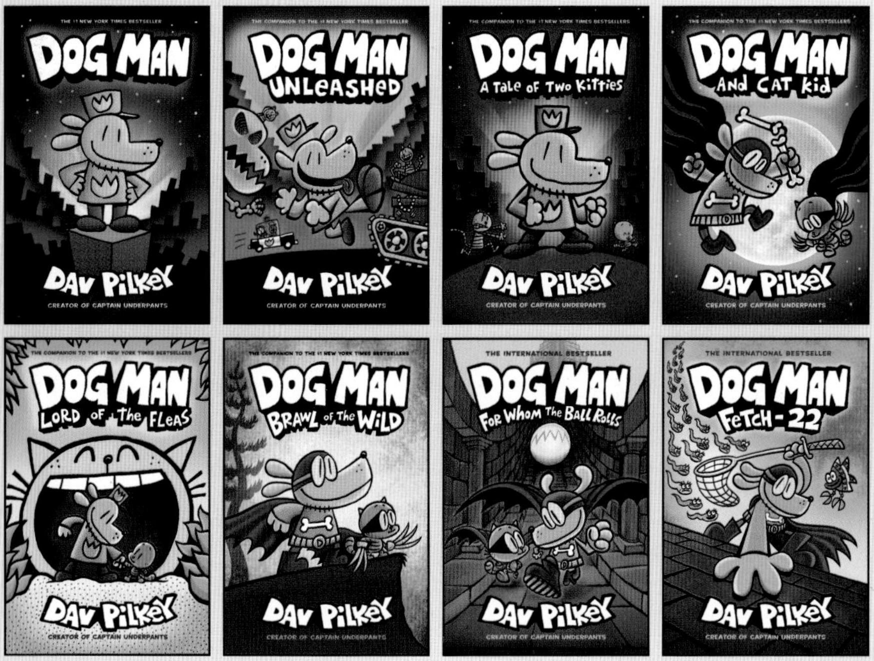
THE #1 NEW YORK TIMES BESTSELLER
DOG MAN
DAV PILKEY
CREATOR OF CAPTAIN UNDERPANTS
THE COMPANION TO THE #1 NEW YORK TIMES BESTSELLER
DOG MAN UNLEASHED
DAV PILKEY
CREATOR OF CAPTAIN UNDERPANTS
THE COMPANION TO THE #1 NEW YORK TIMES BESTSELLER
DOG MAN A Tale of Two Kitties
DAV PILKEY
CREATOR OF CAPTAIN UNDERPANTS
THE COMPANION TO THE #1 NEW YORK TIMES BESTSELLERS
DOG MAN AND CAT KID
DAV PILKEY
CREATOR OF CAPTAIN UNDERPANTS
THE COMPANION TO THE #1 NEW YORK TIMES BESTSELLERS
DOG MAN LORD OF THE FLEAS
DAV PILKEY
CREATOR OF CAPTAIN UNDERPANTS
THE COMPANION TO THE #1 NEW YORK TIMES BESTSELLERS
DOG MAN BRAWL OF THE WILD
DAV PILKEY
CREATOR OF CAPTAIN UNDERPANTS
THE INTERNATIONAL BESTSELLER
DOG MAN FOR WHOM THE BALL ROLLS
DAV PILKEY
CREATOR OF CAPTAIN UNDERPANTS
THE INTERNATIONAL BESTSELLER
DOG MAN FETCH-22
DAV PILKEY
CREATOR OF CAPTAIN UNDERPANTS

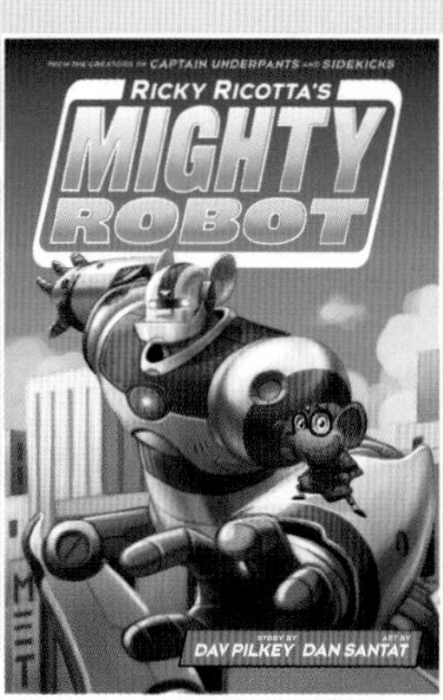
FROM THE CREATORS OF CAPTAIN UNDERPANTS AND SIDEKICKS
RICKY RICOTTA'S
MIGHTY ROBOT
STORY BY DAV PILKEY
ART BY DAN SANTAT

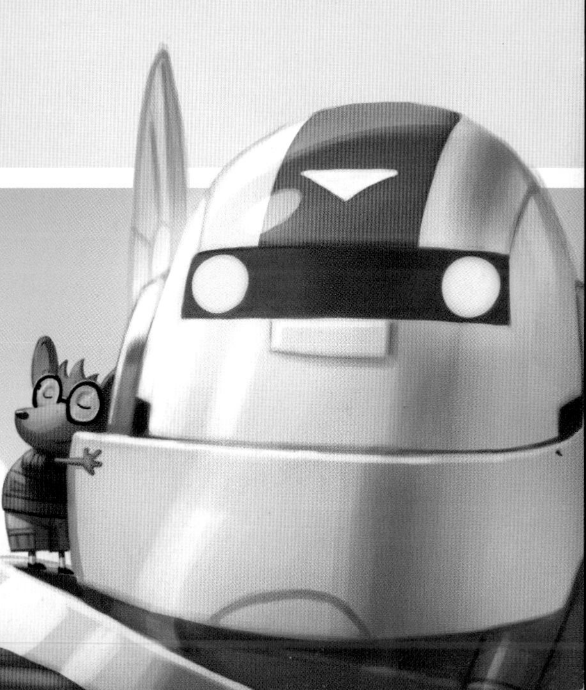

"A fun introduction to chapter books."
— *SCHOOL LIBRARY JOURNAL*

ABOUT THE
AUTHOR-ILLUSTRATOR

When Dav Pilkey was a kid, he was diagnosed with ADHD and dyslexia. Dav was so disruptive in class that his teachers made him sit out in the hallway every day. Luckily, Dav loved to draw and make up stories. He spent his time in the hallway creating his own original comic books — the very first adventures of Dog Man and Captain Underpants.

In college, Dav met a teacher who encouraged him to illustrate and write. He won a national competition in 1986 and the prize was the publication of his first book, WORLD WAR WON. He made many other books before being awarded the 1998 California Young Reader Medal for DOG BREATH, which was published in 1994, and in 1997 he won the Caldecott Honor for THE PAPERBOY.

THE ADVENTURES OF SUPER DIAPER BABY, published in 2002, was the first complete graphic novel spin-off from the Captain Underpants series and appeared at #6 on the USA Today bestseller list for all books, both adult and children's, and was also a New York Times bestseller. It was followed by THE ADVENTURES OF OOK AND GLUK: KUNG FU CAVEMEN FROM THE FUTURE and SUPER DIAPER BABY 2: THE INVASION OF THE POTTY SNATCHERS, both USA Today bestsellers. The unconventional style of these graphic novels is intended to encourage uninhibited creativity in kids.

His stories are semi-autobiographical and explore universal themes that celebrate friendship, tolerance, and the triumph of the good-hearted.

Dav loves to kayak in the Pacific Northwest with his wife.